M d
her s s.
Surp she wasn't crying; instead
she was laughing. "Bea, what in the world is going on?"

Bea's laughing became louder and more intense. Her whole body shook now. "Oh my God, Michael. I just had this vision of us in the back of the car. What would my children say about their mother 'doing' it in the backseat! Oh Lord, I'm so mortified!" She stopped laughing long enough to look into his eyes. "Why did it take me almost losing you to realize that I don't want to live without you in my life?" She cupped the side of his face with her hands. "I almost blew it with you . . . something I promise to make up for as soon as we return home."

Michael dipped his head down to her mouth and kissed her softly. The contact was sweet, but way too brief. "Beatrice, I'll be honest with you, I was ready to abide by your decision. Once we returned to Virginia, I was going to do whatever it took to get you out of my system. The last thing I wanted was to cause you more pain, and that's what it seemed I was doing by loving you."

Special Corruption Unit (SCU) Series

Beatrice McCoy
Executive Assistant Director
Special Operations Section

Michael Spates
Assistant Director
Special Corruption Unit (SCU)

Love Worth Fighting For
Agent Eric Duvernay
Tangerine "Tangy" Taylor

Worth The Wait
Alexander Milbon
Agent Maria Thomas

Undercover Lover
Agent Roderick Radford
Agent Helene Maupin

Deep Down
Alexander Milbon
Agent Beatrice McCoy

Deep Down

KATHERINE D. JONES

Dafina
BOOKS

Kensington Publishing Corp.

http://www.kensingtonbooks.com

DAFINA BOOKS are published by

Kensington Publishing Corp.
850 Third Avenue
New York, NY 10022

All Kensington Titles, Imprints, and Distributed Lines are available at special quantity discounts for bulk purchases for sales promotions, premiums, fund-raising, and educational or institutional use. Special book excerpts or customized printings can also be created to fit specific needs. For details, write or phone the office of the Kensington special sales manager: Kensington Publishing Corp., 850 Third Avenue, New York, NY 10022, attn: Special Sales Department, Phone: 1-800-221-2647.

Dafina and the Dafina logo Reg. U.S. Pat. & TM Off.

First Dafina mass market printing: October 2006
10 9 8 7 6 5 4 3 2 1

Printed in the United States of America

This book is dedicated to Karine Anderson, one of the strongest, most fiercely independent, and bravest women I know. I'm proud to call her Grandma. Rest in peace. . . .

Karine Anderson
November 8, 1920–August 26, 2004

Acknowledgments

To my husband, Ivan Sr., what can I say? You've been there for me for over nineteen years; it is remarkable, fantastic, unbelievable, and so wonderful. Thank you a million times over for all the support and Ivan-isms. You are my rock, my joy . . . my love.

To my boys, Ivan Jr. and Isaiah, I owe you a debt of gratitude. Thank you for hanging in there and *dealing* with me through all the drama!

To Karen Thomas and Nicole Bruce and the rest of the Kensington family, I'm just so thankful to be a part of the team.

To my girls, those sharp, wonderful, fantastic members of the Authors of Distinction—we're taking it to the next level! Thanks for making it fun.

Thanks to Regina and Jonnelda Hightower for offering such great inspiration.

Finally, to my Lord and Savior, through whom all is possible!

Prologue

West Virginia . . .

Jonnelda heard Kharl return with his men. She was filled with dread because she knew if he was back, that meant her daughter and her parents hadn't made it. She ran as fast as she could through the winding maze of the compound, but hearing the shots, she feared the worst. Unfortunately, minutes later, the worst was confirmed. She leaned against the kitchen wall doubled over with emotion.

The plan had been risky, but they'd been through it over and over. Jonnelda would have an alibi—she had been sent to do the grocery shopping for the compound. After distracting the driver, she would take the car to meet her parents at their place of employment at exactly 2:30 P.M. If she couldn't make it because she was being guarded too heavily, she would return to Kharl's place as if nothing happened and her parents would continue without her.

But it hadn't been so easy. After she'd left the compound, things had gone from bad to worse; she hadn't been able to get away from Simeon despite her best efforts. No excuse was good enough—he even followed her into the ladies' restroom at the store. She couldn't make the deadline and she had no way to communicate with her parents without putting them in more jeopardy. She had hoped and prayed for their safety, but the cold realization was that despite their planning, they were never going to be free of Kharl Winton.

Tears fell fast and hot down her cheeks; her breathing came in ragged gasps. Jonnelda knew that there was nowhere for her to hide—Kharl would come for her next.

He seemed to have a highly developed sixth sense; he'd added extra security without warning, almost as if he *knew* of their plan to escape. He hadn't made a sound, but Jonnelda knew when he entered the room. She turned her tearstained face upward.

Kharl said nothing before he drew back his hand. The first blow was so hard it knocked her to her knees. She didn't even taste the blood that trickled from her swollen lips. The second blow connected with her jaw, sprawling her already wounded body on the cold tile floor. After the third blow, Jonnelda didn't have the strength to cry . . . anymore.

Chapter One

FBI Director Michael Spates was on the phone with his direct supervisor, Executive Director Bea McCoy. It was their usual custom to debrief after a mission, but this time she had more to discuss than just the details of their last completed case. Beatrice had also called to confirm the rumor that there would be a major shake-up in the organization's structure.

Michael had heard that there were plans that could adversely affect the unit, but he wanted to wait to hear it from Beatrice personally before he rushed to judgement. He talked about the case first, and then he would deal with rumor-mill gossip. Besides, he preferred to deal with good news over bad. "The San Antonio case wasn't too bad, was it? The budget was a little high, but if you think about it, without our mission setup those guys wouldn't have been caught, at least not without the body count being higher. We can chalk up another successful assignment to the SCU," he said, hoping that he'd managed to keep the tension out of his voice while he spoke with her.

Michael paused before he continued. "The wedding was nice, too. So that makes four of our best agents engaged or married. It makes you wonder who's next."

Michael heard Bea's tender sigh, the softness of which seemed to gently nuzzle his ears. She had caused him no small distraction while they talked, especially since she had absolutely no idea the effect she had on him.

Beatrice avoided the first part of his statement when she answered. "Yes, I'm pleased about the case—even though, I will admit I was starting to become a little worried. Maupin and Radford seemed to take their sweet time about putting away the Wilkens boys, but I must say in the end, the SCU acquitted itself nicely. Now all we have to do is make sure that the right people know about our successes during these reorganization talks and hearings. I've got budget meetings all week and then the congressional hearing. The Department of Homeland Security is really itching to take over the unit. They see it as a real coup to be able to set up missions the way that you are able to, but I'm not comfortable with the proposed change. It would mean that you would have to give up your leadership position and I know the unit is successful because of all the time and hard work that you put into it."

Another soft sigh. "As for your last question, about who's next—I don't really know, but I've heard through interoffice gossip that Max Wilson and Chantal McCorkle are making *eyes* at each other. Zola seems to know everybody's business. If she wasn't such a great administrative assistant, I might wonder about her."

Michael could hear the smile in her voice. Bea presented herself as a serious, no-nonsense supervisor, but he knew she had a fun side, too. Aside from being beautiful, she had a wonderful sense of humor that she showed way too infrequently.

Bea said, "And I agree with you, we need to do what we can to make sure our agents stick around. I don't want to lose any more great talent."

Michael's tone turned serious again. "I'm very pleased

with the way our agents have performed in the face of the toughest situations. There are several things that have come across my desk lately that I think we should take a look into as time and agents permit." He exhaled. "There's also something going on with the Jamaicans, but I'm still waiting on the DEA to get back to me on what they want us to do."

"I looked at the Moroccan file before it was sent over to you. Despite all that's going on go ahead and make the arrangements for the Radfords. Just let me know how it goes in the morning. As far as the Jamaican posses, we've got too much going on—have the DEA put in writing what they'd like us to do and I'll take a look at it later."

Beatrice exhaled. "I think I'm going to head home, it's late and we've been going at this restructuring plan nonstop for the last couple of weeks." She lowered her voice, concern evident as she spoke. "You should get some rest as well. Don't work too much longer or you're going to wear yourself out."

Michael stifled a chuckle. There was only one way he could think of to wear himself out and it was definitely not considered *work*. He had to force those thoughts away so that he could put his attention toward the conversation. He couldn't afford to leave just yet, though he wanted nothing better. The files on his desk were a good indication that he couldn't go home anytime soon. He said, "You know I never get out of here before ten P.M., but thanks for your concern. I'll talk to you in the morning. Be safe heading home."

He placed the phone back in the cradle. The watch list seemed to grow longer with each day, and with the joint assignments that his agents had with other agencies, the unit was stretched thin. Having Beatrice confirm his suspicions sent a chill up his spine.

If his unit were absorbed into the Department of

Homeland Security he would lose oversight of all the current missions and assignments. He didn't even want to think about leaving his agents out there for someone else to oversee. He cared about them too much—they were all the family he had aside from his mentor, Peter.

Early retirement had crossed his mind on several occasions, but the bottom line was that Michael wanted to finish what he'd started. His desk might hold mission requests from Jamaica, West Indies to Jamaica, New York, but he owed it to his cadre of agents to try to stick it out.

Michael was prepared to fight for his job, but he wasn't prepared to beg. He had to have faith that at the right time Congress would make the right decisions.

Michael stifled a sigh. There were several more files that he should read before going home, but with his concentration shot, he knew it wouldn't be a very productive night.

He'd just hung up with the person responsible for his feelings. Beatrice McCoy seemed to occupy his thoughts morning through night. Many nights he went to bed with erotic thoughts of Bea on his mind. Thoughts that rocked his equilibrium and made it difficult for him to stick to his plan to keep his emotional distance from her until she was ready to pursue a relationship with him. It was a time that he'd been waiting for—for far too long.

As a man who was always in control, it unnerved him that he seemed to be so wrapped up in what was going to happen with his position as well as his love life, that he could barely make it through the day. An involuntary shudder passed through him. *How did we get to this?*

The next day brought more of the same for him. His day consisted of dreaming up ways to outsmart either

Congress or criminals . . . sometimes he thought that they were one and the same.

He signed papers, read documents and reports, and made assignments. Michael raked his hands through his hair for the fiftieth time, disgusted that there seemed to be less of it each day. Yet another reminder that time stood still for no one.

He took solace in the thought that perhaps during his upcoming trip to the mountains for their business trip he would find the answers he sought. Maybe the peace and tranquillity of the setting would help.

Later on in the day, Michael looked down at his calendar to organize his week. *Damn! I didn't call Beatrice.* He was so caught up in his own problems that he'd forgotten that the next day would mark one of the worst days of her life. Bea never asked for anything, least of all special treatment, but he had to do what felt right.

Beatrice had come into the office as usual. She hoped the duties and details of the day would take her mind off what she knew she must eventually face. It had worked for awhile, but now in the still of the day with no one making demands of her and the phone quiet, reality came crashing down to meet her. Bea looked at the date on the calendar at a day that she didn't need any help to remember. This anniversary was permanently etched in her memory; she would never forget the day that her life began to unravel.

Beatrice sucked in big gulps of air. She tried to think of pleasant things to be thankful for: the good times and the many blessings in her life. And it worked until the lump in her throat served notice that she was engaged in a losing battle. It hadn't worked last year, either.

The bureau psychiatrist, Dr. Wendy Rose, had told her during their last few sessions to just go with the feelings. Her sorrow was a part of the healing process. Besides, trying to push the tears away didn't do any good. Crying wouldn't bring them back, but it was good for the soul. Today marked the anniversary of her children's memorial service. The attack on their bus had left little for her to bury. Her shoulders shook with the force of her emotion.

As hot tears rolled down her cheeks, she wanted to call Michael. Tell him that she needed him, but she wouldn't . . . she couldn't. She wasn't ready to deal with the consequences of taking such a big risk. *It would be so easy to let go and let you love me,* she thought, but at what cost? She wouldn't be responsible for something bad happening to him, too.

Bea had been putting off his advances with a dual heart. On the one hand, she wanted him to continue to love her, on the other, she wanted him to move on. But she'd made a pact with herself after she buried the three people she loved most in the world that she wouldn't ever make herself vulnerable to love again. She felt as if her heart had been ripped out twice—and that was enough. Because of her past, Bea decided that she would deal with the anguish on her own. What she wouldn't give to have Michael's strong arms wrapped around her in comfort. Many a night she considered giving in to temptation. She wanted to be with him so much that sometimes it hurt.

After several minutes the tidal wave of emotion passed and she was able to function a little better. When she felt she could go on, she lifted her head. Beatrice would learn to get over Michael, just as she was learning to get through the other losses in her life. Problem was, Bea was confronted with her feelings for him every time she looked into the deep brown depths of his eyes or listened, mesmerized by the deep bass of his voice, when he spoke.

It seemed that he didn't intend to make it any easier for her, either. More times than she cared to remember he reminded her that he was just a *call* away if she ever needed anything. Bea knew that if she were honest, the answer that would escape her lips would be *only you*. She needed him to be more than just a good friend. She needed him to be her friend, confidant, and lover. But she would never ask for that, even though she knew he would do it all freely.

A delivery of white flowers on her porch awaited her arrival. She blew out a long breath and shook her head. *Michael.* Yeah, he planned to make it difficult for her to stick to her resolve about not entering into a relationship with him and to maintain a professional distance.

He always found a way to express his concern for her. He would send a bouquet of flowers, or a plant, or a sweet card—always with a handwritten sentiment to let her know that he cared and hadn't forgotten.

Beatrice took the arrangement of white carnations, mums, baby's breath, and Asiatic lilies to her kitchen, where she fixed a soothing mug of hot chamomile tea.

As it cooled, she sipped gingerly. As the years went by it was harder and harder to stay true to her husband's memory. They had been in love, shared a wonderful life with their children, but she had to go on. The way she felt about Michael was a clear indication of that fact. She didn't want to betray what she had had with them, but as the years passed, she didn't want to be alone anymore. If Bea were truly honest with herself, she would admit to the world that she longed for love and fulfillment like anyone else. It was her sense of control, her desire to be in control that prevented her from showing that side of herself to Michael or anyone else, for that matter. Therapy and group sessions had helped when it came to grieving the loss of her loved ones, but it hadn't stopped her from putting a barrier around her heart that she was reluctant to let down. If any man could break through, it was Michael. And that made him a very dangerous man for her to be around.

And even despite her raw emotions, the very notion of spending time alone with him sent a shiver of anticipation through her. Much as she tried to think of their impending trip to Harpers Ferry as just a business trip, her body and thoughts betrayed her true feelings. She had two days to convince herself that throwing herself into Michael's arms would not be the best way to keep business and pleasure separate. And was certainly not the way that she should behave with a subordinate agent. Trouble was, her heart wasn't paying much attention to her sound logic.

Chapter Two

The breathtaking drive to the Hilltop House Hotel through the snow-capped mountains was enough to put them both in a relaxed, lighthearted mood. Maybe it was just the picturesque setting, but suddenly the weight of the world they seemed to carry on their shoulders was lifted. The roads were clear, but temperatures were cool and everything around them seemed dressed in its prettiest winter white.

Hilltop was beautifully situated in the hills of West Virginia, boasting a location on a hill two hundred and fifty feet above the river. And with sixty-two rooms it was the perfect locale for the interagency meeting. They could take over the entire facility and not have to worry about internal security issues.

Senior agents met every few years to keep pace with the division leaders from other agencies such as the State Department Intelligence and Research, the Central Intelligence Agency, and the Drug Enforcement Agency, to name a few. Each participant was responsible for a portion of a group exercise, but it was more typically known as a three-day event where networking was the actual business conducted. And that was the whole purpose. Too much time in the office without some sort of release wasn't good for anyone. These meetings afforded the senior-level operatives a chance to sharpen their skills through the joint workshops and group exercises, while still giving them much-deserved downtime.

The atmosphere also provided a refreshing getaway where they could all complain about how bad they had it and then go back to their rooms with a smile on their faces because they didn't have it as bad as the next guy.

It was an event that was well attended and highly anticipated by the senior-level agents, directors, and investigators.

Michael had important reports to review, assignments to make, and his usual slew of meetings. But sitting next to Beatrice on the way to Harpers Ferry proved to be more challenging than his hectic workweek. He found himself confronted with the feelings he'd worked so hard to avoid while he was alone with Bea during the drive.

Michael looked at Bea out of the corner of his eye. The scent of her Juniper Breeze gently wafted through his senses, and tempted his libido. He knew exactly which fragrance she wore, because he had enjoyed the sweet smell on her for a number of years. She had somehow made it her own, bringing the mild floral scent to a sexy new heat. Many a night he wondered how it would feel to kiss every inch of it on her voluptuous curves. He shifted in the seat. The increased snugness of his pants told him that he needed to change the direction of his thoughts before he embarrassed himself.

"So tell me, Bea. How come you have four bags for a three-day trip? Is this something women learn in a secret class for females only?"

Bea turned to him, her brow furrowed until she saw his wide grin. "Oh, I see, you've got jokes, as the younger generation would say. I'll have you know that I have all the supplies that a well-organized woman would bring with her on a trip, including my 'never leave home without it' emergency kit, and other incidentals."

Michael covered a smirk. "Well, in that case, please forgive my ignorance. I guess us not-so-well-organized men should take a few lessons. I just have one bag; next time I guess I should let you pack for both of *us*."

Bea held his gaze. *Would there be a next time?*

They watched each other uncomfortably for a few seconds. The comment sparked a heated connection that neither was prepared to handle.

Michael's breathing rate increased. Beatrice had been a major part of why he continued to work for the bureau. Her strength and support had been immeasurable to him. He found Bea McCoy to be a very good reason to get up in the mornings—it was just too bad she didn't feel the same way about him. *Yet.*

"Is this your first time back to the area since the last retreat?" Michael hoped his voice sounded normal. It had taken most of his powers of restraint not to say more; not to give in to the desire that rushed heat through his veins.

"Yes. I love the area, but with work . . ." Bea responded.

"Maybe we'll have time to enjoy the sights on the drive back. We can take the scenic route." Michael paused. "Bea, I know this is a hard time for you, but just know that I'm here if you need me, or just want to talk."

Bea lowered her gaze. "Thank you, Michael. And thank you for the beautiful flowers. I know I don't say it enough, but I appreciate your thoughtfulness. You and Zola keep me going during these times. Just knowing that you're such a good friend is enough. The years are passing by and little by little it's becoming easier." *Oh, would that was the truth,* she thought, even as the words were spoken from her lips.

Michael wanted to reach out to her, just to touch her hand, but he didn't know what he would do if she pulled away. "Okay, Bea, but the offer stands. I'm here for you—anytime."

Bea nodded her head, but was quiet.

Michael had let her get away from him before, but he wasn't going to do it again. He had made up his mind; this time would be different. He was encouraged by the deep respect they had for each other; it was a good thing—for starters. But he wanted more—no, he wanted it all.

With music from the radio playing softly in the background, they drove through the scenic hills in amiable silence until either found a topic of particular interest. Bea read through a couple of reports during periods of quiet. Suddenly, Bea spoke after several minutes of reading. "Oh, Michael, would you turn that up, please? I love that song. He was truly a musical genius and a man born before his time." She absentmindedly hummed along as Marvin Gaye's song, "What's Going On" played on the radio. "Can you believe that is from 1971? And the lyrics are still so appropriate thirty-plus years later."

Michael felt his heart tighten in his chest. She had such a melodic, sweet voice it seemed to wash over him like a warm breeze. There was something about the way she called his name that made his hard shell soften just a little more.

The temperature in the car was now several degrees higher than the outside even with the heater on the lowest setting. He grimaced, thinking as he drove that this was definitely proving to be more difficult than he'd expected. Much to his chagrin, he was acting like a hormonal teen. He gripped the steering wheel a little tighter and checked to see how many more miles they had. It shouldn't be much longer, he told himself. This was embarrassing. He was way too old for this kind of behavior. Folks his age had grandchildren, for Pete's sake!

Michael waited until her humming faded and the

song was over before he spoke. He needed conversation, about anything. How to make a mosaic, strip a chair, or change the oil in a car would work just fine as topics. Marvin may have stopped singing, but his own body still hummed—and it was becoming painful. He gritted his teeth. "I didn't eat much before we left. Would you like to have some lunch together once we get settled?" *Why did I say that?*

Bea looked at him curiously. His jaw was very tight, which meant he must be worried about something, she thought. "Sure, just give me about thirty minutes to get myself together."

Her first inclination had been to decline, but she changed her mind after seeing his facial expression. Besides, the sexy way he filled out the black cable-knit turtleneck that peeked out from under his wool jacket was messing with her sense of propriety. He was the definition of tall, dark, and handsome and in excellent shape. She successfully resisted the urge to run her tongue over her top lip. He reminded her of sweet milk chocolate and it made her taste buds water just to look at him. Bea was embroiled in a battle with her emotional and physical feelings and she needed to regroup. Quickly. She took a deep breath as they pulled in front of the lodge.

This is it. Bea told herself not to be so nervous, that it was just *three* days. And, it was just *business*.

Michael unloaded the bags while she went to check in. He left her briefly to park the SUV. Bea noticed several of their peers were already milling around and looked comfortable. The earlier tension she felt started to ooze away. They could do this—she and Michael were well past the age of not being able to handle this simple assignment. They were mature, highly capable agents.

Finally, it was her turn at the counter.

When Michael returned with the bags, the look she gave him sent shivers down his back and up his spine. She was livid. He walked faster to meet her. "Bea, what is it?"

She was silent for several seconds, seemingly in an attempt to control her anger. She had him worried now. The desk clerk looked visibly shaken, too.

Michael looked confounded. He hadn't been gone that long—what in the devil had happened?

Bea spoke through clenched teeth. "Michael, this will not do. When we get back to the office, I am going to line up Karen and Zola and shoot them both. I know this was their doing, their little scheme. The hotel doesn't have reservations for Beatrice McCoy and Michael Spates; they only have a room with a king-sized bed for Mr. and Mrs. McCoy."

Bea placed a hand on her hip while she spoke. "They will pay for this, oh yeah, for this they will pay. The hotel staff has apologized, but since the entire facility is booked and the majority of the folks have checked in, we're stuck until six P.M. After then we can check for cancellations or find out if anyone is willing to switch. They've graciously offered to put a cot in the room, as this was not their mistake. But that's not the point!" She shook her head in frustration. "Do you believe this?"

Michael shook his head, too. "No, actually, I don't. Looks like we will have two vacant administrative positions when we return." His deep voice dropped to an even lower octave as he spoke. He was as upset as Beatrice, considering this wasn't quite what he had expected, either.

Michael had looked forward to his time alone to think about his situation. The last thing in the world he needed was the sight of Bea McCoy in a nightgown floating through his subconscious, or worse, Bea in nothing at all. He shook his head free of those visions.

"I'll order a cot or sleep on the floor. I'm sorry about this, Bea. Karen usually does an excellent job with my travel arrangements." *Forget shooting her, the woman is going up by her toes.*

Bea gripped the key tightly as she and Michael rode the elevator up to *their* room on the sixth floor. The room was magnificent, with traditional period pieces from when the house was built in 1888. Heavy solid wood bureaus, chests, and consoles furnished the room.

The location of the room also allowed for a beautiful panoramic view of the countryside. She clutched her hands to her chest when she walked toward the window to take in the gorgeous snowcapped scenery. Bea stood by the window for several minutes to take it all in before she spoke again. Her earlier disappointment and outrage were diffused by the beauty of her surroundings. She stole a furtive glance at Michael and couldn't help but think about how romantic this would be in another time . . . another place.

Bea turned to find him looking at her with a capricious smile. Michael was always so serious; seeing him like this was out of the ordinary and a pleasant surprise. Their relationship had always been different from the others in the office. She was probably closer to him than anyone else, but it was still hard to classify what they shared. It was more than a deeply affectionate, platonic relationship, but what she would call it, she didn't know.

"Have I done something to amuse you?" she asked.

The smile never left his eyes. "Not at all, I was just enjoying the view."

She turned back to the window, not quite sure how to take his remark. Bea felt herself melting, but she couldn't afford to allow herself to warm to him. The consequences could be *deadly*.

She hardened her voice to a tone that didn't match the feelings in her heart. "Do you mind going down to the lobby while I freshen up? I want to change my clothes before we meet the others for the first session."

Michael started to protest. He wasn't going to turn into some Peeping Tom or pervert, and was insulted by her tone. Why was she so hesitant to be in the same room with him? He blew out an exasperated breath and prepared to walk out the room.

Bea closed her eyes. She wasn't handling this very well. She knew she was being childish, so she put her hand up to stop him. Her voice was soft, gentle when she spoke again—the harsh edge gone now. "Michael, I'm sorry. Just stay. I'll be out of the bathroom in a few minutes. We can head downstairs together if you'd like. I know you're hungry, so I'll be quick."

He smiled despite himself. Few people called him by his first name and he liked the way it rolled off her tongue when they were in private. In the office and most other places of his life, people called him "agent" or by his surname. She was one of the few people who called him Michael and one of the fewer still who called him by his middle name upon occasion.

Michael didn't comment, sitting at the table in front of the window to watch the view. Being treated like he was some sort of masher didn't sit well with him, so he was grateful when her tone changed.

He didn't want their weekend spent with this kind of awkward interaction. They had a lot to discuss about the future of the unit. Besides, they were too old to play these kinds of games. He would never do anything that Beatrice wasn't willing to do and she knew that. He listened to the spray of the water and contemplated his next moves.

* * *

When Bea was finished, she came out of the bathroom to find an empty suite. She hoped she hadn't angered him with her unpredictable behavior. She had to be honest with herself—maybe she wasn't worried about him at all . . . maybe it was her own behavior that was cause for concern. She looked anxiously toward the door, not quite sure whether to go down to the lobby or wait for him. Fortunately, she didn't have to wait long for an answer. A quick knock on the door caused her heart to stir. *Michael.* She rushed to the door, hoping he was on the other side.

Beatrice was nearly breathless in her rush to open the door. "Hi! Where'd you go?" He had changed his clothes, too and she could smell the minty freshness of his breath after he'd entered the room.

Michael looked at her intently as if trying to gauge her demeanor. "I went down to see what was on the lunch menu and then ran into Jake Peterson from defense intelligence. I went to his room to change so I wouldn't hold you up." He gave her appearance the once-over and smiled inwardly. "Looks like my plan worked. So, are you ready to go to the restaurant?"

Bea grinned. He definitely looked better than anything that she could possibly find on the restaurant's menu. He was so handsome in a sharp-edged, masculine way. There wasn't much softness to his features, but then again, she wasn't attracted to that kind of guy. She didn't want some baby-faced, model-looking man. His large dark brown eyes were perfectly proportioned to his nose and high cheekbones. He was tall, powerfully built, and brilliant. She studied his head, deciding that he would probably be one sexy devil if he shaved bald.

Beatrice inhaled and smothered a smile. The thought of running her hands over the smooth brown skin of his head was very appealing. *What was she doing?* She shook those thoughts free from her mind as they headed downstairs together. Minutes later they carried on pleasant conversation in the restaurant as they waited for their order.

Maybe it was a woman's intuition, but Bea sensed something different about him lately. Michael seemed like he was looking for something or it could be that the stress of the job was getting to him. Maybe she'd assumed he wanted to continue to work with the bureau. After all, he had given over twenty years to the job. He might be ready to throw in the towel, though he hadn't said that to her earlier. Perhaps Michael was trying to spare her feelings. She found herself trying to read between every line while listening to him.

As they considered what to have for dessert, Bea plunged in. "Tell me something, Michael. With all the madness that's going to be happening soon, do you even want to stay with the bureau?"

Michael looked surprised by the question. "Bea, how could you even ask me that? I've made the job and the unit my entire life for more years than I care to admit. I'm no less committed now than I've been in the past. As long as the SCU is around and I have something to contribute, I want to be the director. I would think you, of all people, would know that." His comment was sharper than he intended and he instantly regretted his answer.

With an eyebrow raised, Bea responded, "Zeke, I'm not questioning your loyalty or ability to do your job. I know what you can do; I've watched you and been in awe of you since I joined the bureau. You had a reputation to envy even before I came onboard.

"What I want to know is what's in your heart. Do you still have the will to do this or are you ready to move on to the next phase of your life? I know that you are too young to retire with full benefits, but there might be a buyout if DHS takes over and the unit is dissolved. I don't want to think gloom and doom here, but I want to remain realistic about the future."

She paused. "Besides, I know the hours you work; the time, energy, and effort you put into your agents and your cases. It has to be getting old by now. Not too many people would be able to give this job all that you do. If we had any sense, either one of us, we would be showing pictures of our grandchildren around the office instead of wondering if the next round of budget cuts will do us in." Bea exhaled. "I have a certain amount of frustration with all this as well, to be honest with you."

Michael listened quietly. When she called him Zeke, and she was the only one, either she meant business or he had touched a nerve. He would tread a little lighter from now on. Michael had enough experience with women to know how to look properly chastised. He reached for her hand.

Bea hesitated, then put hers in his warm touch. "Bea, I didn't mean it the way it came out. I know this has been rough on you, too. I guess I got a little worked up because there are times when I'm unsure. The thought of not having the unit as part of my life bothers me." He looked deeply into her eyes. "No, it terrifies me. I've let this job define who I am. I'm not complaining, just stating the facts. Everything that I do has something to do with the Federal Bureau of Investigation. I can't remember the last time that I went to church, or did anything for the hell of it. Seems without the bureau, I don't know who I am."

Bea squeezed his hand. "You're a wonderful, thoughtful, hardworking man, and that's what you'd be no matter what you did. But let's not have negative thoughts, we'll figure out some way to show Congress why we're worthwhile. Besides, no other agency, department, or unit can do what we do so well."

The heat from the innocent touch of his hand turned up as she looked into his eyes. Desire simmered beneath the surface, then threatened to take over their friendly meal.

Bea sighed as she pushed away those feelings. She would not *allow* anything to happen between them no matter how much she wanted it. She eased her hand from his and concentrated on the other occupants of the room. When her gaze rested on someone she'd known from her past, she knew it was her chance. She seized the opportunity to put some distance between the two of them.

Without much warning, she excused herself, leaving Michael on the pretense of wanting to socialize before they started their assignment. They both recognized her thinly disguised attempt at control, but this time he made no move to stop her.

Michael watched her walk away while he struggled to regain control of his emotions. He felt the energy that coursed through his body from their brief touch and knew Bea's effect on him would always be the same—she set him on edge. Gone was his self-controlled and rigid demeanor. Gone was the comfort he felt in being alone. Gone was the denial that they could work together and he wouldn't want her every second of each day.

Michael wanted two things in his life. His job and the woman that he loved so deeply.

Two hours later, the hotel was able to find them proper accommodations. Michael moved his belongings out of her room and settled into another room down the hall. There was a little disappointment for both of them because of it. Would being in the same room have been so bad?

Beatrice Lynette McCoy, you ought to be ashamed of your-

self! Acting like a teenager instead of a responsible adult. She didn't want to lead Michael on, but by the same token, she couldn't help her feelings toward him, either. She was very attracted to him; she had been for a very long time. Why can't things ever be simple? she questioned. She really wasn't asking for much—a little peace as she moved into the next phase of her life. Turning fifty would be her next milestone. Didn't she deserve some measure of happiness?

Bea watched as the wind rustled through the trees, blowing the powdery white snow into a swirl. She studied the flurries of snow and likened them to her roiling emotions. One minute she was ready to give in, let the chips fall where they may, the next she reined in her emotions. She had the urge to pace the room, like she'd watched Michael do so many times. She shook her head as if that would banish all thoughts of him. But it wouldn't and Bea knew that. Michael was a part of her, part of her heart; and despite her best efforts to negate how important he was to her, the facts were obvious. Her heart had botched the assignment . . . failed in its duty to remain detached and unmoved. She knew that she couldn't act on her feelings. She'd made a *deal* and she needed to keep up her part of it. A single tear rolled down her cheek. Wasn't that the deal *they'd* made—she wouldn't love, so she wouldn't lose.

Bea looked at the clock on the nightstand. She didn't have much time to make herself presentable. She stood quickly then went into the bathroom to splash cold water on her face. It would be time to start the first session in a few minutes.

Right on time, the meeting coordinator knocked on doors to assemble the analysts, agents, and investigators for their activities. Bea and Michael met in the lobby with other members of the team to discuss their assignment. Both had had time to sufficiently cool their heated emotions and met each other with professional decorum. The activities of the retreat provided the opportunity to distract them from thinking about each other. Their focus returned to the job at hand—even if only temporarily.

Beatrice was headed toward the elevator at the conclusion of the evening when she and Michael made eye contact across the room. His smile disarmed her and she stopped walking away from him and began moving toward him.

Michael met her in the middle and it seemed as if all the chatter from the restaurant, bar, and lobby disappeared. The world consisted of the two of them for that moment and time.

"The night is young, don't tell me that you're going up so soon?"

Beatrice grinned. "The night might be young, but I'm not. I think I'm going to read a little before I go to bed—I need some time to decompress. Emotionally it feels like it has been a very long week. I think the weather makes me want to hibernate, too."

He didn't know what got into him, but he said, "Yes, this is perfect snuggling weather."

Beatrice said seductively, "Oh my, is that an invitation?" Heat smoldered in her gaze and Michael wanted to take her in his arms. He inhaled deeply. "Only if you're going to take me up on it. Just say the word and I'll carry you up to my room right now."

Beatrice laughed aloud. "Okay now, what exactly is in that coffee you've been drinking?"

He played along. "Nothing yet, but I'd love a cup with Kahlúa, how about you? You want to join me in the bar before you go up? We haven't exactly ironed out our strategy anyway, so we do need to spend more time together." *Was he begging?*

"One drink?"

Michael held up his hands in acquiescence. "One drink." He led her to a corner booth in the bar, where they munched on snack mix until their drinks were ready.

Beatrice soaked up the atmosphere. He'd only chosen the most intimate spot in the entire bar. She needed conversation . . . lots of it. "I know a little about Peter Anderson and your association with him, but tell me more of how he helped you become involved with the bureau."

He grinned. "I thought you said one drink. This story could take awhile."

"Has anyone ever told you that you are a brat, Michael E. Spates," she teased.

"You wound me, woman." His grin was infectious and soon they sat across from each other like a couple on a first date.

"Okay, here goes," he said after their drinks arrived and each had taken a sip.

Beatrice loved his smooth, melodic voice and listened carefully. The swells and dips of his intonation were hypnotizing. She pinched herself so she would stop staring at his lips.

"I think I was in the right place at the right time. The bureau was putting a new program in place and they needed young minority recruits. They were looking for young men and women who didn't feel the same angst toward authority most others felt and who wanted to make a difference in their lives as well as the lives of others through a career in law enforcement.

"Anderson was honest with me when he told me the new recruits wouldn't be fully embraced by the bureau." Michael paused to sip his coffee again.

"Maybe it was just timing, maybe it was providence,

but I met Peter Anderson in Detroit at a polling center. I was looking for more direction in my life. The devastation of the race riots of July 1967 was not forgotten. I'd never seen anything like it before, seven days that brought a city to its knees. The fires had stopped burning, but the air was still singed with apprehension and mistrust of anything related to law enforcement and government." He exhaled slowly as if reliving the moment. "Anderson struck up a conversation with me as I waited to vote."

Bea noticed the faraway look in his eyes. He was so passionate about Peter and the bureau. *DHS couldn't take it all away from him!* She would do all that she could to make sure that didn't happen.

Michael said, "During that first meeting, we talked about everything from sports to politics. I had no idea at the time that I was being interviewed for a job. Peter told me Director Hoover was making the necessary changes to integrate the bureau, though not by his choice alone. He had been the director of the Federal Bureau of Investigation since 1924, and it was now 1970. His spying, secret files, and other antics weren't as tolerated as before and he had been told to toe the line."

Beatrice was fascinated. "So you're saying Anderson had been sent around the nation on a major recruitment effort, and our very own Michael Ezekiel Spates was his brightest selection, and the only choice Hoover was pleased with out of the hundreds of applicants that were approved for admission into the bureau."

Michael chuckled. "No, I'm not saying all that. I don't know if out of all the applicants I was the best. All I know is that I got the job. Anderson was my biggest supporter back then and a great mentor."

"Wow, I'm still impressed, that was no small feat." *But then again, Michael was no ordinary man.*

By the time they finished their drinks and talking, it

was late into the night. They returned to their rooms, exhausted. Not just from the daily activities, but from the emotional efforts of trying to hide their feelings. Bea went to sleep with thoughts of Michael on her mind. And with a touch of regret that she was alone in her bed. Despite her earlier protestations, she thought of how nice it would have been if the hotel hadn't found him another room.

With the solitude of late night as his backdrop, Michael stood in front of the large picture window similar to the one in Beatrice's room, with a mug of coffee in his hand. This time it was strong, black, and with lots of sugar—just the way he liked it. *What happened earlier?*

He alternated between watching the gentle swirl of snow outside and the swirl of steam in his cup. Then he looked toward the cold, empty bed. How nice it would have been to look over and see Bea there—warming his sheets and his heart.

Maybe he had overestimated his ability to woo her or to be able to deal with the amount of patience it would take to wait for her to be ready. She seemed so fragile to him still . . . it was killing him, but he didn't want to push too hard.

The next morning Bea and Michael were organized into separate teams and spent much of the day apart. Bea worked with senior personnel from the State Department and the Central Intelligence Agency while Michael worked with Drug Enforcement Agency and National Security Agency people.

It was late evening by the time they met again. Michael walked down to the lobby after changing into a casual outfit. He was surprised to see Bea sitting alone with a drink in one of the alcoves. He debated whether to intrude on her peace; with so much going on he understood the value of quiet downtime. She must have felt his gaze as he watched her because as soon as he was about to turn to go into another direction, she waved him over.

"Michael, I had hoped to run into you sooner or later. I didn't want to knock on your door in case you were trying to catch up on some much-needed rest."

He smiled his response.

Beatrice motioned toward the empty chair. "Sit down, have some dessert with me. I was just about to order some of their famous chocolate cheesecake."

"With an offer like that, how could I refuse?" Michael patted his belly. "I don't usually pass up cheesecake, especially if it is accompanied by strong black coffee. I saw you, but I was about to head to one of the other little seating areas. I thought you might want some time alone."

Bea smiled. "I think I spend enough time alone. I welcome the company. Besides, we're supposed to be strategizing about the plans for Homeland Security."

Michael sat, pulling his chair closer to hers as he did. He detected a faint hint of Juniper Breeze and smiled.

"What is that little grin for?" she asked.

Michael shook his head. "Nothing, just my own private thoughts. You look especially lovely tonight. I noticed your new haircut earlier and I like it. Short hair becomes you, the style shows off the delicate features of your face."

Bea's hand went instinctively to her recently shorn tresses. "Thanks. I wanted to try something a little different. So, tell me. How does a cheesecake-and-coffee lover stay in such great shape?"

"I think I can eat anything because I don't splurge too often. I usually watch what I eat better than this, but on those rare occasions when I'm away from the office, I feel like I should treat myself. I know I don't do all the things I should, but I try to treat myself right when I can. After all, if *I* don't do it, nobody else will."

Bea gave a wry look. "I suppose you're right. I've become more comfortable with the realization that it will always be just me. With most of my family gone now, I've sort of accepted my fate. Like you, though, the cheesecake and other desserts are my splurge. I'll never be a fitness fanatic, but I do try to do the absolute minimum. I want to be around to enjoy those twilight years." She chuckled again. "I've even stopped plucking at the grays—I was losing the battle anyway."

The remark garnered another smile from Michael. He appreciated everything about her, the tiny laugh lines around her eyes when her face lit up in a smile, her graceful maturity, and her amazing strength. He loved the gray hair that peeked out gently from her temples. It gave her a regal look with her new shorter hairstyle. She was more beautiful now than she ever was to his mind. Michael wanted to grow old with her, to face the grays and challenges of moving through the next stage of their years together.

They continued in amiable conversation for several minutes, though the question hung heavily in the air. *What about us?* But neither seemed willing to ask it.

Chapter Three

Michael wondered how he could be straightforward in every other aspect of his life and not about romance. He was not a man prone to indecision, so this was uncharted territory for him. At what point did patience cross the line to inaction? He wasn't afraid to tell her how he felt; yet they never seemed to move from a certain point.

Michael looked directly at her as he spoke. "You are so beautiful, Bea. The way your hairstyle frames your face is just perfect. I know I'm not supposed to say things like that, but I can't help what I see."

Bea inhaled deeply. "You're right, you shouldn't say things like that." She combed her fingers through her short tresses. As much as she liked hearing the words spoken from his lips, she had to put a stop to this. Her willpower and resolve only stretched so far. "I think you're hoping for more between us than I can give. Michael, I can't lo—can't have a relationship with you." Bea bit her lip and looked down at her coffee. "Besides, I don't feel right mixing business with pleasure. You work for me, and I'm not very comfortable with the idea of that kind of relationship, especially considering how it might be perceived by your subordinates."

Michael didn't know how much more his ego could be affronted. "Bea, I won't pretend that I'm not attracted to you. I also won't pretend that I give a damn about office politics. What's important to me, is you . . . us. I've been patient because I respected your need to grieve. But I'm not in the habit of pining away indefinitely. If you say we have no chance, I can accept that—I'm perfectly capable of letting go, but I don't think that's what *you* really want me to do."

Beatrice sat quietly. Michael's message of displeasure with her was clear, but his voice was low and velvety sexy. His words were spoken like the lyrics of a love song. Beatrice wanted to say something appropriate, needed to say something, but nothing came to mind. It wouldn't be right to say, *Michael, I love you, promise me you'll never leave me!*

Michael held her gaze for a few more seconds. Then he shook his head in disappointment from her lack of response. "I think I've overstayed my welcome." He stood and pushed his chair back. "I'll let you get back to whatever you were doing before I came. Good night, Beatrice."

With a damper on what had started out as a promising evening, Michael went back up to his room. Bea watched him leave, mad at herself for pushing him away. The deep hole in her heart was proof positive that she was in no way ready to love. Bea made up her mind. There could be no more personal conversations; they would have to be satisfied with the civil and functional relationship that they'd enjoyed for several years. No more comparisons, no more thinking about how damn good he looked in his clothes, and no more fantasies about what it would be like to have him make love to her.

The next day would be their final day of activity after which they would be alone in the car again. She would need to pull it together long enough to spend that kind of intimate time together. She would try to keep conversation to a minimum.

Bea continued to wrestle with her thoughts; sleep evaded her as she spent another night with Michael consuming her thoughts. She struggled with whether her decisions made any sense at all. Part of her wanted to forget her new resolution, knock on his door, and tell him that she felt the same way, too. Forget what might be office politics—they would accept the consequences of developing an office romance. But the part of her that won out, dictated that she stick to her decision. Again she let the tidal wave of loneliness and unhappiness wash over her until it disappeared. Tomorrow was a new day and as long as she kept waking up, there was a chance that it would be a better day. That's what she kept telling herself . . . and that's what kept her going.

After the final session had been completed, Michael and Bea were in the last group to leave the hotel. At the risk of spending more time alone with him, Beatrice asked him to delay their trip back so that she could savor more time in the beautifully white, picturesque setting. She bought souvenirs from the gift shop then took photos of the hotel and its surroundings for her travel scrapbook. Past experience had taught her to cherish memories and experiences.

Michael looked up at the sky. A cold front was moving into the area and the temperature had dipped noticeably. "I think we should head out now. The weatherman may have been a little too optimistic about us missing the storm coming out of the Ohio Valley."

Bea furrowed her brows, but looked around, too. She clicked two final pictures and then put her camera in its case. As they packed up the SUV with her luggage, a few light snowflakes had begun to fall. It was still early afternoon, but they wanted to make it back in plenty of time to prepare for work on Monday.

Beatrice decided that on the way home they could discuss their strategy. It would be a lot better for both if they focused on work and not on each other. She situated herself in the seat and placed her portfolio pad on her lap. That way she could write as they talked.

A few minutes into the drive, the snow began to come down in blinding white sheets. The storm seemed to come out of nowhere, taking them by surprise. Michael couldn't see an inch in front of him and knew he would have to find a safe spot to pull over.

Bea put away her papers and looked at him anxiously, but didn't say anything that might distract him. She clasped her hands together and began to pray in the silence.

Michael looked around carefully for a place to stop, but before he could make a decision, he heard a loud *pop!* The vehicle lurched violently to the left, spinning out of control. The wheels of the SUV hit a patch of ice and then skidded across the narrow roadway. The car spun around and around for several seconds, then finally rested with a hard thud against the embankment, slamming Bea and Michael against the dashboard. Michael thought he heard a scream, but before he could check on Beatrice his world turned black.

Time passed in a blur. In the silence, seconds turned to minutes. . . .

Dazed, Bea looked around the vehicle to see if there was any damage. As reality set in, she remembered she wasn't driving, moreover she wasn't alone in the car. Feelings of panic sped up her breathing. *Michael.* Bea looked toward the driver's seat for Michael. He was slumped over the steering wheel and there was a deep bleeding gash on his head. She noticed his eyes were

closed and how still he was; Michael wasn't moving.
Wasn't . . .

Fear snaked through her as she thought about the
possibility that he had been mortally injured. With a
shaky hand she reached out to feel for a pulse. As soon
as she moved, he moaned, so she stopped. Bea exhaled.
He was alive. She tried to assess his injuries without
touching him; she didn't want to move him in case
there were internal injuries. There was blood on the
steering column. Apparently, the air bags had failed to
inflate. He could have a nasty concussion or worse. This
had to be part of a bad dream; she couldn't lose him,
too. She didn't know if she could take being responsible for another person's death.

Michael tried to move, but grunted in pain, she noticed. Bea shoved her fear to the background. "Michael,
are you all right? Can you understand me?"

He moved his body again and his eyes fluttered open
and closed.

Without realizing it, Bea started praying again. She
looked at him intently and made the decision that she
would have to risk checking him out. She was concerned
by the amount of blood he was losing—she needed to
find a way to stop it. She felt for his pulse. Thankfully, it
was strong—she turned her attention toward his bleeding head again. "You need to clean this wound," she told
herself quietly, trying desperately to keep panic at bay.

Bea turned her body so that she could check the
back of the SUV—it, too, was intact. The front had sustained some damage, and they seemed pretty well stuck
wherever they were, but she could move her body
around to the rest of the vehicle. She half climbed, half
reached for her emergency bag in the back. She didn't
want to jostle him too much, but she needed her supplies. "Michael, hold on, we're going to be fine." She

hoped her voice sounded reassuring, because, Lord knew, she didn't feel confident about anything!

After she found her bag, she made a mental list of what she'd learned in her basic first aid training. She wasn't sure how far they'd driven from the hotel or if they had been spotted by anyone prior to the accident. She needed to try to call for help. She reached into her purse for her cell phone. Her battery was good, but she wasn't sure about signal strength. She dialed 911. There was an answer, though the reception was poor and crackly. "This is federal agent Beatrice McCoy. Put me through to the supervisor."

She waited until she heard another voice on the line. She repeated her identification then described Michael's condition. "We've been in a car accident not far from the Hilltop House Hotel. I'm not sure how long we traveled . . . maybe about fifteen minutes. Michael has a head wound. It looks bad because there is a lot of blood, but I don't really know how deep it is."

The dispatcher on the line asked, "Ma'am, is he conscious?"

Bea was losing the battle to keep her anxiety at bay. "Yes, no, sometimes. He has a strong pulse. He's breathing and making some mumbling noises. His eyes seem cloudy—no, unfocused. Just tell me what to do!"

"I know things look bad, but you're going to be fine." The voice was calm and soothing. "Ma'am, can you reach outside to get some snow? If you can, wrap it in something to apply it to his head. You need to put pressure on the wound to stop the bleeding."

Bea struggled with the window, but managed to make it go down enough to make a small snowball that she wrapped in the silk scarf she'd had around her neck. She rummaged through her first aid supplies until she found a 4 x 4 gauze bandage to put on his head.

Michael woke fully from the cold of the compress,

but seemed just as dazed as she had been after the accident. It took several minutes before he became fully cognizant of his surroundings. Bea breathed a sigh of relief when he began to make intelligible sentences. The EMT told her to keep him talking, as it was a head wound. Though she didn't really call their disjointed communication *talking*, it served its purpose.

"Michael, do you have any pain anywhere else besides your head?"

When he answered no, his voice was hoarse and sounded dry. Bea was glad she'd also packed water in her bag. She reached inside for a bottle to give to him. She took that time to inspect the rest of the contents. She had more water, and some things to eat, but what really worried her was that she didn't know where they were and how long they might be there. The EMT had said the roads were impassable, and after giving her general advice, suggested she turn off her phone for the next couple of hours to conserve the battery. Bea was glad she had worn slacks, because the temperature was noticeably cooler now.

"Michael, we have to move to the backseat. It is getting colder outside and we have at least a couple of hours before anyone will find us. If we move to the back, we can use our combined body heat to stay warm. I have a small neck roll and blanket in my bag. Do you think you can move?" she asked uneasily.

Michael winced as he nodded his head. "Okay, you go first, I'll help you."

Bea ventured a small smile. "No, I think you should go first. I moved the bags out of the way so that we can have the entire trunk area. If you have any trouble I can help you better from here. I'm not even sure you should move, but we could freeze to death if we stay like this. We need to get to the back and do the things we were told to do. How's your head?"

Bea looked at Michael in concern. She wouldn't know what to do if something happened to him now. . . .

"It's not bad now—hurts a little, but I know I'll live. I have a great nurse."

Bea started making preparations. They would need to put all of their supplies around them for easy access. She had no idea how long they would be stranded, so it was better to be overly prepared than under. Out of habit she put on lipstick, then wondered why in the world she did. She turned back to Michael to help him. He shrugged off her assistance, saying he was fine, then moved to the backseat, making small grunting noises all the way. Men, she thought. *Guess pride wouldn't let him appear helpless!*

Bea gathered the rest of her things and began to climb, but almost jumped out of her skin when she felt Michael's strong hands almost lift her over the seat. Once they were both in the back, they lowered the backseat to allow them to be able to recline. With Bea's neck roll pillow and the blanket, it wasn't exactly comfortable, but it would do.

Michael held her gaze. There was a sweet sincerity in his voice that intimated his feelings. "Bea, we're going to get out of this. I know things don't look very good now, but something will work out. The unit will send someone to look for us when we don't show up tomorrow. If the local guys can't find us, you know our agents can."

She didn't want to even entertain the idea of spending the night in the backseat of an SUV with him. She wanted to be at home in her nice, warm, lonely bed. This was too much for her senses and her imagination. She almost preferred the idea to tending to his injuries all night—such close proximity to a healthy Michael Spates was too dangerous for her. Bea's hormones kicked into high gear with just the thought of his nearness. She tried to think of something to say, but words escaped her. She hoped her eyes weren't telling the *untold* story. She needed desperately to believe the desire she felt for him was masked by her disbelief of their circumstances.

The fog in his head cleared. Or maybe it hadn't, Michael thought. The air around him and Bea seemed to cackle with the heat of desire. What was he doing thinking about making love to her when they were in a fight for their lives!

Michael reached for her to draw her closer. "I don't know if this is right, but I want you now more than ever. If we don't make it, I don't want to leave this world without telling you how much I love you. I have for a very long time, but I wanted to give you time and space while you healed. I know these last few years have been rough for you—but it didn't stop me from falling head-long for you. I need to hear how you feel—say it, Bea."

Bea looked down. "Michael, please don't talk like that. I can't . . ."

Michael interrupted. "You can't what, Bea? Love me? I don't accept that. I know you feel something for me. I can sense it, even though you pull back from me. We may never get the chance again—tell me what's in your heart."

Bea struggled. Conflicting emotion threatened to tear her apart. A slow trail of tears made a path down her cheeks. She had come face-to-face with the possibility of losing him after the car had spun out of control. There was no way she would tempt fate now. "Michael, don't make me." She was whispering now, the pain evident with each word she spoke.

Michael exhaled in disappointment. He wouldn't make her beg. "Come." He wrapped his arms around her as the tears came faster, with more force. "Shush, shush, it's okay." He stroked her hair. "I'm here, Bea. I'll always be here for you."

Outside the storm raged and temperatures continued to drop. Bea shook in Michael's arms, as much from the cold as from her emotional ordeal. They needed to be rescued soon or she wouldn't have to worry about her deal—she wouldn't have to worry about anything at all.

After a few moments she was able to calm herself. She knew she wasn't being fair to him, but once they made it to safety, what would they do? She wasn't prepared to carry on an office romance with him; furthermore, with the reorganization efforts that were currently underway, they both had more than enough to deal with on their plates.

Bea turned her focus back to the matter at hand—survival. "Michael, I'm going to turn to put my back up to your body. We need to create more body heat—I'm really cold. The EMT said for you to stay alert, so I want you to tell me why you chose the SCU and all about your family, okay?"

Michael grinned. "I thought I was supposed to stay awake—I don't want to bore us both into a permanent slumber."

"Zeke!" Bea cuffed him on the shoulder as she twisted her body into a new position. They adjusted the thin blanket over them and hunkered down.

His head hurt again, but he didn't tell Bea. They would be rescued soon enough—besides, it was probably nothing. He wrapped his arm around her to pull her closer before he spoke. "I'll tell you all about me, on one condition."

Bea sighed. "Yes, Michael?"

Passion thickened his voice, his words sounded rough and edgy. "One day, you agree to stop fighting so hard. One day, just give in and let go."

Bea closed her eyes. She didn't know if she could live up to the promise, but she made it anyway. She rubbed her brow with the back of her very cold hand. "Yes, Michael . . . one day."

Michael forced himself not to focus on the pain and began to tell his story. "Most of it you know, but there may be some tidbits that I can fill in for you. I came to the Special Corruption Unit because of my mentor, Peter Anderson. He was more than a mentor actually, he was my idol. I wanted to be just like him and then later as we worked together, I wanted to make him proud. After he retired and suggested that I become the agent in charge, I knew I had achieved something in my life." Michael paused, he was talking too fast and it was making him breathless. "I've stuck around the unit and given up promotions because I believe in my agents. I want them to feel the same sense of nurturing and accomplishment that my work with Peter gave to me. Every one of the agents that I've trained is special. They have untold talent and ability and it's my job to pull it out of them. We have a wonderful crew, Bea. I would hate to give them up—I would hate to give *us* up. We need to find a way to make sure the unit survives the shake-up." Michael paused, and waited for Bea to respond.

"Oh, Michael, I wish we could. There's so much going on though, I don't know if the unit can survive the budgetary ax. Unless we are to concentrate only on terrorism, I don't see a way. . . .

"Seems Washington only understands a few buzz-words. When I think about all the programs that I over-see, the SCU holds a special place in my heart. Agents like Eric Duvernay, Maria Thomas, Roderick Radford, Helene Maupin, Steven Caldwell, Chantal McCorkle, and Max Wilson don't come along all the time. We're blessed to have them."

Though her back was to him, Michael nodded in agreement.

"Michael," Bea began slowly, hesitantly.

"Yes, Bea?"

"Michael, how come you never married?"

He chuckled. "Is that all you wanted to know? Your tone was so ominous, I wasn't sure what to expect." Michael exhaled deeply. "I came close a couple of times, but when it came down to it, the women in my life decided that they wouldn't play second fiddle to my career. And also, I guess I don't believe in ultimatums. Anyway, then you came to work for the bureau and I knew you were the one. But, that little thing called your marriage stopped me from pursuing you. After Harold died, I kept my distance, but it broke my heart to see you in such pain."

Bea backed down. His answer was much more than she bargained for and it made her uncomfortable. "I'm sorry. This was none of my business and I shouldn't have asked, that was too personal. How is your head?"

"My life is an open book to you, Bea, and don't worry about my head. I'm fine now." *It's my heart that I want you to concern yourself over right now.*

The wind swirled and howled outside, making the car untraceable. It would be several hours before a rescue could be attempted. Michael and Bea were in more danger than either realized as temperatures approached subfreezing levels.

Bea turned on her phone to make contact with the fire station.

"Ma'am, we're monitoring the situation, but we can't put any vehicles out in this weather, not even with chains. Visibility is zero and the wind is making it too dangerous to mount an effective search. I suggest you stay put. Please don't attempt to leave the vehicle, use it as your shelter, and as soon as we can, we'll find you.

Remember to conserve your battery, we'll need you to leave the phone on later so that we can locate your exact position. Also, just to let you know, we have contacted your headquarters to apprise them of the situation. It seems everyone else made it back from your meeting before the worst of the storm hit."

Gee, how lucky for them. "All right then, we'll be here when you get here. I'll turn off the phone again. Thank you." Bea turned back to Michael. "I guess you got the gist of that. Looks like it is just you and me, kid."

Michael looked around the back of the SUV in jest. "Yep, looks that way. So, what do you have in that trusty emergency kit of yours to eat?"

Bea smiled for the first time in awhile. "Oh, so now you want to see what I have in my stash. I'm not sure I should even share with you after the way you teased me about my packing. Hmmm, let me see what *I'm* going to eat."

"You wouldn't treat a wounded brother so poorly, would you?" Michael responded.

Bea raked her eyes over him. "Oh, I don't know, a brother looks pretty healthy to me." It was an innocent gesture, but it stoked an already unchecked flame.

"Yeah, come here to find out." Before she could resist or respond, Michael had taken her into his arms. He began gently at first, nuzzling her neck, and trailing kisses along its length. In the quiet of the vehicle, their breathing had become regular and rhythmic . . . they were perfectly in tune with each other.

Michael increased the tempo as passion heated to a boil. All attempts at control, lost.

Bea forgot to protest—she felt too good. She kissed Michael with reckless abandon, nothing else mattered. . . .

Michael received her acquiescence. He drew her

closer, he wanted to feel her body next to his, and wanted her to feel the desire that welled up in him so strong.

He wanted to take his time, love her with a slow hand, but they were impatient, insistent, and insatiable. He found the bottom of her blouse and jerked it up so that his fingers could find their prize—her deliciously soft skin. Michael caressed the warm skin of her back, feeling it prickle with each touch. Bea moaned. He found the hooks to her bra and dispatched them in short order, then his fingers made their way to her full breasts. She wasn't large, but neither was she small. She felt every inch a woman. The supple skin of her breasts seemed to call to him. He dipped his head low to kiss the mocha-colored skin of her areola before he took one chocolate brown nipple between his teeth.

Bea arched her back to give him more. His kisses uncovered the desire she had tried so hard to bury. She was the aggressor now. She could feel him stiff and large through his clothes. Bea wanted to feel him skin to skin, caution be damned. She unzipped his pants to feel him—and she wasn't disappointed. His body responded immediately to her touch. He lurched forward in her hand, as he keened for her fingers to continue their sensual caress. His response was heady to Bea the idea of giving Michael pleasure made her feel deliriously powerful. She continued to stroke him as he sucked harder, moving from one nipple to the next. She felt the hot wetness between her legs . . . *Lord, how long had it been since that happened?*

Michael moved from her nipples back to her mouth. This time his kiss was softer, longer, and deeper. He moved his hands from her back to her zipper, which he slid down in a quick motion. Bea gyrated toward him in anticipation. The temperature may have been below zero outside the vehicle, but inside it was hotter than a Texas summer. Her body hummed and tingled in the most intimate places. Michael had definitely started something now.

"I hope we don't regret this in the morning," she panted between kisses.

"I would never regret you, Bea. I love you and I've never wanted anything else more than to share my love with you."

"Michael . . ."

"Shush, it's okay. I'll settle for now. You don't have to say anything more. Just let me make love to you." He helped her remove her pants and blouse and in short order was completely naked beside her. Bea continued her exploration of his body, which was firm and muscular, caressing the most intimate parts of him. Her lips found his nipples and they were treated to the same erotic loving that she'd received from him.

Michael moaned and pulled her head closer. She was much more the delight, than even in his fantasies. His hands moved across her body, he caressed her hair and the soft skin of her back as she gave him pleasure. He felt her gyrate her hips along his full length, which grew harder and longer with each passing second. He didn't know how much longer he could hold out before he had to feel himself inside of her. Bea moved from his nipples to his mouth, just as he had done. They were perfectly in tune with each other, like experienced lovers. He slid his tongue over the length of her lips, reveling in her taste and feel. She felt like warm silk . . . soft, smooth, delicate.

Bea felt like her heart would explode. She had denied herself physical pleasure for so long, she didn't know if she could handle him. He was so hard, so strong, and so damned virile. Her breath caught in her throat. Michael sensed her hesitation. "Bea, are you okay?"

Bea smiled to hide her embarrassment. "Yes, Michael, I'm okay . . . it's just that . . . well, it has been a long while. I don't want to disappoint you." She whispered her confession.

Michael drew her to him, wrapped her in his arms, and repeated the words of love that he'd uttered earlier. "Bea, nothing you do could disappoint me. You're everything that I've ever wanted."

Bea's shoulders slumped in relief. This was an important step for her, not one she took lightly. She was ready to do with him exactly what she'd promised herself she wouldn't. She was giving herself to him body, mind, and soul. "Michael, I can't make any promises about what happens after today. I hope you understand. I want this, I need this, but I don't know what the future holds for us."

Michael regarded her intently. "Bea, the only thing we're promised is right now . . . we can let that be enough." He sought to close the distance between them. Right here, right now, that's all he knew about. That and how happy he was to have the woman he loved in his arms.

His kiss was even more patient this time. Michael sought to reassure Bea, let her dictate the pace. He was handsomely rewarded with the passionate way she returned his kiss. She sucked lightly on his bottom lip; the sensation sent spirals of ecstasy coursing through him. His body felt like it was on fire, hot, blazing, liquid fire. He grasped her exposed buttocks, pulling her closer. He returned her gentle nips, while enjoying the feel of her curved bottom in his hands.

Bea wanted to give pleasure, but her body's need made her impatient. "Now, Michael, I need to feel you in me," she insisted.

"Gladly." His voice was rough and ready, just like he was.

Michael protected them, and then entered her, hard as a rod and stiff as a brick. He felt hot, wet, tightness encircle him almost immediately. It may have been a long time since she had been intimate with anyone, but she was definitely ready. He felt her engorged lips shudder and pulse each time he pumped into her and withdrew. Michael varied the pace, he moved slowly at first, and then faster, plunging deeper into her womanly embrace.

He kissed her, he plundered her, and he captivated her essence.

Bea moved higher to receive him; he felt heavenly. She scored his back with her perfectly manicured nails, willing him to take her to new heights. No one should feel this good, she thought.

Michael drove himself deep into her, filling her completely. Bea's body begged for release, but he made her hold on a little longer. She shuddered, feeling a powerful orgasm beginning to build. He felt her pulse and quake as he brought her closer to completion. He kissed her nipples again, toying with the hard buds, heightening her awareness of herself. She needed to be reminded what brought her pleasure.

Michael aimed to find out and spend a lot of time showing her. He sucked on her bottom lip, while his fingers did delightful things to her breasts. She felt his large hands moving across her body in a tantalizing dance. She felt cold where his touch abandoned her, but on fire wherever his hands rested. "Michael, I can't hold on much longer, baby, please . . ."

Bea shattered into a million pieces, screaming out his name as she did. Hearing his name in such an erotic octave pushed him closer. Her body bucked, and pulsed beneath his, sending him completely out of control.

Michael moved to place his hands on her bottom to pull her closer as he exploded into an earth-shattering orgasm of his own. "Bea, God, I love you so much." He cried out her name again as he fell over that same deliciously pleasurable edge.

The storm had broken, but neither one cared. Michael

held Bea close and they fell into a lovers' slumber, oblivious to the world around them. Sated, happy, and in love.

Northern Virginia . . .

Zola covered her face with her hands. She couldn't believe that she was about to betray her boss. She had worked with Bea McCoy for five years. A lump the size of California formed in her throat. What choice did she have? Her hands trembled as she dialed the phone. "It's me. I have some information you might find useful. After this we're squared. Don't call me and I won't call you." She hoped her voice sounded more forceful to the other party than it did to her own ears. If the laugh on the other end was any indication, she'd failed.

She gave him the information and hung up quickly. Who was she kidding? Zola thought miserably. Once a person was in with those guys there was only one way out. And that's what she had been trying to avoid all along.

West Virginia . . .

Bea woke up with a start. There was loud tapping on the window that nearly caused her to jump out of her skin. She nudged Michael, who was still sleeping soundly. He awoke to the same insistent tapping she'd heard. The EMTs probably wouldn't expect to find a naked couple in the back of the vehicle. They dressed hurriedly, bumping awkwardly into each other with every movement.

It was pitch-black outside so their first thoughts were that they were being rescued, but the loud crack of the breaking SUV windows and seeing the cold black of gun barrels that were pointed at their heads showed them otherwise. This was no rescue.

Michael and Bea looked at each other. Neither had time to locate their weapons. Five very hostile looking men surrounded them. Michael nodded his head toward Bea, imperceptibly. "We'd better do as they say—for now."

A heavily accented voice, behind the barrel of one of the guns spoke. "Good choice, mon. Now, exit the car slowly. You're coming with us."

The cold air raked through Bea and Michael's clothes, causing them no small amount of discomfort. As soon as they stood beside their vehicle, their hands were bound and they were ushered toward a large SUV outfitted for the weather. The chains on the tires had made it easier for these people to find them than the rescue vehicles.

"What is this about?" Michael asked calmly. He wouldn't show fear, wouldn't give them the pleasure. He directed the question to the man closest to him. He looked strangely familiar. Michael tried to place him, but he knew the face wasn't from an active case. He always remembered his mission profiles. The man was tall and thin, and he had long black locks that reached the middle of his back. His eyes were dark brown, with little spark—Michael didn't like that. If the eyes were truly the windows to the soul, then this man didn't have one. Instinctively he moved closer to Bea, as if to protect her. She seemed thankful for the gesture.

Michael looked at the man again and posed his question, but this time his voice reflected his loss of patience. His answer was a gun butt to his already wounded head. Bea screamed and lunged toward him, but heavy hands restrained her. Michael's slumped body was placed in the vehicle beside her. Bea trembled. His head was bleeding again, and their captors refused to do anything about it. Bea raged, "What have you done? Are you crazy? You could have killed him."

The one who appeared to be the leader responded to her in a harsh tone, which made Bea quiver inside. "Relax, woman, he's still breathing, now take care you hold your tongue before you end up in the same state."

Bea checked a sarcastic retort as she surveyed their situation. She and Michael were in the back of an SUV barreling through the snow to God knew where, Michael had been knocked out, and nobody from the bureau had any idea that they had been taken—perfect, just friggin' perfect.

Juniper Breeze. Michael's head throbbed, but he knew he was all right as long he recognized the fragrance and the woman he loved was beside him. With his eyes still closed he listened to sounds around him. He heard footsteps, muted conversations, and an odd pattern of speech. After a few minutes he realized what he heard was the distinctive pattern of the Jamaican dialect. He could feel Bea beside him, but he didn't move toward her.

He continued to listen, trying to glean what he could through his senses. They were in a large building from the way the voices carried around the rooms. He thought he could detect two or three men in his immediate vicinity. He and Bea appeared to be sitting on the floor, and his hands were bound in front of him, though his feet were free. *That was their second mistake.*

He opened his eyes, he needed to see Beatrice, make sure she was safe. His blood ran cold at the sight of her. Both of her hands and feet were bound, her mouth was gagged, and she looked terribly uncomfortable. Tear stains streaked her lovely face, though she didn't appear to be harmed. Michael was livid. *Oh, they would pay dearly for this.*

Bea made eye contact with him, but didn't attempt to communicate. The fear he saw in her eyes was enough.

Michael hoped he'd silently communicated his resolve to get them out of this situation to her.

"Simeon, seems our boy is awake now. Shall we have us a little talk?"

"Augustus, don't do anything more to him. We need him alive, remember? His dead body is of no use to us. And leave the lady alone, too. Our contact says she is a valuable asset." He snickered. "She even outranks him."

Augustus kicked at Michael's feet. "So you planning to climb the corporate ladder by sleeping with the boss lady? Tsk, tsk, I wonder if the boys back in Washington know about this?" His tone mocked them and Michael knew the man was enjoying himself.

Michael checked his temper before he spoke. He wouldn't be of any use to Bea—dead. He used the most conversationally pleasant tone that he could muster. "My name is Michael Spates, assistant executive director of the Federal Bureau of Investigation. Why have you brought us here and what do you want?" He lowered his voice. "If you think you can negotiate for something with us, you've wasted your time. In case you haven't noticed, the U.S. does not negotiate with terrorists."

Augustus seemed insulted by the comment. He brandished his weapon, waving it in front of Michael's face. "Do I look like a terrorist to you?" He paused. "This is strictly business, mon—don't worry, you and your pretty little lady friend here will have lots of time to catch up where you left off. In the meantime, you need to make a phone call. We wouldn't want any unwelcome company snooping around."

The tough-talking Augustus backed off when he noticed a man coming into the room. He immediately deferred authority to him. . . . Michael surmised he must be the boss. A tall, lanky man with thick, unkempt hair and noticeably bushy eyebrows entered, Michael recognizing his distinctive features instantly.

Michael pierced him with an icy glare. He'd seen his face before . . . from one of the files sitting on his desk in Virginia. Their situation took on new meaning if this man was involved. Adrenaline pumped through his veins and his level of concern for Bea's safety increased one-hundred fold. He thought wryly, *this just keeps getting better and better* . . .

Michael recognized the man as Kharl Winton, head of one of Jamaica's most notorious posses. His operation was responsible for the import of more cannabis to American soil than any other drug trafficking entity. His reach was deep, and his connections solid enough to keep him out of jail despite his many criminal activities. Somehow he had eluded DEA arrest for years.

Michael looked toward Beatrice again. She was watching everything, but not making any attempt to draw attention to herself. He assumed that she was trying to figure a way out of the mess they were in, just as he was, too. He grimaced inwardly. Alone he could handle the situation, but with Beatrice . . . he swore quietly to himself. He wanted to hold her hand, stroke her hair—anything to give her comfort. Winton would regret this particular move—he may have been able to cover his tracks with his other activities, but this was a very bad move. A bad move indeed and soon enough Michael would let him know that fact.

He fought hard to concentrate, to process the information of their capture. Disappointment, anger, and dread filled him in equal parts. How would the Jamaicans have known about them being stranded, including an approximate location? This was no random act of violence. If Kharl had the information to kidnap them from their snowbound location, it meant one thing—they had a *traitor* at SCU headquarters.

Chapter Four

"This is Executive Director Beatrice McCoy. I've managed to find us a house to stay in while the storm subsides. Call off the search and we'll contact you again in a few hours."

The paramedic seemed relieved, but needed to be sure that they were all right. "Ma'am, what is your exact location? Do you still need medical treatment for Agent Spates?"

Bea noticed that the EMT seemed a little skeptical. Her heart pounded in her chest. She looked over at Kharl who held a gun to Michael's head as she spoke. "No, everything is fine. . . . I followed the medical procedures as I was told earlier and he's better. He's resting comfortably by the fire." Kharl handed a piece of paper to her indicating that she should read the note. "We managed to make it to the old Johnson place. It could use a little work, but it'll do for shelter right now.

"We're just going to rest for awhile, let the roads clear, then start out probably sometime tomorrow. We'll contact our headquarters to let them know that we're fine as well. Thank you for your assistance, but we can handle it from here." That seemed to satisfy the dispatcher, because he rang off the line. Bea's heart thudded again as she felt hope fading.

Kharl grabbed Bea's phone after she was finished. "Very good." He smirked. "Now, let's get to know each other a little better, shall we?"

Bea looked toward Michael. He wore a stoic expression, but seemed no worse for the wear, for which she was thankful. She held Kharl's gaze while she spoke. "Whatever you're thinking, just forget it. The bureau won't let you get away with this."

Kharl gave her a bored expression. "Seems I've heard that before. Do you mind changing the tune, this song is getting old." His smug expression gave her pause. Why was he so certain that there would be no repercussions? "And in case you haven't noticed, I get away with whatever I want. The DEA has been chasing after me for years—always a dollar short for the dance." He looked from Bea to Michael. "I think you need to be more worried about yourselves than about me—especially if you don't prove useful."

He motioned toward one of the men. "Show our guests to their accommodations. I have some more pressing business to take care of right now. I'll be back for them later."

Augustus moved toward them, pointing the gun in a menacing way as he did. They were both bound and led down a narrow hallway going to who knows where, she thought as she walked. An involuntary shudder passed through Bea. She looked at Michael again and hoped that they wouldn't be separated. She noticed his jaw flexed as he struggled to control his temper.

Michael took note of everything he saw as he walked. His field training kicked in as he began to examine his options. They were outnumbered, had no weapons to speak of, had no idea where they were, and between the gun butt to the head and car accident he felt significantly less than 100 percent. But none of that mattered because he had to protect Beatrice. He thought, *yeah, this was going to be good.*

In the room where they were first held, Michael had noticed old bloodstains and the cloying smell of industrial-strength antiseptic. He hadn't committed Kharl's full profile to memory from his file, but he knew enough to be concerned about their fate. He would never give up information that would be useful to the man, but he wondered about Bea. No doubt Kharl would want the names and contact information that would allow him to continue to operate with impunity . . . lives would be at stake. Could he stand by while she was tortured? Michael knew that as long as they were held he would be forced to make a choice between the woman he loved and the organization that he served.

They proceeded through the winding corridors in silence. Augustus walked deeper into the structure, which inside looked nothing like one would expect from a West Virginia farmhouse. Kharl's compound was a large sprawling structure, full of long halls and small rooms. It was clean enough to be decent, but far from comfortable. The rooms were drafty and apparently no attempt had been made to modernize the front rooms of the structure. But as they walked further into the house it began to take on a new life. These were the rooms that housed the heart of his operation. They were larger, held more amenities, and were more comfortable. Bea sniffed, and she smelled something not totally unfamiliar. . . .

Michael edged away from Augustus and moved toward her again. She felt his thumb brush up against her thigh. It was a welcomed gesture, because she needed to know he was there for her. She wasn't a field-rated agent, but she knew enough to know that this situation wasn't good.

Michael's gaze met hers and he held it as long as he

could. He wanted her to know that they were in this together and he would do anything to keep her safe.

They stopped beside a small room that looked like a replica of a jail cell, secured by a see-through door that locked from the outside. Once inside they realized that the glass was not clear . . . they couldn't see out, though their captors could see inside. The room was cold, cramped, and held nothing more than a small metal toilet and sink and a cot. Augustus had unbound them and shoved them into the room. "Make yourselves at home, supper's in one hour." The man then walked away, leaving them stunned and confused.

Beatrice reached for Michael, and her grip around his body was tight enough to indicate the extent of her fear. Michael held her close and whispered reassuring words in her ear; as he did he looked for surveillance equipment and anything that could be fashioned into a weapon. He felt Bea's heart race against his body, making his heart surge with the need to protect her— Kharl Winton would pay dearly for this, Michael would make sure of it.

Michael didn't like the looks of anything in the room. There was a drain in the middle of the floor with a hook that was suspended directly above it in the ceiling. The floor was sloped to accommodate the . . . flow.

The room was obviously designed for more than just *holding* people. He continued to study the area, looking for their best means of escape. They would have to think fast, he wouldn't give Kharl the opportunity to come up with a ransom plan, or any other type of plan, for that matter. His first priority had to be getting Beatrice out of the compound safely. He stroked her back as he held her.

Before being tossed into the room, everything of use had been taken away. He needed some *MacGyver*-like inspiration about now.

"Bea, I'm sorry for getting us into this mess. . . ."

Beatrice held up her hand. "Michael, you had nothing to do with this! If I hadn't delayed our departure to take those damned pictures we would have beaten the storm and would be home right now. I'm the one who should apologize to you. We're in the middle of Lord knows where with madmen and gangsters. Do you recognize anybody? No one's face looks remotely familiar." She paused, while she looked around the room. "And judging from the appearance of this place, it's not going to be a very pleasant stay."

Michael smoothed her hair again. "When the food comes, let's see if we can overtake the guards. I don't want to know what he has planned for us, but he's not going to get it. If we can work our way out of here, I'll provide enough of a distraction for you to run. We're on farmland, so stay in the tree line and run as fast as you can!"

Bea raised an eyebrow. "Michael Ezekiel Spates, if you think I'm leaving you here, just forget it. We either make it out of here or not—*together.*"

Michael shook his head vigorously. "Don't be stubborn, woman! We don't have time to argue. You're the ranking officer, so *you* need to get out of here and to safety. Contact the unit, let them know where I am, then we can shut down this operation. The DEA had their chance, now it's up to the SCU to clean up their mess." He hoped his voice held the reassurance that his heart didn't feel. "Don't worry, we'll get through this."

Un-shed tears shined brightly in her eyes. There was no way she could comply with his request. "Michael, I'm not leaving you here. Not now . . ." She placed her face on his chest. "Michael, I've been such a fool. I should have given in to my feelings a long time ago, and now it may be too late." She whispered, "I love you, I guess I have for a long time. I don't want to lose you."

Michael kissed the top of her curly tresses and held

her closer. He sighed inwardly. How long had he waited to hear words of love from her? How long had he prayed for his chance to show her how much he loved her? And now time might be against them. "Beatrice, now that I know you love me, I'm never going to let you go. Just get to safety, I'll be okay—I promise."

They were both silent for several minutes. The gravity of the situation slowly seeped into perspective, making them realize that their professions of love just might be too late.

Michael felt Beatrice's body tremble. He positioned her so that he could see her face to wipe away her tears. Surprised, he realized that she wasn't crying, instead she was laughing. "Bea, what in the world is going on?"

Bea's laughing became louder and more intense. Her whole body shook now. "Oh my God, Michael. I just had this vision of us in the back of the car. What would my children say about their mother 'doing' it in the backseat! Oh Lord, I'm so mortified!" She stopped laughing long enough to look into his eyes. "Why did it take me almost losing you to realize that I don't want to live without you in my life?" She cupped the side of his face with her hands. "I almost blew it with you . . . something I promise to make up for as soon as we return home."

Michael dipped his head down to her mouth and kissed her softly. The contact was sweet, but way too brief. "Beatrice, I'll be honest with you, I was ready to abide by your decision. Once we returned to Virginia, I was going to do whatever it took to get you out of my system. The last thing I wanted was to cause you more pain, and that's what it seemed I was doing by loving you."

Bea shook her head in disagreement. Michael looked at her for a few seconds and then slowly a smile crept along his lips. "And, technically, it wasn't the backseat of a car. It was the trunk area of an SUV. I think that elevates us above horny-teenager status."

Bea laughed again. "Yeah, but only slightly. I can't wait to get you home to *my* bed. I don't want to waste any more time being scared or hiding my feelings. I'm ready to be with you now—no more apprehension. I promise."

Michael smiled again. He liked the sound of those words. But a small part of him wondered just how they would mesh their two distinct lives together. *No, not your bed . . . our bed,* he thought. He didn't intend to be her lover. He wanted all or nothing and he fully intended that Beatrice McCoy become Beatrice Spates.

Michael enjoyed his house, his surroundings, and the things that made him feel comfortable. Beatrice hadn't moved from the house that she'd shared with her husband and children, and he wasn't willing to share the bed that was once her marriage bed. That was definite. They also had work issues to resolve . . . he didn't even know if he would have a job after the next few months. *Yeah,* he thought.

There was a lot to work out, but knowing that Bea loved him, helped him focus on the future in a way that he hadn't dreamed of before. *But first things first . . .* he had to get them out of there and away from their captors.

Zola stared out her window. She didn't know what else to do. Once they found out that she was the traitor, her life would be over . . . who was she kidding, it was over the moment she traded her soul for the life of her drugged-out little brother. And why?

She cursed herself under her breath as she looked around her tiny apartment. She used to have a nice place, a nice life, but every time he came around, he stole something else to sell for drug money. His habit was out of control and he didn't give a damn who he took down with him. And now, even after the last bit of money she'd given him, she didn't know where he was—ungrateful bast—. "No, why curse him, you made these choices," she said aloud.

Zola felt like she needed a drink. She walked away from her perch at the window toward the refrigerator. Inside, she had a bottle of Riunite, but that was as strong as it got—and it was definitely not strong enough!

She took stock of her present situation; Zola wanted to cry, but she was long past that . . . the tears were all dried up. All she had now was a little bit of time.

Once Karen figured out that she had been lying, they would force her to tell them all she knew. The sad part is, she didn't know much, but it was enough to endanger the lives of everyone in her life who really mattered. She looked at the file on the cocktail table that she'd made from an old trunk. Zola had taken it from Spates's desk and brought it home. She was supposed to report in to Kharl, but hadn't been able to force her fingers to dial his number. He would come looking for her soon enough if she didn't do as she was told.

She considered her options. Beatrice McCoy had always treated her more like family than the losers who were related to her by blood ever did! She thought if she tried to help her brother that she could will him to clean up his life. If she could just prove to him how much she loved him, it would be enough . . . but it was never enough. He would smoke it, shoot it up, or ingest it—he took her love and turned it into something evil.

Zola glanced at the clock on the wall. She probably still had it only because it had come from Wal-Mart . . . from anyplace else, he'd have stolen and sold that, too!

Zola walked back to *admire* the . . . view. She wanted to laugh out loud at the irony of her life. Yeah, time, she thought. She had a little more time to look out this window to consider what a colossal mess she had made out of everything in the name of love.

The lump in her throat threatened to choke the tears

out of her. She held onto the windowsill for strength, willing the sensation to pass. She didn't want to cry. Again.

Bea and Michael sat on the edge of the cot, poised and ready. They had a plan, and as soon as the door opened they would attack. They heard Augustus speaking to someone as the door was opened, but he didn't enter the room. Instead a little girl about ten years old balanced a large tray precariously in her small hands. Bea jumped up to help her before the girl and the tray hit the floor. The girl mumbled something about coming back for the tray in fifteen minutes and scurried out the door at the insistence of Augustus, who stood at the entrance.

"Damn," Michael uttered, upset that they'd lost their opportunity.

Kharl took a long drag on his pipe before he spoke. "I hope they enjoy da meal . . . it just may be der last." He watched the pungent smoke swirl in the air around him. He turned his attention to Augustus again. "Call on Zola, we'll give her one last opportunity to get back on the right track. She should have the file we're looking for, but if she don't want to give it up, that's fine—we'll just kill the whole lot of 'em."

He put the pipe back in his mouth, satisfied with this course of action. He had a business to run and no time for distractions. It was too bad his DEA snitch had let him down, he thought with a grunt. But, if Zola hadn't called with the new information he might not have known there was another agency for him to worry about. Kharl smirked in disgust; he felt like he spent more time paying off government informants than selling his product!

He walked back to his office preoccupied with

thoughts of his business dealings; Bea and Michael were just a minor consequence.

Bea picked at her food with the tip of her plastic fork. She noticed that Michael ate with relish. She stifled a giggle. This was too serious a situation for levity, though in some ways there was a comically cruel irony to their predicament. She had promised herself she would never give in to her feelings for him out of fear something bad would happen to him—just like with her husband and children.

She guessed that she should thank Zola and Karen for trying to make them see that they belonged together. Their little scheme with the reservations had almost worked, but more importantly it planted enough of a seed to make them recognize there was much more between them than boss and employee. Bea regarded Michael as her equal.

She sighed inwardly; well, she had given in to her feelings . . . maybe she could take some consolation in that, because they would probably die together.

Bea's stomach grumbled, but she ignored the sensation. The truth was she was hungry, but she was more worried about how they would escape than anything else.

The food wasn't fancy—oxtails, rice and peas, and a roll—but it was hot and spiced just the way he liked it. Michael noticed that she hadn't eaten anything and stopped stuffing his mouth. Bea appeared to be deep in thought. "Bea, you need to try to get something down. There's no telling when they will feed us again, especially after they begin to . . . question us. Conserve your strength."

Bea nodded her head in agreement. "Michael, if they send that little girl back, what are we going to do? I assume she's Kharl's daughter or maybe one of the other guys' and I doubt we can recruit her help. We aren't going to get anywhere with these plastic utensils, either. . . ."

Michael finished hurriedly and stood up to pace the small room. He hated the expression in her eyes; it pained him to know that she was so scared and that there was little he could do about it. Bea had no business in a situation like this . . . she was trained to take care of people, real estate, and material, not for field duty. This was not her domain and for once he wished she weren't right by his side. He could handle the escape a lot better if he didn't have to worry about her safety as well. He was more worried about her safety than his own. He was going to have to force himself to focus, if either one of them were to get out alive.

"Michael, what are you thinking?"

He turned to look at Bea. How honest could he afford to be right now? He stopped pacing the floor and sat down next to her on the cot. He held her close as he whispered in her ear, "Just follow my lead."

After Michael brushed away an errant lock of hair, he said, "I knew during this trip that I'd have to make some hard decisions, but I never dreamed it would be like this. I was looking toward the more mundane things, like what to do with over twenty years of federal service, how long to wait for the woman I love, whether to buy a new car or a truck."

Michael shook his head. "Maybe something so simple as whether that circular saw at Home Depot was a better deal than at Lowe's." He paused to gaze at her in earnest. "I have forced myself to live such a lonely existence, that now I don't want to even think about a life without you, Bea. No matter what I've thought about my life before, I know now that you have to be in it. You fill a void in me, Beatrice McCoy. And I can't lose that—I've waited too long to get to here."

Emotion welled up in Bea, threatening to spill tears

over her long black lashes again. Michael saw her glistening eyes and wanted nothing more than to hold her in his arms forever. He spoke louder. "Bea, I'm going to give them what they want."

Bea jumped from the cot. "No, you're not! Michael, don't be crazy, they will kill us either way it goes. They've allowed us to see too much of their operation . . . why do you think they were so nonchalant about our being here—we're not a threat anymore."

Michael nodded in agreement. "I know, I've thought about that, but maybe I can convince them that two high-ranking FBI agents are worth more alive than dead. I've got to give it a shot—" Michael winced. "Okay, poor choice of words. But I have to give it a chance—it may be our only way out of this mess."

Bea looked at him in consternation. "And what if you're successful . . . then what? We go back to Washington as moles for the Jamaicans? I don't think so. I'd rather die in this rat hole than do that. I swore an oath to uphold the law and that's what I'm going to do until I draw my last breath. I can't believe you would even remotely consider betraying those who mean so much to me."

Michael reached for her, but she pushed away his hand.

"Beatrice, you can say whatever you want to at this point, but my mind is made up. If I talk, we live—if I don't, you know the consequences." He paced the room again. "And as far as duty and honor go, I've given my entire life to this job and my country. The nights I've watched over missions, the weekends and endless hours, my blood, sweat, and tears . . . my soul. Beatrice, enough is enough. If you think that I'm going to stand idly by and watch you die, too—forget it."

A cold hush descended over the room, as neither appeared ready to budge from the position that each thought was right.

* * *

Kharl watched and listened to the couple from his office in amusement. Everyone had his or her price. And for all their position and high-and-mighty ideals, these folks were no better than the agents he had under his thumb at the DEA. He smirked as he decided that he would wait to question them after Augustus returned with Zola.

Satisfied that he would find out the information he sought, he leaned back in his chair to read over his spreadsheets. Despite the occasional threat his operation faced, he was pleased with the numbers . . . business had been very good . . . very good indeed.

Chapter Five

Northern Virginia . . .

Karen had a strange feeling in the pit of her stomach. She hadn't heard from either the executive director or the assistant director. She'd expected that either she or Zola would have received a phone call about their little prank, but she hadn't heard a word. She tried Agent Spates's cell phone. Nothing but the voice mail. She left another message, then started to think about her options. She called Zola next, and was also immediately connected to her voice mail system as well. "What is going on here?"

As much as she relished the thought of the boss being out of the office for a few days, she couldn't understand why she hadn't heard from him . . . this wasn't the way they operated. Discomfort gnawed at her, something was definitely wrong—she needed to figure out what.

Karen looked out the window to check the weather. She wasn't afraid to drive in the snow, but considering that most Virginians didn't manage very well even with less than an inch on the ground, she had an important decision to make. The area had received a few snow flurries, but now the roads were all clear. Tugging on her shoes, she grabbed her coat and keys, then headed out the door.

"Jerk!" Karen yelled as she jumped onto the sidewalk outside Zola's building. The man had been in such a hurry he'd almost hit her as she walked across the street from her parked car. *You shouldn't be going so fast on these slick streets anyway!*

Angry with the inconsiderate driver and cold from the frigid temperatures, she rushed inside the building to the bank of elevators that would take her to one of the upper floors of her coworker's building. She had been trying to reach Zola on the phone for hours to no avail, so she hoped she was home and the trip wasn't wasted.

When she reached her apartment she stretched out her hand with the intention of knocking, but then she noticed the door ajar. "Zola?" she called as she pushed it open further and took a few cautious steps inside. The apartment was dark; she felt for the light switch, but she stumbled over something with her next step. A scream erupted from her throat that seemed to come up from her toes. Karen braced her body for impact as she landed spread-eagle with a thud on the bare hardwood floor. Seconds later she tasted blood from her cut lip. Dazed, she realized the moan she'd heard was not from her own lips. *Zola!*

Karen wasn't badly hurt, just disoriented; she struggled to push herself up so that she could find Zola. The pitiful moan sounded like the woman might be in real trouble. Karen felt her way to the wall and eventually to a light switch. With the room illuminated her worst fears were confirmed. Zola lay on the floor in the middle of her ransacked apartment, battered and bloody. Karen forgot about her own injuries and rushed to her side. She looked bad. . . .

Karen flipped up her phone to dial 911. While she did, she spoke to Zola; unsure the woman could even understand her. She tried to offer words of reassurance, though in her heart she knew they would be of no use. She held Zola's head in her arms as she waited for help to arrive. She fought to keep the tears from spilling from her eyes.

Zola's unfocused eyes didn't seem to notice Karen's battle. Another moan escaped her lips, before she said, "Didn't tell Jamaicans . . . didn't tell."

"Shush, shush, help will be here soon, just hold on, Zola." Karen thought she must be in shock or even delirious. But her lack of response seemed to agitate the young woman.

"Didn't tell . . . find the file . . . file . . . sorry . . . so sorry."

She looked down at Zola, trying to make sense of her words, but before she could Zola released a long, tortured gasp. All that remained was an eerie silence; Karen knew Zola was gone.

Karen continued to hold Zola in her arms, tears streaming down her face until the EMTs burst into the room. They took one look at the two women and began working immediately on Zola, but they were never able to reestablish a heart rhythm for her.

Karen was crushed, she couldn't believe that her friend was gone. Zola had been her friend, confidante, and most recently her coconspirator in trying to get their bosses together . . . and now she was just . . . gone.

The police arrived next on the scene. Two detectives approached her with questions. The taller of the two men extended his hand toward her. "I'm Detective Cranton, and this is my partner, Detective Casey." He paused as he noticed her lip and bruised face. "Ma'am, are you sure you don't need medical attention?" he asked with concern.

Karen's hand instinctively went to her mouth. She could feel the cut from the fall, but it wasn't bad enough to warrant a trip to the hospital. "No, I'll be fine. I just can't imagine who would do something so horrible. And just look at this place!"

Her eyes wandered over the plundered contents of Zola's apartment. The couch had been ripped apart, cupboards and drawers were open and their contents spilled carelessly to the ground. Karen was just about to say something else to the detective when she noticed the tiny edge of an SCU file folder sticking out from between some newspapers. *The file.* "Detective, would you excuse me, I think I need to use the bathroom." Her voice sounded forced and hollow—even to her own ears.

"Yes ma'am, but please remember this is a crime scene." He gave her a weary look, then continued to look around.

Karen turned the water on in the sink as she leaned against the vanity. She had to think. . . . This wasn't some random act of violence—Zola died to protect the file that was stashed in her living room. That meant her murder had to be related to SCU business—and that *might* explain why she hadn't heard from Director Spates. *She had to find a way to get to that file.*

Letting out a stream of blasphemous curses, Kharl threw several objects from his desk up against the wall. He had never been known to keep his temper in check. Simeon and Augustus were nervous.

Kharl fumed. Zola had proved tougher than he'd thought after all. His men had completely failed him; they hadn't come back with either the file or the woman.

Still angry, he realized now that he would be forced to rely on information from the two agents that he held. Then he would have to dispose of them carefully . . . he didn't want the Federal Bureau of Investigation breathing down his neck, too. There was enough to worry about without that little complication.

Kharl was a coldly calculating man; he assessed risk and made decisions with little hesitation. He decided that he didn't need both agents on his payroll—one was enough. He breathed out heavily.

The woman would have to go; besides, Spates seemed more malleable. He would work for him in spite of McCoy being eliminated. However, he doubted that she would do the same. Her insistence on duty and honor would probably spur her to self-sacrifice and he could do without all the drama.

Kharl looked again at the routes his distributors would run this month before he calmly unlocked his desk drawer to take out his gun. He loaded the CZ-85 then went to the back part of the compound where Beatrice and Michael were being held.

The way he figured things, there was too much at stake for a disruption in business. He didn't like incompetence or failure in his operation. Unfortunately, Augustus and Simeon's performance had proved both, which left him to clean up the mess.

Karen returned from the bathroom, then sat down heavily on the couch as the coroner prepared to remove Zola's body from the apartment. Large tears flowed steadily down her cheeks as her friend was taken away. She was visibly shaken and inadvertently knocked over the papers on the small side table. She didn't have to stay, but she felt compelled to for Zola's sake. Although she had known her for years, she didn't know whom to contact in case of emergency, so she thought that she would leave that up to the police. It was still a very surreal experience. *Zola, disloyal to the FBI?* It just didn't make sense.

The detectives ignored her clumsiness as they went

around cataloging evidence. In the blink of an eye, the opportunity presented itself. She had to take it. With courage she didn't know she possessed, Karen deftly removed the file and placed it under her shirt. Now she just had to get out of there.

Karen gripped her purse and several tissues tight to her body while walking toward the door. She looked back as she was about to exit. "Officers, you have my contact numbers. I don't think that I can take any more for tonight. Please call me later if you need me."

With her heart seemingly about to jump out of her chest, Karen hurried across the street to her car. Her hands shook like fall leaves as she took out her phone. She placed the file on the seat next to her while she dialed. Tension coursed through her every cell. If Spates and McCoy were in trouble, they would need help from the unit. And there was only one person she trusted enough with such a delicate situation—Agent Eric Duvernay.

She breathed a sigh of relief when he answered the phone. "Eric, it's Karen. I know it's late, but this is important. Something terrible has happened; I need you to meet me at SCU headquarters right away. I need your help."

Bea watched Michael pace in the silence. He was her rock—the strongest, most capable man she'd ever known outside of her father.

She grew more tired as she watched him, tired of the charade, tired of not getting what she wanted. More than anything, she wanted him to caress her the way he had recently. Bea hadn't realized how much she missed a man's touch until he awakened the feelings she'd thought she'd successfully suppressed for all time.

She looked toward the ceiling and whispered, "Why

now?" Even as she did, she felt a stab of guilt. She'd always been taught not to question God, but boy oh boy, did she have a few comments for Him about her current situation! Wasn't this trip supposed to be about finding a strategy to keep the SCU going? Networking with the other agency and department heads, and just enjoying a part of her history?

You made love to him in the back of a car! Are you nuts? she thought. Even then her body ached with the need to be touched by him. Her hormones had been activated by their little tryst . . . and she wanted more. Michael Spates had her womanly desires kicked into high gear. She turned away—she would just melt from embarrassment if he knew what she was thinking about him as he paced the room trying to come up with a way to secure their safety.

Bea wanted to feel some shame, some regret, but the simple truth was she wanted to be back at the hotel snuggled in bed with Michael . . . under the comfy down covers . . . the roar of a fire crackling in the background. The fantasy brought a smile to her lips. But her joy was short-lived as she watched creepy-crawly things head for her unfinished food. A shiver of disgust brought her back to reality. She was about to say something to Michael when the cell door opened again.

The young girl had returned to pick up the tray but this time Augustus didn't accompany her and she seemed even more skittish than before. After she took the tray, she appeared to slip. When Bea helped her up, she whispered harshly, "Take this." Bea noticed the tremble of her hands and the fear in her eyes. She slid the piece of paper under her sleeve inconspicuously.

After the doors shut she went to Michael and wrapped her arms around him. Instinct took over. "We need to read this note. I don't think that little girl belongs here, otherwise she wouldn't be so scared."

Michael nodded in agreement. They stayed very close to each other to prevent the possibility of being overheard by the recorders that they knew were hidden in the room. Their nearness was necessary . . . but also distracting.

Bea suddenly found it very routine to be in Michael's arms—a position that before today she wouldn't have imagined. So much had changed in so little time. Would things ever be normal again? For that matter, what was *normal* for them?

Bea lay on the cot in the fetal position. Michael came over to rub her back in an attempt to apologize to her and comfort her. Bea slipped the paper from her sleeve and found inside a small knife and a hastily scrawled note.

Help me. My name is Jamela. Mr. Kharl killed my parents and he will kill you too.

Bea turned so that Michael could read the words as well. He furrowed his brow. Both wondered if they could trust the girl. Bea spoke first in hushed tones. "It could very well be a trap, but I don't think that she is sophisticated enough to fake the fear in her eyes. I think we have to believe her." Bea sighed. "When we run, we're taking Jamela with us."

Michael almost chuckled. There was no way he was messing with Bea when she sounded so authoritative and so maternal. Mother hen had spoken. Good thing he agreed with her assessment—dragging an under-dressed kid would definitely make escape a little more difficult, but Jamela may well have saved all their lives by providing them with a much-needed weapon.

"Slow down, Karen, and tell me what's happened . . . from the beginning," Eric responded. "I'm leaving the house right now, talk to me."

Karen took a deep breath and put the car in gear. She put him on speaker and her words tumbled out in a rush. "Zola McNeil has been murdered. The police are in the apartment now, I'm just leaving her place." She hesitated as she fought to get her emotions under control. "I think it has something to do with the director, because she had a file that I know was on his desk. It was in her apartment and you know we never do that! Also, it didn't look like robbery because whoever did this didn't take anything of value, but they tore up the place pretty badly. I had gone over there to ask her about Spates and McCoy."

Fresh tears fell as she recounted the details. "Eric . . . she died right in my arms, it was horrible. She kept trying to tell me about the file. Apparently, she was able to hold out from her attacker . . . she was beaten badly."

Eric listened quietly. He needed to process the information that Karen provided to him—all intelligence was critical at this point. "Whose name is on the file?" he asked simply.

Karen responded, "That's the strange part. It isn't from an active case; the name is Kharl Winton, who's currently under DEA surveillance. The SCU doesn't even have him on the radar."

Eric blew out a ragged breath. He spelled out the name to double-check. "I know of him. Winton is head of one of the most vicious Jamaican posses on the eastern seaboard." *Damn, this just got a heck of a lot more complicated.* "Karen, get to the office as fast as you can and make sure you aren't followed. I'll call ahead for backup."

Karen listened to the concern in Eric's voice and a shiver passed through her that had nothing to do with the cold temperatures outside. Eric was still an active trainer with the bureau, but for as long as she'd known him he had never openly reacted to any situation. If he was concerned, then she was frightened out of her wits. She pressed on the accelerator. Her heart rate increased with each second that passed, until she reached the SCU office.

The darkened building appeared eerily quiet. She wanted to laugh at herself for being so scared. It was a Sunday evening, of course the building was dark. Karen looked at the file again. Kharl Winton was bad news.

Her cell phone rang, the shrill sound nearly making her jump out of her skin. She looked at the display; it was only Eric checking on her. Karen said, "I'm here at the office, but I don't see anyone. How close are you?" She wanted to sound calm and self-assured, but even to her ears she sounded like a woman on the edge. She was no agent—just a very accomplished administrative assistant and her nerves were frayed from the day's events. After she finally made it home she was going to need a glass of white Zinfandel—a very tall glass.

Karen waited until she saw Eric park his vehicle and approach her car before she got out. They headed toward the building together in relative silence after a quick greeting. Eric said, "You did good, Karen. Just hang in there, we'll get through this."

After they entered the building, Eric asked her to wait while he spoke with one of the guards. Several minutes later, they went upstairs to the SCU space. Karen used her keys to open the door to her boss's office as well as to his private conference room and that's where she and Eric settled. Karen noticed the intensity of Eric's gaze as they prepared to talk, which contributed to her sense of unease, but his words soothed her.

"Karen, I know that you're frightened, but you know the team and I will make sure that we do all we can." He paused to let his meaning sink in. "I want you to tell me everything that you know so far. If Kharl is involved in their disappearance then we have to do our best to be prepared for him." Eric shook his head to punctuate his words. "I won't lie to you. Mr. Winton is the head of one of the most notorious gangs to come out of Kingston, but you know our creed—Spates and McCoy are too important to me for us to fail. Trust me?"

Karen nodded her head slowly. She knew that he would risk his life for her boss. "Yes, I do trust you and the rest of the team. I couldn't think of anyone else to call, even though I knew on some level that I should call Beatrice's deputy officer, too.

"No matter what, I know you'll do your best to bring them back safely. But I have to admit I keep wishing the director will call or just walk through that door. Now, I know that isn't going to happen." She asked softly, "What are we going to do?"

West Virginia . . .

"What are we going to do now?" Bea asked, her voice tight with tension.

Michael knew that they needed a distraction before Kharl came for him. He hated to put all his faith in a child but he needed Jamela to make his plan work.

Michael sat on the edge of the cot and began to complain of a headache. Bea rushed to his side. "Michael, Michael, are you all right? Oh no, your head is bleeding again. We need help," she shrieked. Bea went to the door and pounded on it.

Before he could walk out his office to make his way through the compound his attention was directed toward their room's monitor. Kharl watched the scene in disgust. He holstered his weapon, hoping that Michael wouldn't need serious medical attention. He spoke to Simeon, one of his lieutenants. "Take the girl with you to see what's going on. Call me on the radio when you know something. I need him more than I need her." He waved his hand in a dismissive gesture. "These folks are about to wear out der welcome."

Simeon and Jamela arrived at the door a short time later. Michael lay there on the bed, unmoving. Bea, who appeared very upset, practically pulled Simeon to him to check him out. Bea looked at Jamela and motioned with her head for her to stand near the door. The man was so preoccupied with Michael's condition that he didn't seem to notice the position of everyone else in the room.

With a swift motion, Michael jumped up and swung at the man, sending him to the floor with a loud thud. Michael and Bea moved him out the way and told Jamela to run. They had seconds before Kharl's goons would descend on them.

"Okay, Jamela, you know these passageways. What is the fastest way out of here?" Michael demanded.

Jamela looked terrified, but her little legs seemed propelled by the desire to escape Kharl's compound. The trio made it to the kitchen in minutes, but they had company waiting for them there as two angry-looking men blocked their path.

Bea slipped the knife that Jamela had given her to Michael. They didn't have any time to waste, so Michael didn't. With a single violent thrust forward, he planted his left knee into the groin of the man on his left side while stretching out a right hook that severed the Adam's apple of the wide-eyed man on the right. Both men collapsed backwards in pain and shock.

Bea grabbed two large knives from the butcher-block holder, then they continued with Jamela, her eyes wide with surprise.

As soon as they opened the back door, the frigid temperatures rushed in. Jamela wasn't dressed for the cold weather, and didn't have on a jacket or warm shoes. She paled with the thought of having to go outside in the freezing air. Bea looked at her, took off her sweater, put it on the girl, and nudged her out the door.

Two more men approached from the side of the house, but Michael's SCU training heightened his awareness of the situation. He knew time, the weather, and the circumstances of their kidnapping were all against them, but he moved as though he had a plan.

Bea didn't think—she just acted. Her body was in motion before she knew what happened. With all the force that she could muster she threw the knife in her hand toward one of the men. Both blades, one from Michael and one from Beatrice, connected with flesh and muscle. Michael turned to Bea in awe. "When we get out of this mess, remind me that we have to talk."

Instinct had taken over completely; it was fight or flight, and at the moment they were doing both. Jamela ran with the enthusiasm and energy of youth. Michael didn't need to worry about her keeping up with him— quite the contrary. The three of them ran full throttle toward the tree line. They heard dogs, gunfire, and yelling, but they kept their heads low and just kept moving through the snow.

Michael directed them to a heavily snowed-in cabin. It was obvious that it had not been used in several years; the pane of a single window was the only visible indication that a structure even existed. They walked around the back, where Michael was able to break in one of the windows to gain entry. It was dark and cold, but free from animal habitation, which was a good thing. They could stay there long enough for them to come up with a plan.

Since the building wasn't on his property, with any luck Kharl and his men wouldn't know that the place even existed. The darkness of the evening sky would buy them some much-needed time. The "cabin" was actually little more than someone's old storage shed that sat on the edge of his or her property. Michael had no idea how far they were from Kharl's compound; they had just run as long and as far as they could before total exhaustion had taken over.

Once they were settled, Jamela took a few timid steps toward Beatrice and gave her the cell phone that Kharl had taken away. Bea didn't know how she'd done it, but she was so glad she had. She wrapped her arms around Jamela and squeezed her with gratitude. "Sweetheart, thank goodness for you . . . you've saved our lives with your bravery, you know that?"

Jamela gave her a lopsided grin, apparently appreciative of the praise.

Bea turned to Michael. "My battery is very low, so this call has to count." She handed him the phone, and watched him then begin to dial.

Karen led the other members of the team into the conference room as they arrived, one by one. She said to Eric, "I'll put on the coffee."

It had been quite a while since many members of the team had worked with Eric, but just knowing he was leading a mission was enough information for them. Eric Duvernay was an SCU legend.

He greeted each agent warmly, then proceeded quickly. The feeling in his gut was very similar to what he experienced when he rescued Tangie Taylor, the woman he loved, and who was now his wife. The anticipation, nervousness, and sense of urgency around the mission filled him in the same way. He'd called these agents in because they were proven and true. Max Wilson, Steven Caldwell, Chantal McCorkle, and Marcus King were some of the best agents the Federal Bureau of Investigation had on the payroll. And even with as little information as they had to go on, Eric felt confident about finding Spates and McCoy. He just prayed that when they did, the two would be alive and well.

Eric sat at the head of the conference table and passed out hastily put-together briefing folders. As usual his delivery was short and to the point. "McCoy and Spates are missing. The EMTs found the car they were riding in but there was blood in it, glass from broken out windows, and no sign of them. Their weapons were still holstered in their bags, and all their identification and extra clothing were left behind." He looked down at the photo in the folder. "We believe that the man you see here, Kharl Winton, is responsible for their kidnapping.

"Also, Zola McNeil, the EAD's secretary, is dead and we believe that she worked as a mole for Kharl. Before she died she passed on some valuable information to Karen, and so with that and the information that I've been able to drag out of a DEA contact, we need to move." Eric paused; he needed his team to know exactly what they were up against. "I've been in touch with McCoy's assistant director. This is not a sanctioned mission. We're going out there on our own because he wasn't convinced we had enough information to act. But I know that if we don't act now, it will probably be too late. The Jamaican posses are no less violent than the South American cartels and the Mafia families. Folks, it's now or never. If we wait, I'm convinced that we'll be holding three memorial services instead of one."

The agents shared looks of anticipation between them. There was always a certain measure of excitement when they worked together. Max smiled reassuringly at Chantal. She had grown into quite the capable agent—her female predecessors would be pleased with her performance.

Steven and Marcus both gave the thumbs-up sign. Eric looked around the room and was satisfied that he had everyone onboard. "We've obtained satellite photos of

Winton's compound and all the buildings in a ten-mile radius. This marks where the car was found and these are the three possible spots where we can stage an operation. Intelligence is weak and with so little time, we won't be able to wait for much more. Kharl probably has about fifty to sixty people with him, maybe more, maybe less, but we'll prepare for more. We're going in with 'extreme prejudice' and we're flying by the seat of our pants. In less than an hour from now we'll be there where the conditions are less than favorable for us. It's dark, cold, and we don't know what kind of situation we're walking into—"

Agent Wilson said, "Sounds just about right for most of the SCU operations that we undertake, sir. I'm glad to be aboard." A sentiment that the rest of the team shared.

Eric smiled in response. "Good to be with all of you again, too. I guess I'm proof that you never really retire from this unit. But I'd do just about anything for the director, he means more to me than a mentor—I owe him my life." With that said, he started to pack up his papers. "Grab your gear, check to make sure everything is working, and let's move out."

Kharl showed no outward signs of his feelings, but he seethed on the inside. He didn't care for the interruptions to his schedule or his plans. He would make an example of all three of them as soon as they were found.

"They're on foot, with no food, extra clothing, or shelter. They won't get too far. Bring the dogs back in to rest—at first light we move out again. If they survive the night, we'll find them then, no need to rush." Kharl looked around at the damage. He wasn't too pleased with the fact that two adults and a little girl had managed to take out four of his men and escape—but it was a hollow victory, in his opinion. He took some comfort in knowing that they had just signed their death warrant.

Chapter Six

The temperature was below freezing inside and outside the cabin. Michael knew that he needed to get them to safety. Jamela would die of exposure if they couldn't get her into some warm clothing soon. She and Bea huddled in a corner, trying to stay as warm as possible.

Michael waited impatiently for his call to be connected. He dialed Karen's personal cell phone number hoping that she had it on—he couldn't afford to be connected to her voice mail at a time like this.

He thanked his lucky stars after she answered on the second ring. Michael spoke quickly. "Karen, it's Spates. Don't talk, just listen. We're in West Virginia in a cabin. We're safe for the moment, but they'll be coming for us soon. I need you to go to the office to call for local backup, and while you're on the way, call Eric Duvernay, tell him to come get us the hell out of here."

Karen nearly dropped the phone in her excitement. "Oh thank goodness! I'm in the office now and Eric is on his way to West Virginia with a team. We know about Kharl—the link was Zola McNeil. Eric and the team will be there in less than thirty minutes. Um . . . he *borrowed* a Black Hawk."

Michael paused briefly, then a chuckle erupted from

deep in his chest. "Well, I won't say that I'm not grate-ful, but we'll have to talk about all of this later. For right now, we're here and waiting. I think that we're safe as long as it is dark, but as soon as light comes, we'll be in great danger. Use your computer to triangulate this call to let him know our exact position and if he's not with the team, wake up Agent Banks. Tell him to get his butt down there with you—we're going to need him, too."

Michael paused. "Once I get Beatrice McCoy and the girl back, I've got to take care of some unfinished business."

Karen didn't pretend to know what her boss was talk-ing about and she didn't much care. He was alive and safe, and she was going to do everything she could to get him back where he belonged. Karen wanted to do more, but she had to trust the team to do what they did best—save lives. She followed Michael's instructions, then sat back with a large cup of French vanilla cap-puccino to wait.

Michael held Bea in his strong arms, while Beatrice held Jamela. The three of them huddled together in the icy pitch-black of the shed for what seemed like hours. Jamela was unnaturally quiet and that bothered both Bea and Michael—they wondered what nightmare the poor little girl been through while she was Kharl's prisoner. As they waited, no one made a sound.

The stillness of the night was broken by the loud piercing howl of an animal. The sound nearly caused Bea to jump out of her skin and forced a long, tortured yell from Jamela. Michael sprang into action. He made it quickly back outside the shed to see *what* was out there. The bared teeth of a German shepherd and the double barrel of a farmer's shotgun met him in the inky darkness.

Michael assessed the situation. After short deliberation, he decided that his best course of action was to raise his hands to show that he wasn't a threat. He wouldn't give the person with his hand on the trigger any reason to pull it. "My name is Michael Spates. I'm an agent with the FBI."

The man, unimpressed with Michael's statement, spit out tobacco juice before he spoke. "Hold it right there, mister. This is private property. Besides, I wouldn't care if you was that dress-wearing Hoover himself, I want you off my land right now."

Michael wanted no less, his tone indicating how he felt. "I'd be glad to go, just tell me where I am and how to get to the nearest phone then I'll be on my way."

"What are you doing out here anyway?" The man raised his rifle higher. "You got anybody else in there with you? You don't look like no government man to me—you wouldn't be one of them drug dealers from up the way now, would you?"

Michael considered his choices. He didn't want to have to kill a man and his dog for ignorance, but . . .

"I would suggest that you drop your weapon unless you want to be charged with threatening a federal officer." From nowhere a familiar voice entered the fray.

"Damn, it's good to hear your voice . . . what took you so long, Duvernay?" Michael watched as Eric and the rest of his team surrounded the farmer; with badges waving and guns flashing, they easily took control of the situation.

"Are you okay, sir?" Agent Wilson asked.

Spates nodded his head. "Much better now. We need to get McCoy and the little girl out of here. I hope you have some hot coffee and some food with you." Inside the building, Beatrice couldn't hear what was going on, she just knew Michael had been out there for what seemed like a long time. She released Jamela long enough to peek out the window. As she did, Agent McCorkle reached in to hoist herself through.

The scream died in Bea's throat as soon as she real-ized the cavalry had arrived. "Agent, you are a sight for sore eyes! Stay there, we're coming out." Bea helped Jamela to the ground and they were both wrapped in Gore-Tex jackets. Despite the warmth, Jamela shook like a leaf and refused to leave Beatrice's side.

Michael watched them—taking note of the deep bond that was growing between them. He turned to Eric. "First we get them to safety, then we take care of the Winton *business.* How far away is the *bird* parked?"

Eric grinned at the reminder of how they'd arrived before he answered, "A couple miles up the road, but with this weather it's pretty rough going out here—we should get you guys out of the elements."

Michael nodded and turned to the farmer. "How far is your house from here, sir?"

The man realized his opportunity to make amends and quickly became cooperative. "It's just up the road. Y'all come on and get warmed up. Another storm is fixin' to blow through here."

As they trudged through the snow-covered field, Michael used Eric's phone to call Karen again. The di-rector tried not to mince words whenever possible. "Karen, it's Spates. Tell Banks we need about thirty min-utes to set up completely, and then I want him online with McCorkle. We've got to move quickly if we're going to stay ahead of the game. I'll call you back when we're set." He paused. "And Karen—thank you."

Spates handed the phone back to Eric and they con-tinued up the hill. The man, now identified as Joe Reed, led them to his home, which was a comfortable old farmhouse with one very important feature—a crackling fireplace. Joe sat Bea and Jamela down at his kitchen table while he made hot chocolate with milk and marshmallows for them. After he offered everyone else strong coffee, a new friendship was forged.

Joe watched the group thoughtfully; they looked like no other conglomeration of "agents" he'd seen before. "Did y'all come here to shut those guys down? Ever since they bought that place they been running roughshod over everyone else. Folks have been known to disappear up there, too. I call it in when I know something's going on, but they seem to have the police in their back pocket. They tell me that they're investigatin', but nothing seems to come of it. I've taken to walking around with my dog and gun everywhere I go. It's a lot safer to shoot first and ask questions later, if you know what I mean."

Beatrice had told Jamela that she would be right back and walked into the front room just as Joe made that statement. An eerie shiver passed through her. As she walked toward Michael, the other agents scooted down on the benches so that Bea could sit next to him. Instinctively Michael smiled and put his arm around her, which surprised the other agents in the room.

Bea leaned into his embrace and enjoyed the warmth of his body, but she was all business when she spoke. Kharl Winton had tried to kill her and she didn't take the threat lightly. "Okay, now that you guys are here, what's the plan?"

She smiled sweetly at Joe, before she intended to ask him to leave, but he knew the conversation was not for his ears. Joe excused himself to the kitchen to check on Jamela.

Michael looked at Eric. "The first thing we need to do is set up camp away from here. As soon as it is light outside, this is one of the first places that Kharl will come to look for us. I'm not going to put that man in any more danger. Winton has probably not fooled with him before because he didn't see him as a threat, but with us here that changes things. Maybe we can set up a camp near the bird." He turned toward Beatrice. "As soon as we leave here, my other priority is to get Director McCoy and little Jamela back to Karen at the SCU office. She'll take your report and then set you up in a safe house. We've been compromised so you can't go home until things have been checked out."

Bea looked ready for a fight, but before she could object, Jamela walked into the room. She looked from Bea to Michael as she made her plea. "Miss Bea, Mr. Michael, please don't go back there. That man kills everybody! He killed Augustus, my parents, and many other people. He doesn't care about anyone. He would have killed me, too, but I think he was saving me until later. . . ." Jamela looked down and her voice trailed off as she fiddled with her flimsy dress; however, her meaning was clear.

Anger welled up in Bea. "I stand corrected." She changed her mind about objecting to Michael's suggestion. "You're right, I need to take her away from here." She turned from Michael to the rest of the team. "Whatever you *need* to do—do it. I'll cover it when you get back to the office." Eric, Marcus, Chantal, Steven, and Max nodded in agreement.

Beatrice rose from the bench where she was sitting next to Michael to take Jamela back into the kitchen, but before she left she leaned in to give him a sound kiss on the lips. Pleased with the dumbfounded expression on his face, she turned back to her new charge. "Come on, sweetheart, they have a lot of work to do, so let's go get ready."

Jamela smiled for the first time as she took Bea's outstretched hand.

A shocked silence covered the room, until Michael spoke. "Dammit, now don't act like we're not grown. Let's get to work!"

Eric thought he would bite his tongue clean off, but managed to regroup in time to make a contribution. "Sir, we will need to borrow a vehicle from Joe to get the EAD and Jamela back to the helicopter. Then we can decide the best place to set up camp. It will be light soon and the first search parties will be coming out to look for you."

Bea looked at her newest little charge. The girl had been through a lot, but Beatrice needed her again and so did the rest of the team. "Jamela, those people in there are very good at what they do, but we might need your help some more. You were very brave back at Kharl's house and you helped save us. But before they go back in to make sure he doesn't hurt anybody else, is there anything that we should know?"

Jamela hung her head again. "I'm not the only girl they had. He would come and get some of the older girls when he had big parties on the weekends. We always had to stay in our room until he called us to do something. There are about ten others locked in a room. Miss Bea, I'm so worried about them—whenever someone tries to run away he punishes everybody." Tears rolled down Jamela's cheeks. She tugged at Beatrice's sleeve. "You have to help them, too. I know Kharl was probably very mad that we left . . . he's . . . he's going to hurt them."

After hearing her plea, Bea could barely control her breathing. She wanted Kharl Winton in a body bag! "Jamela, we're going to do everything in our power to help them all. But to do that I need to ask you a big favor. I'm going to ask Mr. Joe for a piece of paper, do you think that you could draw the room where they are right now?"

Jamela brightened. "Yes, I'm good at drawing. I can make a nice picture of his whole place."

Bea smiled. "Okay, honey, you do that." She smoothed down the little girl's hair, which was in desperate need of washing. Her thick cornrows were almost matted to her head. And the girl was definitely going to need new clothes. Bea found herself making a mental checklist for her. When Jamela was finished, Bea returned to Michael's side with the little girl's drawing. She looked nervously at Agent King, who was an explosives expert. "You guys be very careful. We don't need the deaths of those children on our heads. Is Banks here yet? We need eyes on that compound—our margin for error is very narrow."

Michael nodded in agreement. He wouldn't argue the point that he knew his job, because he knew her concern was for the safety of the innocent in the compound. He shared the same feeling, but Kharl Winton and his crew were another story. He raked his hands over the stubble that now covered his chin. "Yes, he's here, let's go."

Beatrice gathered Jamela and they said good-bye to Joe. Through the swirl of the wind and fresh snow flurries, Michael said, "You're going to have to go back in Banks's SUV. The wind is too bad for the helicopter."

Bea moved toward the vehicle, and after she and Jamela were seated she looked back at Michael with a worried expression. "I love you, Michael," she shouted, but the words were lost in the high wind.

With equal measure of relief and disappointment he watched as Bea was driven away. After they were out of sight, Michael turned up the collar of the jacket that he had been given and walked back toward his group. With Banks added to the equation they numbered seven agents compared to Kharl's few dozen men. A wry smile turned up the corners of his mouth—it was *almost* a fair fight for Winton.

Kharl nudged the young woman sleeping next to him. He made it a practice never to wake up next to a girl—they tended to become too clingy. The women that he chose to sleep with on the property were strictly for entertainment purposes only. He didn't need or want a personal attachment with anyone. Besides, any attachment to the women who worked for him could prove to be costly. They served a purpose—his purpose, and when they ceased in their usefulness he usually rid himself of them anyway.

Kharl stretched his body, working out the kinks in his muscles as he did. He had never been an early riser, as he was usually up late at night, but here it was nearly 4:00 A.M. and he was awake. He felt a restlessness he couldn't quite identify. He wasn't worried about the FBI agents, he would find them and dispose of them as he did any other problem in his life, but it didn't stop the feeling that coursed through his body. It was a sense of uneasiness that not even his female company could soothe. He nudged her again, and when she didn't move, he decided to be the one to leave the bed.

Kharl dressed quickly and walked out of his room where he ran into several of the guards on patrol. They were surprised to see him up so early, which seemed to unnerve them. Kharl strode through the halls, opening doors and checking on things until he had been through all the rooms. His actions woke several of his men whose disgruntled moans were quieted as soon as they recognized him. He gathered some men to assemble his search parties. Kharl knew the agents couldn't have gotten far so he concentrated his efforts on the immediate vicinity of the camp; if they were still outside they would have died of exposure. Just in case, he sent a small unit out to the further reaches, concentrating on homes where they might have been given assistance.

After he had given out instructions, Kharl went back to his office to wait. He had twenty-five men and ten women and children on the compound with him. No matter how they felt about him sometimes, they knew that their fate depended on him. No one would take care of them; they were just poor illegal Jamaican immigrants with no future except what he provided for them. It didn't hurt that he wouldn't be able to conduct business without them, the folks on his compound were a vital part of his drug operation. He couldn't allow the American government to make him look bad by undermining his authority to his followers—he was Kharl Winton, after all.

He sat alone for awhile trying to collect his thoughts. He wouldn't accept anything less than success—he wanted that government man's head. Kharl looked at the security monitor, which showed the outside of the compound. His restlessness increased just thinking about the situation. He didn't like feeling out of control. The escapees needed to be found and quickly. "Nobody makes a fool of a Winton," he growled through tightly clenched teeth.

"Damn, they're up already," Chantal said into her radio. "I see lots of movement on the compound."

She rolled on her side, keeping her targets in sight at all times. She couldn't afford to be engaged in a gun battle right now, not until they were in the proper position. With her heart in the pit of her stomach she worked her way toward the correct spot in Jamela's drawing. As soon as she reached it, she inched up toward one of the windows to look inside. Thankfully, she found the girls sleeping in cots, just like Jamela said. Two cots were empty, though, one she knew was Jamela's—the other one made her pause. This mission was dangerous enough without adding the noncombatants into the equation. She planted a small camera then moved on to her next location.

As she moved, a low growl echoed through the quiet. Chantal froze after she realized she had company—of the four-legged variety.

The beast bared its teeth in an act of aggression, but fortunately didn't bark.

Chantal stared at the large dog but didn't attempt to move—she didn't want to give it any reason to attack. Instead she put her hands where the dog could see them, and told him firmly, "No, now go away." The dog eyed her warily, but didn't heed her command. Chantal inhaled deeply, then lowered her voice the best she could. "Be a nice dog and go away, dog." Her tone was firm and in command. Despite the roiling in her stomach, she knew she couldn't allow him to smell her fear. With a sigh of relief she watched the animal's stance change. She figured that her guardian angel must be working overtime because the dog turned and walked away. It was all the time that she needed to shoot him with a tranquilizer dart. After a small yelp, he was down, asleep instantly. She moved him behind some brush and continued her progress forward to set up more cameras.

Michael turned his attention to the other agents in the makeshift shelter they'd erected as their command post. "Banks, be ready to go with minimal surveillance. We're going to have to depend on intel from the heat signatures inside the buildings. King, put as much of a delay on the charges around the civilian area—all other spots we detonate with extreme prejudice." He paused, as he remembered what Bea said to him. "We also have to pray that he isn't paranoid enough to move the other girls." He looked at Eric. "As soon as McCorkle plants the cameras, we move out."

Eric nodded his head in understanding. He didn't even have time to register that this was his first search and rescue mission since his wife's rescue. He'd accepted his duties and moved into the role that he needed to play effortlessly. Before they left the camp he checked the ammunition and sights on his weapons— just as he'd always been taught.

Agent Wilson would take point. He watched McCorkle move away from camp with more than a little trepidation.

They had been dating officially for four months, but he knew she was the *one*. He watched her lithe body, laden down with gear, move across the field from them and wished that he were there to provide backup. But Spates was right—too many bodies moving would increase the chances of detection. Besides, he told himself, Chantal knew her job. She'd proved that fact many times over since they first worked together on the Russian Mafia case with Agent Maria Thomas-Milbon. Max watched and waited—and checked his weapon repeatedly.

Agent Caldwell snickered. He watched Max practically pull out all his hair with worry over McCorkle. That's why he was an avowed bachelor. There was no way he would allow himself to be tied in knots on a mission like this—no way. He preferred to operate with a clear head and conscience. He looked back at Max again and then edged toward the camp line. He would be ready as soon as they were given the order.

Agent Banks blocked out everything except his computer screen. If things went wrong it would be on his head—he was the eyes and ears of the group and they depended on him. He had each agent marked with an infrared signature so that he could determine his or her position. He could also determine if an agent went *down*.

Agent King readied his explosives by checking the charges and repacking them for his tromp through the snow. He'd always liked a challenge—and as usual, working with the SCU provided one. His mission was to plant the explosives around the compound to create a total collapse of the structure. If anyone remained inside after the initial attack, they wouldn't survive.

McCorkle returned to their encampment out of breath, with disturbing news when she addressed Agent Spates. "Sir, I've planted the cameras, but from what I can tell, one of the girls appears to be missing."

Chapter Seven

Agent Spates swore vehemently. *Perfect, just frigging perfect.* He wanted to complete the mission with minimal loss of innocent life, but if they didn't find her soon she would become collateral damage. He wasn't going to turn tail now that he had the opportunity to take Winton down. He turned to King and in a firm voice and with dispassionate eyes, he said, "You have your orders."

Agent King nodded his head in understanding, moving toward his first position. Agent McCorkle opened her mouth to say something, but Agent Wilson touched her shoulder and shook his head no.

The plan was the plan and they had to go forth. As Spates walked, everyone else fell in step. Agent Duvernay flanked to the left to cover King with the explosives. Wilson and Caldwell were with Spates and they fanned out along the perimeter on the right of the compound.

Spates felt the familiar adrenaline rush—this was like the old days before he was relegated to working a case from the administrative position of his desk. He enjoyed the feeling . . . the action . . . the hunt . . .

Within minutes the unit was in position. Everyone

had a target, ready to go. Agent Banks gave the signal that he had them tracked and they moved ahead.

Kharl's men were engaged almost immediately. There was no element of surprise—bullets flew and screams in several different accents were heard. Posse members came streaming out of the buildings to find out what the hell was happening as well as to help their fallen comrades.

Banks yelled, "Duvernay, you've got six hostiles headed your way—McCorkle, back him up."

McCorkle aimed her weapon and squeezed off ten rounds. She took out three—and Duvernay did the others. The entire scene turned into a complete melee— with Winton's men down in all directions.

Spates made it to the door first, followed by Wilson. Max tossed in three canisters of tear gas, then they moved in quickly with masks on. Chantal reached the door and was followed in by Caldwell. They took the sections of the compound that they were assigned, making their way carefully and shooting anything that moved. Chantal headed to the area where the girls were supposed to be and peered inside the door. "Banks, give me a status."

On the other side of the building, Spates and Wilson found the resistance dwindling. Posse members laid down their guns in surrender.

Jonnelda was jarred from her sleep by all the noise. It sounded like a war zone to her—almost like the devastation she knew from the posse wars in Kingston. Despite the confusion, she dressed quickly and made her way toward the room with the rest of the girls. She'd almost made it when she felt a warm hand clamp down over her mouth and her body pushed to a corner. She might have felt some relief if it had been anyone other than Kharl. He half carried, half dragged her toward the room with the others.

"Chantal, get in the room now!" Banks could see Kharl's movement toward her, but the other team members were too busy to help. Banks had no way of knowing that it was Kharl, but he knew the body moving toward her was not a member of the team.

King had also moved into position—he had strict orders to start his countdown.

Chantal walked into the room and plastered herself against the wall. Everyone else looked at her wide-eyed in terror. She motioned for them to be silent.

Kharl. The hairs on Michael's neck stood up in a chilling sensation. Intuition told him he needed to act. He felt the adrenaline course through each vein as it surged through his body. He radioed Banks. "What's going on?"

Banks responded immediately. "McCorkle is in a room two hundred yards ahead with a hostile right on her position."

Spates ran toward her, and arrived in time to see the back of Winton's head just as he moved into the room and out of his line of sight. "Damn!" He looked at his watch—they were down to minutes. "Banks, call everyone back. Duvernay, Caldwell, Wilson, and King, clear the area. I'm going after McCorkle." He clicked off his radio before anyone could respond and positioned himself with a small mirror outside the door so that he could see inside. He checked his watch again . . . three minutes.

Inside, Kharl and Chantal were at a standoff. Chantal had her weapon leveled against his head, but he had his leveled against Jonnelda's temple. The frightened girl was begging for Kharl to let her go.

Banks was screaming into her ear, "Take the shot!" But Chantal couldn't risk Jonnelda's life. She saw Spates and told Kharl, "Okay, okay, I'll put my weapon down, just don't hurt the girl."

Kharl snickered, as he let down his guard. He held

Jonnelda by the arm, but away from his body. "How many are with you?"

From behind him, Spates said, "Now see, that's your problem, you need to focus. There's only one person that you need to worry about—and that was your last mistake." Michael squeezed three rounds into Kharl as Kharl aimed his gun at him.

Michael checked his watch—there was no time left. "We don't have time to make it to the door." He shouted, "Everyone out the window—now!"

King looked from his watch to Agent Duvernay, who motioned for him to proceed. He breathed out heavily before he pushed the button on the remote. Explosions rocked the early morning sky.

The explosion rattled the windows of their hotel room. Jamela nearly fell as she jumped out of her chair, the brows of her large brown eyes creased in worry. "Miss Beatrice, what do you think that was?"

Bea knew that it was the Winton posse compound being destroyed, but she didn't know what to say to the little girl. Her nerves had been on edge since they'd been dropped off at the hotel. She and Jamela had made it as far as the same hotel Bea had checked out of before she demanded that the driver stop the vehicle. No way was she going to be stuck in Virginia wondering what happened.

The hotel staff regarded her a little strangely, but they were accommodating, which was all she needed. Beatrice made reservations for three more rooms for the rest of the team, then settled down.

Although the weather was still very cold, the snow-plows had performed admirably and the roads were passable. Bea decided that she wouldn't leave until she was able to wrap her arms around Michael Spates again. She preferred not to let him out her sight for awhile. They could return to Virginia together. Besides, they had to figure out what to do with Jamela. Beatrice smiled down at the tiny girl, who she thought was much smaller than she should be for ten years old.

Beatrice assumed that her luggage was either still in the car or at the compound with Kharl. So, once they checked in she and Jamela stopped by the gift shop for a few sundries and other miscellaneous items. Fortunately, they managed to find enough supplies to get them through the next few days. Bea was even able to find a sweat suit that fit Jamela with the hotel's logo on it.

Bea shrugged her shoulders—the girl managed to pull at her heartstrings . . . and in the process shred every ounce of self-control that she possessed with one look of her big brown doe eyes. Between Michael and Jamela, she was just a big ole emotional sap.

"Come on honey, let's get you into a nice warm bath. Don't worry about what's going on out there—you're safe and sound and I'm not going to let anything happen to you." Beatrice spoke the words with much more conviction than she felt, but she put up a good front for Jamela's sake.

"Michael Spates, if anything happens to you, I'll never forgive you," she said to herself after Jamela was in the bathroom. While she was alone, Beatrice walked around the hotel suite, talking to herself, praying aloud, and watching out the window for any sign of the unit's arrival. She wanted the mission to be over—and over right now.

It wasn't so much a matter of a lack of patience as much as it was that this was the first time she'd acknowledged her feelings for Michael. Now his life was in jeopardy, and she was finding it hard to hold it together—this wasn't just another case. It was much more personal and she knew that Michael, the same Michael Ezekiel Spates that she'd vowed not to love, was in grave danger. It would be time to get Jamela out of the tub soon, so Bea sent up another short prayer, then let it go.

She'd called Karen as soon as they were in the room to inform her of the change in plan. Bea supposed years of work with the SCU had made Karen very flexible—because she hardly seemed surprised by the call. Bea told her to go home and that she would talk with her later. Bea wanted to hear more about Zola, but she had to put those feelings aside. Michael was her first priority; when they returned to the SCU office in northern Virginia, they could deal with work stuff. . . . Bea nervously looked at her watch. "Please let them be safe," she whispered.

Sirens blared in the darkening sky. Police, fire department, and bomb squad personnel as well as other federal agents swarmed around the now demolished Winton posse compound. Cadaver dogs were also brought in as a result of the information Jamela had provided earlier.

As early morning turned into early evening, Michael and his exhausted team made way for the local police to round up Kharl's men and take care of their charges. The SCU didn't have an arrest rate and didn't care how many posse members were apprehended. No, they were just thankful that everyone was safe and were tired from a long day.

McCorkle and Wilson talked quietly away from the hubbub of activity. "I've got to hand it to you, that was good work, but it was a close one, McCorkle."

Chantal tried to massage the kinks out her neck while she responded. It was a bit too close for her own comfort, but she wouldn't tell Max that little fact. "It may have been close, but isn't that true to SCU form?

The residents are safe and we got a bonus with Winton. The DEA should thank us, but they won't. They need to find out where their leak is first." She looked at Max in the moonlight of the winter sky. "Don't tell me you were worried about me?"

Max rubbed his neck now—she was great for the unit, but bad for the health of his heart.

Eric Duvernay watched from another corner as he waited for Agent Spates. He had to chuckle to himself; he remembered well the days when he thought he had *control* over his emotions. *Max may as well just throw in the towel,* he thought.

Suddenly, a strong gust of wind drew his attention away from the couple. The storm kicked up the wind and blew snow with gusto. The helicopter wouldn't be able to return them to northern Virginia tonight, he thought, disappointed about being unable to see his family. He would call his wife Tangie as soon as they were settled. Another strong gust spurred him to walk toward Spates to find out what was happening.

Michael was in the middle of a conversation with the INS and social workers from the state. "Look guys, I'm a federal agent, I don't know anything about these kinds of things. In less than thirty minutes I'm going to take my team and vacate the area. You can decide what to do with whoever is left."

"Sir, can you tell us anything about them? Do they have identification?"

Michael was perturbed. "Whatever they might have had went up in smoke with the compound. I don't have extensive information on Winton or his operation, but I'd be willing to bet they're not naturalized Americans. Folks, I understand your need for information, but there just isn't too much that I can give you. I suggest you do your own interviews and meet with the DEA personnel who had this place under surveillance." Michael started to walk toward Duvernay to tell everyone to prepare to leave when he was stopped cold by a voice that he hadn't expected to hear so soon.

"Agent Spates, on whose authority did you mount this operation?"

Michael turned around to face the man who was next up in the food chain and his ranking officer. He didn't blink when he spoke. "Sir, I understand your desire to make it to the next level, but I didn't know you were willing to do it over Beatrice McCoy's dead body. This operation was mounted on the only authority that I respect." Michael walked away, and stride-for-stride he and Eric headed toward the rest of the team.

Michael blocked out all other distractions. "Listen up, folks, I've talked with Karen at headquarters. We have lodging arrangements at Hilltop for the night. Tomorrow morning we'll head back in for the debrief, but for now, we're finished."

Eric looked back at the deputy director, wondering how he made it to West Virginia so quickly. After his conversation with Michael, Eric figured that his face was red from more than the cold. It would be an interesting few days once the fallout from the mission rose to the surface.

Eric watched the police uncover bodies from the frozen ground. CSI units were everywhere marking the scene and cataloging data. The coroner was also on-site to pick up the bodies of Kharl's men. He blew out a long sigh. The whole scene was going to be hard to explain—especially since this was an unsanctioned operation. He didn't envy Michael's position, but he knew he would have made the same choice.

He turned to Michael, speaking in low tones. "Are you sure you want to do this? Most folks who go up against him don't survive. Besides, it was my idea to come out here to look for you—I have a lot less to lose than you do."

Michael looked at him intently. "The hell you don't—a wife and two children plus the career that you've built over the last fifteen years is plenty." He exhaled slowly. "Besides, it was my idea to go after Winton. Let the *deputy* take his best shot! If he wants my job, he can have it, but I won't allow any of this to fall back on Beatrice."

As they continued to walk toward the SUV that would take them to the hotel, both appeared to be deep in thought. They rode in silence, thankful that it was *almost* over.

Michael hadn't mentioned Jamela to the INS or the social workers. He had the feeling that it was that little omission that would cost him . . . maybe even more than his decision to conduct an operation without the proper authority. Michael rubbed his chin in thought, he knew the deputy wasn't going to make things easy for them. As a matter of fact, he knew the man was probably going to bring him up on charges. Beatrice wasn't going to be happy once she learned that bit of news.

Thinking about that reminded him how much he wanted to see her again. By this time she should be safely in northern Virginia, however, so their meeting would have to wait until the next day. How quickly had their relationship gone from business to personal—as amazing as their story was, it just went to show that God was happy . . .

The team arrived at the hotel a short time later. Michael was given a key and since he had no luggage to speak of, headed to the gift shop. He bought a few items to make himself comfortable for one night. The hotel graciously offered to hold the dining room open for them and they were given the choice of eating in the dining room or being offered room service. Michael wasn't looking forward to either, but chose the dining room with Eric, since they were both missing the women they loved.

Eric sliced his medium-rare steak with gusto while he spoke with Michael. "Sir, is there anything that I should know or that I should do?"

Michael checked his grin. "No, agent, but thank you for asking. I have things under control and when we get back to Virginia, I'll do what I need to . . . on all fronts." Michael knew Eric was asking about Bea as much as the job.

Eric decided to go the more direct route. "Okay, are you sure you know what you're doing with the ED? This could be a dicey situation since you work together."

Michael bit back a stronger retort. He was almost fifty years old; no way this kid was going to question him about his romantic life. "Eric, what did you say to me when I tried to warn you about going after Tangie?"

Eric blinked. "Nothing, sir, you never warned me about going after her—you supported me."

Michael nodded. "Yes I did; even when I had reservations, and that's exactly what I expect from you and the other members of the team. My relationship does not have to get 'approval.' Bea and I are well past the age of majority." He was silent for several seconds. "I know you mean well and I appreciate your concern, but I know what I'm doing. Beatrice means more to me than anyone in this world."

Eric smiled. It was about time the director thought about his own happiness for a change. "Then I'm happy for you. So now, what about Jamela?"

Michael took a long sip of his Shiner Bock beer. Bea and Jamela would be settled in Virginia by now. He hadn't asked Karen where they were staying because he didn't want to be tempted to call her. Besides, it was late and Jamela was probably asleep, he reasoned.

This was a conversation that he would definitely save until later. He just wanted to relax for a few minutes before going up to his room. "I think we can go over all of this during the debrief, besides even though I thank you, we're going to have to figure out a way to get your ass out the sling, too. We could be facing similar charges if the deputy wants to push it—need I remind you that neither was this a sanctioned hostage rescue nor are you a member of the Hostage Rescue Team!"

Eric's fork stopped midair. "Are you purposely trying to ruin my dinner?"

Michael met his gaze and both men laughed.

"Not at all, but you and I know we're going to have to wade through a bunch of crap when we return. As much as I look forward to my own nice warm bed, my kitchen, and amenities . . . it's going to be tough. We're laughing now, but in a few months we may both be crying the blues. We're going to need serious divine intervention for this one."

Eric sipped his beer before he responded. "I know, but I have faith. We'll come out this with a few bumps and bruises, but we did what we thought was right. I stand by my decision and so does the rest of the team. If the bureau wants me to put my papers in—you know I'm more than willing to fall on my sword. Just tell me what you need from me and it's done."

"I'm proud of you, son. You've come a long way from that cocky young man I first met at Quantico—more years than I care to remember-ago. You've given more than your fair share to this agency and I'm not going to ask for any more." He added quietly, "If there's anyone who has to fall on their sword, it has to be me. I want you and Beatrice to be protected." Michael exhaled slowly. "My time with Beatrice showed me something that I've been avoiding for more years than I care to admit. I think it's time—"

Eric interrupted excitedly. "Are you saying that you're ready to settle down now?"

The question hung in the air. Was it such a foreign concept? Michael wondered. Maybe there was such a thing as too much information. He decided against sharing more about his budding romance, though he wanted nothing more than to talk about his feelings. Put it out there that he loved Beatrice McCoy and he didn't give a darn who knew. He inhaled deeply. "No, what I'm saying is that I'm tired. Maybe I need to reevaluate what I want from my life. Over the past few years I've fielded several offers from other companies to provide security. I've even turned down some very lucrative offers. Government service is very rewarding in many areas—but wallet ain't one of them."

Eric laughed and nodded in agreement. Between his inheritance and investments he was very comfortable, but he knew others on the team had a lot more to lose. "If it turns *ugly* I'll do what I can for the other agents."

Michael's voice dropped an octave. "No, you won't. As director you all are my responsibility. The deputy can have my head if he wants it, but I'll be damned if anyone in the unit will be touched. Russell is just an ambitious, backstabbing bastard."

Eric raised an eyebrow. "Okay, tell me how you really feel."

Michael shook his head. "I know, I know. But he wouldn't even have the position if I hadn't turned it down to stay with the SCU. As far as I'm concerned, he ought to be licking my damn boots. People like that never learn—they get something that they don't deserve and instead of being thankful they continue to look for more. Well, this time he may have bitten off more than he can chew. I don't give up *anything* without a fight."

Eric nodded and though unspoken, knew Spates meant both professionally and personally. He picked up his fork again and continued to eat in the silence that accompanied Michael's statement. Each had a lot to think about and tomorrow was soon enough to deal with all of it.

Several minutes later, after completing his meal, Michael said good night to Eric. He headed up to his room for much needed rest, though he didn't know how much sleep he would get without talking to Beatrice, who remained heavily in his thoughts.

He fingered the key in his hand before he put it in the lock. He missed Beatrice. The past four days with her had transformed his life. He realized that he didn't want to spend another night away from her as he prepared to go to bed . . . didn't want to think about life without her in his arms. He chuckled to himself. This was a pretty damnable way to figure out he was just human—with the job on line, Beatrice in his heart—everything he wanted could go away in one fell swoop.

As soon as Michael entered the room, he caught a slight whiff of Juniper Breeze. His heart beat double-time. *What was Bea doing here? In his room?* He stepped farther into the room and the light was turned on immediately. The smile on his face froze, as he looked headlong into the gaze of a furious Beatrice Lynette McCoy—complete with hands on her hips and flashing angry eyes. *Uh-oh . . .*

"Michael Ezekiel Spates! Where have you been?" Beatrice demanded. "It has been hours since the compound was imploded, but I haven't heard a word from you. I was worried sick!"

Michael closed his mouth. What was Beatrice still doing in West Virginia and why was he given the key to her room? "Well, number one, I thought you were gone and number two, it is very late so I planned to call you in the morning." He put down the gift bag. "And number three, take your hands off your hips before I show you what I want to do with them. So, are you going to tell me what you're doing here?"

Bea lowered her tone and looked toward the door of the adjoining room. Jamela slept soundly there and she didn't want to wake her up. She took Michael by the arm and led him to the bed. "I know that you're tired, but I was so worried about you. But, you didn't really think that I was going to go back to Virginia without you? I've talked to Karen half a dozen times, but she hadn't heard from you, either. I could have called Tangie, but I didn't want to wake her or worse, worry her. The longer I waited, the more nervous I became." She blew out a long breath. "I'm just glad you're safe."

Michael hid his satisfaction that she'd stayed behind for him. "That, my dear, was a mouthful. If I had known you were here, though, I would have called. I've been downstairs for over half an hour having dinner with Eric." Michael lowered his voice to a sexy low timbre. "When I could have been here with you instead."

Once he took off his jacket and shoes, Beatrice moved instinctively into his arms. He cuddled her to his chest. All the trauma of the past few days seemed to dissolve away in his embrace. Michael enjoyed the feel of Beatrice against his chest, the only problem was that it wasn't his *bare* chest. He hated to ask her to move, but he needed to do a few things—there was the little matter of a few days' grime attached to his body. Michael kissed the top of her head. "Give me ten minutes on the clock. If I don't get in the shower my clothes are going to start a mutiny." Michael favored her with a devilish grin. "I have to warn you that since I didn't know I was sharing my room I don't have pajamas."

Beatrice smiled. "Who says you need pajamas?" She

pulled against her nightshirt. "I guess I'll just have to take these off so that we're even."

Michael headed toward the bathroom door but turned back. "Make that eight minutes on the clock." His expression turned serious. "Do me a favor, though, and check on Jamela. I don't want her to be afraid . . . maybe we should turn a night-light on for her."

Now, how did I get so lucky? Beatrice was pleased by his concern for Jamela, because during the last few days with her, the little girl had completely captured her heart. Bea opened the door and found Jamela still sleeping soundly with her new teddy bear. She adjusted her covers, turned on the bathroom light, and, satisfied that she was fine, went back to Michael.

By her calculations he still had a few minutes left to his shower time, but she couldn't wait that long. From the moment she had seen him, she'd wanted to eat him up. Bea undressed quickly then went to the bathroom where Michael hummed softly in the shower. He had his eyes closed while he washed his face.

Bea stood silently in the doorway to admire the view. She started at the bottom and worked her way up. He had the nicest legs she'd seen on any man in a long time, smooth chocolate brown, muscled, chiseled, and strong. Her eye moved higher. *Hmmm . . . very nice . . .* she lingered there for several seconds before she moved up to his washboard abs . . . *nice again.* His chest, the one she found so enticing to lay against, was another muscled feature, with just a hint of hair for her to run her fingers over. Something she itched to do right now, but she showed remarkable restraint. His arms rivaled the beautifully sculpted arms of David Robinson, formerly of the San Antonio Spurs basketball team. Damn, then he turned around . . . the back was just as nice as the front.

Beatrice giggled to herself. She *almost* felt like a voyeur.

"Woman, if you don't get in here!" Michael turned around to face her, eyes open, and sultry with desire.

He had only but to ask. Bea opened the shower door and stepped in before he could utter another syllable. Michael took her in his arms and kissed her with the need he'd felt from the moment he laid eyes on her—it was anxious, potent, fervid . . . complete. Beatrice received him with the same zeal, and returned his kiss with eagerness. The heated water from the shower was nowhere near as hot as the passion that raged between them. Michael kissed her jawline all the way to her ears. Then he lovingly nuzzled and kissed the sensitive skin of her neck. Bea moaned in pleasure, as her hands skimmed along his back to bring him closer.

Michael moved down her neck to the tops of her breasts, slyly tormenting her before he would dip low enough to take her protruding nipples into his warm mouth. His hand cupped her apex, massaging the delightful triangle before he slipped in a finger to tease the bud that begged for his attention. His mouth found a nipple and he teased without mercy, nipping and licking until she called out his name. With a slow hand and masterful touch he brought forth the quivering release from Beatrice that he longed for—"that's right, baby, let go for me."

Bea closed her eyes, leaned against the shower wall panting for air, struggling to regain control . . . she felt like a spineless tingle of sensation. Michael had expertly pushed her over the glorious edge of orgasm. When she opened her eyes again it was to the self-satisfied smile that he wore on his face. Bea took him in her hands. The shower water glided down her back, energizing her underused muscles. She was emboldened by his unspoken challenge. She was determined to give as good as she'd just received. She gently teased his rounded sac, running her nails against the skin . . . then moving her hand up and down along his length. Michael responded immediately. He grew harder, and incredibly, still longer. Bea unconsciously licked her lips in anticipation. He brought her close and kissed her again, just as soundly as before. Beatrice enjoyed the sensation, but this was about him now. She massaged in earnest now, loving the feel of him, large against her abdomen and stomach. She broke the kiss and turned around with her bottom against him.

"You do like to live on the edge, don't you," he teased.

She reached outside the shower stall to retrieve the gold foil condom packet that she'd brought along . . . just in case.

She waved it in front of Michael and that was all the motivation he needed. He brought her close and kissed her again, just as soundly as before. Beatrice enjoyed the sensation, but this was about him now. She moved up and down on him in response and was rewarded with the words that she wanted to hear. "God, you feel good." She could tell he was the one struggling for control now. Bea smiled wickedly and continued. She placed her hands on the wall, while the water continued to fight a trail down their bodies. Michael entered Bea from behind and almost groaned aloud with the sheer pleasure he felt from being inside her. His hands found her breasts and he caressed them while he pumped slowly into her, he felt her push back and together they found their way toward a little piece of heaven. Beatrice felt her toes curl as the feeling snaked up along the entire length of her body . . . it coursed through her, hot . . . electric . . . and all encompassing, until she felt herself shatter. Michael recognized the now familiar signs and gave in to his own feelings. He followed her almost immediately with a powerful release that rocked him to the core.

* * *

Several minutes later, they lay naked in the bed, holding each other close . . . satisfied, complete, and in love. Michael lay listening to the rhythmic beat of her heart, and knew she was awake. He felt grateful for her presence, but he had questions. He didn't want to ruin the moment, but he needed to know. . . . "Beatrice," he whispered, "why didn't you go back to Virginia to wait?"

There was silence for a few seconds then Bea turned around to face him. "The truth is, I needed to know that God answered my prayers. I needed to know for myself—with my own two eyes that you were safe." A single tear rolled down her face. "I've been so afraid to love you . . . afraid to lose you . . . Michael, if anything awful had happened, I don't know what I would have done." She stopped, while she regained control of her emotions. "After Joshua and Janice died—I couldn't even pray. . . . A loving, just God wouldn't have taken away everything that I cared about . . . so this was a test of my faith . . . I had to know that God still heard me."

Michael wiped her tear away with his finger. "Bea, I know your pain has seemed unbearable, but God has heard your prayers all along and has never left you. I know that because you're here with me now . . . and this was my prayer after everything . . . happened.

"I hated to see you in so much pain and not be able to do anything for you, but He answered my prayers and here you are in my arms. Beatrice, I love you and would gladly have given my life to spare yours, if that's what was required. My commitment to you is eternal."

"I know . . . I feel it every time you look at me." Bea kissed the tips of his fingers. "I've found in you something that I thought was lost forever. Michael, with you beside me, I feel like I could conquer the world—you make me strong . . . you make me happy to be alive again."

"Miss Bea," Jamela's sleepy voice broke the stillness of the night. "Miss Bea, I'm thirsty."

Beatrice hastily pulled the covers up. "Sweetheart, just take a bottle of water from over there on the dresser and go back to bed—I'll tuck you back in if you just give me a second."

"Busted. Too bad I don't have pajamas or I'd tuck her in myself."

Bea pinched his shoulder. "Yeah right—I bet you would have been a big help with two A.M. feedings. Keep the bed warm, I'll be back in a minute."

Michael stretched languidly. "Yes, ma'am, I know how to support the woman of my dreams. I'll be right here when you finish."

It took Bea a little longer than expected to settle Jamela and when she returned, Michael was fast asleep. "Of all the things—" She started to swat him with her pajama shirt as she took it off, but she knew he had to be exhausted. Bea climbed into the bed instead and curled up behind him. In minutes she was asleep, too—a contented smile on her face.

The next morning the three of them, Michael, Beatrice, and Jamela, shared breakfast in the room before they prepared to return to Virginia.

Jamela buttered her toast before slathering more orange marmalade on it. She spoke in a matter-of-fact manner, like most children her age. "Mr. Michael, I'm glad that Mr. Kharl didn't kill you."

Michael almost choked on his coffee. "Um . . . thank you, Jamela. I'm very glad that we're all safe. You were very important to our success. I think that I'm going to tell the president that you deserve a medal, or maybe I should just make you a deputy agent."

Jamela grinned wide, showing a mouthful of teeth.

"Forget the president, I want to be a deputy agent so I can be tough just like you and Miss Bea."

Bea smiled. "Being an agent isn't just about being tough. It means you have to use your head, too, you have to be able to think your way out of tough situations. Each case requires a different set of skills, but sometimes it is just a matter of luck, like with you. You were our good-luck charm." A thought mulled around in her head. "Jamela, when was the last time you were in school?" Bea looked at Michael. She knew she treaded on shaky ground. . . .

Jamela looked down. "My mom and dad came over from Kingston to work for Mr. Kharl when I was in third grade. He said I could go to school and he would give us a free house to live in, but since we moved here, I've been at the compound. My mom's job was to clean up at rich people's houses and my father was a gardener, but that's not really what they did. They would go to deliver drugs for Mr. Kharl. My parents knew some of his family in Kingston and that's why they trusted him. My mom thought we were coming here so that I could go to American schools, but they didn't know . . ." Tears fell from her eyes, but she continued, in a strong, determined voice. "Mr. Kharl made Simeon kill them when we tried to get away. They wanted me to run away when they saw him coming, but I stayed behind and after we got back to the compound, I never saw them again. Jonnelda says he buried them out back where all the other bodies are—Mr. Kharl kills a lot of people."

Bea went to find a tissue for Jamela, and when she returned, hugged the little girl close. "Sweetheart, you don't have to worry about any of that anymore. I'll make sure you're taken care of, and we'll find your relatives soon." Her heart opened for the little girl. She had been so careful to protect her feelings, now here she was openly professing her love for Michael, and wishing like hell she could take Jamela home with her. She kept her own tears at bay while she soothed Jamela's.

Jamela wiped her eyes. "But I don't want to go back. . . . I want to stay with you."

Michael interjected, "Jamela, Miss Bea has to follow the rules. . . . We have to find your other family first."

Jamela said in a tone that questioned Michael's attachment to reality, "Not just at Miss Bea's house. I want to stay with you, too. I want to stay in the house with you both, you know, *your* house!"

An uneasy quiet cloaked the room. They would obviously have to find a way to explain the exact nature of their relationship. And they would . . . as soon as they figured it out.

Michael's eggs went down the wrong pipe and he coughed repeatedly. After she made sure that he was all right, Beatrice hid her smile behind her hand. *Of all the things . . . it took a ten-year-old girl to knock him off his foundation.*

A knock prevented further conversation and Michael jumped up to see who was at the door. He *almost* breathed an audible sigh of relief when it was Eric. "Duvernay, I thought you'd never get here. I think it's time we headed out, don't you?"

Eric looked further into the room where he made eye contact with Bea and Jamela. He effectively covered a grin and responded, "Yes, sir, the weather is clearer now and it's safe for us to return in the chopper. We're all set—if *you* are."

Northern Virginia . . .

When Michael arrived at his office, he had several messages waiting for him. There was no reprieve, no attempt to understand his ordeal. He had to account for his actions . . . and those of the team. He called a meeting to inform them of the bureau's course of action.

"First of all, let me say that I'm very proud of each and every one of you for what you did. I probably wouldn't be here if it had not been for your dedication to the unit and to me personally." He paused, unsure how to let them know. . . .

Michael tapped his pen on the table in effort to steel his nerves. "I regret to inform you that we're all under investigation."

The news fell like a bombshell as he'd expected, but he pressed on.

"The Internal Review Board wants to close us down while they investigate what happened at Harpers Ferry. Even though it was a successful operation—several department heads were overlooked and proper chain of command was not followed. They want to interview all of us, from the executive director to the administrative assistant. We are to report to duty, but only as a way to be available to the board. Effective this morning, after we finish the debrief, we are on administrative leave until the board assembles a team and has the opportunity to look over our records. We have to turn in our badge, weapon, and keys on our way out this evening."

The hush that fell over the room was deafening. He looked into the faces of Eric Duvernay, Chantal McCorkle, Steven Caldwell, Zach Banks, Max Wilson, and Marcus King. He needed them to know that he was as committed to them as they were to him.

Michael exhaled slowly. "I know this feels like a slap in the face, but I promise you—we will get through this. You, each and every one of you have worked hard for this unit and you've given nothing but dedicated, exemplary service . . . which won't be forgotten as all this mess is sorted out."

Eric wasn't looking forward to these interviews. This

would be the second IRB review he'd had in the last few years. One time of being picked apart by his peers was definitely enough. "What do you want us to say, sir?"

"Duvernay, I'm not asking you to say anything except the complete answers to their questions—there will be no cover-up. We need to say exactly what happened and why. The simple fact is the deputy wouldn't authorize a rescue. The HRT was not called in because there was no place to call them to. If Karen hadn't found Zola before it was too late, none of us would be having this conversation." He paused. "Let me make no bones about this— if you hadn't shown up when you did, we'd probably be dead by now. The IRB will want to know who made the decision for the rescue and how we came to mount an operation against Winton. We all know there is no paperwork on either mission . . . and frankly, I don't give a damn. You did what needed to be done in your best judgment . . . that's what we do in this unit. If we didn't, there would be a few hundred people out there who would know the difference."

Max shifted in his seat before he spoke. Michael noticed the movement and turned to him. "Yes, agent?"

"Will this disciplinary action go into our permanent file?"

"I hate to give weak answers, but the truth is, I don't know. The ED and I will do our very best, but there are no guarantees. I'm willing to make whatever deals I can, though, and I'm going to fight for a complete exoneration. We took liberties, but we did it on the basis of saving lives . . . how many more people would Kharl have murdered? No excuses—just fact."

Michael leaned back in his chair. He could continue to entertain questions that he didn't have the answers to or get on with his job. He chose the latter. He sat forward again and began the brief in earnest. "Okay, before the details become fuzzy, let's get this information on paper. Duvernay, we'll start with you and Karen. Give me the chronology of your actions."

The meeting continued over the next few hours until all the information could be translated into an appropriately written report that Michael planned to review with Beatrice McCoy later that evening. He looked forward to seeing her again, but not for reasons of discussing work. The question of "now what" had hung uncomfortably in the air between them after their return. Michael needed some answers.

Chapter Eight

Michael had a few minutes before his next meeting, which was with Beatrice. However, his peace was short-lived. Karen buzzed to inform him of another call. "Boss, the INS is on the line. They want to know where to pick up Jamela."

This was turning into one heck of a day, he thought as he moved to answer the phone. *First the IRB, now this.* Michael closed his eyes—he knew that he couldn't avoid them forever. "Put the call through." He held the receiver in his hand; remembering the words that he'd spoken to Beatrice earlier. . . . *My commitment to you is eternal* . . .

No matter what decision he made—he would betray someone. His integrity as a law enforcement officer, as well as a man, hung in the balance. Michael swallowed into a throat that felt as dry as sandpaper. "This is Agent Spates."

Beatrice inhaled the aroma of her freshly brewed coffee. Sometimes the sweet smell was more satisfying than the consumption of the liquid. She watched the steam swirl before she took her first sip. Bea drank coffee when she had a lot on her mind, and today she felt like she could go through a couple pots of the brown brew.

Michael had come clean about the details of Zola's death. He'd tried to protect her, but she'd demanded to know the whole truth. It was hurtful to hear about the betrayal, but it was also necessary. Zola had been the *mole* in her organization. Bea knew that she had probably hurt them by passing on vital information, but she couldn't be upset with her—if Zola hadn't held out against Kharl's men, the consequences could have been dire, which would have made the future very bleak for her and Michael.

Bea watched the steam rise and swirl as she remembered her conversation with Michael. He'd said, "Zola was involved with Kharl because of her younger brother's drug habit. Apparently, he was a mule who'd made the error of stealing product from Winton.

"Apparently, Zola tried to help her brother work off his debt by providing information to Kharl that would keep him a step ahead of law enforcement. I guess the deal was her brother's life for her usefulness. The irony is that we can't find her brother now, either—he may even be one of the bodies buried on the property. Forensics should be able to make an identification soon."

She blew into the cup before taking her next sip. Her heart ached over the conflicting feelings that surged through her. Hurt, love, loss . . .

It was very painful for Beatrice to know that her trusted assistant of more than five years had betrayed her. Zola must have been desperate not to come to her with her problems—they'd been able to enjoy an atypical work relationship, one that had been good for both of them. Now that was gone, too.

Beatrice spoke with her parents and offered to help with the funeral expenses. It would help to give her closure—Bea had considered Zola part of her extended family.

Beatrice had so much to think about now that she was back from her ordeal and the retreat. She'd avoided INS inquiries about Jamela even though the little girl had been with her since their rescue. Her new secretary, a temp from another department, didn't seem to understand her reluctance to answer certain calls. Beatrice counted about a dozen unread messages on her desk about Jamela.

Beatrice sat alone in her kitchen thinking and planning. She didn't want to diminish the good thoughts she'd had about the day, but she had to be more practical. She would have to come up with a workable plan. After a wonderful day of shopping and a visit to one of Beatrice's favorite hair salons, the little girl was settled in *her* room, reading. Beatrice had even checked on school enrollment.

Bea knew that she was becoming too involved, but she couldn't help herself—taking care of Jamela seemed so natural. More importantly, Jamela seemed to trust her and Michael. Bea couldn't stand the thought of her going to strangers while her immigration status was figured out or her relatives in Jamaica were contacted. It seemed only right that she should stay with her. So why hadn't she confessed to the INS that Jamela was with her?

Michael sent up a small prayer for wisdom while he waited for INS response.

"Agent Spates, this is Officer Hightower, with the Bureau of Immigration and Customs Enforcement. We have information pertaining to a minor child, Jamela Beckford; we understand from the other residents of the compound that she was last seen with you."

The female voice on the other end of the phone had

all the softness of a Brillo scouring pad, but Michael refused to be intimidated. "Yes, officer, that's correct. Miss Beckford is important to the case against Winton and his cohorts. Until we can get this all sorted out, we felt it best that she remain under our guardianship. She is a material witness and may be in danger if she is held with the other Jamaican detainees. You see, there is a certain amount of concern for her safety. If she had not assisted the bureau, we wouldn't have been able to carry out our operation. Miss Beckford was vital to our efforts."

Officer Hightower laughed a low, deep, throaty laugh before she spoke again. "Now, Agent Spates, I've been with the INS and now ICE for the better part of twenty years. That was a pretty good story, but you and I both know that it was a load of crock. But you've caught me at the end of the year and I'm feeling a little generous." She paused. "I'll tell you what—provide all the contact information for the child to me and take Jonnelda Lindo off my hands and we'll have a deal."

"Jonnelda Lindo?"

"Yes. She doesn't get along with most of the other detainees and frankly I'm worried about her. We haven't been able to locate anyone willing to take her in Jamaica and with her background with Winton, I'm afraid she's headed straight for the streets." Officer Hightower sighed. "So, take it or leave it—wherever you have Jamela, you now have Jonnelda and I want complete details on their care plans. You have twenty-four hours to call me back. Have a nice day," she added cheerily.

Michael put his head in his hands. Given the circumstances he was afraid to ask what next. He didn't know if he could handle the answer. Now how the devil was he going to break this news to Beatrice?

* * *

"Beatrice, I need to see you. Do you mind if I come over?" His speech sounded strained to his own ears, even though he tried to sound relaxed.

Bea was surprised by the request, but eager to see him. "Not at all, Jamela has been asking about you all day. But I'm not sure if I like the sound of your voice; is everything okay?"

Most certainly not. "It is what it is . . . I'll explain when I see you." Michael hesitated while he shuffled papers on his desk. "I have a few things to clear off my desk and then I'll be there—say around nine P.M.?"

"That's fine. We'll see you then." Bea held the receiver in her hand; then looked down at the school registration information. She hoped their conversation wasn't going to be about bad news. . . .

Michael arrived at Bea's doorstep exactly on time, as she knew he would. He was met at the door by a very enthusiastic little ten-year-old.

"Mr. Michael, you're home. I've missed you." Before he could say anything, she threw her arms around him in a bear hug.

Michael responded in kind. She was good for the soul. Seeing her smile helped to lift his spirits more than he could have imagined.

Beatrice walked toward the door with a dish towel in her hands. "Come on, I know you didn't eat, so I made a plate for you. Jamela is quite handy in the kitchen and we made some meat patties and plantains for you."

Michael thought the aroma was familiar, but he didn't dare hope. A smile lit up his face. "You know a man could get very used to this." He returned Jamela's hug. "It's very good to see you, young lady, and thank you for that warm welcome." He started to walk toward the breakfast room where Bea waited with his food. Jamela reached for his hand, which he took gladly.

Michael made eye contact with Bea and felt the warmth of her love. This is what he'd craved all his life, whether he took the time to admit it or not. "Thank you . . ."

Bea shook her head. "We wanted to do this, it's not that big a deal. Now, eat your food before it gets cold. Jamela and I are going to frost this coconut cake she showed me how to make." Bea squeezed his hand, then walked toward the prep area in her kitchen where they could still see and talk to him while they worked.

Michael was quiet for several seconds as he gave thanks for the food and asked for strength to do what he needed—he ate quietly until he was ready to speak. "Bea, there have been some new developments that we need to discuss in private." His tone was soft, yet firm.

Bea gave him a questioning look. "Jamela, as soon as we finish this cake, how about you finish that drawing that you started today?"

The little girl looked disappointed, but responded appropriately. "Yes, ma'am. But can I bring it to you when I'm finished?"

Bea smiled and stroked her face. "Yes, you may, but give us a few minutes, okay? There's a lot that has to be settled and I need you to be a big girl for me."

Jamela scrutinized their masterpiece. When she was satisfied that every square inch was sufficiently covered in white icing and coconut, she bounded up the stairs toward her new room.

Bea called after her, "Walk, young lady—remember, no running in the house!" Bea then turned to Michael. "All right, you have my full attention."

He looked at her. "No, I don't, because if I did, you'd be here in my arms."

Beatrice wanted nothing more, but he'd come over

for a reason and she was tired of what her imagination had come up with—she wanted to hear it from him. "If I were in your arms, you would still be stalling . . . tell me what's going on," she said gently.

Michael pushed his empty plate up. "There is bad news and worse news. The IRB seems determined to make a case against us and the ICE wants us to be responsible for both Jamela and Jonnelda or they both go back to Jamaica. I spoke with Officer Hightower; she wants a decision about Jonnelda by tomorrow."

The incredulous expression on Beatrice's face demonstrated her shock. She sat in the chair across from him. "Michael, what in the world did you tell her? I can't be responsible for these two girls! I don't even have a real plan for Jamela. This is awful, there's no way I can do this and continue to work, too!"

A feeling of dread began to course through him. "Bea, what do you suggest we do?" His voice took on a harder edge than he'd intended.

Bea arched an eyebrow. "Well, for starters, *Zeke*, I suggest that we discuss this in a rational manner." She exhaled slowly. Anger flashed in her eyes. She wasn't going to be forced to do something that she couldn't handle. Her life was orderly and controlled just the way she liked it. Michael was crazy if he thought he could come over and just drop the news of a seventeen-year-old girl on her doorstep. And since when did the ICE blackmail people into doing their bidding? This was no casual favor. Bea picked up his plate and walked to the sink. She filled it full of hot soapy water for one plate and one fork.

Michael noticed what she was doing and rubbed his forehead. He knew he was in trouble now . . . why was everything so damned difficult? He took a long sip of his ginger beer, then stood up to pace the room.

Bea didn't make eye contact with him again. Instead, she washed the same plate about six times.

Neither one seemed to care about the IRB process and the impact on their careers when they had such pressing *personal* business to take care of. . . .

"If you keep this up, you're going to end up in juvenile detention, Jonnelda!" Officer Hightower said, her voice tight with tension. She had had just about enough attitude for one long day. She counted to ten in her head and then continued. "We need to have more information. I'm sure there is something more that you can tell us to help us find your parents or some other relatives. You are connected to somebody, an aunt, uncle, older cousin? We need answers."

Jonnelda sat in the interview room with a dispassionate expression on her face. She'd learned how to tune out the world after Kharl began to take her to his bed. She didn't feel and she didn't think . . . she just did what she was told and waited for each assault on her dignity to be over.

After what happened to her parents, she realized that she had to save the one person left in her family, and for her she would make any sacrifice. She choked back the tears; her life had gone from bad to worse since coming to America. This was supposed to be her ticket to a better lot in life . . . to more opportunity and a chance to find happiness. Kharl Winton had managed to take all that away from her, and not just in Kingston, but in the U.S. as well. There was so little left . . . but she had to hold on, if she was sent back she wouldn't know what to do.

Jonnelda listened to the officer and was almost moved to confess her secret, but then she remembered the promise. . . . With her lips in a grim line she remained silent. Besides, no one could understand what she had been through . . . what she had given up.

Officer Hightower shook her head in exasperation and hoped Spates would take the bait and take Jonnelda away from the rest of the detainees. If she were involved in one more altercation, she would have to be locked up with *real* criminals. She made one last appeal to her. "Okay, Jonnelda. We've tried everything to work with you, but you've given us no choice. I'm moving you out of the facility until we can process everyone else. If you stay here, I can't guarantee your safety. You'll be picked up and moved out of here tomorrow."

Jonnelda's eyes were wide with fear. "No, you can't do this to me. I have to stay in the facility! Don't you understand? I have to be here when they—"

Hightower looked at her curiously. "When they what? And who is *they?*"

Jamela walked back into the room with an expectant expression on her face. "Miss Bea, can I show Mr. Michael my picture now?"

Beatrice sighed. Jamela became more precious to her every time she saw the little girl. She and Michael were going nowhere fast, which wasn't going to help Jamela at all. They were going to have to talk it out until they could come up with a workable solution. She looked down at her watch and noticed that it was very late . . . no matter how tired she was, she would have to put in a few hours of work tomorrow. "Jamela, you may show him the picture, but then I want you to brush your teeth and go to bed. I'll check on you before I turn in for the night."

Jamela started to protest, then quickly agreed. She strode purposefully over to Michael, who was back at the kitchen table, and sat down next to him. In her best impersonation of a teacher, she explained each facet of her drawing. "Miss Bea and I talked about my life. She told me that a lot of people love me, even if they aren't here anymore and that I am never alone. So this picture is of my mom and dad in the corner. They are in heaven, see the blue clouds? Over here is the farmhouse and this is Kharl with the big *X* through his face, and this is the sun with you and Miss Bea. This is our house and see, I'm smiling."

Michael followed her direction to each picture that she showed to him, a lump forming in his throat.

She had been through enough turmoil. He would have to find a way to make this work with Jonnelda. He took her hand in his. "Jamela, now that you are here and safe, we are going to do everything we can to make sure that you're safe and well taken care of. Miss Bea and I care a lot about you, and we're very glad that you've come into our lives." He paused before his emotion got the better of him. "Come here, now give me a big hug before you go to bed. I'll stop in to see you before I go."

Jamela smiled and gladly hugged him before she scampered off to her room again.

Beatrice watched the scene with conflicted emotion. She couldn't afford to become any more attached to Jamela, and there was no way she could let her go until she made sure that she would be well taken care of—as if anyone could take care of her better than me, she thought. She looked at Michael—they still had a great deal to work out. It didn't help, either, that her hormones had gone into high gear the moment she'd laid eyes on him earlier this evening. She resisted the temptation to forget all about business and go straight to pleasure . . . and with her bedroom right down the hall . . .

Bea took homemade vanilla-flavored ice cream out the freezer and made a fresh pot of coffee . . . she had the feeling she would need both.

Michael stood right beside her as she poured coffee into two mugs. He tested the ice cream to see if it was soft enough to scoop. Satisfied that it was, he began to fill the two bowls with the creamy vanilla delight. He returned the carton to the freezer and then sat down next to Beatrice. They acted as if this was their normal routine. Bea's breath caught in her throat. This was too familiar . . . too right. She trembled. This was the same routine she'd shared with her late husband after Josh and Janice had been sent to bed. "Michael, this isn't going to work. As much as I love you and as much as I want to be with you, I can't do this right now. . . . I'm just not ready."

Michael pierced her with his intense gaze. "Bea, what just happened?"

Bea fought hard to hold back her emotion. She didn't want to be this weak, snively woman. She had to regain control. She started slowly. "Michael, we have to go back to the way things were before Harpers Ferry. I feel like I'm holding on by a thread here, and when I'm with you, I have to—"

Michael interrupted, "You have to what, Beatrice? I'm not pushing you to do anything that you don't want to do, Bea. Maybe I was out of line about Jonnelda, I'll figure something else out, but don't hold that against me."

Bea almost snapped. "Michael, this has nothing to do with the kids!" She shrank back in her seat. "Oh my God, don't you see? I can't separate the old from the new. I talk to Jamela just like I did to my own daughter. I don't know where the fantasy ends and reality begins. We're sitting here in my kitchen like this is what we do all the time . . . a minute ago I was fantasizing about you taking me to bed . . . *my bed*. Michael, this is not us! You haven't been here in the house since the memorial service for the kids." Beatrice held her head in her hands. "Michael, I'll take care of Jamela and Jonnelda, but I can't carry on a relationship with you, too. I need boundaries so that I can maintain my perspective."

After a few seconds of silence, Michael spoke. His voice was low and soothing . . . it had lost the hard edge from before. Bea touched his heart with her admission of vulnerability. "My life means nothing without you in it. I've watched you and loved you from afar for all these years, and now we finally have a chance at our own happiness. I'm not going to walk away from that because of fear or confusion. This is just a test, Beatrice. A test to see if we have the right stuff to make a lasting relationship. I believe we do, but baby, you have to trust me. You have to know that we're in this thing together—nothing can interfere unless we let it." He shrugged the tension from his shoulders. "There is a solution to all of this that we just have to be willing to face head-on. I can't make love to you in your bed . . . but we can look for alternatives. Bea, I want to be both your fantasy and reality—but I can't if you push me away."

Bea closed her eyes. "Michael, I know you mean everything you say, and that's what makes this so difficult. I know I could just give them over to you and you'd solve all my problems, but I can't do that . . . I won't. I have to figure this out on my own. I have to be able to handle my own feelings. . . . I feel like an awkward hormonal teen again—this is very uncomfortable for me." She looked directly into his gaze. "Michael, we need to end this before we both end up more hurt. As much as I love you and want you and I to be together, I've got to have space." Her voice dropped to a whisper. "At least for now. Please don't fight me on this."

Michael blew out an exasperated breath. He wanted to throw his hands up in frustration, but he managed to calm himself before he spoke. "Beatrice, I never fight you on anything. Maybe that's my problem. I give in to your every whim and I end up with the short end of the stick.

You need to be very sure of your position because I'm not going to continue up and down on this emotional yo-yo. I'll give you the space that you need, Bea, but after I walk out those doors, we go back to the way it was before the car accident." He stood up to leave. "You've set the terms, but you don't get to change them at will."

Bea nodded her head in understanding and with a lump in her throat she agreed. "I know. I'll call Officer Hightower in the morning and then call you with the details later." She stopped when he stood in the door-way. "Don't forget about Jamela."

He remembered the picture she'd drawn and how much it meant. . . .

Michael started toward the bedroom. "I'll do that now. Let me know if you need any help explaining everything to her. It might be a good idea to have one of the psych folks talk with her. She's been through more than any ten-year-old should."

Jamela sat up in bed as soon as Michael entered the room. "Mr. Michael, I made something else for you." She shoved a small package in his hands.

He leaned in to kiss her good night. "Thank you, sweetheart, now get some rest. I'll come by to see you again soon."

In her sleepy child's voice she said, "I love you. Thank you for taking such good care of me and Miss Bea."

Michael's throat felt as dry as sandpaper. He tucked her snugly in her covers and stood up. "You're welcome, Jamela. I'll see you soon."

After Michael left, Beatrice sat on her bed. She studied her room, the place that offered both solace and sadness. Very little had changed during the time she'd lived in the house. Her television was in the same spot . . . her oak-finished dresser held the same lotions, potions, and pills as before . . . her beige carpet and sage-colored silk curtains that coordinated with her plush sage floral-patterned cushioned window seat were much the same as before.

She was living in a time warp. A time when the McCoy family consisted of a father, mother, a son, and a daughter . . . the reality that she was a widow and childless seemed to scream at her in the wake of Michael's departure. Once again, being with him conjured up all the feelings that she'd worked so hard to forget. Why had he been so damned insistent? They could have left well enough alone and her life would be so much simpler. Now look! She would have to deal with how much she loved him every time she saw him . . . every time he looked at her with those intense brown eyes that seemed to see to her soul. Bea didn't bother to stem the tears that fell over her long lashes. She wanted to cry until she didn't feel anymore . . . wanted to cry, cry, cry.

Kingston, Jamaica . . .

"How was he killed?" Vanessa Winton asked as she forced her voice to remain calm. Her brother had done a fine job of building up the organization in the U.S. and now he was dead, just like that. She couldn't accept that.

No one in Kingston would dare attempt something so risky; the Winton posse was too powerful. Kharl had taught her everything she knew about how to run a successful import-export business. Her tactics were ruthless, but that seemed to guarantee success like no other motivator.

Vanessa leaned back in her chair. She trembled inside, but with a roomful of people looking to her for strength, she would express her grief at a later time. Right now she needed information. . . . Someone owed her a debt. In her world it was a life for a life.

Vanessa spoke carefully. "Get me names and addresses, I'll be there in two weeks. I need time to put some things in play."

Chapter Nine

"Jonnelda, if there's something that I should know tell me. If there's someone who needs protection, we can do that, but I can't help if I don't know."

Before the young lady could answer, another officer peeked into the room to motion for Officer Hightower to take a call in another room. She turned back to her. "Jonnelda, I have to take this call, but we're not finished yet—I'm still waiting for your answer."

Jonnelda stared blankly ahead . . . waiting for the next disaster to happen. She hoped the phone call wasn't about her physical. She felt like a spectator watching her life unravel before her very eyes. She had to hope that she could accomplish her goals before she was sent back or the government made *other* arrangements for her.

In the interview room, which was nothing more than a cell with a one-way mirror, she fumed as she realized that she had been so close—so close to getting away from Kharl, from the life she'd been forced into and now here she was back in *captivity* again. She could curse the FBI.

The longer Jonnelda sat the heavier the weight of her reality seemed to burden her shoulders. She held back the tears that threatened to spill over her thick black lashes, though all she wanted to do was put her head down and cry her eyes dry.

Officer Hightower breathed a sigh of relief. "Yes, Agent Spates. That sounds reasonable to me. I'll have her taken over in the morning and then if all goes well, I'll release her to your custody. Thank you, I know I didn't make this an easy choice, but I really do believe this is her best option. I'm meeting with her now and she is . . . complicated. She'll be better served this way and so will we. I'll see you tomorrow."

"Doc Rose, what I need is a quick assessment. I know that you don't usually work with kids, so I'm glad that you've agreed to do this."

"Michael, psychology is not like ordering fast food. I can't just make a quick assessment—there are no fries with that diagnosis of schizophrenia. I'll agree to see the girls, but you may be biting off more than you can chew. What are you prepared to do if they need further treatment? You and Bea have too much to do to handle troubled children or a troubled child. Are you prepared for regularly scheduled appointments, possibly even medication or emotional outbursts? It is no easy feat to take care of a child with behavioral issues."

There was silence on the line for several seconds. "Spates, what's going on here? Why are you even involved like this? What's in it for you? Or is this about Bea?" Wendy heard the long exhale on the other end and knew that she was on to something.

Michael responded defensively. "Doc, why does there have to be something going on? Why can't I just be ready to do something different in my life?"

Wendy almost fell off her chair. "Because people don't

take on the responsibility of raising children for a change of pace. Jamela and Jonnelda aren't toys that you can re-gift after you're tired of them. It sounds like they have been through an extraordinary ordeal. Michael, I'm alarmed at what I'm hearing." Dr. Rose had always thought she could depend on Michael's levelheaded way of behaving, but now she wondered if she'd made the right assessment. "You need to start making sense real quickly before I call you in here for an evaluation." She decided to push harder. "Michael, tell me everything or I'm going to cancel the appointments."

Michael's displeasure at being bullied was evident in his tone. "Okay, but this stays between us. And no matter what you say, you can forget about getting me on your couch. I like my skeletons right where they are. . . ." He breathed out.

"The truth is that Jamela has touched a very special place in my heart. I'll be fifty this year, but when I see her I feel young again. I guess I never thought about having a legacy. I'm not trying to sound sappy here, but Jamela represents the future, a future that I want to share with her and Beatrice. Bea loves that little girl so much. I've always thought that work was enough, but I know now it isn't. I want a family . . . I want it more than I ever thought possible and it starts with Beatrice."

Michael paused for a brief second. He needed the doctor to understand his perspective. "Don't misunderstand me, I do want what's best for Jamela, but if there is no place else or no one else, then I'd like her to stay with us. We have to find out if she has another family member willing to take her on, though; we're not in the business of ripping families apart for personal gain. Beatrice is very taken with Jamela, but she understands that there is the possibility that she may have to leave."

"What do you think her response would be to that?

Is she too emotionally involved with the child to be objective?"

Michael arched an eyebrow. "No, Beatrice is handling herself just fine. She has been through a lot these last few years, but she is one of the strongest, most capable women that I know. She'll handle whatever comes her way, and of course, I'll always be there to help."

Dr. Rose made a few notes, but seemed satisfied with that explanation. "So you and Bea are serious now? When did this happen?"

Michael cleared his throat. "I'm not on your couch, *Wendy*."

Dr. Rose chuckled. "Touché, I'll call you after I've met with the girls."

"I'll meet you at the office, we can talk then," Michael said before he disconnected the line. He planned to follow through with the process to the end. Beatrice may not like his involvement, but he was just as invested in seeing the girls safe as she was. . . .

Besides, he thought selfishly, as soon as Jamela and Jonnelda were settled he and Beatrice could concentrate their efforts on each other, again.

Irritation peppered her tone as she spoke. "Michael, I really don't think that this is necessary. Don't you think that this will make the girls feel uncomfortable or like they're under a microscope?"

Michael's response indicated his own displeasure. Why did they have to fight every time they talked? It wasn't like this before. . . . "Beatrice, I'm doing this as much for them as for you. The girls have been through a traumatic experience, there's no telling what secrets they are hiding out of fear, or even what kind of post-traumatic stress they may be feeling. Let's just give the process a try. It really can't hurt to have Dr. Rose talk

with them. If she feels uneasy she will refer them both
to a pediatric psychologist, but at least we'll know if
something is going on with them that we can't handle.
And more importantly, they will be able to share their
feelings with someone."

Bea listened quietly. He made perfect sense, but she
didn't want him to be right. She didn't want him to
come over . . . or to feel desire for him . . .

This internal battle she fought over loving him felt
like it would take her over the edge. She missed him
and that made her angry, too. Where was all that self-
assured control she'd possessed not so long ago? She
shrugged the tension from her shoulders before she
responded. Her voice was barely above a whisper. "All
right, Michael, we'll do it your way. I'll meet you at Dr.
Rose's office."

Officer Hightower arrived with Jonnelda and
Beatrice with Jamela at Dr. Rose's office. But they
didn't meet right away, because Bea and Jamela were
behind closed doors to talk with the doctor about the
purpose of the meeting.

"Jamela, my name is Dr. Wendy Rose, but you can call
me Doc Wendy. Most people do around here. I work
with Miss Bea and Mr. Michael. We're going to talk
today about some things . . . mostly about what happened to you. I'd also like to discuss the changes that
are going to be happening in your living situation.
Above all, I want you to know that you can tell me anything that you want." Dr. Rose paused for a few seconds
to allow Jamela to hear what she was saying. "I've heard
that you are a very good artist. We're all good at doing
something; people tell me that I'm a very good listener."

Jamela smiled and seemed more at ease. "Doc Wendy
sounds funny, but I like it. Do you know how to shoot a
gun and throw a knife like Miss Bea?"

Beatrice nearly choked as she swallowed. Dr. Rose

looked toward her. "Maybe now is a good time for Miss Bea to go get some water. There's some in the reception area. Have Gizzelle get it for you."

Bea nodded her head and left Dr. Rose and Jamela to talk. As she walked out, obviously distressed by what she'd just heard, Michael walked into the reception area. Jonnelda sat in a chair next to Officer Hightower looking very much the sullen teenager. Beatrice glanced her way, but when the girl refused to make eye contact, Beatrice again focused her attention on Michael. She motioned for him to follow her to a corner.

She stood very close to him so that they wouldn't be overheard. Michael tried hard to concentrate on her and not the scent of her Juniper Breeze, which reminded him of the last time they'd made love. He looked at her intently. "Bea, what just happened? You seem shaken up."

"Well, I can say with assurance that what she witnessed from us did more damage than a thousand hours of watching violent television shows. Michael, she thinks that we're some sort of vigilante superheroes, with guns, knives, and bombs blazing!" She hesitated, after she realized how dramatic she sounded. Jamela must be having a more profound effect on her than she noticed.

Michael smiled, not at her statement, but at her. There was so much he found that appealed to him about her, so much he loved . . . so much he wanted in his life . . .

"I have a niece in Detroit who talks about a dramameter. I think she would be proud of you, that rated pretty high up there."

They both chuckled and some of the tension between them abated. He held her by the shoulders. "Take a deep breath and tell me what happened from the beginning."

Inside the office, Dr. Rose said, "Jamela, sometimes adults have to do bad things for a good reason. Guns, knives, and bombs hurt people and should never be used unless absolutely necessary. What Mr. Michael and Miss Bea did was so that they could protect you and other people from Mr. Kharl. Do you understand that—does that make sense to you?"

Jamela nodded before she answered, then she spoke with the unbiased clarity of youth. "I know they did what had to be done. Mr. Kharl's men were chasing us and they would have killed us, too. I've seen him do lots of bad things, some of the ladies in the women's section would call him a 'bastard.' I'm not really sure what that is, but they made it sound really bad."

Wendy hid a smile behind her hands. "The way they meant it, yes, it was a bad thing. Jamela, Miss Bea and Mr. Michael seem like they are important to you?"

The little girl nodded yes.

Dr. Rose continued. "Can you tell me about the other important people in your life?"

Jamela sighed. "When we left Kingston, I was very little. I don't remember my grandmother or my other aunts and uncles. Some of the older ladies, the ones that Mr. Kharl kept around to cook and clean, would tell me stories about my parents and other family, but they are just names. I don't have any pictures . . . not even of my mom and dad." Her eyes glistened with moisture. "Jonnelda's important to me. She would make sure that the other kids didn't pick on me when I did or said something wrong. She always made sure that my clothes were clean and that I ate, especially after what Mr. Kharl did to my parents. She was like my big sister, but she's been so sad lately. Sometimes she won't say anything to me at all; she won't talk to anyone. She just sits and looks sad enough to cry, but she doesn't. One of the other ladies said that she was too strong for her own good." Her look of consternation changed to one of brightness. "I don't really understand what that means, either, but I know Jonnelda loves me."

Dr. Rose smiled gently. "Jamela, what things make you sad?"

Jamela looked down at her hands. "It makes me sad that all the men, Augustus, Simeon, and Kharl are dead and that the compound is gone. It was the only life we had, even though they were bad men. Now we don't know what is going to happen. I would hear some of the older women talk at night. Some of them can't go back to Kingston because they would be killed, it's not safe when you don't have the protection of the posse leader." She paused and looked earnestly at Dr. Rose. "I don't want to go back, though; I want to stay here with Miss Bea." Jamela grew quiet. "*And* Mr. Michael, but they don't live together, so I have to wait until he comes over to see her."

Dr. Rose's assessment was almost complete, but she had a few more questions that she hoped the little girl was up to answering. She began gingerly, "Do you think you'd like Jonnelda to live with you and Miss Bea for a time?" Dr. Rose asked in a gentle tone.

Jamela brightened noticeably. "Yes, ma'am . . . I mean, Doc Wendy. It would be good to have my 'big sister' living with us. I know she gets worried about me and this way, she can watch me when Miss Bea has to work late or travel. She told me sometimes that she has to go out of town. With Jonnelda there, I wouldn't be afraid."

Dr. Rose was relieved. "Okay then, let me talk with Jonnelda privately for a few minutes and then we can all meet. You are such a big and brave girl, Jamela. It seems there are a lot of people who want to make sure that you stay safe. You can add me to the list, too. There's no more reason to be afraid, because we're here when you need us."

Jamela smiled as she stood to leave the office. Dr. Rose walked out with her, prepared to meet with Jonnelda, but as soon as the older girl saw Jamela, she jumped up from the waiting room chair to hug the little girl.

Dr. Rose, Bea, Michael, and Officer Hightower watched the interaction in surprise. No one had ever seen the tight-lipped Jonnelda express so much emotion.

"Oh God, Mela! What are you doing here? I was so worried . . . I didn't know what had happened to you or where you were. I didn't want to go back to Jamaica and not know if you were safe or not. I've been crazy thinking about you." Jonnelda's words came out in a rush as free-flowing tears streaked her face. She kissed the little girl's face repeatedly and hugged her close.

"Jonnie!" Jamela squealed. She threw her arms around her in a big bear hug. "I missed you, too. I told Dr. Rose that I want you to come live with me and Miss Bea."

Jonnelda looked around the room with an expression of total confusion on her face. No one had mentioned to her that she would be with Jamela! All her worry and distress had been for nothing—she was safe. Jonnelda was overwhelmed with emotion.

Dr. Rose watched with keen interest. She nodded toward the adults in the room as she directed Jonnelda away from the child. "She's fine, Jonnelda. Come talk with me for a little bit. We'll meet with everyone else in about half an hour."

Jonnelda wiped tears away with the back of her hand and kissed the top of Jamela's head. "I love you," she whispered into the little girl's ear. Jamela smiled from ear to ear and bounded toward Michael and Bea. Jonnelda and Bea said in unison, "Walk, don't run."

Jamela looked from one woman to the other and immediately slowed her pace.

Beatrice fixed Jonnelda with a curious stare before the young lady headed into Dr. Rose's office.

Michael watched the entire scene in silence, making note of all he'd witnessed. An uneasy feeling surged through him.

Wendy walked in first, sat behind her desk, and immediately began to write notes. She looked up when she finished. "Okay, Jonnelda, we can begin now. You can call me Doc Wendy like everyone else. I'm very pleased to meet you, especially considering it looks like you've had a lot on your mind. Maybe I can help you."

Jonnelda blew out a tired breath. "Why did they send me to you? Do you work for the FBI like *they* do?" The snide meaning when she referred to Michael and Beatrice was unmistakable.

Wendy sat back in her chair. Her suspicions were slowly being confirmed. "Jonnelda, I think that you are old enough to understand the truth. Yes, I do work for the bureau. I have worked with agents McCoy and Spates for longer than you've been alive, and I know that they are good people. They'll take very good care of you—of you both."

Jonnelda looked down. "I know that I sound ungrateful. I just need a minute to collect my thoughts. Since they came and shut the compound down, I've been sick . . . everything happened so fast. Kharl was acting crazy, I thought he was going to kill me. All I have been able to think about is Jamela, keeping her safe . . . and then she was just gone. No one would say anything about what happened to her. At first I didn't even know if Kharl had done something awful to her—I've been a mess without her."

Dr. Rose steepled her fingers. "She means a lot to you."

Jonnelda looked up. "You have no idea."

Dr. Rose continued. "So does this mean that you are willing to move in with Beatrice McCoy until your return to Jamaica?"

Jonnelda's eyes turned cold. "You mean my deportation. Since we're being honest here, let's call it what it is."

Dr. Rose countered. "We'll have to cross that bridge when we come to it. Nothing has been set in stone. But in that spirit of honesty, tell me why you're having such a tough time with the other women that you are being boarded with and also tell me if you plan to cause problems for McCoy."

She breathed out long and hard. "Jamaicans, like most other West Indians, have their own superstitions and taboos. I was the last one with Kharl, so they're just taking out their frustrations on the only viable scapegoat—me. They're treating me like I'm cursed, but it's all just a silly old wives' tale. And no, I won't cause problems for the FBI. Now that I know where Mela is and that she's safe, nothing else matters."

"Did you know Jamela back in Jamaica?" Dr. Rose asked, her curiosity piqued again.

Jonnelda rotated her shoulders. She was tired of playing twenty questions with this shrink. She pursed her lips together and remained silent.

Dr. Rose studied her posture and body language. "It's okay, I'm not going to tell anyone. Our conversation is protected by doctor-patient confidentiality." She paused and leaned back in her seat again. "I think you should consider coming clean with Beatrice McCoy and maybe even Jamela."

Jonnelda's large expressive eyes grew worried and she shook her head vigorously. "Please don't say anything, I'll do whatever you want me to do, I promise."

Dr. Rose said, "Jonnelda, it's all right. Nobody is going to force you to do anything that you don't want to anymore. I'm just making a suggestion. It has been my experience that secrets never stay hidden for too long. I'm here for you—I'm willing to help you sort it all out with Beatrice and Michael."

Jonnelda shook her head no. "I can't . . . not right now . . ."

Dr. Rose looked down at her notes. When she raised her head she said, "Okay then, when you're ready. Maybe now we should talk about Kharl."

After the revelation, conversation was kept to a minimum between Jonnelda and Dr. Rose. In the waiting room things had changed as well. Officer Hightower had to rush back to her office and excused herself, which left Michael with Beatrice and Jamela in the doctor's waiting room.

Jamela sat down at the magazine table, which she'd turned into a desk, and focused on her drawing for Dr. Rose. After a rocky start this morning, all was right in her world—she hummed pleasantly while she drew.

Michael conferred several times with Karen in the SCU office. Everything was under control, but there had been no word yet from the IRB agents, so he and the rest of the SCU were on hold still. He looked over at Beatrice and successfully fought the urge to reach out for her hand. The expression on her face telegraphed her feelings—she wasn't happy. He was concerned now about her ability to handle both girls without his help . . . especially if there was going to be friction with Jonnelda.

Michael cleared his throat before he spoke. He didn't want to offend her or put her on the defensive, which he seemed to do regardless of what he said nowadays. "How are you feeling about this?"

Beatrice rubbed her neck. "Honestly, I'm not sure. Before we walked through those doors, I thought I had everything under control, but now my gut is telling me something isn't right." Bea was pensive as she watched Jamela draw. With a quiet exhale of air, she added, "There's more going on with Jonnelda Lindo than she

is willing to let on . . . if her secrets are going to impact
Jamela, me personally, or the bureau, I want to know
about it. How much do we really know about her relationship with Kharl? I know according to the report that
he used her as a hostage, but how close were they before
we took down the compound? I don't like where my
thoughts are headed concerning her, especially since
she will be a guest in my home. I know the ICE did a
background investigation, but I'd like you to run one,
too." She searched Michael's face for understanding.

He nodded. "Consider it done. Like you, I don't want
any surprises over the next few days. We don't know
enough about Jonnelda to give me a warm fuzzy, either.
I hope you don't mind if I check in on you regularly to
see how things are going?"

Bea smirked. She hoped Michael didn't think he
wasn't transparent. But she would give in for awhile,
the truth was, and she wouldn't turn down his help as
she tried to navigate these totally unfamiliar waters.
She looked over at Jamela again and nodded her head
in silence. Despite her desire to be more independent
and self-assured in this area, she didn't feel entirely
comfortable. Moreover, as much as she hated to admit
it, she needed Michael—he was still her rock.

Dr. Rose finished her assessment then asked to speak
with Beatrice and Michael privately. "Well, you asked
for my professional opinion so I'm going to give it to
you. I don't see any overt signs that Jonnelda or Jamela
will need continued therapy. I think that they both
show signs of being under extreme emotional stress
and they exhibit signs of that through interrupted sleep
patterns, loss or increase of appetite or other ways, but
my best advice to you both is to be aware and be concerned. Let them grieve the loss of Kharl, their way of

life, their friends, and their families. As time goes by they will improve and I suspect that though you'll have growing pains, you'll adjust. What concerns me more than the girls though is the two of you."

Bea gasped. "What on earth for?"

Dr. Rose looked from one to the other. "What they need more than anything is stability. This is a terribly confusing time for both of them. While Jonnelda is older, she still needs the same kind of love and concern that Jamela will need. They have to learn to trust again—they need to know that the world isn't such a crazy place and that they are secure with the two of you. The bond that was formed with Jamela was not just with you, Bea, it was with Michael, too. Michael, you saved Jonnelda's life when you shot Kharl. There's an unconscious bond that she will always have with you."

Dr. Rose let her words sink in before she continued. "I'm afraid before I can sign off on the two of them being released into your custody and not returned to the detainee center, I need to have your solemn oath that you'll work together. I need a commitment from you, Bea, to let Michael participate in the co-guardianship of those girls and I need you to commit to spending at least every weekend and some days during the week with them, Michael."

Dr. Rose came from around her desk and leaned up against its edge. She looked down at them authoritatively. "I want to see the four of you back here for a family session in ninety days to follow up. I'm afraid my terms are not negotiable. You asked for my professional assessment and so here it is."

Chapter Ten

Michael sat with a stunned expression on his face, but said nothing. Beatrice tried to speak, but choked on her words and sat sputtering for several seconds. The incredulous expression that crossed her features said it all.

Dr. Rose arched her eyebrows and waited for the commotion to cease. When both seemed pulled together, she buzzed her secretary and asked for the children to be brought in for a short session before she would send everyone home.

Dr. Rose returned to her chair, leaned back, and waited for everyone to be seated before she began. She finished the meeting by telling Jamela and Jonnelda that it was a pleasure to meet them. "I'm giving you both my card, if you need anything, or want to talk, you just call me, I'll help you to get everything back on track again. Remember, it will help everyone to make the adjustment if everyone stays on schedule." She clasped her hands together and smiled reassuringly. "Okay, I'll see all of you back here in three months—unless problems develop. Have a good time and take care of each other."

As soon as the meeting concluded Michael asked to speak to Dr. Rose alone. However, she anticipated as much and wouldn't agree; as far as she was concerned she was only doing what was best. And maybe there was a little matchmaking sprinkled in there, too, but it was for their own good. "I'm sorry, Agent Spates, I have a full afternoon, so just stop by the desk on your way out to make an appointment with my secretary and I'll be happy to see you then."

Michael stood rigid as a stone . . . any second it looked like steam would come out of his ears. He knew when he was being played and Dr. Rose definitely had something up her sleeve. Bea noticed his silent reaction and took his hand in a calming gesture; together they walked out of the office.

Michael's cell phone rang before they made it outside. He recognized the number and after he answered looked at Beatrice apologetically. "I've got to go, but how about I take everyone to dinner tonight?"

Bea considered the proposition for a moment. "No, I need to help Jonnelda settle in. Come over when you're done at the office and we'll have dinner together." *As a family*, she didn't add.

Michael said good-bye to the girls, brushed a kiss on her cheek, walked to his truck, and was gone in less than a minute. As Beatrice watched his tail lights disappear, she felt a twinge of trepidation. A shiver ran up her spine, as much from the December cold as from the feeling that coursed through her. She pulled the belt on her camel-colored cashmere coat tighter, then inched up her brown leather gloves higher to cover more of her hands.

Christmas was in less than three weeks and for once she could buy for the people in her home instead of her extended family. It was the end of the year and there were so many challenges and changes to deal with—all of a sudden she didn't like the thought of doing everything alone, when just forty-eight hours prior she was ready to have Michael exit her life. There was school registration, gift buying, work issues, and above all a conclusion to their situation. They had so much to settle in their relationship and now they were thrust into a situation that neither of them was prepared for.

Bea felt if someone would just pinch her, she could wake up from it all. After a couple minutes in deep thought, she turned back to Jonnelda and Jamela to say, "Well, I guess it's just us for the time being, let's go get you two settled. Then we can decide what we'll eat."

Beatrice, Jonnelda, and Jamela headed toward Bea's home in her champagne-colored Lexus RX 330. Jonnelda loved the feel of the vehicle, it had been so long since she had been in anything nice—she tried to put away all thoughts of her experience at the compound, but it was going to take some getting used to. She fingered Dr. Rose's card—she had the feeling that she would need it. She didn't know if she was strong enough to pull off what she planned. Jonnelda wondered how long it would take. . . .

Beatrice was grateful for the quiet. She had a difficult enough time trying to concentrate without the distraction of conversation. She looked at the children through the rearview mirror. Jamela was content to play games on her new Game Boy and Jonnelda seemed deep in thought. Bea wondered what was going on with her. It was something that she resolved to find out once they made it home.

Jonnelda fidgeted with her sweater as she rode silently in the back of the vehicle with Jamela. So many troubling thoughts swirled through her mind. She watched Beatrice fawn all over Jamela. She treated her like a precious child—like *she* was *her* precious child. It hurt, yet in some way it was also strangely comforting. Because now at least she knew Jamela had been safe while they'd been apart and that's all she'd wanted anyway.

Jonnelda sighed. They were driving through a very nice neighborhood. *So, this is what the real American Dream looked like.*

She took note of the tree-lined streets filled with stately houses—each had perfectly manicured lawns, and either two-or three-car garages. This was an older neighborhood with mature trees, totally bricked structures, and where the neighbors beeped and waved in greeting to each other.

As they drove further in, Jonnelda noticed that some of the garage doors were open to reveal the family treasures that they contained—like bicycles, lawn equipment, plastic storage containers, and brown boxes. What the heck did people keep in those brown boxes, anyway? Every garage seemed to have a few in different sizes.

Jonnelda knew that she allowed her mind to wander because it was safer that way. It was much easier to focus on the mundane facts of her current condition than to face the reality that her life was very screwed up.

They arrived at the house where she would stay until the state decided her fate. Jonnelda decided that she wouldn't beg to stay in the country. But if she were allowed to, she would do all she could to make things right. Kharl had taken so much away, but not anymore, she wasn't still a victim –she had the opportunity to live her own life now. Dr. Rose had helped her to see that everything wasn't her fault, and she had control now.

Hurumph, she thought. She hadn't even managed to fool Dr. Rose for more than fifteen minutes. Jonnelda's heart beat furiously in her chest. How in the world was she going to keep up the charade with these FBI people? If they were able to take down Kharl's whole operation, how was she to match wits with them?

Jonnelda shifted uncomfortably in her seat, ready to exit the vehicle. She was thankful that the only conversation in the vehicle had been between

Jamela and Beatrice—she couldn't have handled anything more.

She stared at the lovely two-story colonial-styled home. It was picture-perfect, complete with a white picket fence to surround the property. Jonnelda could just imagine Beatrice in the home, baking cookies. Bea had so much more to offer Jamela than she did. Jonnelda reached into the vehicle to gather the small bag that contained all that she owned in the world: two pair of jeans and five pair of underwear, courtesy of the immigration service.

Maybe Dr. Rose was right and she needed to come clean about her relationship to Jamela. Every time she looked at the child—*her child*—her heart broke over the decisions that she'd made.

Beatrice shrugged off the uneasiness she experienced and led the way into her home. She'd watched Jonnelda from the car mirror during the drive. There was something very troubling about the young lady—she seemed so sullen at times. Bea made a mental note to talk more with Dr. Rose about her. This girl was going to be in her home alone, sometimes even alone with Jamela. Beatrice needed to be sure that she could trust her. She turned to Jamela once they were inside. "Honey, why don't you go to your room for a few minutes. I'll call you down when it's time to cook for Mr. Michael. I need to speak with Jonnelda alone for a few minutes."

Jamela sucked her teeth, before she asked, "But when you're done can I show Jonnie my room?"

Bea smiled. "Of course you *may*, now scoot."

Jonnelda looked around curiously as she followed Bea into the kitchen. Bea turned to her. "I'll give you the fifty-cent tour after we're done. This won't take long, I just have a few things that I want to say."

Jonnelda regarded her with a grim expression on her face.

Beatrice sat down. She needed to collect her thoughts. After a few seconds of silence, she dove in. "It has been a long time since this house was filled with laughter or joy. Since Jamela has been here, I've been able to enjoy it again and I've found that I missed it more than I knew. I want to continue to enjoy those good feelings and the peace that I've come to know. . . ." Bea paused to catch her breath. She was nervous and she had no idea why.

"Jonnelda, I know that it must have been difficult for you at the compound. It sounds like Kharl was nothing more than a snake, but if there are things that I should know, I wish you'd tell me. I want to be your friend while you're here in my house. I don't want you to be a guest, but rather part of the family." Bea paused to wait for Jonnelda's response.

Jonnelda's gaze was intense, when she made eye contact with Bea her expression held a certain amount of defiance. "You want to know who I really am? I'm not Jonnelda Lindo the Jamaican posse queen. I'm just a young lady who was forced into a bad situation, like so many others of my Jamaican sisters. We believed the lie—the one we were told about life being so much better in this country than in Jamaica.

"I came here expecting some kind of utopia. Yes, I was naive, but this life was never what I wanted or expected. This is not who my parents raised me to be." Jonnelda hesitated, she couldn't say much more for fear of saying too much.

"Yes, ma'am, it was difficult with Kharl, he took everything from me, and left me with nothing, least of all my dignity. I'm bitter, I'm humiliated, and I'm angry, but it won't affect my ability to behave normally. I know you're probably concerned about whether I'm safe or not . . . I'm no threat to you. You can trust me alone in your house, nothing will come up missing and I promise not to burn the place down. Jamela is safe with me, too. I'd never do anything to hurt her." She hesitated again before she said exactly what was on her mind.

"Respectfully, it really is none of your business whatever's going on in my head. Just know that I can handle it . . . but I do thank you for your concern."

Bea swallowed hard as she checked her tongue. Trust was earned. And this girl was going to have to do more than tell Bea to get out of her business to earn hers. Beatrice said, "Fair enough. You're right, I don't need to know all of your business. . . . I just need to know that we understand each other. I don't have a lot of rules, just one that is very important to me—respect my house and me. No boys, no smoking, no drinking or other drugs, and no cursing. I'm trying to provide a wholesome environment for Jamela and I don't want that kind of drama in my home. It will take some time for the government to sort things out, and frankly, I have no idea how long both of you will be here, but I don't want us to treat this as a temporary situation. I want to do everything I can to create a family environment, as much for the two of you as for myself."

Jonnelda nodded. "Ma'am, my family is dead, nothing will change that, but since I don't do any of the things that you've mentioned, I guess we'll get along just fine. I can see what you're doing for Jamela . . . and . . . I'm grateful. It hasn't been easy for her, especially after her parents were killed, but she's strong and she cares about everybody. She managed to make life worth living in that hellhole of a compound of Kharl Winton's. She's more important to me than you'll ever know, so you don't have to worry about anything."

Bea made eye contact with the young lady and believed her. Something about her sense of conviction about Jamela, told Bea she would rather die than see harm come to her—and since she felt the same way, she guessed it would be all right. "Okay Jonnelda, you have a right to your privacy, but my door is always open to you. I mean that."

"I might just take you up on the offer after a little while. I just need some time to sort out how I'm feeling and what I think I should do." Jonnelda's shoulders visibly relaxed as she leaned back in her chair. She finally let a smile tickle the edges of her mouth. "Now that we have the big stuff out the way, may I have the fifty-cent tour of the house? I love what little I've seen."

Beatrice brightened, too. They couldn't solve all the world's problems in fifteen minutes. She resigned herself to taking it slow. "Yes, you can. But, I'm sure you're tired, too. Do you want some time to relax?"

Jonnelda shook her head. "No, I think I'd like to spend some time with Mela, maybe I'll color with her, that's one of her favorite things to do—that girl has quite an imagination. She creates whole worlds around her drawings sometimes; at one point I thought about entering her work in some contests—"

Bea listened—taking note of the pride that oozed from every syllable that Jonnelda spoke. She couldn't help but wonder about the *exact* nature of their relationship, though she supposed in large part it was because Jamela was such a lovable child, a sentiment to which she could attest personally. Bea dismissed the disquieted feeling that being around Jonnelda gave her and put the kettle on for coffee. "Sure, take some time to catch up with her. I'll call you both down after awhile. I think we should make a special dinner to celebrate."

Jonnelda looked around the room again. She could learn to do great things in the space. She loved the great cabinet space with the glass cutouts to show off the fine dishes and china, the granite countertops and the large island, perfect for a pastry prep center. The extra-wide double stainless-steel sinks would make for easier cleanups, too. She sighed, this was truly the American Dream. Beatrice McCoy seemed to have it all.

Her heart constricted in her chest before she excused herself—memories of Kharl, and the rest of the Wintons threatened to depress her. She needed to find Jamela fast—she was the one bright spot in her life.

Bea watched her walk away and sighed. Jonnelda was hiding something . . . running away from something, but she was devoted to Jamela. Bea supposed that would have to be enough for right now. She turned her attention toward the freezer. *Hmmm . . . what should we make for dinner?* She wanted to come up with a special menu, because tonight they would celebrate. It was the right thing to do for the girls.

She decided to think about the menu a little longer. In the meantime, Bea picked up a piece of paper from the pad she kept near the phone. A consummate list maker, she began to think of the things that she needed either to do or to check into. There was school for certain, shopping for Jonnelda, Christmas gifts for the office, especially Michael, and, unfortunately, a meeting with the director of the bureau. She simply couldn't put it off any longer. Her deputy was calling for her head on a silver platter—but his betrayal would not be rewarded, she thought.

As soon as she was comfortable with her routine with the girls she would need to return to her long hours in the office. Jonnelda was old enough to take care of them both—as long as she obeyed the rules, everything should flow smoothly. *Yeah, as long as she obeyed the rules.*

She forced away negative thoughts about them and used Michael as her inspiration to visualize happier times. Bea remembered their intimate time in the shower and the SUV—heat flushed her caramel-colored face. It didn't make sense for a woman of her age to

behave in such a wanton fashion—and she'd had the
nerve to warn Jonnelda about boys.

It seemed as though she was the one who needed a
chaperone. Bea groaned as the ache of sexual need
began at her core. She squeezed her legs together in a
feeble attempt to block out the feelings and fixed a cup
of coffee, the strength of which could rival any pur-
chased from Starbucks. Maybe thinking about Director
Michael Ezekiel Spates wasn't such a bright idea after
all. She watched the swirl of steam coming from her
mug and likened it to the swirl of emotion in the pit of
her stomach. Before she could force her attention away
from the man with the ruggedly handsome face who
dogged her thoughts, a bloodcurdling scream cracked
through the air.

Bea raced up the stairs to the source of the cries, her
heart pounding out a staccato rhythm all the way there.
Her eyes were wide with fear as she met Jonnelda going
into Jamela's room. The little girl's hand was covered in
blood as she was near hysterics.

Bea watched speechless as Jonnelda scooped her up in
her arms, taking her to the bathroom that they shared.
Jonnelda spoke soothing words as she assessed and
cleaned the wound. Beatrice watched her movements,
but stood rooted to the spot just outside the doorway.

After cleaning her wound, Jonnelda looked up when
she noticed her. "It's all right Miss Bea, it looks worse
than it is—Jamela always freaks out when it comes to
blood. She's fine—look for yourself. I don't even think
it will need stitches."

Bea blinked several times, while comprehension
dawned on her slowly. Jonnelda was too calm and too familiar. She looked closer at the resemblance between
the two, but pushed out of her head notions that they

were related. If Jonnelda were Jamela's sister that would explain why she was so protective of her and why she had been so worried about her. Why wouldn't she admit that? Why keep that kind of secret—even from Jamela?

Bea found her voice. "Thank you, Jonnelda. Jamela, are you all right, sweetheart?"

Jamela snuggled up to Jonnelda as she sniffed. Her tears were gone and she was obviously better, but she seemed to be very comfortable in Jonnie's arms. "I feel better now, Miss Bea." She looked down at her hand. "I was . . . I was . . . running with the scissors." She looked up between both women, and her words came out in a tumbled rush. "I know that I'm not supposed to do that, but I was in a hurry, I wanted to make another picture for Mr. Michael for when he comes over for dinner. I'm sorry."

Bea gave her a reassuring look. "Sweetheart, I'm just glad that you're okay. And thank you for telling the truth. You know you could have been seriously hurt! Now you should understand why you're never supposed to run with scissors—do me a favor and promise that you'll be more careful." Jamela nodded her small head in agreement. "Now come here so that I can look at your hand."

Jonnelda spoke up. "No, she's fine, I've got—" She looked at Bea's censuring expression and immediately let go of the child. "You're right. Go on, Jamela. I'll just go get ready for dinner."

Beatrice stopped her at the doorway. "Jonnelda, I know she's like your own flesh and blood, it's okay to be concerned, but let me do my job, okay. It's only our first day. We'll work the kinks out." Bea smiled at her and watched as Jonnelda rushed off to her room. But not before Bea noticed the glisten of moisture in her eyes. Bea shrugged her shoulders and attributed her behavior to teenaged hormones.

She returned her attention to Jamela to inspect the cut. It was indeed fine . . . just like Jonnelda had said. She resisted the urge to knock on the bedroom door and went downstairs to cook instead. She needed time to discuss her feelings with Michael. Maybe he could observe them and tell her if she was being too sensitive about the girls . . . and maybe even a little jealous that they were so close. As she hugged the little girl, she said aloud, "You're losing it, woman." Jamela looked at her as if she'd lost her mind, but continued the hug. Bea sighed. "All right, little lady, still think you can be my sous-chef with an injured hand?" Jamela nodded enthusiastically and down to the kitchen they went.

Jonnelda sat in her new room hugging herself close as she rocked on the bed. The tears ran quick and hot down her face. "Lord, how am I going to do this? How am I going to let my little girl go again? I can't bear to watch her move away from me and love someone else as her mother!" Jonnelda rocked, talked to herself, and prayed until she felt better. After several minutes she came up with a way to handle the situation. She went to the bathroom that she would share with Jamela and splashed cold water on her face.

When she was presentable she thought that she'd join Bea and her daughter downstairs to *celebrate* their being one big happy family.

The irony was almost too much.

Beatrice scrunched up her face as she read the directions on the couscous. Jonnelda couldn't help herself and smiled. She took the package from her hands and told her in a soothing tone, "Don't worry, I've got this one. Jamela, show Miss Bea how to make the dough for the apple fritters. We need them to be light and crispy."

During the next several minutes there seemed to be a

shift in the air. Beatrice calmed down long enough to be able to marvel at the way Jamela and Jonnelda worked together—she started to feel a sense of peace again.

Jonnelda said, "Miss Bea, if we are going to do this right, we need to find a proper market. I want to make steamed callaloo and jerk fish, but it needs to be farm-raised trout if you want it to taste good. We can make the grains and other things you've bought, but I'm kinda missing home. I want to share some of our favorite meals with you."

Beatrice grabbed one of her lists and her keys. "Okay then, let's hit the road."

Jamela was excited as she pumped the fist on her good hand. "Yes!"

Beatrice took them to one of her favorite markets. It was open-air during the summer months, but closed-in during cold weather like they had now. She browsed, observing as Jonnelda picked up and inspected several produce items. She thumped, smelled, or squeezed everything. One thing was clear, Bea noticed, she had discriminating taste, which was unusual for a teen.

Most teens didn't care what they put in their bodies, let alone how fresh the broccoli cuts seem to be. Bea decided that she was certainly a puzzle and she was very curious about her, but the atmosphere was too festive to ruin with more questions. She looked around for some fresh ingredients for her contribution to the meal. She decided on sweet potato pie with a pecan crust. With her new KitchenAid mixer, she could whip up some flaky dough in no time. They would have Michael begging for more, she thought.

She turned to Jamela. "Come on, we'll let her commune with the callaloo, while we go pick some yams."

Jonnelda looked up, temporarily removing her nose from the side of a melon. "I thought we were having sweet potato?" she questioned.

Bea smirked. "We are, it's the same thing, Miss Picky. I'll see you in a few minutes."

That girl. Bea walked away shaking her head in wonder.

The return trip was filled with lots of teasing, laughter, and smiles. After showing Jonnelda where everything was located in the kitchen drawers, she let the young woman have her way. Before long the delicious aroma of authentic Jamaican food flooded Bea's house, making it warm, inviting, and just the place that she wanted to be. She hoped Michael would enjoy their recipes.

Michael arrived later than he had intended, but still early for his normal workday schedule. He knocked on Beatrice's door several times. He could hear music blaring with a distinctive calypso beat and every few seconds, peals of laughter coming from the direction of the kitchen. He stood quietly listening for about a minute . . . enjoying the sound. It seemed as if the "girls" had gotten off to a good start. It was Beatrice who finally opened the door.

Michael noticed her flush skin, and how radiant and alive she seemed. She looked beautiful . . . complete. He marveled at her, his mouth open for seconds before he found his voice. "Sounds like all of you were having a terrific time in there. Do I dare come in?"

"You'd better! We want you to come join the fun. We're calling it a 'night in Jamaica'—and that's not in New York. What do you think? Can we take our show on the road?" Before he could answer, she pulled him by the collar into the house. He thought he detected the slight bouquet of Cruzan rum fruit punch on her breath . . . *hmmm* . . . *that would explain the good mood.*

Michael allowed himself to be drawn into the house.

His jaw dropped when Bea began to sway her hips to the rhythm of the music, which was now on a slow, sultry song. She tried to entice him into dancing with her, but when he shook his head, she moved particularly close and slid her body up and down his. Michael dropped his briefcase. The giggles behind Bea and in front of him made them both realize and remember that they were not alone. Bea waggled her eyebrows. "Until next time . . ."

Michael cleared his throat as he prepared to greet the girls. He wasn't sure if he could handle coming home to this kind of treatment very often. Especially considering that the uncomfortable tug in his pants proved that he still wanted her every bit as much as she wanted him.

Michael pushed those thoughts away and walked fully into the kitchen, which had apparently been turned into a Jamaican restaurant. The smells swirled around his nostrils and he inhaled deeply. He loved ethnic cuisine, and Jamaican dishes just happened to be some of his favorites.

All three stared at him in anticipation. "So this is what happens when you guys are left to your own devices." He looked around with a sweeping gaze—"I like it!"

Jamela ran to him to give him a big hug and he swung her small frame around as if she were light as a feather. Her giggles were heard above the sound of the music playing in the house. Bea and Jonnelda were caught up in the moment, too, and soon enough there was a chorus of laughter reverberating off the walls.

While Michael swung Jamela, Beatrice and Jonnelda continued to work on the dance moves Jonnelda had been showing her before Michael arrived. They were doing their own version of a Jamaican line dance and cracking up all the while.

Tensions had eased between them and both seemed

content to *just be*, he noticed. His heart was full, almost totally overwhelmed by a sense of peace and contentedness. Maybe Dr. Rose wasn't so off base after all . . . though he doubted she would have envisioned this particular scene.

Music playing, fingers popping, and hips swaying . . . on second thought, he could get very used to this kind of greeting . . .

Chapter Eleven

Michael stared at the Korean War picture on his wall. It was a print entitled *Easter Sunday, March 29, 1951.* It served as just one of the reminders of why he came to work everyday, but this day he could do without. He wanted to pace the room, but remained rooted to his chair as he spoke on the phone. His eyes moved from the print to the photo of Peter Anderson and a much younger Michael on his wall. The photo was taken right after he was sworn in as an agent. Michael exhaled . . . sometimes that seemed like a hundred years ago.

Michael closed his eyes in disbelief. "Banks, are you absolutely sure and does anyone else know about this?"

Agent Banks was patient with his senior agent; he knew the news was hard to take. "Yes, boss, I checked a few times before calling you back . . . I'm sorry. The answer to the second question is no, I had to dig deep in order to find out what I did. I doubt the ICE has the desire to delve this far down into a returnee's past. I doubt further that even the DEA knows as much as we do. I had to play connect the dots with a lot of fragmented information."

"Read the information to me again and then forget you ever found it out," Michael commanded.

"Yes, sir." Agent Banks blew out a puff of air then began: "Jonnelda Lindo is actually Jonnelda Lindo Winton. She is Kharl's sister-in-law. She is not a teenager, but in fact an adult—we think twenty-five, based on school records—and mother of one child. Her child's name is Jamela Beckford Winton. Her grandparents have raised Jamela since she was a toddler. She was placed in their care while the Winton posse rose to power. Kharl's brother, Moses, was killed during a turf skirmish in Kingston about four years ago. I found most of this in the DEA database—but don't ask me how, we'll both be better off."

Michael listened, taking notes as he did. "Go on. How long has she been with Kharl and can you tell her level of involvement with the posse?"

Michael heard as Agent Banks shuffled some papers around until he found what he was looking for. "Well, it looks like shortly after Moses Winton was killed Kharl rose to power. He set up a few operations on the West and East Coasts, and then decided to make West Virginia his home base. From some of the surveillance chatter that I've been able to get my hands on, it looks like Jonnelda Winton was just one of his many personal-use women. Just because she carries the Winton name, it didn't get her too far; she became a part of his harem, like some of the others that he brought over. I guess without the protection of her husband, she was at his mercy. Anyway, Jamela arrived with the grandparents three years ago. There are surviving relatives that both could go and stay with, but given the situation, I wouldn't advise it—the Wintons are a powerful family now; unless Jonnelda and eventually Jamela are going to take their place in the power structure, they will become fish food."

Michael grunted, but kept writing. "Okay, what do you have on the rest of the family?"

Agent Banks chuckled. "They are an interesting bunch. . . . Women don't typically have much power, but apparently Vanessa Winton has bigger balls than both her brothers. She runs quite a successful operation, which expands across that island and several others. Ms. Winton is well protected, elusive, ruthless, and a remarkable businesswoman."

"Should I arrange a date between you two?"

Agent Banks cleared his throat. "I'm sorry, sir, powerful women have always fascinated me."

Agent Spates grunted again. "Is that all you have?"

"For now, but I'll keep digging around. I'll call again as soon as I have more information for you."

Michael shook his head at the thought of what his young agent could do and all the information that he could access with his computer. "Thank you. And please stay out of trouble." *Damn, now how do I tell Beatrice? She is going to be livid with Jonnelda!*

As soon as he replaced the receiver, Karen buzzed him. "Sir, two agents from the IRB are here to see you."

Michael closed his eyes again. *Of course they are . . . this is the perfect ending to a perfect day!* He checked the time. . . . It was late, and he should call Bea, but he decided to wait until he was finished. He carefully slid his notes into an unmarked folder. "Thank you, Karen. Show them in and then you can go home, there's nothing more we can do today."

Karen responded, "Yes, boss. Tomorrow is another day and another fight. I'll see you in the morning."

"Vanessa, are you sure you want to take on this battle?" Delroy asked. It was his job to keep his boss out of trouble, but she seemed determined to bring on the fight.

Vanessa Winton sat at the head of the table surrounded by the five men she trusted with her life. The slightly sweet aroma of fried plantains and cocoa bread hung in the air, the smell wafting from the kitchen nearby. It was a warm Jamaican evening, perfect for entertaining, but this wasn't a social meeting. This was strictly business—the business of revenge.

Her cold brown eyes indicated just how sure she was of her decision to engage this enemy. "There aren't too many things that I do that I'm not sure of," Vanessa responded irritably. "This is about family honor. No one gets to do what the FBI did to my brother. . .

"And that worthless sister-in-law of mine! I've heard that she took Jamela and she's now living with one of them. I sent her and her whiny family to the U.S. out of the goodness of my heart. Her parents wanted a chance to make something of themselves and those girls and I did what I could out of respect for the memory of my brother Moses." Her voice rose, her tone incredulous. "And this is how they repay me?"

Vanessa twisted a napkin in her hands. "Jonnelda was sent there to help Kharl, not stab him in the back." Anger swirled around the dark depths of her eyes, giving them a dangerous appearance. Her voice was a low whisper when she spoke again . . . her meaning perfectly clear to all. "But she'll pay for her betrayal . . . I'll see to it personally." The napkin fell apart, a mess of fragmented and broken fibers. Vanessa looked down at what she had inadvertently done and a smile curved her lips. She imagined the bodies of the agents responsible for the death of her brother.

"Agents Williams"—he pointed to his partner—"and Jackson, sir. We've been asked to look into the case of Kharl Winton. We need to see your briefing material and all other information that pertains to the case—no matter how minute. We'd also like to set up appointments with the rest of the agents who participated in the . . . operation . . ." He hesitated, but then spoke forcefully. "As always, we expect full cooperation."

Michael motioned for them to sit down as he took a stack of files out of his desk. He'd been expecting them, after all. "Gentlemen, let me just tell you that you'll find that we are all above reproach on this one. We made judgment calls based on the information we had at hand. Feel free to go through everything, we don't have anything to hide." He looked down at his empty coffee mug. "Before my secretary leaves, is there anything that I can get for you?"

Agent Williams spoke again. "We'll be fine, if you could just direct us to your conference room we can begin." He picked up a handful of files and then handed the rest to Agent Jackson. "We'll call you when we're ready for you," he said with a note of finality.

Michael's outward appearance gave no indication of the internal battle he fought to keep from tearing this cocky guy a new one. He realized that these guys had a job to do, but he'd earned the respect that they needed to show to him. He looked them over—they were still wet behind the ears, he thought. *Boys in men's clothing.* Unfortunately, these green agents controlled his fate at the moment.

Michael checked his tongue and motioned for them to follow him into the adjoining conference room. "I trust you'll find this satisfactory, gentlemen. I'll be in my office." He shut the door with a little more force than necessary and started for the outer office door. Yeah, he would give them his full cooperation, but he would be damned if he would wait to be called on the carpet at their will. He wasn't going to act like the naughty little child sent to the principal's office. He was the damned principal. Michael went to the break room and made a strong cup of coffee. He needed the caffeine. Just two weeks ago, everything was fine in his life. Beatrice, Jonnelda, and Jamela were doing well and getting along with each other. He was able to spend more time with them with the bonus being that he and Beatrice were becoming more comfortable with each other, and now this—Jonnelda's betrayal and the Internal Review Board investigation. He said, "What next, or should I even ask?"

The jingle of the bells welcomed them into the mall. Jonnelda and Jamela were like two kids at Christmas—which was exactly the case. They ran excitedly through the doors of the entryway and stood in awe of the many decorations. The amount of fake snow inside rivaled the snow on the ground, and several Santas with elves greeted customers, Christmas carols played throughout the mall, there were lots of people milling through the halls and in and out of stores. The scent of holly berries, cinnamon, and vanilla hung in the air.

For the first time in years, Bea was giddy. She held Jamela's hand as they negotiated the crush of people, with a smile that warmed her face.

"Jonnelda, if we get separated, just call me with your new cell phone. We'll meet over here by the fountain."

Jonnelda nodded her head and disappeared through the crowd. With a gleam in her eyes and two hundred and fifty dollars in her pocket, she headed off to find Christmas bargains. It was their first time together in Pentagon City Mall, and all were delighted. Bea watched her disappear and shook her head. "Guess it's just you and me, kid."

Jamela tugged her arm impatiently. "Come on Miss Bea, I want to buy presents for Mr. Michael and Jonnelda."

Jamela dragged Bea into the Limited so she could find the perfect outfit for Jonnie. "Oh Miss Bea, can we

get it, look, it's perfect. Look at the design on the shirt."
Jamela was talking fast and repeating herself often in
her excitement. "And look at these pants—everybody
wears these now."

Bea raised an eyebrow. "I don't know, Jamela, aren't
these pieces a little . . . revealing?"

Jamela blew out an exaggerated puff of air. "Miss
Bea, that's the whole point. This will show off her
dragon tattoo!"

"Her what?!"

Jamela backed away from the rack. "Oops, well,
maybe you're right. Let's go look over there."

Beatrice pursed her lips. *Note to self, find out about that
darned tattoo.* "Yeah, let's go do that. The tops are *longer*
on that rack."

Vanessa eavesdropped from the next rack. She was
just another harried shopper looking for last-minute
gifts, or so it appeared. She followed Bea and Jamela,
making sure not to get too close. She doubted that
Jamela would recognize her Aunt Vanessa, but that
didn't matter. She was there for research . . . she was
still a few days from making her move.

Jonnelda looked around several times. She couldn't
shake the feeling that she was being watched. She spotted a pair of jeans with a pink cuff and matching denim
and pink shirt and all thoughts of being followed disappeared. Jamela would be too cute in the outfit with her
long legs and slight build. The girl seemed to grow
every day, she marveled. She turned around abruptly
and thought she recognized the man with the baseball
cap and Hilfiger shirt. Hadn't she seen him at the Gap?
she wondered. *No, it couldn't be.*

Jonnelda chastised herself for being so silly. She
could have sworn she recognized him as someone from
Jamaica, but then again, why not? People came over
all the time . . . she was being silly. Her thoughts turned

to more positive possibilities as she spied a pair of earrings that would look great on Bea with her short hairstyle. She fingered the glittery bobs; she looked at her time with Bea, Michael, and Jamela as the best in her life. Both agents had started to become so special to her in just the three weeks she'd known them. And she did owe Michael her life. Kharl would have gone through with his threat to kill her—he'd never cared about anyone but himself. She felt tears spring to her eyes. Jonnelda had always suspected Kharl of murdering Moses . . . he'd always been jealous of his younger brother. She supposed that's why she had been forced into his bed when Vanessa sent her to the U.S. "All water under the dam." She picked up the earrings and walked purposefully over to the counter. "I'd like these in a gift box, please."

Delroy watched with interest. He'd followed her through at least five stores in the crowded mall, making sure that he kept from making eye contact with her. He had to admit, he'd never seen Jonnelda look so good, so content . . .

He shook his head in disappointment. His long thick braids swayed with the motion. Too bad she had crossed the line with Vanessa . . . he had a job to do and nothing would stop him from completing it. Vanessa Winton hated failure almost as much as she hated betrayal. If Jonnelda Winton had to die, the way he looked at it, then so be it. He continued to trail her until she met up with the woman named Beatrice. Delroy was ready to call it a night; he had what he needed. . . .

Three hours later, laden down with packages, Beatrice, Jonnelda, and Jamela headed home too exhausted to even think about cooking. Bea called Michael, but only reached his cell phone voice mail, so she left a message: "Michael, we are going to grab some take-out for dinner. If you get this message, call me back to tell me what you're in the mood to eat. I love you. Talk to you soon."

She looked down at all the bags that filled her arms; this was turning into a marvelous Christmas, she thought.

Michael pulled up to Bea's driveway loaded down with packages. He had received her message but missed her, too. He hoped everyone was hungry, and in a festive mood because he'd brought it all.

He didn't know what had gotten into him—maybe hearing her message with her words of love touched his heart. As bad as things were, just knowing that she loved him seemed like it was enough. What had started out as a drive to certain disaster now seemed brighter; he and Bea would face the future together.

As usual, Jamela greeted him at the door. Her large doe eyes grew wider. "Oh, Mr. Michael, is that for us?"

Michael leaned down to kiss the top of her head. "Yes, it is and there's more. Put your shoes on and help me unload."

Jamela squealed with delight—he didn't know the girl could move so fast. She assisted Michael with the six-foot, live Christmas tree and after a couple of tries, they actually managed to get the monstrosity in the doorway.

Beatrice came running after hearing all the commotion. "Oh my God, Michael. It's a tree! Where in the world did you get it?" Too late, she realized how silly she sounded. She stood dumbfounded. She hadn't had a Christmas tree in her house in almost ten years. It was gorgeous and smelled wonderful. Bea had always loved the scent of pinecones and cinnamon.

Michael righted the tree and walked to her. "I hope you don't mind. You inspired me this afternoon. I've been out shopping for the past three hours." He grinned in embarrassment. They both knew his behavior was extremely out of character. Beatrice wrapped her arms around him and planted slow kisses on his lips and along the strong angular lines of his jaw.

Jamela tapped her foot impatiently. "Mr. Michael, there's more stuff in the truck."

Jonnelda had finished setting the table and came to rescue them. She took Jamela's hand. "Come on, squirt. I'll go out there with you. Let's leave these two lovebirds alone for five seconds."

Beatrice laughed. "Okay, okay, we're coming."

It took another five minutes to bring everything into the house and it looked like Michael had spent a month's salary. Aside from the tree, decorations, Christmas music, and gifts, he'd also bought traditional Christmas dinner fare—including a turkey and a ham.

After Michael blessed the food, they began to eat. Dinner was a combination of take-out from three different restaurants—Indian, Moroccan, and burgers.

Michael and Bea couldn't keep their eyes off each other . . . or their hands. A gentle brush of fingers, a hold when passing food, or a touch to make a point during conversation . . . it was indicative of their need to be together. They were suffering from a serious case of missing each other.

Jonnelda eyed them with the wisdom of understanding. It had been like that during her early days with Moses. Before she understood what his last name meant in the context of the posse system. She came up with an idea. "Agent Spates, how about I decorate the tree with Jamela and read Christmas stories with her while you take Miss Bea out for awhile. I'm sure you two have a lot of *work* stuff to catch up on. Besides, it will be fun for us to just hang out for awhile."

Bea smiled. "You trying to get rid of us?"

"Not at all, sometimes it's just nice to spend time with

the one you love, that's all. There was a time when I had that," she said, almost whimsically.

Michael was reminded of his earlier conversation with Banks. He needed to discuss the situation with Bea, but he refused to do it now—Bea had too much on her mind as it stood. He made a note to talk with Jonnelda soon—he needed to know her plans. Thus far she had been the perfect "big sister" to Jamela, but he needed to make sure she wasn't playing them for her own endgame. "Thank you, young lady, that's very considerate of you. You don't have to call me Agent Spates, though, Michael is fine." He turned to Beatrice. "How about we get the tree situated and then go out?"

Beatrice nodded. "Just let us clear away this mountain of leftovers and we can get started. Why don't you get started organizing the bulbs, and we'll handle this?"

Michael smiled. "No, we'll all do it, this way the task will be finished faster; besides, how often does a man get to work in the kitchen with three beautiful girls?" He stood and immediately started clearing dishes away or wrapping them in plastic. A short time later, with Nat "King" Cole singing the Christmas Song on the CD player, they began to string bulbs along the tree.

"Jamela, hand that gold bulb to me and I think we'll be done," Bea said, with a look of consternation on her face.

"What's wrong?" Michael had noticed the furrowing of her brow.

"Hmmm . . . I'm not sure, but it seems like something is missing. . . ."

Jonnelda stood back. "It needs the star on top—where is it?"

Michael began looking through the bags that had contained the decorations. He'd picked one up, but it was nowhere to be found. While they looked, Beatrice had an idea.

"Let me check the attic, I think mine is up there. I'll just go upstairs; give me a second."

Bea rummaged around the small space. She'd packed away her ornaments many a Christmas ago. After pushing several boxes to the side, she found her special box. She lifted the lid and her hand froze midair . . . there was the star right next to an ornament that Josh had made in second grade. Her fingers trembled and she felt powerless to move; she stood there, tears streaming down her face. Oh God, how she missed her children. Joshua, Janice, and Harold had been her entire life and now they were gone.

Michael looked at his watch. Bea had been gone for over ten minutes. He climbed the stairs to the attic to find her. He heard the tears of her anguish and moved faster. "Sweetheart, what is it?" He reached out to her and placed her in a protective embrace. Her tears came faster and stronger, until her entire body shook with the force of her emotion. Michael looked around, searching for whatever could have caused this change in emotion. She was happy and smiling just fifteen minutes ago. His eyes rested on the childlike creations in the box. He understood immediately. "Shush, sweetheart, it's all right. I'll get the star, you just sit here." Michael wiped a spot clean for her to sit on, retrieved what he needed and quickly closed the box. Through it all Beatrice still had not spoken. He put the star on the floor next to them and held her in his arms again. Blood pumped through his heart at an alarmingly fast rate. He was concerned now . . . maybe it hadn't been such a good idea to buy the tree. If Beatrice wasn't ready to deal with moving on, then he didn't have the right to push, even though that was not his intention. *Dammit, Michael, you really blew it this time!* He thought, angry with himself.

Her tone was barely above a whisper. "Joshua always

hated that picture because his two front teeth were late coming in. All the other second graders had their two front teeth except him. Josh said, 'did the tooth fairy forget to bring my new tooth?' And I told him no, she was just making a very special tooth just for him so he had to be patient." Beatrice closed her eyes. "I've always loved that picture, he looked so handsome . . . he was just starting to lose some of his baby fat and his face was starting to look grown-up. He had also grown three inches that year—I couldn't keep that boy in shoes or pants. I kept telling Harold his six-four genes were going to bankrupt us." A long sigh. "Oh Michael, I'm so tired. I'm so tired of the pain, when will it ever go away?"

Michael hated the feeling of helplessness that engulfed him. He would do anything for her, but he *couldn't* do this. He stroked the side of her face. "I love you Bea, and I'll always be here for you." It felt and sounded inadequate, but it was all that he could promise her. As long as he took a breath, he would protect her.

After a few moments longer, Bea felt stronger. The beating of Michael's heart calmed her as he held her close. His words were comforting, and somehow she knew if she just stayed with him, everything would be fine. She listened to the sound of his breathing, the timbre of his voice and inhaled the masculine scent of him. . . .

This Christmas would be different. It wasn't the same as what she'd had before, but that didn't devalue what she shared with Michael or the girls. Beatrice wiped the tears away with the backs of her hands. "Thank you. I'm okay now. I think we should probably go back downstairs. The girls are probably starting to wonder what happened to us." She picked up the star and handed it to Michael. "Will you put this on top of the tree?"

Michael captured her lips in a long, slow kiss. "It would be my pleasure," he answered.

* * *

Being with the girls over the past few weeks had been nice, but they really missed time alone. Jonnelda reassured them that she would take good care of Jamela and after an exhaustive list of dos and don'ts and phone numbers, Michael and Bea set off. They rode in his truck like a couple of nervous teens on a first date.

Once they were seated, Beatrice reached into her pocket. "Michael, I meant to give this to you before, but I kept forgetting to do it with all the things that have been going on lately." She handed him a key. "I want you to be able to come and go as necessary. . . . I certainly don't want you to have to knock every time you come over."

Michael smiled. "Thank you, I didn't want to ask myself, I wanted the decision to be yours. I have your key right here. I want you to always feel welcome—my home is your home, and I mean that. And just so you know, I've never done this before."

The rest of the ride was made in silence. Both had so much to think about . . . and the possibilities of what might happen once they arrived at his home weighed heavily on them. They hadn't talked about intimacy, but it didn't stop them from craving each other's body.

They arrived at Michael's modest home in Tysons Corner in record time. It was the perfect size for a small family, or in his case, a family of *one*. It was the first time she had ever been to his house and butterflies fluttered in her stomach. *How could he still have such an effect on her?*

They'd worked together for so many years and she had been able to contain her feelings; now, she was running hot and cold. One part of her wanted him more than breathing, the other part wanted to run back home where it was safe, where she didn't have to acknowledge her feelings. Bea had so many questions, yet should she ask?

Michael showed her into his living room. She sat down on his overstuffed sage-colored couch and sank back into the cushions. Bea noticed that his home reflected the way she saw him: it was warm, smartly decorated, and filled with soothing colors. Nothing about it indicated the austere environment that he worked in—there were no sharp angles, no modern gadgets or shiny chrome. Michael knew how to separate work and home—she was impressed by that knowledge.

After a protracted silence, she said, "Michael, you don't owe me explanations about your previous relationships. Besides, I don't have a right to pry. We're both adults with past lives . . . I'm okay with that—I'm a big girl."

Michael shrugged. "I wish you would ask. I want you to care." His tone was flat.

Beatrice hadn't meant to offend him. "Michael, don't be silly. Of course I care, but I'm not willing to let it interfere with what we have now." She slipped off her shoes and swung her legs on to the seat. "Our time right now means more to me than anything. I love you and nothing will change that. But I have to admit that sometimes I compare you to Harold, and the truth is, I feel guilty when I do. . . .

"Michael, we had two beautiful children and were married for nearly twenty years, but I never felt the same desire, the same wanting for him as I do with you. Honestly, it scares me."

That was an admission he wasn't prepared for—he'd always felt the sense that he would have to compete with her deceased husband. He'd never been married before and had to admit he didn't quite understand the dynamics. Would she ever really get over him? Would there always be a part of her heart that he couldn't capture because it belonged to Harold? Michael stood up abruptly, leaving Bea alone on the sofa for a few minutes. He needed to do something with his hands as he mulled over her words. He went to the kitchen and leaned against the sink. *I can control a whole unit of agents, but I lose my head around this woman!*

Michael mixed a drink for both of them and then sat down next to Bea. His expression was serious, his brow furrowed. "I don't want there to be secrets between us when it comes to matters of the heart . . . for so long I've been satisfied with work as my mistress. My physical relationships have been few, but I want you to know, I've made love to you a million times in my dreams."

The air Bea was about to breathe in caught in her throat. "Michael," she whispered.

He reached out and stroked her face, the tenderness of his touch brought tears to her eyes. She loved him just that much. Bea took a sip of her drink to calm her nerves. Every nerve ending seemed sensitized to his presence.

Beatrice leaned into his touch, then kissed the inside of his palm. He took her hands in his and kissed them. His lips were so warm and soft, a slight shiver traveled up her spine. Bea tried to slow down her breathing. They were supposed to take it slow as per her own rules. Where she once thought she had a full life with her job, she now realized that without Michael's love her life didn't have the same meaning. Her gaze traced his features. She loved his hands, his smile, his eyes . . . his everything. In the short amount of time that they'd been intimate, Michael had become her reason for being.

Michael took a slow sip of his drink. He turned on the fireplace with his remote and then turned on the stereo system that he had encased in a large oak armoire. The sounds of Marvin Gaye's "Distant Lover" filled the room. Beatrice grinned. She knew he was smooth, but this was a pleasant surprise.

Michael caressed her arm, then reached for her, unable to keep his hands to himself any longer. She moved fluidly into his arms. His lips found hers and their kiss was passionate and loving. He heard the moan from deep in her throat. She tasted like sunshine, with the remnants of the fruity drink still on her tongue. He deepened the kiss, as she moved closer. He held her so tight that he could feel the outline of her bra. A particular piece of clothing that he couldn't wait to relieve her of . . .

Beatrice felt herself melting into that pool of molten lava that kissing Michael seemed to create. She was hot, wet, and wanted nothing but the feel of this powerful man inside of her. They should slow down, she told herself. *The hell we should!* Beatrice tugged at the shirt, tucked so neatly inside his trousers. Michael had always been such a smooth dresser, but at this very moment, she didn't give a darn about clothes, except that she wanted them off right now! She pulled at his shirt at the same time she fought to unbutton it.

Michael started to chuckle. He broke the kiss long enough to say, "It's okay, we have a few hours. Let me do it before you ruin this shirt that you bought for me." He unbuttoned it slowly, painfully slowly, until Beatrice could stand it no longer. She tore at his shirt, popping off the last three buttons in the process. "Come here," she demanded.

Michael chuckled again before she reached for him and tangled him in a passionate embrace. Her tongue slid easily into his mouth, where she tasted and teased as much as he just had. Breathing became a commodity.

Damn, why did she have on so many clothes? Beatrice wondered. She tried unsuccessfully to kiss him and pull off her silk blouse and cashmere sweater. It was just as hard to pull off her pants without pulling off his lips.

Michael stopped her groping to sit her down on the couch. He was just as hot for her, but he wanted their time to be special. They hadn't made love or even talked about it again since leaving West Virginia. Now, here, they were on his living room sofa back to acting like teenagers. He didn't want to stop, but they *needed* to. He knew the time they'd spent together with the girls was wonderful, but he hadn't told her about Jonnelda yet and there was still so much unsaid between them. "Beatrice, you take me over the edge, woman, but we need to talk."

Beatrice stood before him naked. She cupped her full breasts and teased the nipple to a tight bud. "I don't want to talk any more, Michael. I want to kiss, I want you to suckle me before I dip my head low and suckle your—"

Like I said, too much talk. Michael grabbed her in a rough embrace, he told her, "you don't play fair." Then he licked the taut bud until her skin dimpled with goose bumps. She moaned again and Michael thought he would burst. He took her nipple deep into his mouth and loved it tenderly. Beatrice felt her whole world sway.

He moved to the other nipple and bit gently until it protruded like a ripe chocolate berry. He caressed her full rounded bottom with his large hands and knew she was ready. The rich aroma of her femininity filled the space and Michael breathed deeply. He loved her . . . he loved everything about her.

Beatrice held on by a thread. She'd waited so long to be in his arms, desire threatened to make her release before she intended to, but she didn't want a quickie, she wanted to experience several hours of his expert touch. It felt like years instead of mere weeks since they were last together and she needed him . . . no, she just loved him so much she wanted to be one with him. She willed herself to calm down and enjoy the moment.

Michael moved from her breasts to her mouth again and then dipped his hand into her warm space. His fingers felt immediately wet and he was satisfied. She wanted him as much as he wanted her. . . .

He slipped his fingers in and out, simulating what he wanted a certain part of his anatomy to do, her moans mixed with his as he increased the tempo and the temperature soared about eighty degrees. Beatrice moved with him, driving him deeper into her; he felt for her bud and once he found it, he played with it, applying just the amount of pressure to bring her pleasure. He felt her body go rigid, then begin to quiver as he brought her to orgasm. She screamed his name in his mouth as he covered her lips with his own seconds before she released. He had intended to take her to his bed, but he couldn't wait. He laid her down on his couch and covered her body with his. He reached for protection and then slid into her waiting body. He gripped her buttocks, keeping her slightly lifted off the leather and began to stroke her. Her body felt like pure heaven.

Beatrice welcomed him. She wasn't completely recovered from her orgasm, so her body still bucked and trembled underneath him. She called out his name repeatedly, and sweat began to bead around her hairline. Bea lifted herself higher and higher to meet him. The room filled with the sound of their bodies crashing into each other in a perfectly rhythmic tune . . . almost like the beat of drums being played.

Michael kissed her neck and the smooth skin between her breasts. Her chest heaved as he pulsated her body.

Michael drove harder, longer, faster until he, too was calling her name. Beatrice reached for his nipples and as he drove hard, she pulled the buds between her nails until they were as rock hard as other parts of him. Their joining was primal, intimate, loving, and powerful.

The feel of her nails against his naked flesh pushed him to climax. In one long drive, he was deep inside her, releasing all he had. Beatrice received him and the tiny explosions of her climax matched his own until they were both plunged into a world of bright light. Nothing else registered except the sound of their breathing and thump of their hearts.

Moisture glistened on both of their bodies. Michael rolled to the side to lie beside her. "Bea, no one has ever made me feel the way you do. I love you more than I ever thought possible." He grinned. "I may have to put you under citizen's arrest."

Bea giggled, "Only if you promise to frisk me daily." She stopped talking to allow her breathing to become normal again, then said, "I think I owe you another shirt."

Chapter Twelve

Michael awoke after sensing something was wrong. His bed felt cold as he looked at the clock—it was 3:00 A.M. He watched Beatrice dress in silence, but conflicting emotions tore at his insides. One side he was angry, on the other, he was disappointed. *What happened?*

In a husky, sleep-deprived voice he asked, "Why are you leaving?"

Beatrice shrugged on her sweater as she answered. "Michael, I don't feel comfortable leaving them by themselves. I know that Jonnelda is capable of taking care of them, but I really think that I should be there. Besides, this is probably not the best example to set for them. They need to know that our lives are above reproach." She paused. "Besides, what they witnessed at Kharl's was immorality at its best."

What she didn't tell him was that she wasn't ready to spend the night at his place yet.

Michael hid his disappointment, he just wanted to wake up with the woman he loved in his arms. "Then why didn't you wake me? Remember I drove, so you don't have your car."

"I know, I called a cab." She gave him a slight smile. "You looked so handsome sleeping there, that I couldn't do it. I've been awake for about two hours battling with myself over what to do." She sighed. "Too much is up in the air right now—I need some closure on certain issues. I've taken enough time off, so I've decided to go into the office on Monday. There are some things that I've been avoiding that I can't put off any longer."

Michael nodded. "I understand that, but don't bother with the cab, just give me five minutes to get dressed." He rubbed his tired eyes. "As far as the office, Beatrice, that's right after Christmas. Are you sure that whatever you have planned can't wait until after the first of the year?"

Beatrice sat down on the edge of the bed to put her shoes on. "Michael, I don't expect you to understand everything that I do. Suffice it to say that there are people and things that need my attention." Her tone matched his. "Have you noticed that when you go off half-cocked, I don't question you? Do me a favor and even if you don't think that I'm right, respect that I have the sense God gave a chicken. Michael, with or without you in my life, I have a sound mind."

Bea watched as Michael sat upright in the bed. She knew that he was completely naked on the crumpled sheets that they made love on. She stood up again, in a move to put more distance between them before she gave in to her desire to stay with him. She needed to hold on to her anger—otherwise she might never leave. Beatrice felt that she couldn't tell him her exact plans—as much as she hated secrets she had to keep this one.

When Beatrice looked at him again, he was fully dressed and walking toward the bedroom door. Her tone softened by the time she spoke again. "Michael, I'll be fine in a cab, go on back to bed. I'll call you later on today—I'm sure the girls will want to spend time with you and we still have that mountain of food to finish." She tried to smile, but the end result was weak and she knew it.

Michael continued toward the front door. He said simply, "Pull your coat close, it's cold out there." He clicked the button to start his vehicle and disappeared out into the early-morning darkness. A cold, biting wind whipped inside the foyer as soon as he opened the door.

Bea stood still for several seconds as tears sprang to her eyes. She didn't know which was worse—the cold from Michael or the bitter weather. The ride back to her house started off in awkward silence. After a few minutes, Michael turned the radio on to WHUR and they lost themselves in the music and their own private thoughts.

From a million miles away it seemed, she heard him say, "Beatrice, I love you."

Rousted from her thoughts, she turned to look at his profile. She said quietly, "I know you do, and I love you, but it doesn't mean that we don't have problems to work through."

Michael continued. "When things settle down, will you marry me? I know this is a terrible way to propose, but my heart is breaking. I don't want you to have to leave my bed again."

Beatrice clutched at her heart, the beat was so fast. "Michael . . . Michael, I don't know what to say. I mean . . . I can't . . . what about Jamela and Jonnelda, and work and—"

"And the budget deficit and global warming. Come on, Beatrice, this is our one shot! What we have has nothing to do with anything or anyone else—this is about what we want and us. If you say you love me, why not prove it? Marry me and let's get through all that life has to throw at us together."

"Dammit, Michael. What makes you think things are that simple? What world do you live in? I can't just throw caution to the wind because of love—as important as you are to my life, there's much more that I'm responsible for. . . ." She watched as Michael bristled and instantly felt guilty, but it was the truth.

The peacefulness of the drive on the near-empty roads was interrupted by the tension that had crept into the enclosed space of his vehicle.

Michael inhaled deeply, then exhaled long and slow. "Beatrice, I have been patient with you for years. I've loved you on the sidelines through the thick and the thin, the good and the bad." He paused, then said, "I'm not going to do it anymore. At our age we have more years behind us than in front of us. . . ." He shook his head in conviction. "We need to decide how we want to spend the time that we have left on this world.

"I don't want to lose more precious time with you, so I need you to examine your heart and then decide how you want us to proceed. This emotional roller coaster that we've been on is more than I can take."

The finality of his tone was disturbing. Beatrice listened quietly and the fight was gone from her spirit. *Emotional roller coaster,* the words seemed to echo in her broken heart.

They arrived at her home, but before she stepped out she said, "If that's the way you feel, then I guess it's time to stop the *ride,* huh?

"Michael, I'm not playing games with you, I'm just trying to keep my sanity while we sort everything out, but if it's too much for you then you're not quite the man I gave you credit for being." Beatrice stared into his eyes for several seconds, then slammed the door before she hurried into the house.

Michael opened the driver's-side door to go after her, but closed it after seeing that she was safely inside. "Dammit, dammit, dammit!" he swore before leaving. As he drove, Michael questioned himself. "Why do you insist on pushing so hard? Why can't you just enjoy the moment?" It seemed that they had moved from passionate to pathetic in the blink of eye.

"Aw, shucks," Vanessa Winton said with a sneer. "Looks like the lovebirds had an argument. Well, that's too bad, because it doesn't matter if they are together or separate—they're both dead." She added dryly, "We're just waiting for the funeral."

Delroy started the engine. "Can we go home now, boss? My eyes are burning so bad that I don't think that I can see straight anymore. I want to get you back to the hotel safely."

Vanessa nodded her head and said, "Yes."

Although they had been conducting surveillance for the past forty-eight hours almost nonstop, she was exhilarated, not tired. "Now that we know where he lives, too all the pieces are put together. Besides, I know you're tired. Let's go back to get some rest—we're going to have a few days of long hours ahead of us." Vanessa paused in thought. "I think we'll have our best opportunity to strike pretty soon since the house will probably be full with all their friends and family on Christmas day. They won't see us coming and won't be prepared.

"Also, remind me to call the ICE, I need to speak to one of the officers there to make sure that we have all the right equipment. Thank goodness for government corruption." Vanessa chuckled. "Yes, what I have in mind will be just perfect."

Vanessa's smile caused Delroy an inward shudder. He turned on the lights and pulled onto the road.

Jonnelda woke up suddenly. Sweat formed a thin line around the edges of her hair and pooled beneath her breasts. She awoke with a sinking feeling of dread. She'd learned at an early age to pay attention to warning signs—a sixth sense that warned her trouble was coming.

She thought back to the mall, maybe she should mention her observations to Beatrice. She lay still trying to quell the feelings that surged through her. She couldn't take the chance that Jamela would be harmed. She wouldn't worry Bea; she would call Michael instead. Jonnelda listened as cars moved on the residential street. She heard Bea come up the stairs and to her room. But then after a minute or so, she heard Bea's footsteps pad toward Jamela's room and then hers before she went back to her room again and closed the door.

Jonnelda pretended to be asleep when Bea peeked in because she wasn't ready to talk yet. She glanced at the time. It was pretty late for the amount of activity she listened to, but she supposed with the holidays, there was more going on with everyone.

In the stillness of the night with only the blinking of Christmas lights outside to disturb the darkness, Jonnelda marveled that this would be her first Christmas in relative freedom since Moses had died. She concentrated on good memories of her husband and Jamela as a baby. It had been four years since the police took away his bloodied body. He was gone, but she had a second chance with Jamela. Tears of joy mixed with tears of sadness until eventually she drifted back to sleep.

Beatrice sat in the middle of her bed, box of tissues next to her and gulped air between her sobs. "Damn him!" she lamented. She was tired of feeling so down about Michael. He had the ability to take her to such soaring highs and then sink her down to such devastating lows. She would let things be—maybe she was out-thinking herself?

Bea swore softly as a fresh wave of tears trekked down her face. The confusion and attempts to control herself had worn her out. Bea exhaled slowly; there was only one way to settle this—she picked up the phone to dial Michael's number.

He answered on the first ring and sounded out of breath. "Bea, I'm sorry—"

"No. Michael, I'm the one who is sorry. We need to be able to talk openly and I'm afraid I didn't give you the opportunity to do that—can we start fresh in the morning? How about a nice breakfast over here in about six hours?"

"How about the three of you come over here and I'll do the cooking. I've been spoiled for the last few meals. Maybe we can get past the earlier unpleasantness and have a good weekend after all. I realize that my kitchen is smaller than yours is, but I think we can manage. It's the least I can do to make up to you. What do you say?"

"Funny, I was just there, but don't even remember the color of the room. Okay, you've got a deal on one condition."

"Yes?"

She chuckled. "You have to agree to come over later in the evening for dinner. We still have all these left-overs to eat."

Michael smiled. "And have the chance to spend most of the day with you—you've got a deal. Do you mind if I bring over a movie?"

Bea was quiet a second too long.

"Bea, are you still there?" Concerned laced his voice.

"Yes. I'm sorry, I'm here." *Just a momentary flashback.* "That's fine—look forward to it." She heard Michael stifle a yawn. "Okay, well, get some sleep. We'll be over there to demand our pancakes and sausage soon enough. I love you."

"I love with you all my heart, I'll see you soon."

Beatrice lay awake in her bed for several hours. Something had to change. Everything reminded her of her time with her husband. She and Harold often curled up on the couch that she would share with Michael to watch movies. It wasn't fair to him or to herself; Bea lamented that she should be getting stronger, not trying to continue to hold on to what she used to have in her life. Her thoughts, her emotions told the story, she was living in the past. Bea had to admit that it was time . . . it was time to let go . . .

She drifted to sleep with thoughts of Michael's marriage proposal on her mind.

Michael looked over the brochures, including the pamphlets for children's activities and dress-code information. It promised to be an interesting adventure, but he was certain that he'd made the right decision. They needed to find neutral ground. . . .

He enjoyed spending time with Bea, but not necessarily in the home that she had shared for twenty-five years with another man.

Michael placed everything in an envelope and went back to bed to rest before he turned his kitchen into Chez Spates, breakfast restaurant extaordinaire. With a certain amount of satisfaction in his decision, he slept comfortably until his alarm sounded four hours later.

Dressed and out the door thirty minutes after the blare of the alarm ceased, Michael dashed into the store armed with his list. He had to be crazy to invite everyone over—without even an egg in the refrigerator. He moved swiftly down the aisles until he reached the chilled foods section. He stopped so abruptly, a woman behind him nearly ran over him with her cart. He'd stopped after the sensation of being watched became too strong to ignore. Michael apologized, let the woman pass him, and then casually began to look at food items as well as the other shoppers.

Gotcha! He watched a man curiously reading the contents of a box of Cheerios. Michael noted his dress and demeanor. He seemed interested in the contents of the box only after he noticed Michael glance in his direction. How long did it take to read *low fat* and *heart smart?* He decided to test his theory. Michael looked around to see if the man was alone. After he didn't notice anyone else he continued to move. He placed eggs, butter, and cheese in the cart and kept walking toward the dairy refrigerator for milk, but before he reached in to grab the bottle, he turned to the man, which caught him completely off guard. Michael placed the cart between the man and the doors. "You've got exactly five seconds to tell me who you are or we take a walk outside and only one of us returns."

The man shoved the box of cereal at Michael's face, knocked over the cart and made a dash toward the exit. Michael gave chase, but the man disappeared into a waiting SUV that sped away before he could copy down the license plate. "Damn!" he muttered before walking back into the store. Curious onlookers asked him if he was all right. "I'm fine, but did anyone get a good look at the man or the vehicle?" The answer was a few nods and noes as people moved away and back to their own business. Michael muttered again and went to retrieve his items. He would have to talk with Bea about the incident. He couldn't be sure that she wasn't being watched, too. He took out his cell phone and began to dial. As soon as his call was answered he spoke, his words a barrage of threats and curses.

Eric chuckled. "Well, boss, I'm glad you got that out of your system. So what's going on, in ten words or less."

Michael paused. He knew better than to let his emotions get the best of him. "You need to let the team know that we may have a problem. I'm being followed, but when I tried to get more information from the guy he bolted. I didn't get anything from him. I'll tell Bea, but I'd like you to let everyone else know to watch his or her back. Meet on Monday for a strategy session, not in the office, though. Those jerks from IRB have moved into my space. Make it coffee in our 'secure' spot—you know the one."

Eric exhaled. "Yeah, I'll be there. I'll see if Tangie can go to her mom's house for a few days. I'm sure Pop would love to see the boys anyway. Thanks for the heads-up—I'll get right on it."

Michael hung up and made his way through the checkout without further incident. He checked his car thoroughly before he headed back to his house. He had just finished mixing the pancake batter when the bell rang. He answered it immediately and swept Beatrice into his arms. Before she could respond, his lips sought hers and captured them in a passionate kiss. Jamela and Jonnelda watched from the doorway. Jonnelda turned to the younger girl. "Not all old people act this way, so don't worry."

Michael broke the kiss after hearing the snickers behind him.

"Wow! That was some greeting," Bea teased. "Okay Jonnelda, breakfast is over, see you girls later. Drive carefully."

Jonnelda feigned disgust, "Oh, Miss Bea! We're going to have to hose you two down. Now, where's my breakfast? I'm so hungry that I could eat a whole side of pork!"

Michael hugged both girls and invited them in. "Come on, let me show you the kitchen. I guess you guys didn't know you were going to have to work for your meal." He tweaked Jamela's nose. "Especially you, young lady. Let me give you the ten-minute, two-dollar tour of the place and then we can start."

Jonnelda looked around appreciatively. The house was everything that she expected; neat, orderly . . . functional, just like its owner. She noticed that he had chosen relatively dark and muted colors, but it didn't make the house appear to be depressing. She liked his use of black and burgundy cushions on his leather sofa. His use of military art gave his place a masculine feel without being overbearing, too. From his prints detailing an event from each time period of war, she could tell that he appreciated service and duty. But it was his picture over the fireplace mantle of Dunn's River Falls in Jamaica that she fell in love with . . . its scenic beauty was a pleasant reminder of home.

After touring the rest of the house to include a lovely black-and-white half bath, she deduced that Michael was either never home or he had a great cleaning lady, in order for his place to be so immaculate.

She caught up with Jamela again, while she held court with Beatrice and Michael in the kitchen. She smiled inwardly at her child's precocious behavior. "Hey, don't tell me you guys started without me?"

"Yeah, you took too long. We've been snacking and talking for the last fifteen minutes."

Jonnelda smiled again. "So I see. I was just admiring your house, Michael. I really love what you've done with it . . . it's so tasteful and you used several of my favorite colors. You've got a great eye for a—"

"For a man," he finished for her with a laugh. "Actually, I've been in this place for over ten years, but I'm home so little, that I had a designer complete the basic concept and I just filled in the gaps with my most personal possessions." He waved his hands around. "So what you see, my dear, is a joint effort. I just didn't want to come home to a barren, undecorated space. But enough about my handiwork, let's get these pancakes on the griddle. I'll pour—you flip. I've got to get the bacon going, too."

Bea chimed in, "I'll second that motion. We need to get going or we're never going to eat. He's got me over here peeling potatoes for the hash browns—I think I'm going to protest. And look at poor Jamela, she's on strawberry duty. So you two hurry up," she urged.

Two hours later, after eating and teasing and laughing, breakfast was finished. Jamela found her corner to relentlessly punish whatever villains she fought on her Game Boy and Jonnelda found a book from one of Michael's massive shelves in his den/study and sat next to her on the couch.

With the dishes washed and dried, Michael and Bea continued to sit at the table and enjoy each other's company. They could see the girls, but they were out of earshot. Michael took the opportunity to talk privately with Beatrice. He watched the swirl of steam from his mug for a few seconds before he began. "I think that you should take extra precautions for a few days. There was an incident at the store earlier today."

Bea sounded alarmed. "What kind of incident?"

"I was followed, but when I cornered the guy he got away. I don't want to worry you, though, because to be honest, it could be nothing—maybe I just spooked him. . . ."

"Or maybe, this case isn't over yet." She motioned toward Jamela and Jonnelda. "What have you been able to find out about them? And don't give me that look—I know you've been digging. I've known you for a very long time."

Michael raised his hand in surrender. "Guilty as charged, but I prefer not to discuss it here and now. Let's table this for a more private time. In the meantime, let's try to come up with a tighter schedule. Call me when you go out and I'll do the same. Tell Jonnelda to keep her cell phone on at all times and please make sure that it stays charged—no sense in having the darn thing if the battery dies when she really needs it." He smiled. "So now you think you know me?"

The lines of worry on her forehead eased. "Yeah, I know you. But I didn't know you could put together such a wonderful spread like we just ate. I see you've got undiscovered talents. . . ."

Michael's eyes turned a sultry brown as he licked his lips and said, "Oh, there are definitely some undiscovered talents that I'd love for you to discover . . . or uncover, as it were . . ."

Beatrice giggled. "You do inspire the imagination, Mr. Spates."

Michael placed her hand in his; the warmth caused a tingling sensation to surge through her. Bea closed her eyes. She wanted to be in his arms again, the memories of their time together came flooding back, causing no small measure of discomfort in certain areas.

"I don't know if I can handle being any closer to you. I seem to turn into this love-starved harlot, with carnal, lustful thoughts at every turn."

"Wow, I'm impressed that I can inspire all that—I'm better than I gave myself credit for, after all." Michael curved his lips in a sexy smile.

Bea cuffed him on the shoulder. "What am I going to do with you?"

He waggled his eyebrows in response. Bea giggled again. She loved this side of him.

Michael figured there was no time like the present to spring his surprise on her. "Give me a second, I need to get something to show you."

He returned immediately with a stack of brochures. "I hope you won't be mad about this. . . ."

Beatrice looked at him curiously. "Let me see what you've done," she said, reaching her hand out for the material. It took a few seconds for the information to register. She jumped up from her chair when she realized what he'd done. "Oh, Michael! This is wonderful." She threw her arms around him and planted a passionate kiss on his lips.

Jonnelda and Jamela looked up to see what all the fuss was about. Jamela said conspiratorially, "They're at it again."

"I know—they seem to have one-track minds," Jonnelda responded, as she laughed.

Bea stepped back, remembering that they were not alone. "Girls, come here, let me show you where we're going to spend Christmas."

Jamela and Jonnelda jumped up from where they sat, excited to be included in Bea and Michael's plans.

"There is a resort in the mountains of White Sulphur Springs, West Virginia, named the Greenbrier. It is wonderful and very exclusive, so for Michael to be able to reserve two rooms for Christmas is just short of a miracle. Anyway, they'll have activities for both of you, with dinner, dances, games, and lots of shopping." Bea waved the brochures around. "But we are going to have to buy more new clothes because formal dress at dinner is required. Maybe we can have our hair and nails done before we go, too."

Michael moaned, "Oh brother, another small fortune."

Beatrice cuffed him on the shoulder again. "Never mind that! I hope you've got a nice tuxedo—we don't want to show him up, do we? Well, not too badly anyway."

Jonnelda teased, "I'll go on one condition—that you two agree to act your *age* while we're there. If not, I promise to pelt you with as many snowballs as I can make."

Bea hugged her. "You wouldn't dare, besides, I am a snowball-making queen. I think you might be in trouble."

"Great, then it's settled. We leave in three days, which means I need to alert the malls of an impending invasion." He was joined in his laughter, and could tell that they looked forward to a good time together. Michael excused himself after his cell phone rang.

"Hi boss, sorry to call on a Saturday. I just thought you should know that Vanessa Winton is in town. She flew into Dulles International Airport last week. Do you want someone on her? My contact at the DEA told me, but nobody is tailing her, they want to toe the line on her—if she is here for business reasons they don't want the charges dismissed on some stupid technicality. They are taking a wait-and-see approach. And since that has never been your specialty . . ."

"Yes, Banks, thank you for the heads-up. I'll have Eric put someone on her. I'll be out of town for the next five days. I may have already had a run-in with one of her people earlier today. I was at the grocery store, and noticed that I was being followed. The man bolted when I approached him, though, so I didn't get any information out of him." Michael paused. "I've already told Bea to be a little more careful until we leave."

Agent Banks chuckled. "Oh, *you* and *Bea* are going out of town, now that makes it a little more interesting."

"Do you want to direct traffic at Quantico for the next three months?"

"Sorry, boss. Well, you have a great time and I'll keep you posted."

Michael grunted, "Yeah, you do that. Out."

He returned to the kitchen to find Bea, Jonnelda, and Jamela knee-deep in Christmas plans. He sat down quietly to listen, hearing their excited voices seemed strangely comforting to a man who'd spent most of his time enjoying the peacefulness of his surroundings. He smiled to himself and continued to watch as Bea began to write a list.

Monday morning came too soon. Bea sat on the edge of her bed trying to steel herself for the day that she had in front of her. Even though they'd had an exhaustive conversation about her going into the office, Bea still felt a little guilty about leaving them alone. On an intellectual level she knew they would be fine, but in her heart she still felt like she was deserting them.

Sitting on her bed, Beatrice said a prayer for strength and then went about her routine until she left the house. She kissed Jamela good-bye and left a note for Jonnelda with all her pertinent work information.

Beatrice sat behind her desk, coffee cup in hand at 7:30 A.M., sifting through her messages. It was strange to be back and not to see Zola behind her desk as well. . . . Bea knew that she would have to replace her soon enough. Unfortunately, she was in no mood to do that at the moment. She would consider her options after the new year began. Today she had a few important tasks to take care of—beginning with her deputy. As soon as she heard him enter his office, she buzzed for him to meet with her. She noticed that Russell Watson seemed surprised to see her even though they had maintained regular phone contact.

"Russell, I'm glad that you made it in before the rest of the staff. There are a few things that we need to discuss in private."

Russell sat down across from her and crossed his legs, his stance immediately on the defensive, Bea noticed. However, she didn't take steps to alleviate any of his stress.

"Yes, ma'am, what can I do for you?" Russell casually placed a piece of paper on the table next to him.

The question was posed good-naturedly enough, but Bea didn't give a damn about niceties.

Bea sat forward in her chair with her hands clasped together. "Russell, I'll speak as plainly as possible. I'm disappointed in you. We've worked together for the better part of ten years. I recommended you for the position personally, yet when it mattered most, you chose to try to walk over my dead body to advance. I want you to stop this ridiculous investigation into Michael and Eric's actions. This is beneath you, and you know it!"

He cleared his throat. "If you mean that you'd prefer that I call off the IRB for agents Spates and Duvernay, you know I can't do that. Once the board finds just cause to investigate, they can take over from their office. I'm afraid it is out of my hands."

His cocky smile grated on her nerves. "Well then, you give me no choice but to request a transfer for you into another department."

Russell picked up the paper that he placed on the table. "Well then, you'll give me no choice but to execute this complaint against you for harassment. As you can see, I anticipated a negative reaction to my actions. I'm just doing what I think is best for the bureau. We can't have our agents going off half-cocked. You run an undisciplined department and I happen to think that I can do a better job. There was no threat posed by the Winton posse. Your agents were wrong on all counts. I'll hold onto this letter until after the first of the year. That's when I'll expect you to step down." Mirth twinkled in his blue eyes before he walked out of her office.

Beatrice was livid. "This isn't over yet, Russell!"

Chapter Thirteen

Beatrice picked up the phone immediately to dial Michael's number; she gritted her teeth as she waited for him to answer. Her chest heaved in anger. How dare Russell betray her trust! Thankfully, Michael answered on the fourth ring.

"Michael, it's me. It's been a *heckava* morning, do you have time for a lunch date this afternoon?"

"Sure," he responded. "But what's wrong? You sound so tense."

Bea counted to five before she responded. "I'm just mad as hell, but we can talk about it when we see each other. Obviously, I should have cleaned house at my office a long time ago. Russell Watson just made a play for my job. I never realized what an ungrateful back-stabbing lot I had here until now—this is unbelievable!"

"Okay, don't get your blood pressure up. We'll hash it out this afternoon, how about one P.M. at the corner restaurant?" He paused. "Whatever is going on, we'll deal with it together. Listen, I've got to meet with the IRB guys in five minutes, so I'll see you soon."

Bea relaxed a little. "I'm sorry, Michael, for being so wrapped up in my issues. You know that I can't get involved, but let me know, off the record, if you need something. I'm going to do all I can to support what we did when they come to question me. Good luck with them and I'll see you this afternoon. Thanks."

After he disconnected the call, she held on to the receiver for a few seconds. She loved the velvety smoothness of his voice . . . she also loved that he said they would deal with things *together.* Those words had more appeal than she'd given credit to in times past.

Bea looked down at the souvenir snow globe from the Hilltop Hotel that rested on her desk. Heat flushed her skin as she remembered their intimate time in the shower . . . he made her feel like a beautiful, desirable woman again. And desire was what she felt every time she laid eyes on him. *How am I supposed to finish any work when all I think about is you?*

Michael had quickly become a constant in her life. She didn't even want to think about life without him. "How do you fall so deeply, madly in love with someone?" she asked herself.

Bea leaned back in her chair. Maybe she should consider stepping down . . . had falling in love with Michael clouded her judgment? Was she less competent because of her feelings? What if Russell was right and he was better for the job than she? Beatrice sipped her now lukewarm coffee. Then she pushed away those negative thoughts that prickled around the edges of her subconscious and forced her attention to the stack of papers on her desk for review. She definitely wouldn't be productive if she allowed self-doubt to get in her way. "Russell Watson, I'm not going to let you walk away with my job." After a few more minutes of contemplation, she came up with a course of action. *We're just going to have to handle this situation like adults.*

Bea completed a couple more hours of work and then decided to try again with Russell. She didn't want to create an environment of animus to detract from the mission they were set up to accomplish. He entered her office looking like the proverbial cat that swallowed the proverbial canary. Beatrice bit her lip to stop the caustic remark that begged to spring free from her mouth.

Bea adopted a very professional tone when she spoke. "Russell, I think we need another opportunity to discuss the changes that need to happen in this department. We can't afford to let emotion derail us, which is something that I preach to the agents under my supervision all the time. And while we don't always do things by the book, we always complete our missions and that has to be a testament to something. We've made a good team until this point . . . and I'd like us to continue. So, if there are specific areas that we can address, I'd like us to begin to do that now."

Russell swallowed hard. Bea concluded that he must have come back expecting round two in her office. His blue eyes turned dark sapphire before he spoke, and the bitterness he felt was apparent in his tone. "Agent McCoy, you say we make a good team, but frankly I've seen no evidence of that. You seem to have more regard for everyone else on the team except for the person who is supposed to make decisions in your absence. I could have told you that something was going on with Zola, but I knew that you wouldn't hear me."

"Russell, what are you saying?"

He crossed his legs and leaned back. "I thought I was being clear. I'm saying that you trusted everyone with information except the person with the real need to know. I can't tell you how many times I've sat in meetings with you and had no idea what would come out of your mouth. Real comforting for the deputy!" He sneered. "And Zola had been acting strange, kind of cagey for weeks, maybe even months, but I didn't want to become embroiled in an EEOC investigation if I called her on her behavior. But more than that, I'm sitting here on the outside watching as you and *Michael* become thick as thieves. Even though I outrank him, I don't have near the access to you that he does. In this office it has been hard-assed Agent Beatrice McCoy's way or the highway."

Bea reacted as if she had been struck. "Oh God, Russell, why didn't you come to me sooner? I had no idea that I was doing that to you. You've been wonderful to work with; I would never have knowingly treated you the way you are saying. My behavior has nothing to do with race. . . . Russell, I have always respected you—but more importantly, I value you, your contributions and judgement tremendously. Please forgive me. With Zola's betrayal, all the budget cuts and reshuffling of departments to DHS, we need to have stability in our unit." She added softly, "To achieve that, I need you."

Bea made direct eye contact again, "Threats and counterthreats are not going to help us get the job done, so can we call a truce while we work things out?"

Russell let out a long breath, but before he could respond, Beatrice's phone rang.

Bea answered immediately. "Oh, okay, I understand. No, now is not good, but we can discuss this later. I'll call you after lunch. Thanks." She replaced the receiver, then turned to Russell. "I'll tell you what, I'm starving and my lunch date just cancelled. How about I treat you to a gourmet meal? We can continue this over a nice juicy steak."

Russell smiled for the first time since he entered her office. "Yes, I'd like that." His earlier animosity seemed much reduced now that he'd said what was on his mind. He looked at Bea and nodded in agreement. "You've got a deal, but let me make a quick phone call, I need to change my plans. I'll meet you in the lobby in five minutes."

* * *

Vanessa watched the afternoon sky darken like her mood. She had no appreciation for winter in the District. All the cold weather made her long to take care of business quickly so that she could return to her pleasantly warm Jamaica. She didn't know how her brother stood the mountains of West Virginia. It made her realize how great a sacrifice he'd made for his family because not even for a successful operation would she have given up home. Thoughts of Kharl only served to dampen her spirits more. While she listened to the information that her DEA informant provided, she tapped her fingers on the hotel desk in irritation. "What are they looking for?"

The party on the other line answered, "Looks like a subtle look-see. The questions were very broad and were more focused on Jonnelda and Jamela. It seems like they are trying to determine if the wayward Wintons should be sent back home with the rest of the deportees from the compound. The agent seemed very interested to find out that the two are connected and more importantly that Jonnie is Jamela's mother. But when he asked about you, I thought I should call."

Vanessa sighed. He would probably want a bonus for the information. "Yes, you did the right thing. I may have to do something to get their attention. Maybe with a little incentive they will concentrate their efforts on someone or something else." She reached for a piece of paper and pen to copy down the information. "What's the agent's name?"

"Agent Michael Spates."

Damn him! Vanessa hung up abruptly and called Delroy from the adjoining room. "Our timetable has just been moved up. Get your coat, we're going out."

Bea stood at the door and pulled her coat closer against the blustery winter wind. She was relieved to see

Russell come down to the lobby of the building so that they could leave. She and Russell exited the building to take the short walk to the restaurant on Ninth and E Streets—a popular spot for bureau personnel who worked at that location.

A few minutes into the short journey, the swirling of the late December wind blew Bea's hat onto the sidewalk. As she bent down to retrieve it, she heard a quick succession of spurting noises above her head.

Bea looked down at Russell's fallen body and watched in horror as blood spilled from his chest. The acrid smell of gunpowder and burning flesh assaulted her senses. Instinctively, she ducked down to shield her body.

She searched frantically for the shooter amid the scrambling of the other pedestrians on the street. Beatrice doubted that they would risk another shot, but to be sure, she reached into Russell's jacket for the gun she knew he carried. She needn't have worried, however, because in less than a minute several federal agents surrounded her.

"I'm sorry, boss. She moved just as I aimed."

Vanessa shook her head. "Don't worry about it. I don't know whom you shot, though; he doesn't look like anyone in the pictures here. But he came out of the building with her, so that's good enough for me. Now we can go back to the original plan, this ought to keep them busy for awhile. Put two men on her house; if she makes a move, I want to know about it."

Delroy nodded in understanding. Inwardly, he breathed a sigh of relief; he knew her stance on failure all too well.

They passed by the Spy Museum, ignoring the confusion behind them. People stopped to find out what was going on, but they continued walking—just another tourist couple on the way to the Gallery Place Metro station. It would take the police a few minutes to secure the area, and that was all the time that they needed.

Delroy inconspicuously dropped the gun in the trash can before they boarded the train—the last one to leave before the station was shut down pending the investigation. Vanessa watched from the moving train as police combed the platform. She turned to Delroy and encircled his hands in hers. She whispered in his ear, "Don't worry about it at all. Well done—we got their attention, and that was exactly the point."

They ignored the curious murmurs of the other passengers as police searched the station and a uniformed policeman walked up and down the aisles. They pretended to be a young couple only interested in each other and completely in love. The policeman glanced their way but continued to the next car. A smile curved her lips as she thought about how she would avenge her brother's death.

Despite the cars in front of him, Michael pressed on the accelerator. Sweat rolled unceremoniously down his back, indicating a high level of tension. Between the beeping and the aggressive lane changes, he made it to the hospital in record time. Albeit, by breaking several traffic laws driving the distance between his Springfield, Virginia office and George Washington Hospital where Beatrice had been admitted. He created a parking space in the middle of the lot and ran into the building. He spotted an agent that he recognized from Bea's office and went directly to him. "Where is she?"

The young agent appeared stunned, but Michael didn't have time for that, he needed information. He flashed his badge and repeated his question, his tone sterner the second time. "I said, where is she, dammit."

This time the agent recognized his name. "Right this way, sir." Michael was led down a private corridor to a room with a guard at the door. Michael flashed his badge again, then was allowed in.

Beatrice sat on the hospital bed in a gown, looking stunned. As soon as she saw Michael she ran into his waiting arms. "Oh God, Bea, I'm so glad that you're safe. I was out of my mind with worry. What in heaven's name happened? Karen said there was a shooting outside the bureau building and that you were there." His voice became choked with emotion, so he stopped talking to kiss her.

Beatrice held on for dear life. She didn't want to ever leave Michael's arms. She kissed him back with abandon. She didn't want to think, didn't want to talk.

After the kiss, he held her for several minutes in silence. He felt a small jerk at first that was soon followed by full body shaking. Bea lost control, nearly collapsing from the force of her cries. Michael steadied her in his strong embrace, holding her until she was spent. After a few minutes he sat her down on the bed again.

Bea began slowly. "We were walking and talking, then the wind blew my hat and I went to pick it up. One minute we were discussing what to eat for lunch and the next he was on the ground dying. Michael, it was awful . . . I . . . I . . . think that I was the target. I think Russell died because of me—the shots were fired when I bent down. . . ."

Michael caressed her hair. "Shush, shush . . . it's all right now—you're safe."

Beatrice took a deep breath. "The director wants me to go to a safe house until this mess is sorted out. I can't believe this happened. The police found the gun, but whoever did this knew what they were doing. This was a professional hit, no prints, no serial number—nothing. They had multiple escape routes—they might have boarded the train after the shooting, or jumped in a cab, car, or the bus. How could this happen? I keep replaying the scene in my mind, I just see his eyes . . . they were full of shock . . . he just laid down on the ground . . . blood spurted from the holes in his chest and he just . . . he just died."

Beatrice held on to Michael closer. "Oh Michael, we said such hateful things to each other. I was so mad at him for making me feel incompetent and telling me that he thought he could do the job better. I was livid until I decided that our office didn't need the added turmoil of strife between us, too. I invited him to lunch to smooth things over. Before we walked out, it seemed like we had come to an understanding, but I don't know . . . he was unhappy being my deputy and it was all my fault. I dumped on him when I needed him and undercut him when it came to important decisions. I was a terrible leader.

"Oh God! Michael, look at me, first Zola, now Russell. We've lost more people in a month than we've lost in over a decade." She took a deep breath. "Maybe I should step down or at least consider what I'm doing. I can't even think of going back to that office right now. While the guys check out the house, will you take Jonnelda and Jamela over to your place?"

Michael nodded. "I'll take care of them, don't worry. I just want you to take care of yourself. I'll go by the house and pick up some things before they move you from here. I feel terrible about Watson, but I'm so thankful that you're alive. We've been through too much to lose each other now."

Bea nodded her head in agreement. "What would I do without you—my rock! I love you so much, Michael. I don't want to live without you."

Michael stroked her cheek. "Is that an answer to my proposal?"

Beatrice looked at him so intensely she seemed to lose herself in his brown eyes. "The answer is yes, yes, I will marry you. Let's just get through this crisis, then we can plan a small ceremony. We'll have a lot to do with moving your things to my house and putting your house on the market, but we can talk about all that later. Please check on the girls for me. I'm so worried about them."

Michael stiffened in response to what she said, but did not acknowledge her with words. Now was not a good time for this kind of discussion. "You're right, I should get going. I'll call you after I get to the house. Try to rest." He walked down the long corridor in deep thought. There was no way that he was going to sell his house or move into hers. Problem was, he knew what he wouldn't do, but had no idea what he would do.

He arrived at the house less than two hours later. He'd had to prepare his home for two guests. Michael was used to being a loner, so this would be an interesting experience for everyone. He didn't know why he was so nervous . . . but when he opened the door to her house it was with no small amount of trepidation.

Jonnelda seemed just as anxious as he was; she waited with a packed suitcase almost at the doorway. Michael appreciated her cooperation and told her as much. "I see you spoke with Beatrice. This won't be for long, because we leave for the Greenbrier as soon as Beatrice is released. How's Jamela doing?"

Just then Jamela walked into the room. "I'm fine, Mr. Michael; how is Miss Bea? She sounded funny on the phone, but I told her not to worry, if you could make us a delicious breakfast like you did before—we'd be just fine. She laughed, but I could tell she wanted to be with us. So, I told her we could talk every day until the bad people are caught."

Michael smiled. "I'm sure that made her feel better. Thank you two for being so helpful. So, who's ready to hit the road?"

"Just let me check the house one more time and I'll be right with you," Jonnelda responded. In less than a minute it seemed, she was locking the front door. Michael marveled at her behavior; she seemed almost spooked. Their talk was long past due; he needed to find out her intentions before he intervened on her behalf with the ICE.

The ride back to Michael's house was uneventful. The girls shared his spare bedroom and seemed to settle in with no problem.

After taking some time to sort out the events of the day, Michael called Jamela and Jonnelda into the living room to talk about Beatrice. He made hot chocolate for Jamela and coffee for Jonnelda and himself. As he stirred he tried to think of the best way to discuss what was going on around them without causing a sense of panic. After little thought he settled on the direct, honest approach. "There's still a lot we don't know, but I wanted to take some time to answer your questions. I know this is a peculiar situation—the whole darn thing is peculiar, while we're at it, but I want you to feel secure in knowing that we will do everything we can to make sure that you're both safe. We suspect that there was an attempt on Beatrice's life. We don't know if it is related to a particular case or not, but the FBI is in the process of launching a full-scale investigation. I feel pretty confident that we'll know what we're dealing with soon enough. I'll keep you informed as appropriate and we'll continue with our plans to go away for Christmas.

"I think your lives have been disrupted enough and you certainly don't need this kind of nonsense going on—so we are going to do what we can to find out who is behind the shooting and take them down. You'll be safe here and by the time we return from our getaway, the bureau will have taken the necessary steps to see that Bea's house is safe, too—you two will be more protected than Fort Knox." His attempt to lighten the mood garnered a small smile. Michael sipped coffee during the pause. He hoped he was doing and saying all the right things. His agents had stirred paternal feelings, but he'd never experienced anything like this . . . it felt like an overwhelming desire to protect and make the world safe just for the two of them.

"In the meantime, we've got three more weeks before school begins and we'll need to look at permanent solutions for the two of you. I would love for you to become a part of our family, but that decision has not been made yet and we probably need to sort the rest of this out before we take on the next big issue."

Jonnelda's heart lurched at the thought of being sent back to Jamaica. To see her child happy kept her going. And as strange as it felt sometimes, she had started to care about Beatrice and Michael as if they were family, too. She let out a long sigh before she spoke. "Michael, I can assure you that there is no one in Jamaica who would welcome Jamela or me back with open arms. If the immigration service is looking for somewhere to send us—they may as well forget about it."

Michael gave her a censuring look. "Maybe we've said too much already. There's still a lot to be settled before any final decisions are made. Do you two have everything that you need? I can make a run to the store before we turn in for the night."

Jamela looked from one to the other, trying to figure out what was going on. "I'm fine, Mr. Michael. Jonnelda brought almost everything we had—I thought we were running away." Jamela laughed, but neither Michael nor Jonnelda joined her. She noticed and wished she hadn't said anything. The tension between them became so strong, Jamela simply rose from the table and left the room. She didn't want to be in the middle of something between two of the most important people in her life.

Jonnelda held Michael's gaze. She wasn't going to back down without a fight and she wanted him to know that fact. He could intimidate most anyone, but she had a strong will of her own. Right or wrong, she wouldn't go down without at least speaking her piece. She'd learned those lessons the hard way after becoming a Winton.

Michael spoke, striking the first blow. "Were you planning to run away and disappear in the middle of the night?"

"What do you want to do now? He's waiting on me to get back to him with more information—this is crazy!" Agent Banks looked down at the surveillance photos of Vanessa Winton and shook his head. He couldn't believe she would risk a trip to the U.S. to target one of the bureau's top officials. In his book, Vanessa had moved from having moxie to just plain stupidity. "Thanks for driving halfway around the city to meet with me."

Agent Eric Duvernay gave a wry smile. "Yeah, welcome to the world of the SCU. I think I want to talk to McCoy first. I know Spates wants the information, but with everything that's been happening, we need someone in leadership to determine if we have enough to begin an operation. I don't want the IRB on my ass for another damn thing. Besides, this involves her as much as anyone else."

Agent Banks nodded in agreement, though now he wished he had contacted AD Spates first. "I'm glad that

I'm not in your shoes—I don't know which is worse, to have the AD or the IRB crawling up your *assets*."

Eric chuckled. "Yeah, I know. This Winton thing has made it very crowded up there. Thanks for calling me—Tangie is probably going to make me change my phone number after this. . . ."

Banks teased, "Just remind her that her husband is responsible for saving the world on several occasions. She'll understand a few more middle-of-the-night calls, disappearances for days at a time, and your reluctance to talk about work. All wives of super-agents do."

Eric grinned. "If it weren't so late, I'd probably knock you on your butt for your insolence. As it stands, I still have to drive back halfway around this city to return to my nice warm bed."

Agent Banks laughed. "Hey, I was just trying to be careful. One of my instructors taught me that."

Eric laughed, too. "Yeah, yeah, that guy should have flunked you! Okay, I'm out of here. I'll be back in touch after I talk with McCoy. It will be her decision about what we do next. Keep your eyes open, though. And in case I didn't say it before—good work. You may have just saved our collective tails."

Agent Banks blew on his nails and feigned buffing them on his shirt. "Saving tails is what I do."

Eric clapped Banks on the shoulder as he rose from his seat. "Oh brother—what a monster we've created. Good night, or good morning, as it were. You'll hear from me soon."

The all-night diner was almost empty, but he checked out the sparse crowd on his way out the door anyway. After he walked out into the frigid parking lot, he found himself looking around cautiously. If Vanessa Winton had the guts to go after Beatrice McCoy as they now suspected, no one was safe. Eric decided that he would have Tangie and the kids spend more time with heir parents. He would join them for Christmas and hen return alone. *Guess the old saying is right, you never really ever retire from the SCU.*

As they continued their conversation, Jonnelda eyed Michael warily. "Never mind that, you know perfectly well that I have no place to go. Which makes me wonder what else you know." She arched her eyebrows as she posed the question, "Why did I get coffee and not hot chocolate, like Jamela?"

Michael finished the last sip of his drink and pushed the cup forward. "Because I figured someone your *age* would want a more adult drink."

Jonnelda's laugh was dry, without mirth. "I happen to love hot chocolate in the winter, but yes, a woman of my mature age does usually drink coffee. You've known for awhile, yet you chose not to tell Beatrice. I can tell by the difference in the way that you and Beatrice treat me. That makes me question you—what are your motives?" She sighed again. "So is this the part where I beg forgiveness for my duplicity? Or maybe we just skip all that and you tell me what you and Bea intend to do."

Michael appeared slightly exasperated with the direction of their conversation. "How about we just skip all the drama. This is not an episode of *Knots Landing*, so why don't you tell me everything—from the beginning." His flat, authoritative tone brooked no room for deceit.

Jonnelda sucked in air through her teeth, then exhaled slowly. She knew this day would come, but she preferred it not be today. "Fine. But remember you asked for it—I didn't bring this fight to you."

Michael nodded. "I'm ready. Tell me what's going on from your side of the story."

Jonnelda nodded, then began. "As you probably know, my name is not simply Jonnelda Lindo, it's Lindo

Winton. I'm not a teenager, but an adult widowed woman. My husband was Moses Winton. And yes, he was a member of the Winton posse, but he was nothing like his demented brother and sister. He was the middle child and seemed to miss out on their craziness and viciousness. Moses was wonderful, kind, and a good father—which is why they killed him. No, I don't have proof, but I know it in my heart.

"At first I was so heartbroken I could barely function. Jamela was so young, she had just started to talk and would get into everything—she needed a mother and a father and in my condition, she basically had neither one. My parents begged me to give her to them while I got myself together and I did. I was nineteen and a wreck, no good to her or anyone else. I stayed with my *loving* sister-in-law for a few months and then we worked out a plan. I would help in posse business like Moses was supposed to, get myself on solid ground, and then resume caring for my child. What actually happened was a nightmare. Vanessa was a lying, double-crossing psychopath—and those were her good traits.

"My parents brought Jamela to West Virginia and in short order discovered Kharl was no better than his sister. We talked about escape, but before they could get away they were killed. I watched him bury them— he didn't make me watch them being shot, but I knew the exact time that it happened; it felt like a knife pierced my heart." Jonnelda stopped to wipe the tears from her cheeks. "I held Jamela in my arms and cried for hours. How do you explain that kind of death to a child?" She shook her head. "I didn't bother to tell her the truth. . . . I guess at some point I expected Kharl would kill me, too. Sometimes, I actually wanted to die, but there was Jamela. I did what I was told and began to despise myself as much as him.

"Kharl used me like an old towel. He would send for

ne whenever he needed *drying off*—I was an object to
him, to be used at his leisure. I hated him more than
I've ever hated anyone in my life. There were times that
I imagined killing him with my bare hands, but I had to
be sure that my baby was safe.

"Jamaica was no option—with the Wintons still in
power and those still loyal to them—I wouldn't know
whom to trust. I can't go back to my home and expect
to live very long, but I'm okay with that as long as Jamela
is going to be all right. I got into so many fights at the
deportation center, because there are others like me.
They know the minute they step back on Jamaican
soil—they're dead. No one wants to go back to face
Vanessa and her crew. And even though it makes no
sense, like I told Officer Hightower, I became the scapegoat for the operation. They would have killed me at the
center, but they were too scared—fear saved my life."

She paused. "I wasn't too happy about leaving the
center because I didn't know when Jamela would be trans-
ferred in. I was so afraid of losing her or never seeing her
again if we didn't leave at the same time. But I'm glad now
that you agreed to take me in, because you never know
when someone will get the courage to do what they
shouldn't—someone may have decided I was too good a
target to resist. I fought so hard because I needed to stay
alive long enough to find out what had happened to my
child."

An involuntary shudder passed through her. "Especially after all that we went through at the compound
with Winton. Jamela was only nine years old—I couldn't
let her Uncle Kharl get his hands on her, so I did whatever he told me—I let him degrade me, peddle my flesh,
use me for sport . . . But I knew his day was coming. I
knew with everything that I had in me that he was going
to die and that I would have something to do with it—

the one thing I hadn't counted on was the FBI. I'd always thought that he was untouchable."

Michael blew out a long breath. Her life had certainly become complicated in the short time she'd walked the earth. He felt compelled to help her now that he understood her position. She was just a desperate mother trying to do right by her child. But it didn't stop the question that still burned to be asked. He looked directly into her eyes. "What about Jamela, what do you intend to do with her now? You know Beatrice really loves her. . . ."

Jonnelda sighed again. "Yes, I know and my heart has been tugged and pulled every which way. What are my options? I don't seem to be the one in power here. What do you want?" Her tone was just a bit too suggestive to Michael.

Michael reacted as if he'd been slapped. "Jonnelda, I know it seems every man wants something from you, but I don't! I love Beatrice McCoy more than you'll ever know, so I don't want anything like *that* from you. I know this has been tough on you and I admire your grit in being able to make it through each day, but you are not on the streets—you don't have to think like a hustler." He slowed down to control his emotions. "Not everybody you come in contact with is out to get you—at least not from where I sit. You need to ask yourself some questions, like what you want and where you want to go from here. This is your life, just know that Beatrice and I will support your decisions."

Fresh tears fell down her face. "Michael, I'm sorry—I should have known better. You see—I don't even know how to act with you and you saved my life. How am I going to take care of Jamela?"

Michael's tone softened. "Jonnelda, just remember that you're not alone. We're here for you and we're going to face this as a *family*. I care deeply about you and Jamela, even in just the short time that we've all known each other. I can tell that Beatrice feels the same way. We could have all made different choices, but we didn't, so I think this is right for all of us—part of the divine plan, you might say." Michael paused to let his words sink in. "Guess you're stuck with me for a little bit. You probably need to finish school and think about what kind of career you want to have in the future. Also, you should know that Beatrice has agreed to marry me. Once we work out all the details, we'll all live under one roof. I don't want to sound like Dr. Rose, but how do you feel about that?"

Jonnelda had to chuckle at the reference to the psychiatrist. "I'm fine with that—and thank you for such a generous offer. I need to be able to pull myself together—get my life back on track. Even with my pregnancy and Jamela's birth, I was able to complete school, but I do want to go to college, study something related to office management. I've always dreamed of working in corporate America. The romance and adventure of people doing important things. The notion of people being movers and shakers has always held a certain appeal. I never had grandiose ideas of being a power broker myself, but I think I'd like to work in an office atmosphere in a major company."

Michael noticed the faraway dreaminess of her expression and it brought back memories of his own youth . . . the days when he was a new agent to the SCU and on a personal mission to save the world. He could appreciate her goals, but couldn't resist the chance to tease her. "Oh, you do like to live on the edge." He chuckled. "That's a good goal, though; after we get this business settled with the ICE, maybe I can help you find a training program. We'll need to work on your résumé as well." Michael's tone was much more relaxed now, more conversational and at ease. "Thank you for being straight with me, I needed to know that I could trust you again. And before I forget, you are quite welcome. Life has been rough on you, but we're going to make sure that your circumstances drastically improve. Looking back, it's been one hell of a month."

Jonnelda nodded in agreement. "Yeah, but for me it has been a hell of a decade. I'm ready for a positive change in my life. Thank you for having a measure of faith in me—even if I don't have it in myself right now. I'll help you tell Beatrice whenever you're ready—but hopefully it will be some time after Christmas. I'm looking forward to going to the Greenbrier and seeing how the other half lives. The spa sounds heavenly and if you need some free time with the future Mrs. Spates, I don't mind hanging out with Jamela at all. She is growing so tall, next year I'll be looking up at her." Jonnelda's smile turned serious. "Besides, I'd like to spend some time alone with her to find out how she really feels about everything that is going on around her. She really loved her grandparents. . . . I'm not so sure that she is as over their deaths as she pretends to be—I know it was awhile ago, but they were really the only parents that she knew. I've allowed so much to happen to my little girl . . ."

Michael heard the pain in her voice as her words trailed off. "Jonnelda, you and your parents did something right because Jamela is a bright, talented little girl. The wonderful part of life is that sometimes we get a second chance. You can't change anything that happened, but you and that little girl have a lot of living to do yet—just make the most of it. You're not alone anymore and you have a bright future ahead of you."

Moisture glistened in her eyes. Jonnelda touched his hand. "Yes, I know that now. I know I'll never be able to repay the both of you for all you've done for me. I am forever in your debt and I won't forget it. Jamela will miss your pancakes, but how about I make us breakfast tomorrow?"

"You two go ahead in the morning, I'm going to have to leave early to check on Beatrice and to find out how the investigation is progressing. But make yourself at home. You should be able to find everything that you'll need."

Jonnelda couldn't resist teasing him about the orderly way he kept all his things. "That won't be a problem, I'll just look for the labels. You have to be the most compulsively neat and organized person that I know."

"You just call if you need anything, young lady. Now, aren't you supposed to be going to bed?"

On her way to the room she called back to him, "*Knots Landing*, huh? Wow, you reached back."

Michael laughed. "Go to bed! You young people just have no appreciation for the classics."

Chapter Fourteen

Beatrice sat up in her hospital bed wide-awake despite the lateness of the hour. She gave up staring at the clock; knowing how much sleep she wasn't getting served no purpose. She reached for the phone several times to call Michael but she wouldn't allow herself to complete the call. She'd tried to convince herself that she needed to say good night to Jamela, but as much as she wanted to, it wasn't the truth. She just wanted to hear Michael's words of reassurance in her ear. She wanted to borrow some of his seemingly unlimited strength. "Michael, where do we go from here?"

He scrunched his lips as he read the time on his watch. It was fairly late, but he needed to hear Bea's voice once more before he went to bed. He hoped he wouldn't wake her.

Beatrice answered on the first ring, her voice sounded almost breathless. "Michael, I've been thinking about you for hours—what took you so long to call me?"

He smothered a chuckle. "I didn't want to call you so late, but I needed to hear your voice. I have to tell you, I'm not disappointed. How are you feeling?"

"I've been a little restless, but I'm better now. I've done nothing but think about you and the girls. I hate being cooped up here and knowing that it will be at least another day before I can be with you. I wish I were there in your arms—I miss you."

"I miss you, too. Jamela and Jonnelda are both doing fine. Which brings me to my next subject. I've been giving this some thought. I don't think that we should share a room at the resort. As much as I want to wake up with you in my arms, I think that we should set a better example for Jamela, she's too impressionable and at the compound she was exposed to much more than she should have been without understanding what real intimacy is all about. I want to show her how responsible adults behave . . . though I want to be anything but responsible when I'm around you. Like the kids say in their own special vernacular—you've turned me out!"

Bea chuckled softly. "I agree—reluctantly, just for the record. After the ceremony and we work out the moves, we'll have plenty of time to be together. I love that you are so honorable, but my body hates the fact right now. I've been in this bed imagining all sorts of new and sexy positions for you to put me in. I think that maybe I should join a yoga class again—you know, to increase my flexibility." Bea grinned and felt like a teen talking dirty with her boyfriend. Michael made her feel young again. "In all seriousness, though, I want to be in your arms letting you have your wickedly loving way with me." Bea could hear the laughter in his voice and it warmed her through to her core.

"Oh, you little vixen. What are you trying to do to my resolve? I'm doing the best I can as it is, so don't make me come over there and break you out of the hospital."

Beatrice laughed out loud. "Hmmm, I like the sound of that. Promise?"

"No, I most certainly do not. Try to get some rest,

we'll all be together soon," Michael retorted. Bea's yawn confirmed to him that he should let her get some sleep, though he doubted slumber would come to him even after hearing her sweet voice. "I love you, Beatrice McCoy."

"And I love you, Michael Spates. Sleep tight. I'll call you in the morning."

Michael lay in bed waiting for sleep to claim him. He could just picture her in her hospital bed, black curls mussed, no makeup and a flimsy gown to cover her luscious body. Beatrice had wound herself firmly around his heart—what he wouldn't give or wouldn't do for her, he thought painfully. He didn't know what his life would be like without her front and center.

Which brought to mind the real reason that he could not sleep. Michael felt badly about not discussing Jonnelda with Beatrice. He didn't have a problem performing any of the secrecy of his profession, but the one thing he did not want to do was to keep secrets from Beatrice. Through the years until now, their relationship had been predicated on friendship, trust, love, and honesty. He felt almost as if he had betrayed her.

Turning on the night lamp, Michael decided to read a little more information from his case files about the Winton posse. The Winton family both puzzled and troubled him. How could a family that claimed to value loyalty so much continue to stab each other in the back? He believed Jonnelda's assertion that Moses had been purposely killed . . . and if he had to bet, he would say it was probably by Vanessa. She seemed to have a much greater affinity for her brother Kharl and seemed to want him to lead the family. *Unfortunately.*

Michael leaned back in his bed. After the Greenbrier they would have to take a serious look at their living arrangements. He wouldn't feel safe with Beatrice back in her house until he knew for sure the culprits had been apprehended and no longer posed a threat to her. He couldn't believe someone actually had the temerity to target a federal agent. Anger welled within him, further threatening his peace of mind. They couldn't be certain yet that the Wintons were behind Russell Watson's death, but until they were sure—everyone was a suspect. He studied Vanessa's face to make sure that he would recognize her if she dared to come around.

Bone-weary tired, Michael turned off his lamp just before dawn's early light peeked through his bedroom windows.

Michael dressed quickly then left the house early as planned. He had a lot to do despite a lack of sleep. He'd called Karen and asked her to meet him at the office a little earlier than usual—it promised to be a full day at SCU headquarters.

Karen sat behind her desk as he walked in; he was surprised, but grateful to see a steaming cappuccino waiting for him as he entered the doors. She greeted him cheerily. "Hi boss. Good to see that we're back to our old schedule."

Michael smirked. "Hi Karen. Don't you worry, with Christmas just days away, I'm not going to keep you. I need to check on a few things before I head out for the holidays."

Karen nearly choked on her coffee. *What did he just say?* "Um, excuse me? Did you just intimate that you're doing something special for the holidays?"

Michael looked at her with a gleam in his eye. "Karen, you know I love you like a *secretary*, but you don't need to know my every move. If ever you require my assistance, I'm just a cell phone call away. As for today, I've come to see if there are any leads on the shooters. I also want to schedule a meeting with the rest of the team for right after the New Year. Now, is all that agreeable with you?"

Something had definitely happened to the otherwise impassive agent—something good, she had to surmise. Karen struggled to pick her jaw up off the floor as he spoke.

"That's fine, sir—now tell me what you did with the real Michael Spates. I can tell that you're just a cheap replica."

Michael held his hands to his chest. "You wound me. Cheap, I am not. But if you want to have a job in the next fifteen minutes you'll let me get some work done."

Karen smiled. "That's better. Oh, by the way, you have a couple of handwritten messages from the IRB guys and a few voice mails, but I didn't check those—I figured you would do it when you were ready."

Michael stopped before entering his office and called back, "Thank you. Santa just might have a little bonus in your check for all your hard work."

Again she was flabbergasted. Beatrice McCoy was nothing short of a miracle worker if she had been able to thaw her stiff, ultraprofessional boss. Karen tuned her radio to the WHUR morning show and began reviewing files to pass to Michael for signature. It felt good to be back in their old routine. As for the bonus—he'd always been generous, but to joke about it was a very good sign. Things were looking up again, even if the IRB had her momentarily spooked.

Karen enjoyed her busy, fast-paced job and didn't want to have to leave it—she couldn't imagine working for anyone else. Before long she found herself singing a Christmas carol along with Johnny Mathis.

Michael listened to her sing and smiled again in his office. It was good to be back—no matter how long it would last. He took a look at his messages. What did the

IRB want with him? It had been a few days since their last session. He sat back in his chair to listen to the first message. What he heard made him drop his pen. "Spates, this is Watson. I've had some time to reconsider—I've decided to call off the review. I know you and your team did what was best, probably saved the DEA years of investigative work. I'd like to meet with you next week to discuss where we go from here—I have a proposal for you." Michael's breathing became harder. Listening to a message from a dead man was disconcerting, to say the least.

He took a minute to collect himself before he listened to the next message. It came from the IRB to confirm that the investigation had been completed and the findings inconclusive. Michael grunted, *how generous—inconclusive*. He picked up the phone. "Karen, it looks like we're back in business—get Eric on the phone for me."

He felt a small sense of satisfaction because of the results, but total vindication would have been best. With the IRB behind them, it was time to finish the Winton case then look at how to save the SCU from the Department of Justice chopping block. Michael wanted to talk with Beatrice, but felt that he needed to speak with Eric first. He and the rest of the unit had been sweating out the conclusion of the review, so this would be welcome news.

He fought the need to throw caution to the wind to celebrate—this one small victory anyway.

Eric was on the phone in minutes. "Karen says that you're in a good mood. What's going on?"

"I hope that you enjoyed your time off. Because, effective today there will be no more unpaid vacation for SCU agents—even ones that we borrow from Quantico. I hope that you're available right after the Christmas holiday."

"I'll be there. Tell me what we know so far."

* * *

After two days, as promised, the foursome was off to spend Christmas together. Beatrice noticed that the drive to the Greenbrier resort was as picturesque as the one to the historic Hilltop Hotel. Originally built in the late 1770s, the resort was nestled in the hills of White Sulphur Springs, and had a long and distinguished history. It had even been used as a secret hideaway spot for the president in the event of an attack on the White House. It was steeped in tradition, formality, and grandeur.

"Oh my," the words escaped Jamela's mouth, but were felt by all as soon as they stepped into the lobby. From the vaulted ceilings to the exquisite molding that surrounded the rooms, it felt lush and rich.

They were shown to their rooms and Jamela and Jonnelda both let out squeals of delight as soon as the bags were set down and the door closed. Beatrice couldn't even admonish them because she wanted to take her shoes off and jump on the sumptuous bed herself. Michael had arranged for a two-bedroom suite for them and a single room for himself. The Christmas package was costly, but worth every penny. There were several activities the girls could participate in and even though Jonnelda was there without male companionship she looked forward to the Gingerbread Ball Dinner Dance on Christmas eve. Jamela looked forward to the puppet show and the fashion show. Jonnelda had noticed that the little girl was becoming quite the little fashionista. In the month that they had been at Beatrice's house they'd both gained weight, but it looked good on them and mother and daughter had a healthy glow that hadn't been present at the compound. As the days wore on it seemed the similarities between them outshone the differences. Jonnelda knew it would be time to tell Beatrice the truth soon.

But for now, as she threw a pillow at Jamela and laughed—they would play. This was a once-in-a-lifetime trip. Everyone she cared about was right by her side.

Beatrice unpacked her clothes for their four-day excursion and placed them in the drawers of the beautiful mahogany dresser. Satisfied that Jamela and Jonnelda were fine and would eventually settle down, she went to Michael's room to spend some time with him. Bea knocked softly on his door.

"Come in, it's open," he answered. His gaze went directly to her lips as she approached. Michael stopped hanging up his clothes and scooped her into his arms. Doing just what he had longed to for so long.

Beatrice welcomed the heat from their first touch. She felt spirals of liquid fire course through her as his tongue dipped in sensual exploration. It seemed like a hundred years had gone by since they had been in each other's arms. Beatrice wanted to make up for all the lost time—in that very instant.

Michael caressed the skin of her back and stoked her desire. He seemed to know just which buttons to push to move her from prim and upright to definitely improper. She deepened the kiss and gloried in his taste and feel. His muscled chest begged for her hands to outline each ripple, and she obliged. Her breathing became heavier and more labored with each passionate touch of his lips. Heat seemed to rise around them, wrapping them in a warm cocoon. Bea wanted to say something . . . perhaps warn them to slow down, but she couldn't. She didn't want to slow down—she wanted nothing more than for Michael to make mad, passionate love to her through the night. "Umm . . . Michael . . . do you think that I can come all the way into the room?" Beatrice asked as she stood in the entryway of his room.

Michael stopped nibbling along the line of her jaw

long enough to pick her up and carry her to his bed. Beatrice protested. Standing was one thing, but a compromising position on his bed was another. She did not have the resolve to resist being *that* close to him. "I think we should go back to the living area to talk."

With a gleam in his eye he answered, "Why? I happen to like where we are quite a lot."

Beatrice smacked his hand as he reached to cup her breast. "I'm just so sure that you do, but I'm not prepared for that right now. I'm having a hard enough time already trying to tamp down my feelings for you. How I thought I could be alone with you in the same room and not want to jump your bones, I don't know. I guess in some ways this is going to be a long four days."

Michael recaptured her lips in a slow, hypnotic kiss before he helped her off the bed. Beatrice sighed. If he was looking for a way to make her regret her decision, he'd succeeded. As soon as they parted, her body began to cool and she missed his touch.

"Is that better?" His eyes mocked her with phony concern.

But she could tell from his body's reaction to her that she had the same effect on him as he did on her. He was just a little less vocal about it. Bea had to take some satisfaction in that knowledge. Though intellectual satisfaction was the least of her . . . desires.

She straightened up her clothes and swiped at her hair to return her appearance to some semblance of propriety. After several seconds, her breathing returned to normal. "Yes, much better. Now, are you going to behave while we are here or am I going to have to keep our interaction limited to public places? I really thought a man of your mature age would know how to control his libido . . . guess I was wrong." Bea tried to jump out of the way, but she wasn't quick enough. She erupted into uncontrollable giggles as Michael immediately picked up where he left off. His kisses were urgent, insistent and above all, sensual. The flame that flickered just below the surface erupted into a volcano of passion. He sat her down on the love seat and kissed her thoroughly.

Her attempt at decorum was reduced to a mere fleeting memory. Beatrice kissed him with abandon now, pressing her open lips to his, giving in to the passion that would not be denied. Her heart beat wildly in her chest, seeming to crash up against her rib cage.

Beatrice allowed Michael to explore her body through her clothes, careful not to let desire override common sense. She was touched by their intimacy—the sheer joy of sharing space and time with him.

They shared kisses on the couch for nearly an hour, until by mutual agreement, their kisses ended. She couldn't stand any more without being able to consummate the act. Michael's arousal had become painful without a way to release his pent-up seed. When she broke away from him, Michael helped her with her buttons and smoothed down her hair. He whispered in her ear, "How was that for a man of my 'mature age'?"

"Well, since you're fishing for compliments, that was . . . incredible. You're probably the most delectable, delightfully sexy, intelligent, wonderful man that I know."

Michael kissed the nape of her neck as he closed the last button on her blouse. "Oh, very good Ms. McCoy, you've passed with flying colors, however your *prize* will have to wait until a little later. For now, I guess we should check on the girls."

With a small measure of disappointment, Beatrice agreed. She was consoled by the fact that it would soon be time for their first formal dinner. She looked forward to the evening in excited anticipation. After one last kiss, she returned to her room.

Michael promised to meet her in half an hour. He needed time to put himself back together—in fact, to recover from Beatrice's delectable touch. He gave his body much-needed time to calm down before he attempted to get ready for the evening.

His black evening suit was ready and hanging on the valet along with a steamed and pressed white shirt, so he took the time to make a couple of phone calls. His first call was particularly important, to agent Steven Caldwell, who he'd given an extra duty . . . one he hoped Caldwell wouldn't screw up. He shook his head in amusement—good thing his agents were priceless— 'cause he didn't think he could give them away.

The next evening was the annual gingerbread ball. Beatrice wore a simple formal black gown studded with black beads. Her curvaceous size-twelve figure filled out the gown in all the right places, for which Michael was duly impressed.

He wore a tuxedo, complete with black bow tie and cummerbund. Beatrice licked her berried lips when she saw him. With his hair freshly cut and mustache expertly trimmed, he looked quite the picture of a *GQ* magazine model.

Jonnelda and Jamela watched in amusement as the couple danced close. They delighted in making comments about them until a young man came by their table.

He greeted them both warmly. "I must say that you two look absolutely ravishing tonight. You must be the best dressed ladies in the house." He extended his hand before he introduced himself. "Hello, my name is Steven and I would appreciate the honor of dancing with both of you before the end of the evening."

Jamela giggled and gave her best imitation of a very grown-up response. "I would be delighted, but I think that my sister is a better dancer, so perhaps you would enjoy her company more." Jonnelda tugged at the little girl's ear before she responded to Steven. "Forgive her, she left the manners line too quickly." She favored him with a bright smile. "I, on the other hand, would love to dance."

Steven winked and shook Jamela's hand. "Maybe next time. Before your vacation ends, I must have at least one dance."

A wide smile spread across Jamela's face again. "Sure, maybe we can dance after tomorrow's dinner."

"That would be fine. I'll see you later." He turned back to Jonnelda. "Shall we?"

Jonnelda furrowed her brow. "Are you going to be okay by yourself? If Bea and Michael don't come back soon, I'll come back to sit with you."

Beatrice looked at Michael quizzically, but said nothing aloud. Michael answered her unasked question. "Just a little added security. I'm not taking any chances."

She kissed him on the cheek. "You're a good man, Michael Spates. Now let's see how well you can cut a rug."

Michael dipped her down low in response. They were dancing and laughing like teens after awhile.

Steven made eye contact with Michael as he spun Jonnelda around in an intricate dance move. He loved dancing with her—she felt soft and silky smooth as he held her in his arms. A bit too closely, but he couldn't help himself. Jonnelda seemed to fit perfectly in his embrace.

Michael looked on with a watchful eye. *So the confirmed bachelor has a soft spot after all,* he whispered into Bea's ear and she laughed.

Steven knew it was about him, but continued to dance with his angel. The night held all the magic of gingerbread, nutcrackers, and sugarplum fairies. When Michael had first approached him about taking the assignment, he'd complained mightily. Not that having a room in a five-star resort was such a hardship, he was just used to being alone on Christmas. He'd trained himself after he lost his parents to enjoy each day like it was a holiday. December 25 became an ordinary day that he enjoyed no more or no less than the other 364 days of the year. But this would go down as something a little more special.

Steven held Jonnelda closer and inhaled the sexy scent that she wore from head to toe. A secret smile curved his lips as he enjoyed the assignment much more than he had a right to. Her cream-colored sequined dress fit her like a glove and the dangerously sexy slit on the side only proved to heighten her appeal. Steven admired her sophisticated updo as it highlighted her creamy neck. He was surprised by his instant attraction to her, especially considering who she was and why he was there. Steven tried unsuccessfully to banish his improper thoughts. . . . He wanted nothing more than to bury himself in her softness.

Jonnelda felt like Cinderella. No man had held her interest since Moses, and now this tall, sinfully sexy stranger was doing that and more.

It was nearly 1:00 A.M. when she went to collect Jamela from the children's retreat area. She'd had a dance or two with Michael early on, then, when she was bored, ran off with several other children to have some "real fun." Jamela noticed the happy expression on Jonnelda's face. She was actually humming. Jamela's curiosity got the better of her. "Who was that man you were dancing with?"

Jonnelda smiled as she ruffled Jamela's hair. "What did I tell you about getting in grown folks' business?" *He was just someone who made me feel special for a few hours.* "There's nothing much to say, besides I'm sure when we leave here I'll never see him again. He told me his job has him on the road a lot." A wide smile spread across Jonnelda's face. "He was very handsome, though, wasn't he?"

Jamela nodded her head. "Yeah, he was okay, but

boys are gross. I only like men like Mr. Michael," she announced emphatically.

Jonnelda ruffled her hair again. "All right then, Miss Priss. Let's get you in the bath and to bed. It's very late—too late for little girls to be up any longer. After I start your bathwater, go in and say good night to Mr. Michael and Miss Bea."

Jonnelda was totally distracted. The pleasantly masculine scent of her new friend Steven wafted through the air and was etched in her memory. He had a wonderful sense of humor and kept her laughing while they danced. She couldn't help but think about the *what-ifs*. She realized at that moment how lonely she was and how she longed for the comfort of a nice, stable relationship and home life. She didn't know exactly where or how Jamela fit into her plans, but she wasn't going to give up her child. Not totally. She needed to finish school and get her own place first, she understood that, but how was she going to be able to tell Jamela the truth? When should she tell her? She hoped Michael and Bea made good on their promise. So far, they had been good as gold, but she didn't want to take advantage of their generosity. *When will my luck run out?* Jonnelda pushed away the question and focused on more positive thoughts. She snuggled down deeper into her goose-down–covered bed and the smile returned to her lips. The sheets felt heavenly and after such a wonderful night she still felt as if she were living a fairy tale. Handsome Steven Caldwell fit the part of prince very nicely, she thought.

Steven waited until he watched the little girl go back to her room, then he knocked firmly on Michael's door. Spates had a knack for giving him assignments that made him stretch beyond what he thought he was capable of doing. Jonnelda Winton had him thinking and saying things that he'd vowed never to . . . again. Whenever he moved, though, he could smell her light, gentle fragrance on his tuxedo jacket. A juvenile grin curved his lips before he knocked again. He had just enough time to return to a more professional expression before Spates answered the door. Michael eyed him suspiciously and his "come in" was spoken in a gruff tone.

The song in Steven's heart stopped playing. By Spates's demeanor, he knew he had committed some infraction—and was in for it. *Again.* He exhaled slowly before he entered the room. "Hi boss, you wanted to see me?"

Chapter Fifteen

The rhythmic clank of silverware against fine china dishes filled the dining room. It was their last night at the resort and a certain air of melancholy pervaded the atmosphere. As nontraditional as it was, the dinners, dances, and laughter that they'd shared as a *family* helped them grow more at ease with each other and closer.

However, the reality of returning to normal life and the possibility that their time together might be limited loomed over them. They tried to make the best of it, and dinner was interspersed with moments of humor and levity. Mostly supplied by Jonnelda and Jamela's banter.

During their three days together, Michael and Beatrice had stolen several intimate moments to share with each other, but they had not been able to share as much time together as they would have liked. It was a situation that they both agreed to remedy—soon. Their new circumstances brought a clearer understanding of the commitment they would be making to Jamela. They couldn't be as footloose and fancy-free as before when they were single people.

During a lull in conversation, Beatrice noticed that Jonnelda couldn't keep focused for more than five seconds without scanning over the room. She watched in minor irritation as Jonnelda picked at her food and her eyes continued to circle around the room. As if she didn't know, she asked, "Jonnelda, who in God's name are you looking for?"

Jonnelda lowered her head. "I'm sorry, Bea. Am I really that obvious?"

"Yes," said Jamela, Beatrice, and Michael, emphatically.

Jonnelda raised her hands in surrender. "Okay, okay. I'll stop. I just thought that I might see him . . . that's all. Steven and I had such a nice time the other night . . . that's all."

Jamela listened to her and responded, "You said that already. I think that you must like him a lot because you keep repeating yourself and last night you were talking in your sleep." Jamela took great delight in imitating her. "Oh Steven, oh Steven, hee, hee, hee. Your eyes are so beautiful and your muscles so big!"

She shot back, "I did not." Jonnelda turned a dark shade of crimson as she tried to sink lower in her seat. "That's enough, Jamela. I'm sure it wasn't that dramatic. Can I help if it has been a long time since someone made me feel so special? He was a wonderful dance partner, but more than that, he was a true gentleman."

Michael didn't know how much more he could take and just grunted. Beatrice listened to the longing in Jonnelda's voice and gave Michael a censuring look. She knew perfectly well how the young lady felt. As much as she would caution against becoming involved with an agent, she had known Caldwell for a number of years and trusted him. After all, he had been a part of the team that saved her life. She agreed with Jonnelda about him being a gentleman, but he also had a reputation in the agency as a *serial dater*.

Beatrice wasn't sure about the age difference, but she wasn't as concerned about that as the possibility of a letdown in her feelings. It didn't appear that Caldwell was one to settle down with just one woman . . . a point, to her knowledge, that he didn't try to hide.

Beatrice was rousted from her musings by Jonnelda's sudden intake of breath. Bea followed her line of sight to tall, dark, and dashing Steven, who stood near the doorway and appeared to be searching for someone, too.

Michael simply lifted one eyebrow and watched the scene unfold with his fork midway to his mouth. Out of the corner of his eye he caught Jamela giggling, and he placed the slice of succulent aged prime rib in his mouth. Michael suspected that she thought all adults were crazy as evidenced by the behavior she had witnessed of late, but his saving grace was that she was about three years from behaving just like the rest of them. Even though he wasn't really ready to entertain the knowledge of raising a teenager. "Don't worry, Jamela, in about six years this will all make sense. And by then, I'm sure what's left of my hair will be completely white. I think you girls are trying to force me into early retirement."

Bea laughed, but in the secret places of her heart, she longed for the day when she would be worried about the boys that Jamela liked. It would mean that the ICE had allowed her to permanently take Jamela in to be a part of her family.

After a few moments in the room, Steven felt Jonnelda's gaze on his face and turned to her immediately. It took him a few minutes to navigate through the dining room to their table. He remembered the tongue-lashing he'd received the night before about using his considerable charms on Jonnelda and decided that he would simply pay his respects and move on. He would have to come up with an excuse to leave the table early. Problem was, Jonnelda took his breath away and he wanted nothing more than to twirl her around the dance floor all night. He pushed those thoughts away and managed to affect a neutral expression on his face by the time he reached the table.

Jonnelda greeted him as soon as he was close enough to her with a kiss on the cheek. "Would you care to join us?" Her voice sounded breathy and full of anticipation, which did terrible things to his ability to just walk away from her. Steven looked at Michael nervously, letting the question hang awkwardly in the air.

"Oh, where are my manners? Steven, these wonderful folks are Beatrice McCoy and Michael Spates. This is the couple that I told you I'm staying with for awhile." Jonnelda smiled. "And you met the brat the other night."

Beatrice was cordial, smiling pleasantly; however, Michael quickly shoved a piece of meat into his mouth so that he wouldn't have to respond. He simply extended his hand before he mumbled a greeting.

Jonnelda regarded him suspiciously, but continued to focus on Steven. "We're almost finished, but you are more than welcome to join us. I'll wait for you to be served and even have dessert with you if you want."

Michael couldn't help but notice Jonnelda's tone—she obviously liked Steven a lot. He felt just a twinge of guilt for laying the man out for his conduct and told him he was there to watch her, not to woo her. He caught Bea's eye and knew that she was thinking the same thing about how happy Jonnelda seemed to be—finally.

After a few more seconds of silence Michael spoke. "It seems you've made quite an impression on our Jonnelda here, so I think it would be great if you joined us. We can get to know each other better before we go back to our individual destinations and *jobs*."

Michael's emphasis on duty did not escape Steven. He sat down next to Jonnelda and was served immediately. "Thank you for allowing me to join you and intrude on

your family time. I had originally planned to spend a
quiet Christmas alone, but this is so much nicer."

Jonnelda jumped in immediately. "Oh Steven, that's
so sad. No one should be alone on Christmas."

Michael grunted again. This was why God hadn't
given him children until now. . . .

"Yes," Beatrice agreed. She ignored Michael's cold
behavior, deciding to make the best of things for Jonnelda. "This has been the nicest holiday in a very long
time for me. At the beginning of the year I would never
have guessed that I would have Michael, Jonnelda, and
Jamela in my life this way. It just goes to prove that the
Lord works in mysterious ways and will find ways to
bless you that you can't even imagine. This year has
been full of rich and wonderful surprises." She sought
his hand, squeezing it gently. "And I have to say a special thank-you to Michael for making it all happen."

Michael squeezed her hand back, enjoying the warmth
that being with her brought. He nodded his head in
agreement. "I feel so fortunate to be able to arrange this
trip. And I can raise my glass to the notion of a year full
of surprises. I never imagined spending Christmas with
these three lovely ladies."

Steven raised his glass. "In that case, I'd like to propose a toast to new beginnings full of exciting events
with special occasions to celebrate." The smile that he
directed toward Jonnelda indicated something . . . a
little more. And once he noticed the sparkle in her
eyes, he was pleased.

Everyone clanked their wineglasses to include
Jamela, who seemed to enjoy the interesting conversation and her sparkling cider with great amusement.

Sounding very grownup, she asked, "So Mr. Steven,
what brings you here to the Greenbrier? Most of the
people I see are with their families, like we are."

It was a perfectly innocent question, almost to be

expected, but not from a ten-year-old. Steven chucked her under the chin. "That is a very good question, young lady. But I think the answer will surprise you. I came here because I've always wanted to spend Christmas in the mountains, but as luck would have it, I never had enough money to do it. This year it seemed I hit the lottery, because I've been given so many unexpected opportunities, it has been so good that I was able to afford the trip this year." He looked at Jonnelda. "Imagine my surprise about meeting your—I mean, it was great to meet Jonnelda and you . . . and of course just now, Michael and Beatrice. I think they are great people for doing what they're doing."

Michael interjected, "Yes, well some things in life we do because of the job, others we do because we love it. The trick is to learn balance, so that you don't jeopardize one or the other. Beatrice and I have learned over the years that sometimes life requires *sacrifice.*"

Steven's gaze was firmly directed toward Jonnelda as he responded to Michael. "Yes, and then hope that there is the happy ending." He paused. "I guess what I've learned is to take the opportunity when I get it, so that I'm not filled with a life of regrets. I want to do what makes me happy while I'm still young enough to enjoy it."

Beatrice cleared her throat forcefully. Both men looked at her sheepishly. She continued in a firm tone. "I'd like to commend you for your take-charge attitude, but what I hope to help Jonnelda and Jamela with is distinguishing between selfish and unselfish behavior. We all have to make choices in life. Some are good ones and we can feel uplifted about them, others . . . well . . . others we have to deal with for a longer period of time." She turned to Michael again. Her hand never left his. "That's why I love Christmas, to me it is about renewal, we get to thank God for our blessings and then start the year in the right frame of mind. To me, this season always means a fresh start. With Michael, especially, I feel that. This time next year, I expect to be Mrs. Beatrice Spates."

"Oh Bea, that is so romantic," Jonnelda gushed. "Have the two of you set the date?"

Michael's expression never changed, though he was stunned by her words. "No, not yet, but soon. We still have a few things to work out. We'll let you know as soon as we know, though." No one else in the room mattered for a few brief seconds. "You are full of surprises. Does this mean, you are ready to talk seriously?"

"I've been ready. Seeing all the couples here and the families has given me new perspective. I really don't want to wait any longer than we absolutely have to— we've waited long enough."

Jonnelda turned to Steven, whispering into his ear, "Guess this means I'll be babysitting tonight."

Steven chuckled in agreement. "I'm always available to assist." Jonnelda swatted his arm. "I think you're incorrigible."

"I can't even spell that, but if it means that I'm cute and sexy, I'll take it."

"Oh, brother!" she said. Steven noticed that her Jamaican lilt became more pronounced as she relaxed.

Jamela watched Bea and Michael and Jonnelda and Steven with preteen delight. She wished that she had a girlfriend her age that she could talk to about them— Jamela had at least a couple of hours of speculation and gossip in her—and bedtime could wait.

The rest of dinner and dessert passed affably with small talk and chitchat about the activities that they had participated in, from the bridge games to the dances and the beauty and grandeur of the Greenbrier resort.

Beatrice tucked Jamela in bed, and then went to spend time with Michael. She dealt the cards for their game as they talked. "I know it wasn't easy for you, so I want to say thank you for being so gracious about tonight. Even though I'm still not so sure we did Jonnelda any favors. I think she's quite smitten with Mr. Caldwell, which makes me wonder how she will react when she finds out his true identity and that he was sent here to protect her. I appreciate him being here, even though I think he confused the term *protect* with wine, dine, and dance."

Michael hesitated, not sure if he was to respond or if this was one of those female rhetorical questions that only served to confuse men. He decided to go out on a limb. "Probably like any other woman who finds out that she has been misled. She'll be upset, but if she really likes him, she'll work it out. In the meantime, I have my own romantic interests to deal with—come here, woman. I've wanted to kiss you all night."

Beatrice moved closer to Michael as requested. "Oh yeah, probably not any more than I've wanted to kiss you."

His kiss was tender yet insistent. He held Beatrice around the waist and pulled her close to him. The card game was all but forgotten, which didn't bother him at all, considering she was up one hundred points in their gin rummy game. Beatrice smiled mischievously. "Now don't think that you're going to distract me from kicking your butt in this game. However, I might be persuaded to take a break for the right reasons."

Michael stood her up and stroked the small of her back with his hands. He ignited her skin with each touch until Beatrice's breathing came in short gasps.

He whispered, "How am I doing so far?"

"Umm . . . ahh . . . not bad . . . not bad. What other moves do you have for me?" Beatrice answered.

Michael moved his hands down her body lower to cup her firm bottom in his hands. He drew her nearer and found satisfaction in their kiss as his tongue explored her mouth and its softness. He loved the way Beatrice felt in his arms, the way her Juniper Breeze scented and softened her skin. It was all he could do to control himself . . . Bea was his everything. She fulfilled him in so many other ways than the extraordinarily wonderful physical way.

Michael broke the kiss so he could speak. "I don't want to ruin this time we have together, but I want to talk about the wedding. . . ."

Beatrice arched an eyebrow. "Why would our talking about the wedding ruin the mood? I would like to think the thought of our spending time together would only help."

"Bea, that's not how I meant that statement. I just mean as much as I would love to devour you right now, I would also like to talk about how we intend to spend the rest of our lives making love to each other in a perfectly carnal and feral manner."

A small giggle escaped from Beatrice. "My, my, you do have a way with words—I especially like the feral part. It brings to mind certain . . . ideas." Her wide grin was infectious and soon Michael found himself feeling like the teen that she inspired in him.

"What am I going to do with you, Ms. McCoy?"

"Well, first make me Mrs. Spates and then . . . hmmm, how about we practice?" She brought his face to hers and kissed him deeply. The kiss lasted until both moaned in pleasure. Michael felt the familiar stir of arousal as she moved her body against his.

Beatrice knew all his erogenous zones and how to tease them to perfection. He held her closer so that he could move his mouth along the gentle swell of her neck. He planted kisses from her neck to the deep cleavage that formed the perfectly rounded mounds of her breasts. He stroked first with his fingers, then after removing the obstacle of the fabric that covered them, his tongue found the two firm nodules. He suckled to satisfaction. . . .

The sound of Beatrice's mews of ecstasy made the sacrifice of their being apart almost bearable. But with so much to resolve he felt a twinge of guilty conscience for not telling her the truth about Jonnelda, as he knew it. He was committed to wait until after the holidays, but keeping the secret cost him. Michael made the decision that he wouldn't make love to Beatrice until everything was on the table. He needed the openness and honesty that sustained a relationship over the long haul. True, they shared a passion for each other, but love needed more than fire to survive, to his way of thinking.

Beatrice needed Michael to help her feel as if all would be well. She sought the comfort being in his arms always provided, but as she prepared herself to make love to Michael she sensed something was wrong. His kiss seemed to lose its passion as he pulled back from her. "Michael, what is it?"

Michael sat motionless for a few seconds. Her concern was unmistakable and only contributed to his feelings of guilt.

"I don't like when you hold back from me. I know something is bothering you, but I've been trying to let you work it out. Michael, don't you trust me enough to share it?"

Tension crept along his shoulders and knotted the muscles into a tight ball. This was more difficult than he'd anticipated. "Beatrice, trust has nothing to do with what I'm thinking. I know that we still have a lot of points to work out so I'm not sure that our making love again is good for our relationship right now. I know it seems like I lead you on, it's nothing like that . . . it's just that I can't right now."

"Oh God, Michael . . . do you need . . . drugs? Are you on Viagra or something?"

Michael burst into laughter. The sound was so unexpected that Beatrice jumped. "Woman, don't even use that word in my presence. No, this has nothing to do with *inability* to function. I don't like the uncertainty between us, I think we need to work some things out, get some things settled before we continue with our physical relationship. I think it just clouds the issues. And you are too important to me to let go of now—I've waited too long for you to be in my life."

Beatrice sighed. "I'm still not quite sure that I understand why you're holding out on me. How long is this to go on?"

Michael helped her dress. His sexual desire was temporarily on hold. "Beatrice, this is about our future. I want a life with you, one that can stand the tests of time."

She shook her head. "And I don't? Michael, what's going on here, and be straight with me because now you are starting to tick me off."

"I don't want to fight with you, but I think we need to take a look at where we're headed. We haven't made any hard and fast plans about anything . . . housing . . . jobs . . . We've put a few important things on hold and I don't want to continue to do that."

Beatrice looked at him plaintively. "And we can't discuss all this right now and make plans? How much do we really have to settle? We're going to fight for your job with the bureau; if it doesn't work out, you're much too young to retire, so you'll move over to DHS. As far as housing is concerned, my house is larger, so once you sell yours, we can take the profit and invest it or whatever else you want to do. Michael, how are these obstacles insurmountable?"

The heat of anger replaced the heat of passion just that quickly, but his voice was even when he addressed

her. "Beatrice, we haven't discussed or agreed to any o
those things. Apparently you've thought things through
and come up with your own conclusions—I'm sorry, bu
I don't agree with any of your plans. I need more time."

Steven left Jonnelda at her door and walked back to
his room alone. She'd looked at him expectantly, but
he managed to walk away without pulling her into a
passionate kiss. Her lips with their red lipstick were
more than just a little enticing. He'd wanted several
times to ask her to join him, but he couldn't bring himself to do it.

Steven decided that he wasn't willing to face the
wrath of Spates just to satisfy some increasingly bother-
some itch. Spending time with Jonnelda was much
more than he had bargained for . . . her sexy voice with
its slight accent did things to him that he'd rather not
admit. Just before he reached his door, his cell phone
rang. Steven checked the number then answered
before the next ring. "Caldwell."

"I can't reach the director, is everything all right?"

"Man, you're really taking this acting director duty
seriously. Yes. Things are just fine. I think he and the
ED are spending some *quality* time. Do you have any
news for us? If so, please tell me that it is good news."

Eric chuckled. "What's going on over there—don't tell
me that you can't handle a simple babysitting job? You
sound like you'd rather be anyplace else, but on this all-
inclusive trip to an expensive resort. The agent Caldwell
I know would normally love that kind of boondoggle."

Steven's response to his senior agent was dry like his
mood. "Yeah, well let's just say sometimes all that glit-
ters ain't gold. I don't like these feelings that being
around Jonnelda conjures up. I mean, I know she is
supposed to be a teenager, but I know she isn't and she

doesn't behave like one . . . and she is sexy as hell. She's really messing with me, man."

"Damn, not you, too. What is it about the women we are supposed to protect that makes us lose our heads?" Eric exhaled. "Do you want Banks to come out there to help with surveillance? If this is going to be too much, let me know now before they head home. I've had McCoy's house checked twice and everything is fine. Winton seems to have gone underground for awhile, but we aren't leaving anything to chance. When you return tomorrow, be prepared to pull guard duty outside the home. I've been working up a mission profile with Banks, McCorkle, and Wilson. We know Vanessa Winton hasn't given up yet so we want to make sure that we're ready for her."

Steven held the phone, pulled off his clothes at the same time, then he sat on the edge of his bed while he spoke. "Jonnelda and Jamela haven't been out of my sight since we left Springfield, Virginia. I haven't seen any suspicious behavior from the other guests, but then again, if she tried to strike here she would be crazy."

"Unfortunately, she has proven just how crazy she is already. Don't take anything for granted, if your gut tells you to check something then do it because lives may depend on it. Remember what I taught you in class, intuition has saved more lives than procedure." Eric paused. "Do we need to talk about Jonnelda off the record? I'm here if you need a sounding board."

Steven blew out a long breath. He wanted to take Eric up on his offer, but decided against it. He'd only known Jonnelda for three days—this was ridiculous. "Nah man, I'm cool. Besides, when this assignment is over, I'll probably never see her again. After the ass chewing I received from Spates the other day, I'm probably going to west Siberia next. I think the director thought I was enjoying myself too much," he said wryly.

Eric laughed. "Well, it may not seem like it, but if h took the time to chew you out that's a good sign. If he' wanted to punish you, another agent would have alread taken your place and you would be on gate duty in Ar chorage. Don't blow this, though—keep that legendar libido in check until everyone is safe and sound."

Steven listened patiently. "Yes, I know. I love my jol too much to jeopardize my future." A knock at his doo shortened his conversation. "Hey man, I'll check ir with you later, I think Spates is here."

Steven hurried to the door and jerked it open. It was only after Jonnelda exclaimed surprise that he remem bered that he was mostly undressed. He quickly slammed the door in her face. "Jonnelda, give me two seconds."

It was very quiet outside his door until he heard her burst into laughter. Steven hurried to put on his shirt when he stubbed his toe. Jonnelda could hear his yelp in pain through the closed door.

When he answered the door, sweat beaded around his face and his appearance was a lot less smooth than it was when she'd seen him earlier. He spoke as if nothing untoward had happened. "Come in Jonnelda, what brings you here at this hour?"

Jonnelda's mouth went completely dry. She had been ready to make some snappy remark about him being clumsy, but he took care of that idea the moment he stood before her with bare, rippled muscles. It was a full minute before she remembered to breathe; she felt light-headed. She had absolutely no idea why she was there . . . at the moment . . . she didn't know anything.

Steven dipped his head low to capture her mouth in an all-consuming kiss. Jonnelda stroked the corded muscles of his back while his tongue dipped deeper, mating with her own. Soon enough the only thing she *knew* was that she couldn't get enough of him.

Pleasure and conflict warred within him; Steven broke

the kiss after his sense of duty prevailed. This was not what he was sent here to do. Warning bells rang loud and clear . . . but damn, she felt good. Soft, warm, and she smelled divine. Steven pushed her away abruptly.

Jonnelda's doe eyes widened in surprise. "Did I do something wrong?" Hurt quaked in her voice.

Steven grumbled that he should kick himself for being so stupid. Several silent moments ticked on the clock. Struggling for control, his breathing came in uneven gasps. He held her in his arms again, resting his head against hers. "Jonnelda, Lord knows I want nothing more than to take you to my bed and love you through the night, but I can't. It wouldn't be right. There are too many things . . . too much has to be settled."

"Steven, what in the world are you talking about? Is it me? Did I do something wrong?" Confusion gave way to frustration. "Are you secretly married or is some- thing . . . else the matter?"

"No, no. It's not you—it's me. It's complicated, I mean, my job takes me away a lot and I don't want to start something with you and then have to move on at a moment's notice. I don't think Bea and Michael would approve of us having a one-night stand, not that I'd ever consider doing that with you. I'm attracted to you, Jonnelda. . . . I don't want us to get started on the wrong foot—maybe we should just slow down. We need to think about what we're doing."

"What's there to think about? Steven, I haven't been able to get you off my mind since we first met. I'm very capable of deciding when and where I want to give my body to someone. So unless there is a medical reason for you not to make love to me, I want you to kiss me right now."

"Now is not the time Jonnelda, though I'd love to, I swear. Spates would kill me and after he finished,

McCoy would again. After things settle down, I promise I'll call you."

Jonnelda sat on the edge of the bed, eyeing him warily. She breathed out a long sigh of disappointment. "So . . . you work for them." Her tone was flat, devoid of emotion. "So what am I? Your assignment—*your* babysitting job?" Her chest heaved in fury. "What the hell is wrong with you people?"

She paused. With frightening clarity another thought came to her. Her shoulders slunk down in defeat. "Do your feelings have anything to do with Kharl? How much do you know about our . . . relationship?"

Steven held her face gently in his hands. "Jonnelda, trust me, this has nothing to do with that kind of thinking. Personal relationships jeopardize lives, especially in open cases. It just wouldn't be very smart of me or very ethical to engage in a relationship with you at this time. I have a responsibility to my unit to see this thing through. Like McCoy said, sometimes you have to weigh your selfish wants versus unselfish needs. Let's just get through this and then . . . when things settle down, we can talk." He stroked her shoulders, caressing her silky skin until she leaned in for more of his touch. "And then we can do more of this." He kissed her deeply, making her forget any feelings of uncertainty.

Jonnelda moaned in desire, but broke the kiss as soon as she was physically able. "What does your report say about my past?"

Steven moved back to study her face. He wanted to be honest with her, but he wouldn't betray his duty. He avoided a direct answer by searching for and putting on his shirt. When he returned to sit next to her on the bed, his demeanor had completely changed.

* * *

"Dammit Michael, time for what?" Their battle raged on with no apparent compromise in sight. "We've already waited long enough. Yes, I know it was my fault, I didn't want to take a chance on us, but I'm there now. I realize how much I want to be with you, how much I would welcome becoming your wife. Is this some sort of twisted punishment for taking so long?"

"Tell me that's not what you think. If you do, then we have no relationship! To use your eloquent phrasing, dammit Beatrice, if you think so little of me, then why are we even here? Has the thought even occurred to you that maybe I don't want to sleep in the same house, the room, and the same bed that you shared with Harold?" His breathing came in short, angry puffs. "What kind of man do you take me for? I'm not one of the underlings . . . we either make joint decisions or we don't make any at all." Michael paced the room— stunned by the words she'd just spoken. It boggled his mind that someone he loved with his whole heart could also make his blood boil.

A deathly calm cloaked the room.

Beatrice closed her eyes, as a tension headache toiled behind them. The pain successfully drowned out all the happiness she'd felt in Michael's presence over the last few days. *How had everything turned to crap in so few minutes?* She opened them again, determined to settle this once and for all. Michael had one shot to make it right, otherwise she decided that she would throw in the towel. "Why, Michael? Why did you hide the way you felt? How was I to know—some damn Vulcan mind-meld? That wasn't fair and you know it—I deserved better than this from you."

The expression in her eyes worried him. Michael had never seen her so hurt and hated that he was the cause. He rubbed his hands through his hair again. "Beatrice," he started slowly, "I never meant to hurt you. I thought it best to give us some time to get on one accord. I don't want to force things between us . . . our decisions should be made jointly. Bea, I'm just trying to learn how to think of someone else's needs over my own. I'm not good at this relationship thing—it's still too new." He held her gaze, seeking to reduce the animus that existed between them. "What do you want me to say? I can apologize, but the facts remain the same, we're going to have to look at some serious issues before we can set a date."

Her eyes squinted, and her heart rate increased again. Somehow, she resisted the urge to shake her finger at him—she was so mad. "Set a date, a date for what? I agree we need to work some of our problems out, but right now I don't know if I can trust you."

"Beatrice, I would give my life for you, how can you say that you question trust in me?"

She paced the room, leaving the question unanswered in the air. "I need to think . . . you've given me a lot to reevaluate in the last few minutes. Maybe we should leave well enough alone—give each other some breathing room."

Michael sat down in the chair in front of the desk. "I'm not going to give up on us, Beatrice. I love you too much to throw in the towel because we've hit a bump."

Tears shone bright in her eyes when she responded. "That's what makes this so difficult. I love you, too. I wanted things to be different between us . . . wanted this relationship to be better than anything else that either one of us has experienced. But I'm feeling . . . hell . . . I don't know what I'm feeling. It just seems that the moment I let my guard down, really let you in, I meet disappointment instead of bliss."

Michael shook his head in disagreement. "Beatrice, that's a bit melodramatic, don't you think? I mean, we have questions to answer and a few things to settle. The relationship is not lost. We can have bliss, but let's be honest—every relationship has its problems. I'll leave you alone for now, but not before we agree on another time when we'll talk."

The comment about melodrama stung, but she wasn't going to nitpick, she would agree. "Breakfast at seven A.M.?"

Michael blew out a long, ragged breath of relief. "Yes. I'll meet you downstairs."

Bea's voice softened. "No, let's meet here in your room. We need private time."

"Yes, we do." He reached for her, his embrace was tender, indicating his heartfelt feelings. "I'll walk you to your room."

Beatrice checked on Jamela, who she was relieved to see was sound asleep in her bed. Jonnelda was nowhere to be found, but she wasn't too worried about her. She suspected the young lady was under the watchful eye of Agent Steven Caldwell anyway.

It had been a long day that turned into an even longer night. Beatrice walked into her private bathroom, gathered her personal shower items along with her robe and towel and then entered the glass-enclosed stall. The steam rose almost immediately, sending feelings of relaxation surging through her body, for the first time in a few hours.

The fragrance of her Juniper Breeze filled the small space, but unfortunately instead of it providing the calming effect she sought . . . there were reminders of the first time she and Michael spent in West Virginia. Desire coursed through her as a moan of frustration passed through her lips. *Why did Michael have to be so stubborn? And dammit, why did he have to be right?* "How could you have been so blind to his feelings? And so darned sure of yourself?"

After her shower, she rubbed lotion all over her body and lay down in her bed to rest. Sleep wouldn't come easy, not that she was expecting it to anyway, so she took out a tablet to help her process what was going on between the two of them. She placed her thoughts and feelings into columns, the things she'd expected, and then what she thought might be on Michael's mind. They needed to use their time during breakfast to come to an understanding . . . one based on mutual respect and consideration.

Beatrice spent the majority of the night thinking about her feelings. Despite her not liking the fact, there was a lot of truth to what Michael said to her earlier. She was angry for him doing it to her, but she was just as guilty of discounting his feelings. She spent the last few weeks making assumptions about his thoughts . . . his desires, without considering the possibility that she may not understand him completely. Yes, they'd known each other for several years, but they hadn't been in a romantic relationship during that time.

They still had much to discover about each other. It settled in her spirit that maybe rushing the wedding wasn't such a good idea. More than anything, she wanted to share the rest of her life with him . . . but at what cost? Bea knew that she wanted to be Mrs. Michael Spates just as sure as she wanted to take her next breath, but she couldn't let haste result in the destruction of the relationship. She'd come too far . . . no, they'd come too far together to give up now.

Groaning, Beatrice glanced at the clock on the nightstand. She would have bags under her eyes in the morning, but she was satisfied with what she'd come up with on the paper. Her late-night cramming session was worth it. She blew out a long sigh after she finished.

"Your entire life on a sheet of paper. This is pretty sad girl," she said quietly.

It wasn't for naught though, her 'list' would help give them a starting point when they talked, and it also served to give her thoughts more clarity. Something she'd taken for granted almost the entire time she'd known Michael. Beatrice thought she'd had all the answers once she told him that she loved him and he returned the sentiment. *Guess life is more than love . . .*

She had no idea why Michael had put up with her for as long as he did, so she determined that hereafter, she would make a much better effort in their relationship. Beatrice shoved everything to the other side of her bed, turned off the night-light and said her prayers. Tomorrow's breakfast would be spent eating a great deal of crow.

Chapter Sixteen

Beatrice met Michael in his room in the morning. Her hands shook with nervous energy as she knocked on the door. How would Michael react to her? Would he still be upset with her? Question her love and devotion?

Beatrice had spent the night alternating between confidence and confusion. One moment she was sure of him and the sanctity of their love, the next she didn't know if he would throw her out of his room. It was a schizophrenic time, worse than any teen dating angst she'd felt thirty years prior. However, as soon as he opened the door, she realized that she needn't have worried. True to his nature, Michael had taken care of everything.

The smell of fresh biscuits, bacon, and eggs awaited her as she walked in, which caused a wide smile to spread across her face. If he had ordered the scrumptious meal to ease her mind, it worked. She walked straight up to him, planting a small kiss on his mouth. It felt deliciously comfortable to be in his arms again, if only for a few brief minutes.

Desire smoldered just beneath the surface when he responded to her. "That's a mighty fine way to begin a morning," Michael said in an easy southern drawl.

"You just keep doing what you do and that can be

arranged," she answered in kind. She sat down at the table, then began. "I've had some time to think about my behavior and my views. I hate to admit this, but maybe I took too much for granted. Michael, I never meant to discount you or make you feel like you had to bend to my will—that was never even a part of my thinking. I guess because I'm so used to planning things and having to think of the big picture, I assumed, incorrectly, that I needed to do it again and that you would automatically agree."

Michael poured orange juice into a glass, then handed it to her. "I've dealt with my behavior, too. I was too hard on you and that wasn't fair; yes, I should have come to you with what I was thinking. I guess in some ways, I was willing to bite my tongue because I didn't want to risk pushing you away. I can't imagine my life anymore without you in it." He took a sip of his coffee. "To that end, I've been thinking about the job, our life, and us almost nonstop." His eyes never left hers. "Bea, I don't think that I can go to DHS if the bureau pulls the plug on the Special Corruption Unit. You know that I like our arrangement, but what we have is more than professional. You're the reason that I get up every day to do this job. No, I'm not saying that I'm not dedicated to the bureau and to my agents, but frankly, if it all went away I know I would be just fine. If I lose you, I can't make that same promise." He paused to let his words sink in.

"I don't want to work for anyone else—so unless my outlook changes drastically, I think this may be it for me. If the SCU goes down . . . like any good captain, I'm going to have to go down with my ship. I have enough money saved and despite the market, I've got a good portfolio, so I'm willing to take a few months off to decide what I want to do. In that time, though, I'd like to work on us and really make some clear decisions."

Bea nodded in understanding. "Michael, I meant

what I said during the toast. This is a time of new beginnings . . . it's our opportunity."

"You should probably eat your breakfast before it gets cold."

Beatrice sighed. "Yes, Michael, I should, and believe it or not I'm quite capable of making that decision." Bea felt the pressure of tension making her head throb. "Michael, I know that you mean well, but you've got to let me be my own person. One of the few things about you that makes me crazy is that you are so overprotective. I understand that you love me, but it doesn't mean that you can always make things right for me. At the compound you were willing to sacrifice your life for me and I had to fight to get you to understand that we could do it together. Maybe that's why I felt like I had to come up with the perfect plan for us—if I didn't, I knew you would."

Michael spread strawberry jam on his biscuit, then chewed slowly. He said, "I don't know how else to behave with you. I would protect you at all costs, and I'm sorry that you feel you have to fight with me. It's certainly not by design. I just look at you and realize how special every moment with you is—I always want it to be perfect. . . ." His voice trailed off as he took another bite. In a contrite tone he continued after a few seconds of silence. "I know that I'm asking for too much. Perfection in a relationship is *not* killing each other, I suppose. I don't know how to do anything else, but just be me. What do you think, can we work out our problems?"

"Yes, I know we can." Beatrice swallowed the last of her bacon, then took the list that she'd written out of the pocket of her slacks. She smiled at Michael's groan of understanding. "Don't you dare look so disagreeable. You know this is what I do. It's another list—get used to it. Actually, it is more than that; I wanted to make sure that we talked about as many issues and problems as we could remember. So, to help facilitate that, I've written down a list of my assumptions. After I'm done, feel free to dispute any and all. Maybe we can come to some common ground after we put everything on the table."

Michael chuckled. "Yes, ma'am."

Beatrice pursed her lips together. "Michael, you know I don't mean it like that!"

He held up his hands in acquiescence. "Yes, yes, I know, please go ahead."

Beatrice sighed in mock exaggeration. "Anyway, I've written down as my primary assumption that I thought you were going to move in with me. I see how illogical that is now and I'm prepared to . . . put the house on the market. It's going to be a big step for me, but it's one that I need to make. And after careful consideration, it is something that I should have done a long time ago. I'm going to need your support, though. I don't think that I can do this alone, the house has been a part of my life for over twenty-five years."

Michael enclosed her hand in his. "Beatrice, just let me know what you need and I'll be there for you."

She looked down at the paper before her emotions got the best of her. Crying on his shoulder didn't exactly meet the qualifications for a productive discussion. "Okay, the other assumption I had was about the job. You've expressed some ambivalence about it, but knowing you, I never thought that you could walk away, especially considering this has been the only life you've ever known. Not that you aren't extremely capable of doing whatever you want to in life, but what else would you like to do? The SCU is in your blood, just like it has been in our other agents."

Michael shrugged. "I don't know . . . I mean, my hope is that the director will recommend that we stay as a part of the Special Programs Branch, but if the SCU has to go, I can't go with it to Homeland Security. I'm not afraid to step out on my own. I've been talking to Peter regularly and I really think that I could take my security expertise elsewhere. There are lots of hot spots around the globe that could benefit from my skills and knowledge."

Beatrice nearly choked on her juice. "Are you suggesting that you would leave the country? What about us, do I get a say in any of this?"

"Of course you do, I'm just throwing out ideas. I'm not ready to put myself out to pasture. I've got too much living to do. . . . I'm just thinking aloud about my areas of interest.

"You know, if you're going to keep getting excited like that, you're going to need blood pressure medication." A mischievous smile turned up the corners of his mouth. "At your age, you've got to be more careful."

"Why you"—she threw her napkin at him before she stood up. She was laughing as she did, though, and some of the tension she felt decreased as soon as she realized she was wound up too tightly. "Okay, okay. I'll calm down, besides I've got plenty more on my list anyway."

Michael stood as well; he took her in his arms and held her tight. He just needed the comfort and strength of her touch before they continued. They would be together, he resolved, he had no doubt in his mind.

After he released her he said, "All right then, lay it on me, what's next?"

"Well," she said, "there's what to do about Jamela. I need to find out about her parents and her other family before I allow myself to get deeper into this, emotionally. But as far as we're concerned, where do you stand?"

"Bea, at my age, children of my own are no longer an option." He exhaled slowly. "I love Jamela, though, and I'm perfectly willing for us to raise her as our own."

A stab of guilt almost caused him to come clean about the information he'd decided to hold onto. He willed his body not to react, but his mouth felt dry. He wanted to tell her about Jonnelda, but this wasn't the right time, they didn't need to derail their talk. They needed to focus on each other.

Beatrice put the paper down and clasped her hands together. "Oh Michael, I am so relieved to hear you say that. I've been so nervous about her . . . about you . . . I didn't want to be wrong about your feelings for her, because she's so important to me."

Michael forced a smile onto his face. "Yes, I know. She's a special little girl and I know we'll do right by her. So what else do you have for me? So far, we're doing much better than I'd expected."

"I guess next would be the SAMs of any good relationship."

He furrowed his brow. "Hmmm . . . surface-to-air missiles?"

Beatrice chuckled. "Not quite, but just as deadly to a relationship. "Sex, alcohol, and money. Sex, I think we have covered. We've both proven that we can wait for each other . . . celibacy and faithfulness shouldn't be an issue."

This time Michael fortified himself with a long sip of black coffee. "I'm glad you brought that up. . . . I think if we are going to be a good example to Jonnelda and Jamela, we need to wait to make love again until we are married and under our own roof." He hesitated to gauge her reaction. "I've been giving it a lot of thought—yeah, a lot of painful thought, but I think this is right. I've been footloose and fancy-free for all of my adult life, so this is definitely a different way of looking at my life. You don't think that I'm going overboard, do you?"

Beatrice smirked. "I'm thinking that wherever we are for the honeymoon, the headboard will need reinforcements. Are you sure about this? I mean, we haven't even set the date yet."

Michael sucked in a mouthful of air, then released it

slowly. "I know . . . I may have to accost the first justice of the peace that I see . . . unless you were looking for a big wedding?"

Beatrice took her hand in his, brushing her lips lightly along the knuckles. "No, I don't want a big wedding at all. I just need you and whoever the magistrate will need to make it legal. As a matter of fact, I'd like to do it with as little fanfare as possible. Just becoming your wife is enough for me."

"That's umm . . . that's very nice." He moaned. "But ah, very distracting."

Beatrice giggled. "Sorry, I was just trying to drive the point home."

"Yeah, well . . . it's home." He paused thoughtfully before asking, "So when do we get married?"

Beatrice took pity on him so that they could continue their conversation. "To answer your first question, no, I don't think that you're going overboard. I do think we have a greater responsibility to the girls to be above reproach. Especially with Jonnelda's growing interest in Steven. Also, I know a lot more went on at that compound than she is willing to admit. I think Kharl may have forced her into prostitution. After we get back, I want to dig into her past a bit deeper. There are some unsettling issues there that I just haven't taken the time to get a handle on."

Michael remained silent, which Beatrice didn't seem to notice because she moved on with her thoughts. Beatrice smiled. "As far as our date is concerned, I suppose we need to look at a calendar. I'm ready right now, but there are things that we should settle first. I need to get back into the office. I feel like I've been away too long—we're going to have to set up an operation to find Russell's killers."

For Michael, talking about Russell also brought up unpleasant thoughts of Vanessa Winton. He steered the conversation back to them. "Work we can talk about later. Now, as for alcohol, that's not an issue, I'm purely a social drinker with no plans to pursue alcoholism—I drink just what you've seen me do in the past, a little Amaretto, a little German beer now and again and I'm fine." His voice was even, with no hint of arrogance as he continued. "As for money, I'm loaded due to some sound investments. I can more than adequately provide for us whether or not the SCU is in my life.

"Incidentally, I think as soon as we get settled another task I should take on is to secure an investment fund for Jamela's college tuition. It's probably a little late in the game for an education IRA, but I'll do it anyway as well as set up a trust for her with some T-bills and savings bonds. That little girl's had enough adversity in her life—I think the least we can do is make the path as smooth as we can for her before she goes to school. She's such a joy to watch—I'm expecting great things from her."

Beatrice marveled at the pride she heard in his voice. Michael was always so sure of himself—despite what he'd said about not knowing what to do. There was a contradiction in his actions . . . Michael seemed to know exactly what to do and when. Taking his hands in her own again, she said, "Michael, what am I going to do with you? You're my everything."

"I'd say that makes me a very lucky man. So, are there any other burning issues? Because if not . . ." He wanted to take her into his arms. "I have a few kisses to make up for from last night."

Beatrice moved from her seat at the table to sit on his lap. Michael caressed her back while he captured her lips in a deep, passionate kiss. He reveled in her feel, questioning why in the world he chose to deny himself the benefit of her passion. Michael groaned, as much from the wonderful way that she felt in his arms as from the fact that kissing was as close as he would get to her for a while.

He broke the kiss abruptly. "Okay, get on out of here, before you make me go back on my word."

She agreed that being this close was dangerous. "All right, I'll meet you downstairs in the lobby after I get the girls together. I can't believe that this is our last day here. Sweetheart, thank you for everything, I mean that; what you did by booking this trip for us went above and beyond."

"You don't have to thank me, but I'll just say simply that you're welcome. I'd do anything for you."

And he meant it, too . . . including keeping the knowledge of Jamela's true parentage from Beatrice until after their return. A decision he prayed that he wouldn't regret.

Jonnelda knocked lightly on the door to Beatrice's bedroom. She walked in slowly after Bea invited her in the room. "Hi Beatrice, there's something that I need to talk with you about if you have a minute or two." *Or a lifetime* . . .

"That sounds ominous, but we need to get ready, can it wait until we get back home?" Beatrice looked up, but continued to stuff her luggage. She needed to finish quickly. "I promise, I'll give you all the time you need, but a storm is headed this way. If we leave now, we'll make it back home in good weather." Bea wasn't especially superstitious, but she wouldn't tempt fate, either— one snowstorm in West Virginia was enough for her.

Jonnelda sighed. "Yeah, sure, it can wait. I'll make sure Jamela has everything and meet you in the lobby. I've already said good-bye to Steven, so we'll be ready in a jiffy."

"Thanks, I promise you, we'll sit down soon." Beatrice placed her Greenbrier chocolates in a separate bag or safekeeping, but continued to address Jonnelda. "I think our talk is long overdue. I'm sorry that I've been so caught up in my own stuff, but I promise I'll make it up to you after we return. I want you to know regardless of your past, I do consider you a part of my family." An awareness of their odd situation dawned on her and made her think twice about the way she treated Jonnelda. They shared familiarity without true depth in their relationship. Bea resolved do a better job of finding out more about Jonnelda and her life. She hoped that Jonnelda trusted her enough to share information about her life's journeys. Her life in Jamaica and with Kharl couldn't have been easy. Although with the way she carried herself now, no one would know.

Beatrice stopped packing while she talked, turned to Jonnelda, then stretched out her arms. Jonnelda came to her and hugged her tight. "Thank you, that means a lot to me," the younger woman responded.

Bright tears shone in her eyes, but she ignored the emotion that welled up in her. She left Bea's room abruptly before she blurted out the whole truth of her life as a Winton.

Bea watched her go and shook her head. "Steven Caldwell is the source of that behavior, I bet. Oh, to be young and in love." Bea made a note to call Caldwell into her office when she returned. Then she laughed at herself, what advice could she give him? She and Michael were in no better shape. . . .

The short trip back to northern Virginia was uneventful, the weather remained cold, yet sunny and under Michael's expert driving, they made it back in good time. White Sulphur Springs had been nothing short of magical. They had shared a wonderful Christmas after all, one that brought with it the promise for a wonderful new year.

In fact, the return to the real world held somewhat less appeal after being wined and dined and living the life of the rich and famous.

The closer they pulled to her street, the more tense energy jumbled her nerves. She was relieved to see agents patrolling the area, though now that she was back, they would turn security back over to the local police department.

Beatrice had had mixed feelings about going back to her house . . . she really didn't want to spend any more time away from Michael. She also didn't want to become a target again.

Michael squeezed her hand as he parked in her driveway. Apparently he felt the same way. "Would it be too obtrusive for me to stay here tonight? On the couch, of course—I would just feel better if I were here for you while we make other arrangements."

Beatrice blew out a sigh of relief. "Yes, that's fine. As a matter of fact, I was going to ask. I know I'm being silly, but I'm just not sure that I want to be here without you."

Michael stroked the side of her face, with the pad of his thumb. "You don't have to be—not tonight or ever." Beatrice's timid smile was all the reassurance that he needed. "Give me some time to talk with the agents on guard detail and then run home for a minute. I'll be back later on tonight."

Michael drove home thinking about all the things and decisions that plagued him . . . he hadn't been totally honest with Beatrice and while it troubled him, he had to have faith that it would work out in the end. He hoped that she trusted him enough to understand his reasons. Until Vanessa was apprehended there wasn't much the knowledge that Jonnelda was Jamela's mother would do

or her—on the contrary, it would just make a mess of
ssues already confronting them.

Michael wanted to pace, probably not a wise idea while
he drove, however. It almost seemed as if things were simpler before the trip to West Virginia. Well, simpler maybe,
but definitely not better. He blew out a long breath. Beatrice loved him . . . and that's all that mattered.

Michael entered his small house, dropped his bags,
and proceeded immediately to his home office. One of
the first calls he made was to his number-two man, Eric
Duvernay. His four days out of the office had felt significantly longer. He checked his fax machine and computer for any news of Vanessa Winton and her clan.
Eric had promised to contact him in case anything
seemed out of place; however, the patrols turned up
nothing out of the ordinary and Eric had personally
checked on Bea's house while they were away.

After reading the reports, Michael thought with grim
determination, that just like her brother, Vanessa would
have to be eliminated before she was allowed to endanger Beatrice again.

Chapter Seventeen

Jonnelda sat up in her bed; her heart pumped blood through her veins so fast, she thought it would explode in her chest. She looked around the room wildly, someone had been in there, she could tell. Her instinct told her that something was very wrong—she just didn't know what. Jonnelda sniffed the air for fire and strained her ears to listen for strange sounds. Her next thought was to check on Jamela.

A hand clamped down on her mouth before she could take her first step out of the bed. She whiffed at the air with outstretched hands trying to find a way to escape. Her hands didn't connect with anything, however, and fear took over after a few seconds. Her attacker said nothing, just dragged her to the floor where she was gagged and bound. Jonnelda couldn't see anything in the jet-black darkness. The street lamps, which normally cast a golden glow down the block, seemed to be extinguished. Her attacker never said a word, but there was something familiar about his frame and scent. Jonnelda knew instinctively that the attack had to do with the Wintons—they wouldn't rest until Kharl's death was avenged. It wasn't their style to let things slide. They would respond somehow.

Struggling against the ropes that bound her wrists, Jonnelda scooted her body close to the dresser in the room. She had a pair of scissors, which she might be able to use, if she could just reach them before whoever was in the house came back.

She had been left alone in her room to wonder madly what was happening in the rest of the house. She prayed Beatrice and Michael were safe and knew that something was wrong so they'd have a chance to get Pamela to safety. Jonnelda didn't care about her own life as long as her child was safe.

At two A.M. Steven had decided to give up his quest to find sleep. Something in his gut told him to move. He dressed quickly, called Spates on his cell phone, and made the short drive to McCoy's house. He passed by the house to throw off suspicion, yet knew immediately that something wasn't right. Steven parked a few blocks away then doubled back. He had to hand it to her—Vanessa Winton was thorough. She had men in various places to cut off potential escape routes. Obviously, the woman meant business.

"Duvernay, I'm here at McCoy's house, something is going on. I think Winton is making a play tonight. So far, I count six men watching the property. I just pulled up, though, and since I can't see anything inside I can't afford to wait. Get here as quickly as you can."

He snapped closed his flip phone, then Agent Caldwell looked for the most unobtrusive way to enter the house. In just a few seconds, he came face-to-face with one of Vanessa's men. The man raised his radio to signal that they had company, but his finger never depressed the button. With lightning speed, Steven grabbed his arm, twisted it until he broke it, then with his elbow silenced the man with a sharp blow to the neck that crushed his

windpipe. He moved him into a hallway closet, then wer
to check on everyone else's status. Steven wasn't familia
with the layout of Beatrice's house so had to feel his wa
slowly through halls and doorways. If there were six me
outside, he had to assume there were at least that man
inside. Spates and McCoy would be equipped to take
them on—a shudder passed through him—if they hadn'
been captured. He stopped outside one of the smalle
bedrooms . . . he heard muffled sounds coming from the
other side of the walls.

He entered the room with his weapon drawn. Jon
nelda lay in wait and nearly took his eye out with a pair of
scissors. Only his quick reflexes prevented the socket
from being gauged out. Once she realized it was him she
slumped into his arms from sheer relief. Steven smiled,
but embraced her just the same. This was no time for
jokes, but he couldn't resist saying, "If I had known it was
only you, I would have announced my presence."

A ragged whisper sounded from the entryway. "Come
on, Casanova, we've got work to do. On my way in, I
took out two of Winton's men. Things will get hairy in
a few minutes once they realize that the men aren't
checking in on time."

Caldwell glanced in his direction. "Agent Duvernay, good of you to join us. Have you seen McCoy
and Spates?"

"Nah, you two are the first *friendlies* that I've run in
to. Now would be a good time to come up with a plan,
though." He smiled toward Jonnelda. "Jonnelda, it's
nice to see you again, although a few less middle-of-the-
night soirees would be nicer."

Jonnelda spoke up. "We need to find them and Jamela,
too. Can we get a move on?" Her tone was harsher than
intended due to her level of anxiety. Caldwell and Duvernay nodded, then proceeded out the door.

Michael had Jamela curl her small frame into a ball

eep inside Beatrice's walk-in closet. He turned back to
eatrice to see if she was all right; after one look in her
etermined eyes he didn't even bother to ask her not
) come. . . .

There was movement outside her bedroom door.
'hey watched, listened, and waited.

In a harsh whisper Vanessa admonished Delroy. "I
vant those agents and my niece delivered to me in the
iext five seconds." He couldn't see her expression but
ier tone told the story. "Your life depends on it."

The man nodded his head in understanding. Earlier,
he'd searched in the inky black of the night to no avail.
Delroy had reached her bedroom seconds too late because Michael had heard the noises outside and
jumped into action. He slipped into Beatrice's first-
story window in enough time for them to hide Jamela
and then themselves. Thankfully, Delroy had just made
a cursory search and hadn't detected them.

With no special patrol tonight, Beatrice had been left
vulnerable. The police patrolled the area, but after a
major disturbance a few blocks away, the house had
been left alone. Beatrice, Jonnelda, and Jamela had
gone to bed under the assumption that they were
secure. Bea knew that Michael would return after
having some personal time and had simply set her
alarm before retiring to her room.

Bea settled down into an exhausted sleep minutes
after her head hit the pillow. However, an hour later,
she was awakened by a noise in her bedroom that
nearly had her jumping out of her skin. The sight of a
figure crawling through her window was more than a
little disturbing until she realized that it was Michael.
She didn't even want to know how he'd bypassed the
motion sensors and security tabs on her windows. Once

he'd made his identity known, she knew there was re
trouble. She gathered Jamela, whose room was close
to hers, then hid her the best that she could.

Once again she and Michael played both the hunte
and the hunter. Beatrice unlocked the safety on he
gun, which she always left in her nightstand drawer. I
made her nervous to still have the weapon with Jamel.
in the house, but right now she was very grateful for i

Beatrice heard a noise and moved to the left. Michae
hadn't heard it and continued moving forward in the
house. Bea crept along the wall until she heard a chil
ing voice behind her. "Looking for me?"

Bea whipped around to face Vanessa Winton. "Wha
the hell are you doing in my house?"

"I'm here to take care of business, of course. Did you
really think that you could kill my brother, then shelter
my good-for-nothing sister-in-law and her worthless
daughter? No! As far as I'm concerned they are no
longer family and will be dealt with as I see fit, but you
. . . you *are* mine."

The words attacked Beatrice's feelings, as if a physical blow. Her sister-in-law and niece? Nothing she said
made sense. Beatrice's wide-eyed shock was enough to
tell Vanessa that she knew nothing about the relationship, so she dug deeper.

"You know, your INS or whatever you call those
people ought to do a better job of finding people. Jonnelda and Jamela Winton should have been returned
to my home in Jamaica immediately." With a tone of
distinct arrogance she continued. "I didn't really understand the problem until I heard about your interfer-
ence. Imagine my displeasure after I learned that my
niece was sleeping under the roof of the enemy. Kharl
was probably rolling over in his grave when that happened. And poor Moses, he probably did a double flip
in his grave knowing that his supposedly devoted widow

was cavorting with the devil and taking his child along. I came to rectify this unacceptable situation. But before you die, I want to know why you killed my brother. Kharl was the light of the Winton family and you destroyed him and everything that he gave to us."

Beatrice found her voice. "If he was the light, you all must have been stumbling around in the dark. Kharl Winton was a gutless thug and I'm sure anything he *gave* was paid for a hundred times over. Jonnelda and Jamela were looking for a way to escape the life you Wintons provided, so don't think they had any problem sleeping under my roof where they knew they would be taken care of without anything in return except love and respect. I think you confuse control with love—Vanessa."

With a wry laugh, she took a step back. Vanessa raised her gun to fire, but the need for self-preservation propelled Beatrice into faster motion. Buoyed by the adrenaline that surged through her, she hit Vanessa's arm with enough force to knock the weapon out of her hand. Vanessa fought back and though she was a woman of medium build, she was also a street fighter. She grabbed Beatrice by the neck to try to squeeze the life out of her. Beatrice struggled for air, waving her hands around in a desperate attempt to grab onto something of Vanessa's. She struggled until she felt the viselike grip weaken for just a few seconds.

A strong kick to Vanessa's leg secured her release and allowed Beatrice to get the upper hand. A hard punch to the body knocked Vanessa down to the hardwood floor. Bea became keenly aware that she didn't want company from the rest of Winton's men. In very unladylike fashion she drew back her fist to hit Vanessa in the jaw—her eyes widened in shock, before Beatrice's fist skirted across the bottom of her jawline and knocked her into oblivion. "Ow, ow, ow." Bea waved her hand furiously from the pain. She was surprised on

some level that she had been able to do it, but very glad
that it had worked. With Vanessa taken care of, at least
temporarily, she went in search of Michael. Despite her
satisfaction that Vanessa was lying on the floor, she
needed to understand what was going on with Jonnelda
and Jamela. The news was disturbing, to say the least.

Michael watched the man's back as he moved forward in Beatrice's room. He couldn't let him get to
Jamela. He felt as if he were in a bizarre amusement
park haunted house, skulking around in the darkness
looking for the bogeyman.

He and Beatrice had become separated, but once he
spotted the Winton henchman, he had to pursue him—
he would find Bea as soon as he was finished. "Put your
hands in the air where I can see them."

Delroy turned around, surprised that he hadn't heard
Michael come up behind him. "Agent Spates." The
words were uttered with some familiarity. "I think you'll
find that you're the one who should raise your hands."

Michael heard a gun cock behind him. *Damn!* Concern for Jamela's safety made him want to move the fight
out of that particular room. "Glad to see that Vanessa is
prepared, we'll have to assume she had the brains in the
family—unlike her brother Kharl. Where is she anyway?
I want to talk to her."

Delroy flashed white teeth in the darkness. "Sorry
boss, I have specific instructions to kill you. I guess you
could say, she ain't taking your calls."

The man behind Michael cleared his throat. He knew
that despite Delroy's claims, Vanessa's instructions were
to have Michael, Beatrice, Jamela, and Jonnelda
brought to her. He suspected she wanted to be the one
to pull the trigger. Delroy would do well to remember
how she didn't like surprises and liked disobeyed orders
even less. "Let's go. Boss lady wants to see you. Delroy,
lower your weapon."

Delroy hesitated just a fraction. Jamela pushed the covers off her body and jumped out of the closet. "Leave Mr. Michael alone," she shouted. Delroy was momentarily surprised, which gave Michael enough time to act. "Down, Jamela!"

A powerful kick sent Delroy crashing into Beatrice's dresser. The gun he'd been holding flew through the air, then skirted on the floor out of his reach. The man who had been standing behind Michael opted to disobey Vanessa's orders, too, in an attempt to regain control. He fired, but missed. Unfortunately for him, Michael didn't. He crumpled with a thud to the floor. The commotion sent everyone toward Beatrice's room with guns drawn. Michael scooped up Jamela to protect her; Duvernay and Caldwell were the first to arrive. Once Vanessa's men realized that they'd lost the upper hand, they began to move toward the door.

"Right this way, gentlemen." Agents Wilson and McCorkle had pulled up moments before and taken up a position right outside Beatrice's house. As per Eric's instructions, they began to load the wagon with the would-be escaping posse members, who'd come to realize that their trip to freedom was a short one.

Banks restored the power to Beatrice's house, allowing the agents the opportunity to clear the house. The bureau medical examiner was called as well as the rest of the forensics team.

Beatrice rushed through the commotion to find Jamela. She found her wrapped safely in Michael's arms.

Bea turned to Eric. "I need a word with you."

He nodded, then followed her out the room. "What's up?"

"I need a place to stay tonight and I'd rather not go to a hotel. Going to Michael's is out of the question, too. Can you help me?"

"Say no more, I'll get you the keys to my town house in Georgetown. But are you sure about this?"

"More than any other decision I've made lately. Give me a few minutes to pack a bag. I just need to get away from here for a few hours—but I'm taking Jamela, too."

Eric didn't like it, but he did as she requested. After a brief conversation with Tangie, she agreed to meet Beatrice and Jamela at Eric's house. They slipped out during the forensic processing of the house. Beatrice couldn't look at either Michael or Jonnelda.

Tangie opened the doors, then gave her the key. She sympathized with what Bea was going through, having experienced her own bit of similar drama a few years earlier. She waited until Jamela, tired, confused, and scared, was settled into the second bedroom. Beatrice tucked her in, then promised to come back to check on her. When she returned, Tangie was making herbal tea, which she placed in front of her, "Beatrice, you are one of the bravest and toughest women I know. Why are you running away?"

Beatrice took a long sip of the calming brew. She smoothed her hair down, thinking she must look a fright. She concentrated on everything except the question. Tangie touched her hand. "Bea, what's wrong, you know you can talk to me."

Her lips twitched, but no sound would come out. Beatrice sat for several moments just trying to process what had happened. Her eyes sparkled with unshed tears. Her words tumbled out, in a rush of emotion.

"Tangie, I can't do this. I can't continue to love a man who doesn't love me enough or trust me enough to tell me the truth. Jonnelda is a Winton and so is Jamela because she's her daughter. He kept that from me . . . like I would crumble in the damn wind. How can I trust him with my forever? I'm too old to play these kinds of games and I refuse to continue on in a relationship with him.

What kind of man does this to the woman he swears he loves?"

Tangie smiled at Beatrice. These were the same questions that she'd had to ask herself about Eric. "Beatrice, the same man that would wake up in the middle of the night to find you, put himself in danger to save you, and give up everything he has just to be with you."

Beatrice grunted. "Like Eric?"

Tangie said, "No, like Michael. This isn't about him and his behavior, Beatrice. This is about you. I know that it has been hard on you over the last few years, but you can put it behind you if you are willing. . . . Beatrice, Michael loves you as much as you love him—trust that if you can't think of anything else right now."

"I'm sorry Tangie, I didn't mean to be insensitive."

Tangie, waved her off. "Oh shush, Beatrice. We're all in this together. I haven't even commented on the number of times my husband has been called into action even though he is supposed to be doing training, not fieldwork. Bea, we can't change who they are—we can only change how we react. If Michael Spates makes you happy and you want to be with him, forget everything else. Be with the man of your dreams—you certainly deserve the happiness." She paused for a moment. "Now, wipe those tears, get some rest and then call Michael in the morning. He's going to be worried sick about you—if nothing else, you owe him the opportunity to explain."

Tangie stood up and prepared to leave. "I've got to get going—Eric will be coming home soon and I want to be there for him. I'm not saying that it's going to be easy, you two have a lot to work through, but if it's really love, then it's worth fighting for."

Beatrice nodded her head in agreement. A long ragged sigh pushed from her mouth. She did have a lot to think about, and right behind Michael Ezekiel

Spates were Jonnelda and Jamela. *How could you hav
missed that?*

Eric found Michael, then pulled him to the side. "Beat
rice knows everything, and to say she's ready to give you
the same treatment as she gave Vanessa Winton is putting
it mildly. I just talked with Tangie, she settled her and
Jamela at my Georgetown place. So, what's the plan?"

Michael rubbed the side of his jaw in thought. This
was not the way it was supposed to happen, he thought
miserably. Just one darn thing after another.

Caldwell had the misfortune of coming to him at the
exact wrong time. "Sir, Jonnelda is pretty upset about
everything. I'm going to take her home with me, since
the ED has already left. Just to let you know, we're ready
to seal the house. Do you need anything more before
we leave?"

"No," he barked, "I'll see you at the debrief tomorrow afternoon." Michael walked away without another
word to anyone else. Once in the vehicle he let several
expletives fly out of his mouth, then banged on the
steering wheel for good measure. "Damn you, Vanessa
and Kharl Winton!"

Traffic on I-395 was light due to the early morning hour.
Michael drove home slowly, however, because he didn't
trust his emotions—he felt like a walking powder keg.

He should have told Beatrice everything as soon as he
found it out. How was he ever going to make her understand? *Beatrice is never going to forgive you for this one.* . . .

Steven watched Michael before he pulled off with
Jonnelda in his car. He'd given the situation careful
consideration for the past couple of weeks.

Jonnelda looked at him stoically. "What the hell am I
supposed to do now?"

Steven reached for her hand. "The first thing we do

find a sympathetic judge." He said nothing more
before simply starting the engine.

In the morning he stood outside the door of Eric's
place for a full five minutes before he could bring himself to knock.

Beatrice opened the door with a calm expression on
her face. She had been expecting him. After a full night
of tossing and turning, she'd made her decision and
was ready to tell him.

Chapter Eighteen

"Michael, tell me what you know and don't you dare leave anything out." Her eyes flashed anger while she desperately fought to control her breathing.

Michael recognized the look and the emotion. "Beatrice, sit down and I'll tell you everything." He needed to gain control before this turned into a shouting match—one-sided of course; he could tell that Beatrice was just that angry.

With her back ramrod straight, she sat down across from him. She didn't dare sit next to him because she didn't want to have to be responsible for her actions depending on what was said. Her voice was barely above a hiss when she spoke. "I'm sitting and I'm listening, so talk."

Michael took an audible breath, then began. "I've only known about Jamela's relationship to Jonnelda for a short time. I had someone check her out only because I wanted to be sure that we could proceed with the adoption. I didn't want to make the emotional investment in making her a part of our family only to have her taken away. I chose not to tell you because I wanted us to be able to enjoy this time together. Jonnelda was

...arried to Moses Winton for a short time before his ...urder. We've talked—"

"Dammit Michael, you've talked to her, but not to ...e? What does that say about our supposed relation-...hip? How could you do this to me . . . to us? Trust was ...he one thing that I asked for from you." Her voice ...racked and she angrily wiped tears from her cheeks. ...Why weren't you able to give it to me?"

Michael reached for her, but she swatted his hands. ...No, don't touch me—answer my questions."

"Bea, I didn't tell you because I love you so damned ...much. I couldn't stand the thought of you becoming ...miserable about losing Jamela. I didn't know Jonnelda ...like I do now and couldn't possibly have guessed her ...motivations. I was doing the best I could to protect the ...woman I love."

Beatrice turned to walk away before she said, "Unfor-tunately, Michael, that's not good enough. I don't want to see you again, it's over between us."

Beatrice returned to work as soon as she was cleared for duty. Her first day back in the office called for her to review and sign all the paperwork that had been sit-ting on her desk. She read quickly, but thoroughly, the stack that Karen had left for her. That was until she read, *Effective immediately, I resign as director of the Special Corruption Unit.* . . .

She tried to will her heart to stop beating out of rhythm, but her mind could barely stop spinning. Michael knew that Congress had agreed to fund the SCU for another five years, why was he resigning? A shudder passed through her as she considered what his answer might be. *Oh God, Michael, I hope you aren't doing this because of me!*

* * *

"This is quite an honor, but are you sure you want to do this?" Eric looked at his mentor and now predecessor with an anxious expression.

Michael nodded his head. "Yes I'm sure. It's time—I'm getting too old for this kind of business, besides I'm very proud of the work you've done since you joined the bureau. I watched you grow and learn over the years, and can't think of anyone else's hands that I'd rather leave the unit in than yours."

He clapped Eric on the shoulders. "It's time for someone younger to take over the helm. You guys don't need an old coot like myself calling the shots." Michael smiled. "Don't get me wrong, I'm not putting myself out to pasture. I just want to start living my life on my own terms again. It's been a wonderful season, but I'm ready to move to the next phase."

Michael handed Eric a nicely wrapped gift box covered in black and tan paper. "What's this?"

"You won't know until you open it," he urged.

The desk ornament read ERIC C. DUVERNAY, DIRECTOR, SPECIAL CRIMES UNIT

Eric was almost speechless. "Thank you—this means so much more to me than you'll ever know. With the new designation, this is truly a new beginning. I hope that I won't disappoint you."

"Don't thank me, I should be thanking you. It means a lot to me that you are taking over and Peter's legacy will live on. We convinced the bureau director that the Special Crimes designation would carry more weight with the administration. You've got the green light to work on any sort of case that the ED assigns. More importantly, this is your operation now; you've got to set your own standard. And bite your tongue—you could never disappointment me."

"I'll tell the future Mrs. Spates what an honor this is when I see her next week." Eric winced after he noticed

he pained expression in Michael's eyes. He guessed
orrectly that the two had not made up yet. But before
e could apologize, Spates went to answer his phone.

Michael picked up the phone on the second ring.
Spates here."

He heard the sound of her relief through the receiver. "Michael, what are doing resigning from the
unit, after we worked so hard to secure new funding?"

Michael chuckled. "Hello Beatrice, nice to talk with
you, too." His tone lost all mirth after he realized this
was their first conversation since Vanessa Winton raided
her house. "How have you been?"

Eric walked silently out the office to give Michael privacy. He sent up a quick prayer for pride to fall away so
that they could talk freely.

Beatrice's tone was unabashedly truthful. "Michael,
how do you think I've been? I'm miserable without
you—I miss you."

He held the phone in his hands for several seconds,
trying to collect his thoughts. "Then let's stop this. Beatrice, let me come over or you meet me at my place. I'm
going out of my mind without you. I love you so much."

Beatrice sighed. "That's all I need to hear. I'll come
by your place on my way home."

If the sweat making his palms cold and clammy was
any indication of nervousness, then he was plenty nervous. He hadn't had time to cook and would probably
have made a royal mess if he'd tried. Instead, Michael
ordered food from one of his favorite restaurants then
settled down to wait. The table was set for two with a
bottle of wine set to chill in the refrigerator.

Traffic seemed interminable while Beatrice made her
way to Michael's place. Every nutcase in the D.C. metro-
politan area seemed to be driving on the interstate. By

the time she reached Michael's she was a bundle of
ragged nerves.

The house was filled with the divine aroma of baked
chicken, apple pie, mashed potatoes, corn, and green
beans. Ummm, she thought. Comfort food! Beatrice let
the bad memories of her long drive over die away and
wrapped herself up in the moment. Michael's welcoming smile warmed her heart. "If this is how you promise
to treat me the rest of my life, all is forgiven."

He held her so closely their breathing became as
one. All the grief, drama, heartache, disappointment
and hurt melted away into oblivion. All that mattered
was right there between them. "Beatrice, I'm sorry for
keeping things from you—it won't happen again. I love
you too much to risk losing you."

"Shush, Michael. Just hold me. I don't ever want to
consider life without being able to do just what we are
at this moment. I love you too much to ever let you go.
We've wasted enough time being apart. Jonnelda and
Jamela are moving on with their lives and we've been
stuck in the middle of the road to nowhere." Beatrice
raised her head to look into his eyes. She said, "I'm willing to work this out if you are."

The following month . . .

The stress of the past thirty days melted into a blur.
Beatrice admired the red, white, and gold decorations of
the dining room and ballroom while she tapped her feet
to the music of the jazz band playing on the small stage.

Beatrice and Michael clinked champagne glasses in
celebration. The annual Valentine's Day ball was a special event. One made even more special by sharing it
with the one she loved. Michael took her hand to lead
her to the dance floor.

The kiss was supposed to brief, and maybe it was, but
er body didn't know that. Beatrice longed for Michael's
uch. She wanted that feeling of safety and security that
eing wrapped in his arms provided. "Do you think that
e could get out of here?"

Beatrice breathed her reply. "I thought you'd never
sk. I've booked a room for us on the seventh floor."

After a final twirl on the dance floor, he said, "This
s why I love you so much! Let's go."

Butterflies danced a wicked rhythm in her belly as
hey approached her room. It seemed like so long since
hey had been intimate, this time felt almost like a new
beginning. Beatrice unzipped her dress, letting it fall to
he floor. The black velvet and satin fabric that had covered her body like a glove slid down into a dark pool
at her feet. She stepped out of it, showcasing her black
fishnet panty hose.

Michael noticed that her demi-bra barely covered her
nipples. The exposed expanse of flesh between her breasts
and the beginning of the hose begged to be touched—no,
caressed—and loved like the rest of her. Michael groaned
inwardly, she looked good enough to eat.

Bea held Michael's gaze, and when she spoke it
sounded like a purr. "So what do we do? I know that I
don't want to live another day without you in my life. I've
already agreed to become your wife, surely we can work
out the details of a little wedding after all we've been
through together."

The next morning after breakfast in bed of fruit and
each other, Michael said, "I want to take you someplace
today. But it's a surprise, so don't ask a lot of questions
or use your considerable charms to break down my
resistance."

Michael took her hand, leading her to the car. "Trust me. I just want to show you something."

Beatrice regarded him skeptically, but followed nonetheless.

Michael drove to Old Town Alexandria, to a brick building that looked like a town house, but was designated for commercial use. He pulled into a reserved parking space. Bea furrowed her brow. Michael led her up the walkway, through the glass doors to a white door. The brass nameplate affixed to it read PETER ANDERSON & ASSOCIATES

"Oh my God, Michael, you really did it?"

He smiled like the proverbial cat that swallowed the canary. "Yep. My new firm is fully operational. We have a waiting list of cases, strictly high-tech stuff. No following cheating spouses. Our specialty is industrial espionage—we open for business in two weeks. So, what do you think, shall we go in?"

"Yes, we should. Michael, I'm so proud of you, but why didn't you tell me, I could have helped you put things in order, could have made your lists and gone shopping."

His full-bellied laugh had her smiling, too. "Actually, I did hire a wonderful assistant who reminds me a lot of you—trust me, she has everything under control. I think she even has a list of her lists," he said as he opened the door.

Just then Jonnelda returned to her desk from the copy room. "Are you talking about me?"

Beatrice simply shook her head. "You two are incorrigible. I can't believe you managed all this without letting me know! And that little sneak Jamela, how did you manage to keep that big mouth quiet?"

They laughed at that remark, because it had not been easy. It had taken several eleven-year-old types of bribes to keep her silence.

"So I take it that Eric accepted the position?"

Michael smiled. "Yes, I spoke with him and Tangie and they are both very pleased with the turn of events. I thought that Tangie would be more resistant, but she told me that she completely supports his decision; she said he's not the same until he is out in the field doing casework, so she is behind him one hundred percent. He is taking thirty days to restructure and then he'll be at the helm. I'm going to help out until my terminal leave ends, then we are going to be open for business full-time here." He winked slyly. "It will mean more time at home for me, do you think you can stand that?"

Beatrice smiled. "I don't know, are there any fringe benefits to it?"

"Hmmm . . . let me see . . ." He moved closer to her, taking her in his arms. His kiss was gentle, yet meaningful, full of promise.

In mock disgust Jonnelda said, "Oh jeesh. Steven, look they're at it again. I think we are going to need a muzzle for them." He and Agent Banks were installing computer equipment in Michael's new office. Looking up from the cables and plugs that he had in his hand, Steven responded, "Don't be jealous, Mrs. Caldwell, when you get home tonight, I'll have a little of *that* waiting for you. Besides, it's their weekend with Jamela. So that means we have the house to ourselves."

Steven referred to the unofficial joint-custody arrangement that they'd worked out. After Steven and Jonnelda's marriage by civil ceremony, he'd started paperwork to adopt Jamela. Officer Hightower had questioned the swiftness of their union, but after interviewing the couple, she understood why the judge was willing to go along with their highly unusual request. They were so enthralled they could barely keep their hands off each other.

Jamela spent one weekend with Bea and Michael, who served as her godparents, and the rest of the time getting to know her new parents.

Jamela had proved to be remarkably resilient a adaptive. She'd welcomed Jonnelda as her mother never questioning the previous arrangement onc after Jonnelda explained what happened to her biol ical father. Jamela had adjusted to her new family wi no problem—Dr. Rose made sure of that fact in h monthly checkups on the group.

Jonnelda smiled. "Yes, that's right. Should I wear t pink or the white outfit?"

Steven waggled his eyebrows. "Hmmm . . . I thin maybe the nurse's outfit. I may need your special hea ing tonight."

"Oh brother, and you two talk about us," Beatrice i terjected as she turned her attention toward Micha again. "Anyway, I have a surprise for you as well. Th deal closed on my house, so now we can begin ou house search in earnest. I guess we'll be roommate until we find our own place. If we can find somethin, reasonable, like under a million, I'd like to start look ing in Potomac. Don't you think a house with a view o the water sounds divine?"

Michael said, "That it does. We can go out this week end." He turned toward Jonnelda and Steven. "I gues: we'll give the newlyweds a break; besides Jamela loves water, so I'd like her to see where she'll be spending a lot of her time."

Beatrice grinned happily. "Perfect!"

Michael took her in his arms. "Yes, you are. Now, when are you going to make an honest man of me?" Michael took her in his arms again, hoping his electric kisses would help speed the process.

Beatrice broke away after she heard herself moan— they were in public, after all, and shouldn't be making out like teenagers. That's what she told herself anyway just before Michael reached for her again and kissed her until her knees buckled.

* * *

The pastor's office was full before he began the ceremony. It didn't seem as if another person could squeeze inside, prompting him to move everyone into the sanctuary. Karen had made a few discreet phone calls and suddenly, Michael and Beatrice's simple marriage ceremony turned into a small wedding.

Beatrice's eyes misted while she repeated her vows: "I, Beatrice, take you Michael, as my lawfully wedded husband, to have and to hold until death do us part. I promise to cherish you as my helpmate and partner as long as we both shall live. I thank you for waiting for me and for showing me that it is never too late for love."

He held her lightly as he repeated the words of his heart. "I, Michael, take you Beatrice, as my lawfully wedded wife, to have and to hold until death do us part. I promise to cherish you as my helpmate and partner as long as we both shall live. I will honor and trust you to the end of my days. I thank you for showing me that love and happiness are possible at any age."

After the ceremony, they returned to the hotel room where they would begin their lives as husband and wife. A fresh bottle of Moët & Chandon White Star graced the table in the hotel room, courtesy of the unit. Michael began to fill the champagne flutes.

Beatrice couldn't contain her giddiness from the three glasses that she'd already had during their reception in one of the hotel ballrooms. She held up her hand after he started to pour. "Just half for me, I don't think I can take much more—I'm going to be out like a light."

Michael's voice had a devilish edge. "Don't you dare. I plan on loving you through the night, Mrs. Spates."

Beatrice's smile widened and her eyes sparkled with delight and some devilment. "Um . . . I like the sound

of that. The Spates part and the lovin' part. But don
you think we should practice . . . the lovin' part so th
we're sure we have it right?"

Michael smiled at Beatrice. Her sexy "come hithe
look and the fact that she was his wife now gave her
whole new appeal. He didn't want to ever let go of th
moment . . . this time when all he needed to do was t
look at her and know that all was right with the world

He crossed the room from the table to the bed. Bea
rice had started to slip off her white hose. He place
the glasses on the night table. "Please, let me."

Beatrice leaned back on the bed and lifted her leg t
an angle for easier access. Michael reflexively licked hi
lips. He positioned himself on the bed next to her an
carefully, slowly began to roll down the thigh-high hos
that she wore. Her body's small quiver encouraged hin
to continue. As soon as he freed the leg, he stroked the
satiny smooth skin, inching along the inside of he
thighs precariously close to her core. She made smal
mewing noises in response to his ministrations.

He felt her breath catch after he slid his hands along
the curvature of her sex. He played in the thin layer of
hair covering it, and teased her to wetness. Bea's breathing came in short gasps. She reached for him, but
Michael caught her hand and simply kissed it. He
reached for the other leg and began to remove its silky
off-white covering as well. His patience was tested, but
he held on, he wanted their wedding night to be special.

Bea was a little less patient; she had waited long
enough and couldn't wait to have him inside her. She
slid the simple off-white satin dress up to reveal her
white thong and demi-bra. It was her turn to take pleasure in hearing Michael's sharp intake of air. It pleased
her to know that he found her so attractive.

Michael helped her slip off the dress . . . deftly he lifted
her off the bed enough to unclasp her bra, revealing her

ll breasts and pointed nipples. He felt himself harden
his pants. He grew longer waiting for the moment
hen they would be joined as one. Bea caressed him
hrough the fabric of his tuxedo pants. He unzipped
hem with a sense of urgency, unbuttoning his shirt immediately after . . . his clothing dropped to the floor in
pool at the edge of the bed, where they joined her gar-
ments. He allowed Bea to help him remove his shirt be-
ween passionate kisses to her mouth, neck, and the skin
between her breasts. The air filled, then crackled with
their burgeoning passion.

Naked on the bed they continued to explore each
other's bodies. Michael put on a condom before he
eased a taut nipple between his teeth, lightly sucking it
and bringing it to a stiff peak. A stiff peak that matched
the hardness he felt below.

Michael stroked the side of her face, before bringing
his lips to hers. She tasted of champagne and wedding
cake. He explored her mouth, deepening the kiss with
each stroke in their mating game. Her fingers raked
across his back, heightening her senses.

Michael moved his strong body on top to cover hers,
gentle yet insistent. His hands found her wet center and
he stroked her. He stroked her hard and fast until he
brought her to the edge, then he slipped inside her
and continued the same hard-and-fast rhythm.

Beatrice screamed his name, as heat burned deep
inside her, threatening to take her over the passionate
edge where Michael dangled her. He kissed her again,
long, slow, and deep, causing her to release to him everything she'd held stored up. She let go of her self-control,
allowing the sensations that he caused in her to take over.
Raspy breathing . . . blinding white light . . . a sense of suspended time and space signaled their climatic completion. Tonight their coming together indicated their
destiny—they were one in love until the end of their time.

Epilogue

Canyon Lake, Texas . . .

The setting sun was a brilliant kaleidoscope of burnt orange, yellow, and red. The colors flowed from the horizon and seemed to blend seamlessly into the dark blue water. Everything seemed at peace, just as Beatrice and Michael were on their delayed honeymoon—one they took six months after their marriage.

Beatrice smiled as she snuggled closer to Michael, enjoying the warmth of his body against her back. He lightly caressed her shoulders, filling her with a gentle reminder of their earlier lovemaking in their private cabin on the water. A shudder of anticipation of what the night would bring flowed through her.

The last few boats pulled languidly into the harbor. Beatrice and Michael watched peacefully from their spot on the shore. They were content to enjoy a lazy afternoon together. His hands moved from her shoulder down her sides and sidled over to caress her breasts. Beatrice moaned from the sensual warmth of his touch. No matter what else happened in life, she knew nothing could replace the happiness and joy she felt right

ow being Mrs. Michael Spates. And it was something
at she planned to enjoy for a very long time.

Feeling blessed and happy, Michael smiled at his
ood fortune. He bent down to kiss her hair; it had
rown out now, allowing her curly tresses to gently
race her neck. He reveled in its texture and feel. A
ontented sigh signaled his feelings, while he held her.

Beatrice was quite attuned to the way he felt because
is feelings mirrored her own. She leaned still closer so
Michael could wrap his arms around her tighter. Beat-
ice turned her mouth toward him angling for more of
is touch; it seemed she lived for his passionate kisses.

After indulging in each other's taste and feel for several minutes, they broke apart. Her smile was slightly
mischievous. "Michael, don't start anything that you
don't plan to finish."

Her teasing tone was all the motivation Michael
needed. He sought her lips again and answered with a
long, sweet, fiery kiss. "And just who said that I won't
finish?" He answered in a voice that was gravelly with passion and desire. His kiss was deep, his love unmistakable.

Beatrice giggled before she felt herself swept up into
another ardent embrace. She marveled at how much
she loved him back. It seemed that God had given her
a second chance at love and happiness with Michael,
proving that despite her circumstance, it was never too
late for love.

Bea's heart was full, but she still wanted to hear the
words. She loved the effect Michael's silky smooth bari-
tone voice had on her, especially when whispers of love
came from his lips.

Beatrice moaned again as Michael continued to caress
her, fanning the flames of her passion. His eyes sparkled
with hunger, causing her to melt into a pool of heated
passion. Shivers of anticipation and delight coursed
through her, colliding with the heat of her desire.

Beatrice peered into the deep brown depths Michael's eyes, asking him, "Will you always love m like this?"

"Yes, *always*," Michael answered truthfully.

He reached for her again, holding her close. "Bea rice, I've loved you all of my life."

Dear Reader:

Thank you for choosing to read my fourth SCU novel, *Deep Down*. I hope that you enjoyed reading about senior FBI agents Michael Spates and Beatrice McCoy, on their adventure to love. It has been a wonderful process to bring the Special Corruption Unit to life through all the stories, *Love Worth Fighting For*, *Worth the Wait*, and *Undercover Lover*.

Please let me know what you think of this story, which incorporated important changes in the Federal Bureau of Investigation, and chronicled what happened to the Special Corruption Unit because of governmental restructuring. The story was set against the snowy background of winter in West Virginia, but Beatrice and Michael managed to keep warm and their story sizzles!

One of my absolute favorite places to shop is my local Bath & Body Works store. If you notice throughout my novels I used Bath & Body Works's fragrances for my heroines: Cucumber Melon for Tangie Taylor Duvernay, Vanilla Sugar for Maria Thomas Milbon, Sheer Freesia for Helene Maupin Radford, and Juniper Breeze for Beatrice McCoy Spates. Try a few of these wonderful scents and maybe one will become your favorite, too.

As always, thank you for the support you've shown to me during my writing career. I hope to be able to continue to bring more stories of love and intrigue to you in the future. Look for updates on my Web site to find out more information about my new releases, contests, tours, and book signings. Until then, keep reading!

Take care,

Katherine D. Jones
www.katherinedjones.com

Resources Used for Writing This Book

The Greenbrier Resort: www.greenbrier.com
Bath & Body Works: www.bbw.com
The Mafia in New Jersey: www.mafianj.com
www.exastriscientia.fateback.com
The Department of Homeland Security:
www.dhs.gov
U.S. Citizenship and Immigration Services:
www.uscis.gov
The Federal Bureau of Investigation:
www.fbi.gov
Jamaican pride: www.jamaicanpride.com

About the Author

Katherine D. Jones sold her first contemporary romance to BET Books in 2003. Born in Leonardtown, Maryland, she spent her early years traveling around the world as a daughter of a Foreign Service officer for the Department of State. She currently resides in San Antonio, Texas.

Jones obtained her Bachelor of Arts degree in sociology from Hampton University in Virginia. She has been married for over eighteen years to her husband, an army officer and Hampton graduate as well, and they have two handsome boys.

Jones says her writing is reflective of her travels and experience with government agencies. She believes in strong characters that are firmly grounded in real-world issues and problems. Jones says she writes contemporary romance with a twist.

Her writing credits include two novels published by BET Books in 2004, a Kensington Dafina romance in 2005, and several magazine articles for *Black Romance*, *Bronze Thrills*, and *True Confessions*.

She is a 2005 Emma Award Nominee for the Favorite New Author category and a co-winner of the 2005 *Shades of Romance* magazine Reader's Choice Favorite New Author award. Her second title, *Worth the Wait*, was a 4.5 star *Romantic Times* top pick for July 2004.

The following is a sample chapter
from Katherine D. Jones's upcoming novel,
Make Me Do For Love.

ENJOY!

For Karine and Simon Peter
and
Nannie Lou and Charles

Prologue

Korea 1952 . . .

The snow fell in ice-cold sheets. His feet were practically frozen, his boots were worn out, and at this point, he didn't even know if he had toes. The frigid temperatures and the weight on his back made him stumble repeatedly. He was on the verge of exhaustion and ready to give up.

"Just keep putting one foot in front of the other," he repeated to himself as he limped along the road. His heart kept a steady beat, jumping whenever he heard a sound too close for comfort. There was mortar fire in the background to help motivate him to move.

Hisss . . . boom. Hisss . . . boom. The sound was deafening and the black acrid smoke the ammunition created against the white sky made the scene ethereal. Private Anderson was the only man from his troop still standing and he was barely doing that. He forced himself to keep moving despite the pain.

Fifteen minutes earlier . . .

Anderson was in the mess tent working his shift. H
liked the solitude of the early mornings, before th
rush of the day would set his nerves on edge. It was 3:0
A.M. and he was preparing pumpkins for pumpkin pi
Humph. *Thanksgiving.*

Instead of being with his family in the States, he was i
some godforsaken place he couldn't even pronounce
He knew that he had it better than most, though. He hac
a set schedule, was away from the worst parts of the war
and worked in a good unit.

He worked efficiently and quickly, but it didn't stop
trivial thoughts from crossing his mind. As he carved
his fifth pumpkin he had wondered why white guys
liked pumpkin so much.

As a Southerner, he was much more partial to sweet
potato pie, but pumpkin it was out here. He had several
pies already completed and the aroma of cinnamon
and spices filled the air.

He was humming Nat "King" Cole's "Mona Lisa,"
when he heard footsteps. Peter remembered looking at
the clock on the small counter that had been fashioned
for his prep area. He smiled inwardly, *right on time.* The
pot was just about done. The smell of strong coffee
perking permeated the air. The captain liked it strong
with lots of sugar and cream.

Captain Wise had been making his way toward the
tent when the first round hit. His sturdy six-two frame
was flung into the tent as if weightless. Anderson's head
registered the look of shock and pain in his eyes. Adrenaline coursed through his veins, whatever the hell had
just happened—escape became the only priority.

He grabbed his company officer when he heard the
second round heading their way, and slung him over
his shoulder in a fireman's carry. His feet started
moving before he knew where he was going. Hisss . . .
boom. Hisss . . . boom.

He didn't know how much time had passed. He
dn't know anything except that his body was wracked
th numbing pain and his feet were too cold. . . .

The captain was getting heavier by the second. Peter
ied humming "Mona Lisa" again and several kilome-
rs later he had worked his way through several gospel
nes. Songs he hadn't thought about in years, songs
om his childhood. The ones that made Mama cry on
unday mornings. "Wade in the Water," "The Last Mile
f the Way," and "Dig a Little Deeper."

Peter could tell from the faint puffs of white air the
aptain was still breathing, but it was labored and shal-
ow. Wise was frigid, and he felt like a block of ice. An-
lerson was concerned for him—maybe he should just
ut him down. And he wasn't sure if he was doing more
harm than good.

Peter knew basic medical treatment, enough to try to
prevent infection and clean out wounds, but he didn't
know what had hit the captain. He couldn't be sure if
he had a piece of shrapnel lodged in his uniform or if
the force of the blow had caused some internal injury.
What he did know was that he had to find help soon.
He just hoped that the enemy didn't engage him
before they reached safety.

Two years at North Carolina A&T had not prepared
him for anything like this. Nothing had prepared him
for something like this. Anderson kept walking. Maybe
he was still in Detroit eating his favorite foods—maca-
roni and cheese and collard greens. Maybe this was all
a bad dream, maybe the pain in his chest, the burning
in his lungs, were just part of his nightmare and he
would wake up soon. He didn't want to think about the
mangled bodies that had become a blur as he sought a
way to survive. Hisss . . . boom. Hisss . . . boom.

Chapter One

Anderson refolded his blanket over his legs. Whenever he thought about his past, how he became involved with the Special Corruption Unit, sometime the flashbacks were so real he would feel cold. . . .

He was the man everyone called "the Colonel." Private Anderson had served in the Korean War for a total of six months before returning home an injured war hero. His nickname had nothing to do with his rank, but was out of respect for how he had rescued his commanding officer. He had braved frostbite, starvation, and the weight of carrying a dying man on his shoulders.

In the process, he took out a platoon of six of the enemy. Captain Wise had a single grenade on his weapons belt. After spotting an enemy camp, Anderson launched it with what little strength he had left. It was the last thing that he remembered doing before he passed out.

Wise and Anderson were eventually found in a makeshift shelter of brush, nearly frozen to death. After their return, Wise had supported an effort to make him a Medal of Honor winner, but the politics of the time wouldn't allow it—Private Anderson was, after all, just a *Negro* cook.

His color and station in life didn't play too well with

the award committee. So instead, the captain was given the medal. The nation owed Peter Anderson a debt of gratitude, but payment would be a long time in coming.

In the coming years, it was a debt that Captain Wise did his best to repay. After all, Wise owed Anderson his life.

While the two were at the VA hospital, Captain Wise jokingly called him the Colonel. For some odd reason, it became a nickname that stuck with him. Even after his return to Detroit as a veteran in early 1953.

Returning to Detroit to live brought back the stark reality of his life. With few job prospects and even less money he ran out of options quickly. His return to the city had to be short-lived, as he decided to return south to finish his education. Anderson completed his degree at North Carolina A&T in 1956.

For the twenty-two-year-old Anderson, serving in Korea had forever changed him. And maybe not for the better. The bitterness he carried inside himself threatened to eat him alive some days. He didn't save the captain's life for the glory, he did it because it was necessary, but it was hard not to resent his maltreatment by the armed forces upon his return. Nothing was made easier for him. Disillusionment and disappointment changed his attitude toward life. His faith was challenged and with the passing of his mother, his foundation was rocked. He moved back to North Carolina a much different man than he had been before the war. Unfortunately, he had learned many *unkind* lessons over the last few years.

Captain Jonathan Wise returned to his hometown a hero. But living in his hometown proved to be too limiting. He no longer shared the same narrow-minded values as his brothers and father. Anderson had given him a new perspective. Twice Wise had ordered the man to leave him during his rescue, but he never listened.

Wise learned the true measure of a man that winter in Korea and it had nothing to do with skin color and education like he had been brought up to believe. Out of the army and considered a war hero, he moved to Washington, D.C. in 1960 to accept a job with the Federal Bureau of Investigation. The District was exciting, full of promise, and he felt the job he would be doing was meaningful. Another way to serve his country. Yeah, it was wonderful for awhile. . . .

Then the trouble started. Wise found the restrictive attitude and rigid work environment of J. Edgar Hoover's Bureau not much better than life in Lido, Ohio.

His liberalism, while not appreciated, was tolerated. He was, after all, a war hero. But tolerance had its limits. And it was his often radical attitude toward the equal treatment of other races that earned him a small windowless office in Durham, North Carolina. Wise was tasked with menial work for several months until finally he got his big break. His first major case had been tracking down moonshiners and owners of local whiskey houses. So there he was, a twenty-five-year-old white boy, in black bottom. After he realized that he was going to need help, he knew exactly who to call. It was the colonel to his rescue one more time.

For Peter, the call couldn't have come at a better time. The job market was almost impossible—he was just another unemployed black college graduate. But after the captain's request all that changed. He was going undercover for the FBI.

North Carolina, 1960 . . .

Bodies moved to the rhythm of the music. They swayed and undulated to the beat and to the vibration of

he latest Motown hits. You had to shout to hear yourself
hink, but no one seemed to mind. It was Friday night
ind the place was packed. People were everywhere,
trying to get a little liquid libation to wash away a tough
workweek. Peter walked into the small, not much more
than a hole-in-the-wall place, to order his drink. It was
twenty-five cents for one shot, fifty cents for a double.
He'd done his best to try to fit in, but these were work-
ing-class folks. There was something about him that
didn't seem quite right with his nice suit and professional
haircut. They were all gussied up for their night of dancing and drinking, but no one looked quite like him. He
wasn't local—that was for sure.

No one approached him because in these parts they
had learned to be wary of strangers. Concordia was a
small town not far from Charlotte. In these parts people
knew when to mind their business.

It took several minutes, but finally a petite woman
came up to him to ask if she could help him. Peter took
one look at her and his breath caught in his throat. She
was beautiful, with large dark brown eyes, and a small
pouty mouth and all this was set to a generous bosom,
small waist, and curvaceous bottom. He didn't want to
stare, but he couldn't help himself. No one since
Cynthia had gotten his attention like this before.

Peter couldn't guess how old she was, but he wondered if she were even old enough to drink, let alone
serve alcohol.

Finally, his deep bass voice seemed to work. "Um, I'll
take a shot. I'll buy you one, too, if you tell me your
name." He flashed a white, even smile.

Lily took one look at him and rolled her eyes. "Then
I guess you'll just be buying one shot. Money first, then
I'll pour your drink."

Peter bit the inside of his lip to keep from smiling.
Her light voice with its Southern charm didn't have

nearly the bite she wanted it to have, but he had to give
it to her, she had guts.

He found himself staring into the dark brown of her
eyes, pulled in with no way to escape. They watched
each other for several seconds in silence.

Finally, she looked down, then away.

Something happened between them. Something
that he would never be able to explain rationally. He
saw so much in her eyes—sorrow, hurt, intelligence,
and vulnerability.

"I'm sorry, I know I shouldn't stare." He needed to
get to know her. He continued with a wink. "The name
is Peter. I came from up Detroit not long ago." Unfortunately for him, she was unmoved by his declaration.
He shrugged his shoulders while he casually glanced
around the room.

He tried again. "Pretty lady, I'm just trying to find a
way to fit in. I don't have any friends in town, but I did
hear some guys talking about this place, so I thought
I'd stop in to check it out."

He looked her over again, his interest purely personal though he knew that it shouldn't be. "I'm glad
that I did."

Momma Jordan watched from the corner a bit then
decided enough was enough. "Lily Ann, you gon' serve
drinks or talk all night?"

Nice. Lily Ann. Peter decided that the name suited her.
He looked toward Momma Jordan, the proprietor of this
fine illegal establishment. She would bear watching. . . .

Peter raised his glass to her. "I was just being friendly,
ma'am. Just making conversation to pass the time away.
I'd be glad to buy another drink to make it up to you. I
wouldn't want to get your workers in trouble."

Momma Jordan looked him over. The expression on
her big round face was none too friendly. She obviously
felt the same way about him as the other patrons in the

hot house. People smiled, but they kept their distance.
eter sat a little longer while he tried to devise his new
trategy. If he waited until the locals accepted him, he
ould be waiting a very long time. As long as Momma
ordan was around, there would be no wagging tongues—
he'd see to that. Ferreting out information was going to
be *even* more difficult than he'd originally thought.

Peter nursed his shot—as long as one could nurse a
shot, for a bit. He figured that he needed to continue
coming around until they felt comfortable around
him. He knew from the outset that this wouldn't be an
easy assignment, but the folks in Washington had insisted to Jonathan that it be done—and done this way.
Peter had remarked to Captain Wise that it seemed
like a surefire way to get "disappeared" in the Black
Hills of North Carolina.

Mary Wells's hit "Bye Bye Baby" played in the background. So he stayed around a little longer. He lit up a
cigarette, tapped his foot to the music, and watched
the dancing.

An attractive young woman with a tight dress on
walked up to him. "You gotta 'nother one?"

Peter smiled. "That depends. You gotta name?"

The woman moved in closer—bringing with her the
mixture of mint and whiskey on her breath. Her face a
mere few inches away from Peter's, he could see all the
way down her throat.

He noticed that she wasn't as young as he'd thought,
or maybe she was, but the years had not been kind to her.

"Sugah, you give me a cigarette and you can call me
anything you like." Her suggestive tone left little room
for misunderstanding. His body physically responded
to the invitation. *Damn*, he thought. It had been a long
time since Cynthia. He needed to get out of there
before he did something foolish.

He gave her the cigarette, then stood to leave. As he

turned he caught sight of Lily Ann out of the corner of h
eye. She'd been watching the exchange. Peter knew tha
as soon as he noticed her expression. He felt guilty . .
there was no denying the anger that flashed temporaril
in her eyes. He cursed again. What was he doing? H
needed an ally and this was no way to go about getting
one. He started to move toward her, but she turned away
Peter watched her serve a drink to another customer, ther
thought better of it. There would be another day.

He needed to talk with Jonathan Wise about how to
proceed, anyway. He'd had enough for one day. He wa:
spent emotionally. Being in the shot house had twisted
his insides every which way but loose. He'd seen it all.
Married, but obviously still looking, single and looking,
married couples blowing off steam, and singles just
looking for a good time. There was a common thread
among the people he'd seen and it reminded him of
the way he'd felt after his return. One part disillusionment and another part resignation. Maybe that's what
drained him. He'd managed to pull himself together
with help, so he especially didn't want to see others
throw in the towel. Life wasn't perfect, but he had hope
for the future.

Peter stole one last glance toward Lily Ann. He
wanted to stay to watch her all night, but he couldn't.
Dabbing the sweat from his brow, he walked out into
the humid late summer evening.

Lily Ann watched his back as it disappeared out the
doorway. Why did she care that he'd left? Yeah, he was
nice-looking and knew how to fill out the suit he wore
. . . but she had enough problems without adding another man to her woes. She washed the glasses out as
she continued to think about him. Her one consolation
was that he hadn't walked out with that tramp, Shirlene. Not tonight, anyway. Shirlene always seemed to
get her way and any man that she wanted.

Lily Ann yelped in pain as she realized that she'd cut her hand. Unfortunately, Momma Jordan had realized, too. "Lily Ann, what the hell are you doing? That's coming out of your pay, gal. Stop being so clumsy and stop bleeding all over my damn glasses."

Lily Ann rushed out the door. Her aunt had always been a thankless old windbag, with a heart the size of an acorn. Tears streaked her face, not so much from the physical pain, but from the ache in her heart—the one that threatened to swallow her whole sometimes.

She was crying so hard that she hadn't even seen Peter, much less known that he was coming toward her so quickly.

They collided into each other, hard enough for him to knock the wind out of her. If not for his strong arms she would have crumbled to the ground.

Peter held her close. "Lily Ann, are you okay? What in the world is going on?"